On the
Breath of the Gods

WHAT PEOPLE ARE SAYING ABOUT THIS INTERNATIONAL BEST-SELLER

"Thank you for *On the Breath of the Gods*. I now feel I have a study manual for building a solid relationship with a loved one. Nothing else has satisfied."

"After fifteen years of study and contemplation your wonderful book gathered all the loose ends for me. It put in clear focus what I need to do to move towards God."

"If truth had weight, one would need a truck to carry your book around! So many of the points you made were helpful to me that I can't begin to enumerate them."

"Your book is so powerful and alive; what a wonderful gift for the world. There are many more people and aspects of myself I understand now. I think I am not the only one ripe for this book."

"Since receiving your book, I have alternated between the desire to devour it in one sitting and the wish to savor it, reading it slowly over a long period of time. Fortunately, the book is so rich in truth, love and adventure that once I reached the end I quite happily returned to the first page to explore it all over again!"

"I just concluded reading your book and felt compelled to share my pleasure. Your keen insights and detailed explanations of male-female roles and relationships opened literally dozens of doors of realization for me. Many thanks for a great reading adventure."

"Reading your book is like keeping company with a very old and treasured friend—a dialogue I recall and keep looking for. I am thankful and so happy this book has been written. Thank you for sharing the gift."

"*On the Breath of the Gods* speaks right to my mind and heart. This book could change my life!"

WHAT REVIEWERS ARE SAYING ABOUT
ON THE BREATH OF THE GODS

"This is a book full of truths, power and love. Both author and reader are challenged to move beyond self-limiting concepts and instructed in what is necessary to become a spiritual warrior in this life."

—*The Light Connection*

"Tomioka blends the practicality of her everyday life with a rich offering of spiritual guidance as she takes the reader on an adventurous journey through the inner dimensions. For those striving for improvement in their personal lives, for those on the path to spiritual awareness, this is a book to be read and re-read for its deep spiritual truths."

—*In Light Times*

"A very courageous work. Nearly every page has an inspired poetic dissertation on spiritual principles."

—*Resonance Magazine*

"*On the Breath of the Gods* is a fantastically rich novel. I loved this book and my only regret is that I did not write it myself."

—Jim Hawkins, author of *Sword of Power*

"A harvest of answers here to age-old problems—shows in a rich, imaginative framework the entire delicate interplay between inner and outer, between spirit and matter."

—*The Book Reader*

"This is one of the most original books about relationships to come out in a long time. Our customers really want to know about the spiritual nature of relationships and nothing like *On the Breath of the Gods* has come along to explain this."

—Linda Brooks, Oxford Books, Atlanta, Georgia

"It's unbelievable how many personal revelations people are receiving from this most beautiful book. They're telling their friends about it and a wonderful chain reaction has begun."

—Claudia Harris, Chapter One Bookstore, Sun Valley, Idaho

On the
Breath of the Gods

Ariel Tomioka

A Helios House Book
"To realize our highest human and
spiritual potential"

International Edition
Co-published by The Pythagorean Press of
Australia and New Zealand

On the Breath of the Gods

Cover art by Jeff Hukill
Cover design by Ron Turner

ISBN: 0-923490-03-5

See last page of this book for individual, quantity and wholesale ordering information.

Printed in the United States of America
First Printing	*December 1988*
Second Printing	*April 1989*
Third Printing	*July 1989*
Fourth Printing	*December 1989*
Fifth Printing	*March 1990*
International Edition	*October 1990*

Library of Congress CIP Data

Tomioka, Ariel
    On the Breath of the Gods

        I. Title
            PS 3570.04405

        1988   813'.54   88-82620

To the Eagles of Heaven

Contents

Acknowledgements

I wish to thank many people who have contributed to this book in various ways. Mairi Huntington and Kent Cowie gave me much needed encouragement on the original manuscript. Mark Cavalenes believed in my book enough to risk money on his belief. The debt is repaid now, but the affection remains. The first edition of *On the Breath of the Gods* reflected the artistic skills of Susan Sarback, Flenn Crestman and Dan Sailer, as well as the editorial assistance of Julia Ross and Kit Bailey. Ron Turner supported me financially during the time I wrote the book and read/edited all my drafts with the same sensitive appreciation and keen criticism he gives to all he does. His belief in me has given me the courage to share myself with others.

This new international edition, published jointly by Helios House and The Pythagorean Press of Australia, owes much to Jeff Hukill's stunning art, Ron Turner's considerable design and organizational skills, and Rick Walters' careful, thorough indexing.

I want also to thank Tere Smith, the office manager of Helios House—a friend and co-worker who combines work with pleasure and lives every day with genuine enthusiasm. My admiration for her is endless.

Most of all I thank you, my readers, for reading my book, for telling other people about it, for writing to me (and being patient for six months before I write back), and for sustaining me with your good will and love. This book is for you.

Preface

This book was originally published two years ago. So much has happened since then. I have become braver, taken more risks, worked harder, "made waves" and changed much in my life that did not fit my own vision of wholeness. I have also learned to relax and realize that the world will still survive if I don't get that piece written or if I miss a deadline. I have learned to live in the whole, instead of its parts. I am not "without flaw." But I know that I am "perfect." That is, I feel complete.

Many people have written to me after reading my book. Some letters give me tears of joy. Others make me agonize over the misunderstandings that I have had some part in creating. But how can we do anything that is not open to someone else's interpretation? We can't. Any insight you receive from this book comes from you. I cannot tell you anything that you didn't, in your heart, already know. In my act of creating a book for you to read, I have invited you into my world. But I will have failed in my mission if you want only to stay in this world, instead of being filled with a passion to create your own.

You were made in the image of God. You are a creator. The "master-piece" of your creating should be your Self—the individuality that is you. From that center, much can be done to bring more truth and beauty into this world. This world badly needs your contributions. The people who are so anxious to transcend this world only add to its terrible burden of passivity and self-loathing. Spirituality will not result from this denial of our humanity; it will come only through the full flowering of that humanity. We will evolve into self-mastery naturally through the unfoldment of our ability to create ourselves and our authentic lives.

But to evolve "naturally" requires a healthy freedom. There is no particular way to reach self-mastery. No path exists that will take there. God is infinite and requires no official spokesman, no rules, rituals, guidelines or special techniques to contact It. Spiritual beings prove themselves by the respect and the quality of instruction they give you. The adepts I work with have chosen me because I was capable of learning what they had to teach. We earn our teachers. We cannot buy them with money or through commitment to a certain faith. To gain greater access to the inner worlds, we must have an authentic purpose for being there. And we must be willing to experience what is, even if what is is not what we have been taught.

Everything I have written in this book is based on fact. Which is not to say that everything I have written is fact. The experiences and knowledge I am sharing is an accumulation of years and years of inner work, not the six months I've depicted here. I've made up names and changed circumstances for various reasons, sometimes for the sake of the narrative, sometimes for simplicity, sometimes because the truth would be too far-fetched even for the parameters of this story. *On the Breath of the Gods* is not a "channeled" book. Like all true "maestros," the spiritual adepts I describe mostly conduct the orchestra of my own playing, sometimes urging me to more fully express what lies inside me, sometimes impatiently tapping the podium in distaste over my "sour notes." Sometimes I want to walk away; sometimes they want to walk away. Sometimes the music we play together is too beautiful for words.

As you read this book—if it is the right book at the right time for you—significant changes may begin to happen. Do not be afraid of change. Change is the "breath of God" that enables you to "live living, instead of live dying." (That's from Robert Henri, not me.) Keep your wits about you. Ask good questions with your whole being, and live your way into the answers. Do not be so anxious to "finish" things. Do not put off happiness until some future point. Do not make the sad mistake of substituting the illusion of security and safety for real life. Real life is scary and limitless and wonderful. Real life hurts and heals what hurts. Pain and joy are always mixed, because they are both a part of God. Avoid gratuitous pain and superficial pleasures. Pursue your authentic purpose and the necessary joys and pains will inevitably follow.

Perhaps this book will help you to see that you, too, are the hero or heroine of your own story. Your day-to-day objective life and your subjective life—in dreams, conscious inner travel, or imaginative experiences—form equal parts of your story. Most of all, I hope that you feel your own inner power quickening, and that your confidence to be yourself and follow your own instincts for wholeness grows greater all the time. Soul is free. I wish for each of you to discover your freedom, which is the God-Self in action. But we can only get freedom for something, not from something. To be free, we must find our purpose for Being and Be that with all the love and courage in our hearts.

May you live richly, love deeply and create a world in your image. May that world give back to you its delicate and profound treasures.

St. Louis, Missouri
September, 1990

CHAPTER ONE
Over the Cliff

Something was in the air. Many small signs indicated that life, as I knew it, was changing. But at the time, I felt only a vague restlessness and an inner questioning, like a wild animal who senses a shift in the pattern of the weather. It was midwinter, but in Northern California that only meant fifty-degree weather and grey skies. It meant sweaters, closed shoes, and the heater turned on in the morning. We raked leaves and pruned back deciduous bushes. The sky blanched, occasionally becoming sodden with rain clouds which wrung themselves onto the summer-scorched land.

My friend Jean, one of those people hypersensitive to the lack of sunlight, became depressed. Sacramento winters, she said, were miserable times.

"I can't see how you can say that," I scolded, cheerfully dipping my pork dumpling into the vinegar and hot pepper sauce. We were sitting in a red-vinyl booth surrounded by classic Chinese restaurant decor: hanging lanterns with red tassels, plastic flowers projecting stiffly from cheap vases, and a tremendous golden dragon climbing sinuously across the length of the longest wall.

This was Jean's all-too-brief lunch break from the bank, where she worked as a loan officer. But for me, lunch could be a leisurely affair. I had the entire afternoon off from teaching creative writing as an outside consultant to public schools. After lunch, I had plans to while away an hour or two at the bookstore browsing through my favorite shelves. Maybe I'd even buy something and take it home to read. I imagined myself snuggled up on the couch, cradling the precious book in my lap. With my husband, an attorney, at work, and a fourteen year-old son in school, I could relax in the silence of an empty house, a cup of tea steaming on a nearby table. Yes, today was a great day, and the gloomy weather was perfect for it!

Jean merely sighed and tried on a brave smile. That, more than anything, made me feel actually sorry for her. It also made me laugh.

"Is it really that bad?" I asked, pushing the point. "This isn't Minnesota, after all. I mean, the worst thing we get here is tule fog, for God's sake! No snow, no tire chains, no frozen breath and frozen faces. Just think, Jeannie sweetheart, this is California. Aren't you grateful?"

"No," she said. Then she laughed too.

"Look," Jean continued earnestly, "It's not the cold. It's the light. When the sunlight goes away I get depressed. It's something to do with the light rays. I read about it somewhere. When I found out it was a physical condition, I thought, thank God, I'm not crazy! But I still get depressed. I start fantasizing about moving to Hawaii or Puerto Rico or Mexico. But I control myself, keep busy, and pretty soon it's spring again!"

She poked at her dumpling desolutely. "But right now spring is still far away."

I put down my chopsticks and studied my friend for a moment. She was a pretty woman, with medium-blonde chin-length hair and olive skin. Her green-brown eyes were generally lively and intelligent. But now she sat listlessly, slightly slumped in her seat.

"Well, what can you do?" I asked, finally sympathetic.

"Buy a sunlamp," she replied, shrugging. "That's what they say helps. It gives off certain wavelengths of light I need to feel good, apparently."

"Well, so why don't you do it?" I asked.

"I don't know," she said. "It's mysterious. I've known about sunlamps for a couple years now. But I never do anything about it. I just tough it out."

2

Our lunch specials came and were deposited unceremoniously on the table. During the course of the meal, we changed the subject and got onto cheerier matters. Jean was getting a raise and a promotion. She visibly brightened as she discussed her new position and all it meant to her career possibilities. When Jean asked about my own teaching career with sincere interest, I just shook my head and smiled.

"Actually, it's going nowhere," I confessed. "I'm past being bored. Now I'm the walking dead."

We both laughed.

"So why do you keep on doing it?" she asked, a little too sharply. I glanced at her quickly and saw her eyes were twinkling.

"Touche," I granted. "Because I guess I don't know what else I can do. And the job—you know, working with the children and their writing—is really worthwhile. Nothing else comes to mind. Jean, I'm good at two things—teaching and writing. I'm not interested in anything else. And don't talk to me about technical writing, either! Or going back to get my credential so I can be a regular classroom teacher. I wouldn't do either of those things to save my soul!"

"O.K., O.K.," she soothed. "Don't get so excited. But you know, I just feel like something else is coming up for you. I don't know why, but I just feel it."

"Yeah," I agreed. "I feel something, too. But it's all so vague and unformed. So all I can do is just put one foot in front of the other, and keep up my responsibilities for now."

In the ensuing silence my gaze wandered to the wall where the golden dragon lifted a clawed foot high into the air and shot out a stream of fire.

"God will show you the way," Jean said softly. I started. In all our conversations, Jean had never mentioned God before.

"Thank you," I said quietly. "I'm sure he will."

I briefly considered this remark, coming as it did from Jean, a self-proclaimed refugee from a strict Catholic upbringing. Any suggestion of religious dogma or authoritarianism had always set her bristling. Her career and material goals seemed to be what she loved best. But a month ago, Jean had started an evening community college class in dream interpretation conducted by a psychologist. At first skeptical, she slowly became converted into an enthusiastic recorder and erstwhile interpreter of her own dreams.

3

Since she had begun the classes, Jean seemed less driven and more in touch with her own needs. Through the study of dreams, she was learning that her inner life was just as real and important as her identity as a career woman. Jean's goals now seemed more balanced between the material and spiritual, and the furrow between her brows noticeably decreased. I wondered if this new interest in her subjective experiences had brought God back into her life, in a way she could accept. I didn't know, but something apparently had.

"By the way," I began, "I've been having a series of odd dreams lately."

"Oh?" asked Jean, her interest immediately piqued. "Do you want to tell me about them?"

"Sure," I nodded. "I haven't been able to decipher them yet. But they seem to be forming a pattern. A big, kind-of-stupid man keeps bullying or threatening me with violence. The last dream, however, was curious. This time, the man was injured. I was determined to save him by carrying him away from some kind of danger. However, I was told, upon pain of death, that I must also save a robust baby boy. I couldn't rescue both of them because the injured man was so heavy. At the end, I was in tears, apologizing to some authority. I kept saying, 'I wish I could have done it. I really tried.'"

"What do you think the dreams mean?" asked Jean, sincerely interested.

"Well, I don't know for sure," I sighed. "I haven't worked it all out yet. Maybe I'm not ready to face the truth. But I have a feeling I should have left the injured man behind and taken the baby."

"Ah," nodded Jean thoughtfully. "I can see that. But I'm not very good at this yet, and I don't think I can help you. When you work it out, will you tell me what it means?"

"I will," I smiled.

For now, I mulled over the themes of danger, threatened violence, and injury that recurred in my dreams. I also wondered a lot about the healthy baby boy I had failed to save. The mood of defeat and guilt carried over into some shadowed corner of my awareness and waited there with dark, furled wings.

Soon our fortune cookies came. Jean broke hers open and started to giggle. It read, "A new development will shed some light on your situation."

4

"I guess that means I'm going to finally buy that sunlamp after all," she cracked.

I was silent, puzzling over the cryptic note that emerged from my own handful of crumbles.

"What does yours say?" Jean asked, curious.

"Uh . . . It says, 'You are now on the verge of a long-awaited change.'"

"Hey! That's good, isn't it?" exclaimed Jean, dusting off cookie crumbs from her lap.

"Yeah, I guess so," I agreed wryly. "I'm ready for it."

After lunch, Jean and I parted company. I drove thoughtfully over to the bookstore as the rain began to fall in a light drizzle, and progressed into a full downpour. Since I had not brought an umbrella, I parked as close to the building as possible and dashed inside. The bookstore was brightly lit and warm.

First, I browsed through the new fiction display, mesmerized by the colorful dustjackets and catchy titles calculated to snare a reader's interest. For me, this activity was about as smart as an alcoholic fondling bottles in the gourmet wine section of a liquor store. It was dangerous. It was a gamble. When I won, I lived to browse in other, less expensive sections of the store. When I lost, I paid the high price of a hardback book and went home to wrap myself between the sensuous pages of print.

Today I resisted well the temptation to buy a twenty-dollar fiction hardback. It was easy, since nothing leaped from its covers to grab me by the collar. I headed over to the New Age section and flipped through some interesting new titles. I was particularly struck by several books written about the occult practice generally termed "channeling." This is the phenomenon in which a disembodied entity—or spirit, for lack of a better word—speaks through a human being, usually for the purpose of giving psychic counsel or prognostication.

As a long-time spiritual student, I was fascinated with people's interest in this phenomenon. Unlike the practitioners of expanded awareness, of which I was one, these "channelers" did not enlarge their consciousness to take in the higher worlds. Instead, they offered themselves as "hosts" to "higher beings" who took over their bodies and spoke through them for a time. These beings sometimes claimed the title of spiritual teachers, but others of them were self-admitted ne'er-do-wells during their stints on Earth.

I wondered by what rationale people believed that, once out of the body, a man who had been a pickpocket or thief could suddenly become a source of irrefutable higher wisdom. Moreover, how could such information, even generally accurate information, be of much use to people without the key to unlocking the higher awareness for themselves? I also considered whether I was perhaps being needlessly harsh on what was probably a harmless diversion for those whose interest in the spiritual was more for curiosity than wisdom.

"Are you interested in that book?" came a deep voice over my right shoulder.

I turned to look at the man behind me. He was tall, brown, and muscular. He was dressed in a conservative pair of tan slacks, a plaid long-sleeved shirt, and a light-weight jacket. On his head a green wool sports cap tilted nattily above his eyes. His dark beard, flecked with white, was neatly trimmed close to his square-jawed face. He did not smile, and his eyes were riveting.

"Well . . . ," I stammered. Something about that face was so familiar, yet completely strange at the same time. I was sure I didn't know him, but nevertheless he felt as intimate to me as my own reflection in a mirror. In confusion, I dropped the book. It landed with a thud on my own foot.

"Ouch! Oh, sorry!" I exclaimed, on reflex. Why am I apologizing for dropping a book on my own foot? I heard myself think.

The man smiled as he lifted the book from the floor and placed it gently in my hands.

"I had been looking through that book myself," he said conversationally. "Interesting concept, this 'channeling' business. Do you believe in it?"

"Well, that's a complicated question," I said, gathering my wits. I returned the book to the shelf, both for something to do and to head off the possibility that it should slip from my grasp once more. I gave the stranger my full attention. "I mean, some of them are probably charlatans. But other 'channelers' are probably sincere in what they are doing. My only reservation is . . . "

"Your only reservation is . . . ?" the man said rather insistently, I thought.

6

I frowned slightly and studied this intruder to my thoughts. He seemed normal enough. Certainly he wasn't a bum, and he was too neatly groomed to be a "crazy." Then I briefly considered whether he was trying to "pick me up." I dismissed the third idea as somehow inappropriate, though I couldn't tell why.

Finally, I shrugged and voiced my opinion. "People are foolish to believe that just because a Soul isn't inhabiting a body anymore, it is qualified to give you spiritual advice. That's all."

"Interesting point," the man said, an amused twinkle appearing in his eyes. "And what about you? You've never 'channeled' anything yourself?"

I frowned slightly. This was a level of conversation that was rather more personal than I liked. So why did I have the compulsion to answer him anyway?

"No," I said, a little irritably. "I do have inner experiences which may seem similar to what they're calling 'channeling' nowadays. But there's a difference between my experiences and theirs."

"And what would that be?" the stranger asked politely.

"I expand my own awareness to take in the higher reality, and I am fully conscious when I do it," I answered emphatically. "I am never a passive vehicle for a higher power. A higher power does exist, but the idea is for us to become responsible co-workers with it instead. This takes more effort than a lot of people are willing to put in. They'd rather give that responsibility to someone else.

"As for the 'channelers' and other spiritual celebrities in this field, I think it's easy to separate the genuine article from the rest. A real teacher will point you in the direction of your own unfoldment. And actually live what he preaches. In other words, one is only qualified to share the truths one can demonstrate in one's everyday life! Everything else is games, speculation, and theory."

My words hung in the silence. I again became uncomfortable. I began to examine myself to determine whether I had said something simplistic, pompous, or just plain wrong. Finally, I decided I had said the truth the best way I knew how and let it go at that.

The man merely looked at me intently, the expression on his face completely unreadable.

It is difficult to explain the sense that I had in that moment. After the events of that day, odd things became normal, and I never

7

felt like this again. But for now, all I could think of was that something had been turned inside-out in my life. It was how one might feel looking out from the wrong end of a dream. The strange sense of the permeability of physical life with subjective states welled up in me, and I made a supreme effort to check the growing sense of mental chaos which accompanied this awareness.

The man seemed to know perfectly well how I was reacting to this seemingly innocuous interchange.

"Have no fear," he said so quietly that the two or three bystanders could not make out what he said. "If you would like to discuss this further, come to the Golden Dragon Restaurant in one hour. Do not be late."

With that, the man stepped silently down the aisle and disappeared around the corner. I stood there, debating my options. Then, with a sudden inspiration, I bolted after him. I could at least see where he was going, or what kind of car he was driving, or who he was with! These measures made no sense, but at the time they seemed like good ideas. But as I wandered in a daze through the bookstore, I could find no trace of him. I walked outside and stood at the door, peering closely into the parking lot, then casting wide glances at the streets surrounding the busy shopping complex. But the stranger had completely disappeared.

I returned inside to question the clerk at the counter near the door. "Did you see a tall, dark man with a beard and green cap go outside just now?" I asked a pale young woman in a black sweater.

"No, I didn't," she replied.

"Did you see him come in, by any chance?" I asked again.

"No," she replied blandly. She turned to the other clerk who was currently ringing up a sale. The man simply shook his head and returned to counting change into a woman's manicured hand.

I shrugged away the question. "It doesn't matter," I communicated silently, and walked outside. In truth, I was very troubled. It occurred to me by now that the stranger looked quite a bit like my spiritual teacher, the Tibetan Adept Haurvata Sampa. The clothes and cap threw me off, as well as the flecks of age in his beard. But the manner was unmistakable.

And yet, and yet . . . it was too odd to be believed. Ever since childhood, I had been secretly leaving my physical body and having adventures in the spiritual worlds. This process, lately called "out of body projection" or "soul travel," was natural to me. My earliest memories of it began with a serious childhood bout I had with pleurisy. Hospitalized with a dangerously high fever, and subsisting on intravenous feedings, I stepped outside my suffering body and found myself as a point of awareness high above the room.

At first disoriented and frightened, I soon felt the reassuring presence of another consciousness. This presence calmed me with an outpouring of strength, wisdom, and love. I had, I was told, a choice to make. Since I had succeeded in making myself seriously ill, I could die if I wished. Then my life as a reluctantly adopted child, "another mouth to feed" in an already struggling household of six aunts and aging grandparents, would be over.

However, if I chose to, I could stay and work out my own way through life. It would be difficult, I was told. Nevertheless, I would not be alone. I would have the inner assistance of a spiritual guide and eventually find the hidden lessons in every one of my experiences. I had the sense of being shown a great deal more, but a curtain had been drawn over it. I only remembered making a decision to get well, which I accomplished in a remarkably short time, much to the astonishment of the hospital staff.

I had kept up the practice of occasionally meeting with my inner guide throughout my childhood. It surprised and puzzled me that while the lives of saints and saviors testified to the reality of traveling in the heavenly worlds, these experiences were considered impossible for the average person. I felt I knew better, but kept this opinion to myself. After all, wasn't I already enough of an oddball? Did I want to call more unfavorable attention to myself by espousing strange ideas?

So today I questioned the direction my senses had taken me. The existence of my spiritual guide was a precious subjective reality for me. Yet, as a "sane" adult woman, I understood that such experiences were in the realm of fantasy for most people. I "knew" that the physical and spiritual were two different planes, and never the twain would meet!

That is, until now.

A turbulence started somewhere around my solar plexus and began sweeping upwards. I stopped it before it got to my head. This discipline was part of my training as a student of the Unmani Dhun Adepts, of which the Tibetan, Haurvata Sampa, was one. I centered myself in the feeling of God's love and allowed the calm to restore my confidence. Suddenly, I felt very normal. Instead of fearing, I began imagining that this could be the start of a wonderful adventure! I felt the first stirrings of curiosity take hold, and checked my wristwatch to see how much time I had before my engagement with the disappearing fellow.

My watch showed about forty-five minutes until the hour would be up. The restaurant the man had indicated was about a fifteen-minute drive away. Oddly, it was the same restaurant where I had had lunch with Jean earlier that very day. I thought with a start about our casual remarks over our respective fortune cookies. Now Jean's words rang again more meaningfully in my ears.

"God will show you the way," she had offered.

My fortune cookie had predicted "a long-awaited change." I wished I had kept the slip to look at again, but quickly dismissed this as foolish. I needed more than the good wishes of a friend and the prediction of a fortune cookie to change my life from the rut it had settled into over the years. Even now, the malaise of my professional work seemed strange to me. Although I was good at what I was doing, I had the perception of running very fast only to stay in the same place. I had the panicky sensation that if only I relaxed my hold, things would indeed change. But would it change for the better or for the worse?

I remembered the proverbial story of the man who stumbled off a cliff in the darkness and clung to a rock to save his life. After hours of struggling to retain his grip, he finally accepted his fate and let go of his hold, sure that he would fall thousands of feet to a painful death. Moments after he did so, however, he hit the ground beneath him with a thud. He had fallen only a few feet. The fate he had accepted for himself had existed only in the terror of his imagination!

I wondered if I was like that man, clinging to a rock in the darkness, creating a "worst case" scenario that filled me with needless dread. If I relaxed my hold . . . then what? One part of me said, "Go ahead and try it." The other part of me said, "Don't be a fool!"

I put these thoughts aside for the moment and went back into the store. In the remaining time, I selected a paperback science fiction story by one of my favorite authors and paid for it. The air outside smelled damp, and puddles had collected along the curbs where cars sloshed by. In the sky to the west a patch of blue was widening. It appeared that the downpour was over for the day.

I remembered my plan to return home with a new book to read while curled up on the couch with a cup of hot tea. It seemed like a long time ago that I had thought that, though in fact it had been just two hours or less. I had a funny premonition that the day was not going to go as I had planned. I smiled wryly, ambivalent as to whether that was all right with me or not. Then I calmly got in my car and drove to the Golden Dragon Restaurant. As my thoughts wandered back to my personal life, I dared myself to jump off that proverbial cliff. Little did I know that this was precisely what I was going to have to do, and very soon, too.

CHAPTER TWO
The Golden Dragon

He was there before me, sitting in a corner booth, his large hands engulfing a tiny cup of reddish-brown tea. I sat down wordlessly and smiled, waiting for him to speak.

"Ah, I see you have unlocked the mystery," he grinned back, flashing his white teeth. "I thought you would. I had confidence in you!"

I sighed heavily. Whether this turn of events was a relief or a curse, I didn't know which. But more than anything, I was pleased to put the question behind me and be in a position to adjust myself to this strange new reality.

"Haurvata," I said, savoring the conclusiveness of saying his name.

"Yes, dear one," smiled the teacher. "It is I."

Finally, I broke up laughing. "How did you get those white hairs in your beard? And those clothes? I love the cap; you should wear it regularly. It updates your look!"

The man smiled with great dignity. It felt awkward to be joking with him in this manner, but somehow the humor made me feel more confident in an unaccustomed situation. I heaved another sigh of relief and poured myself a cup of jasmine tea.

"To tell the truth, I hesitated to do this," my teacher admitted. Clearly, he had taken no offense. "I do operate a physical body on earth, as you know. But I do not appear to my spiritual students in this manner on any regular basis. There are several reasons for this. One of them is due to what you experienced just a while ago. Without a great deal of emotional and mental balance, plus some spiritual experience, most people would . . . what do you call it? . . . 'freak out'! I do not take such risks, as I have said, normally. But I have decided to make an exception for you."

"Really? Why?" I asked quickly.

The waitress glanced at me in an odd way when she saw me here for the second time in the same day. I smiled inscrutably at her as she handed us our menus. Then she disappeared behind the carved wooden screen.

My teacher continued. "Eventually, in anyone's spiritual journey, it becomes necessary to stop separating one's reality into individual pieces and live, instead, one completely integrated life. In other words, to give a mundane example, at first it may seem acceptable to some to go to church on Sunday and verbally abuse their kids on Monday. But sooner or later, it occurs to them that it is impossible to do both. Seeing the contradiction between such choices and doing something about it is a big step for evolving Souls.

"Living the fragmented life of contradictory realities is like living in a dream within a dream. This level of unawareness keeps the pieces separated, but the discontinuity is actually a source of much strain and unhappiness. If this continues for too long, the tension between one reality and the other will either immobilize a person, or force him to choose between the two. Unfortunately, most people choose whatever feels most comfortable, not what is most progressive for them. So there is a certain amount of backsliding in anyone's spiritual progress, without the individual realizing it consciously."

"This reminds me of people who diet to lose weight," I said, "but don't really change the way they think about food. So, as soon as they stop dieting, they find themselves fat again!"

"Yes," said Haurvata, nodding his head. "The realities of being fat and being slim are separated by a leap in consciousness. To make this leap, a Soul must match appropriate behavior with a harmonious point of view—in this case, eating moderately while placing a high value on being fit and healthy. Behavior modification alone is not enough. Nor is merely a change in attitude. Progress requires both, and is not achievable except through a fully conscious state."

I replied, "Maybe that's why I haven't been very successful lately in trying to make a few changes—like going to bed earlier and waking up sooner. I've tried to set my alarm for an hour earlier, and I've done all kinds of other things, besides. But nothing seems to be working."

"Now this would be a good project for you!" the Tibetan said warmly. "The early morning hours are best for clarity of thinking and tapping into one's inner resources of personal creativity. It also gives you a chance to make a graceful transition from the dream life into the waking state, and increases the likelihood that you will carry over something valuable from the subconscious side. As it is, your present schedule forces you to leap abruptly out of your dreams into a very focused mode of tending to material things. This is not the way an Adept would do it!"

"I suppose not," I agreed, surprised by the thought.

"Let me put it another way," Haurvata continued, leaning toward me for emphasis. "You need to harmonize what you know with how you are living to put yourself at a higher level of integration! Mastery is a here-and-now thing! It is not just an exotic achievement won by six-hundred-year-old men with beards and long robes."

I laughed at this, and a sly smile spread across his broad features.

"I can buy that," I agreed. Haurvata ordered a fish soup and I ordered an appetizer of vegetable rolls.

"In order to accomplish this," he explained, "you must be willing to reexamine, as necessary, every department of your life. You must yield old viewpoints to newer and fresher viewpoints to live on a constantly improving level of efficiency and service. It is somewhat like redesigning a city every time a major change in population or lifestyle occurs. On a physical level, this is neither practical nor possible. But as metaphor for Soul, it is not only possible, but essential.

"Now," he continued, gathering momentum, "the challenges one must face for mastership are always found within his or her own personal, contemporary life. The details of your life today are no more or less difficult than the details of mine during the days when I was a student like yourself, struggling for the golden wisdom. Do not be fooled into putting your goal of self-mastery off to some vague time in the future. You do not have any future. All you have is now!"

"Oh!" I said. His urgency startled me and I couldn't say much more. My thoughts drifted to my dream of the injured man and the baby, and I suddenly realized what they represented: my attachment to a self-image of failure and helplessness versus a brand new viewpoint of myself as a vigorous individual ready to face the challenges of life.

"As you've pointed out yourself," I heard the Tibetan grumbling, "just being outside the physical body does not guarantee one a higher degree of wisdom than while dwelling inside the body. True, stripped of the limitations of the sensory consciousness, the deceased is many times more aware of life than he or she was before. This can seem like true unfoldment to the inexperienced. But any serious candidate for self-mastery should know the difference between the carnival performances of attention-seeking entities in the lower astral world, and the systematic guidance of the spiritual teachers."

"It seems to me that real teachers help you to discover truth inside yourself," I put in, recovering my place in these thoughts. "They don't cultivate your dependency on them."

"Aye," the Tibetan agreed, slipping into his old-fashioned speech. He jabbed a finger in my direction. "We expect initiative, imagination, and courage from our students! Many leave us when they discover that they must make an effort for what they expect to get. They wish to cling to their old habits and viewpoints and have heaven handed to them on a silver platter. Bah! I have no patience for ones like these."

His eyes blazed up for a fraction of a second, and it was as near as I've gotten to seeing him angry. For that I was grateful.

"Now to return to you," he said, frowning. "There is something more you must do for yourself. You must break the habit of occasionally slipping into a state of spiritual sleep."

I colored and controlled myself from wanting to slide further down in my seat.

If he sensed my reaction, he deliberately ignored it. Instead, he fixed me with a serious stare and plunged on. "This is not a dream and you are not crazy. Let us settle this once and for all, and allow your reality to adjust to the fact that I am here in the flesh as well as on the inner planes. I am as real as you are. But now, the question remains, how real are you?"

The question hung in the air, unexpected and alarming.

"Whatever do you mean?" I exclaimed. The food arrived, but we ignored it for the moment. Instead, we stared at each other like two gunfighters waiting for the other to draw. Neither of us would break the gaze.

Finally, he stopped and dipped his spoon into his soup. It was clotted with floating green vegetables and small, pale lumps which I assumed to be fish.

"I repeat my question," he said, more mildly. "How real are you?"

"I'm real, I'm real," I protested. "How much more real can I be?"

"Yes, that's it exactly," the Tibetan said with some satisfaction. "That's what you must find out!"

I shook my head. "I am completely baffled. I need you to explain this to me, apparently."

"And so I will," he said patiently. After a moment, his eyes took in the dragon poised above us on the wall. "Ah, I think I have it! What do you know about dragons?"

"Dragons?" I repeated, puzzled. "Not much. I like to read about them in fantasy books. Actually, I think they're the most fascinating imaginary creatures that exist . . . er, or don't exist. Which is it?"

"Large serpents have certainly existed, my friend," said my teacher. "And still do exist in some dimension of the inner worlds. Anything that has ever been imagined is real, for imagination is merely a reflection of what is, in some arena of life.

"Soul incarnates in many dimensions other than that of space-time. Science is only now starting to recognize the possibility of these dimensions, which lie beyond the observational powers of man. Soul often remembers something of its more expanded life in these worlds. Its memories are frequently distorted by the limited mental faculties it must take on in the human consciousness. But these memories represent, at any rate, some lingering traces of Soul's experiences of the higher worlds.

"Flying horses are real, too, though not on earth. The laws of reality on this planet, in this day and age, do not allow for such creatures. Fairies, gnomes—all these exist as well, and very close to this physical plane, yet we cannot see them. They reside in another reality which generally only children visit, and a few perceptive adults. But dragons have retreated even further away than the elementals of the earth. We have only legends and speculative tales to tell us what they looked like and how they behaved."

"Does this have something to do with me?" I asked timidly.

Haurvata laughed. "Yes, my child. Be patient with me a moment longer. Dragons, you see, while banished from the physical plane of reality, still survive in the imagination for an important reason. Haven't you ever wondered why humanity has continued to maintain such a fascination for dragonkind?"

"As a matter of fact, I have," I said.

"And what have you concluded?"

"Well," I began, "it's not exactly a conclusion. But I suppose it's because dragons are powerful and mysterious. Beyond that, I don't know."

"Then listen," the Tibetan said emphatically. "Dragons represent the awesome spiritual potential of man lying below the threshold of his awareness. Scientists say that man uses perhaps only ten percent of his brain. But I say he uses even less of his spiritual powers!

"Dragons are beyond the duality of good and evil, and thus share qualities of both. Man cannot conceive of what may lie beyond such dualities, so he pins his imagination on a mythic beast that represents for him what he cannot intellectually fathom and morally accept. Do good and avoid evil, the moral teachings say. Yet dragons are neither good nor evil, but simply are.

"Soul is like the dragon in this way. Its highest morality is that it is fully itself, and as itself, it serves the higher power, or God. It may be on the side of peace at one time, and on the side of war at another time. This makes no sense to the social man, but Soul is concerned with its own survival more than with the preservation of any particular community, race, or way of life. The language I am using makes Soul seem immoral. But this merely points to the failure of language to adequately describe the glorious wisdom,

17

freedom, and power of Soul.

"Now you may notice that the literature of both Eastern and Western cultures contains references to dragons. Indeed, the Chinese zodiac, which is divided into twelve-year cycles, has as one of its symbols the serpent, or dragon. But there is one important difference between the Eastern dragon and the Western dragon."

"The Eastern dragon has wings?" I asked, tentatively offering my meager piece of knowledge.

"Exactly," smiled Haurvata. "The Eastern dragon is winged and flies through the air. It can breathe fire. The Western dragon traditionally lives in a cave or under water and is more rumored about than seen. Grendel, of the old English tale, is a typical Western dragon. In the realm of symbolism, water is the most unconscious medium, the world of dreams. Land is akin to the normal daily waking consciousness. But the sky is the realm of the superconscious, the "magical" level on which one can perform miraculous feats!

"What this tells us about East and West is simple. It relates, as you shall see, to something you will learn about in greater detail in the future: the male and female spiritual forces. The Eastern cultures, by and large, have recognized the male and female elements as spiritual counterpoints to each other. The two halves thus make a whole, the yin and yang of existence. In the West, on the other hand, life is regarded as essentially masculine, with the feminine as an evil or regressive influence to its forward movement. Thus, the West has denied the feminine an honored and respected place alongside the masculine. It has effectively banished the female to a dark cave or watery prison.

"Up until now, the results of this aberration have not been tragic. Of course, in terms of human creativity and personal development, the loss has been tremendous. But as a culture, the West has benefited greatly from its masculine drive to provide technological advancements for the earthly community. However, without the proper checks and balances to this aggressive approach, there is a real potential for disaster in the future. The hope is that both East and West can learn from each other and proceed with a modicum of difficulties through the twenty-first century.

"In order to accomplish this, mankind must tap the resources of its hidden spiritual power as symbolized by the dragon. The purpose of this change is more for individual growth than for the rehabilitation of the planet, but the results will be the same. The spiritual power—Soul power—is actually a neutral force. But it can only be contacted by one who has realized both masculine and feminine forces within him or herself. To use the metaphor again, the dragon must be coaxed out of its lair in cave or lake and allowed to soar!"

I crunched on my rolls and considered these ideas carefully. They made sense, but I kept coming back to the question the Tibetan had so insistently asked me. "How real are you?" he had said. I puzzled about this still. My preoccupation must have shown, for soon the Adept stopped discoursing and looked at me keenly.

"Have you figured it out yet?" he asked flatly.

"No," I said. "I take it you're referring to what you said about being real?"

"Aye."

"Well," I sighed. "Pinocchio wasn't real. He was a puppet. But Gepetto, the toymaker, loved him so much that he sent him to school and treated him as if he were real. Finally, Pinocchio saved Gepetto from the belly of a whale out of love for him. Then the Blue Fairy made him flesh and blood.

"I don't know what this has to do with anything. I'm just babbling," I said, shaking my head.

"Not at all," replied my teacher, smiling. "It is a useful bridge between the idea of dragons and your own particular situation. Pinocchio wanted to be human, but could not achieve it without first developing within himself a capacity for love and self-sacrifice. You aspire to the Soul level, but cannot win it until you develop the courage to unleash the spiritual forces within you—the dragon, as it were. So you see, like Pinocchio, you are not quite 'real' yourself.

"In both stories, however, there is a higher power at work. In Pinocchio's case, this higher power took the form of the Blue Fairy. In your life, the higher power is represented by myself, the spiritual teacher. And though I may not have a magic wand, I can help you undergo the transformation you seek! But only you can do the proper work and make the required efforts."

"Oh, I see now!" I said excitedly. "In other words, only Soul is 'real' in your sense of the word. The rest is just . . . just personality, human consciousness, instinct . . . is that the idea?"

"True," he grunted, swirling his spoon in the still-steaming soup. "What people normally think of as themselves is actually a whole block of unconsciousness consisting merely of identification with experiences. Men and women are simply genetic entities without the presence of Soul. The mind, emotions, and memories of the subtler bodies are also rather mechanical manifestations. Culture and social training are even more superficial."

"So what can I do to become 'real'?" I asked, cautiously.

Haurvata smiled. "Many things. But at the bottom of them, only one thing. Have the courage and audacity of the dragon! Take risks, intelligent risks. The past and the future are more fluid than you believe. You are swimming in them now. Stroke in any direction and you are liable to meet with yourself, as you were, as you could have been, or will be in the future. Life is dynamic for Soul, and time is merely a mechanical factor which can be transcended when necessary to accomplish your spiritual goals."

"My head is spinning," I groaned, which was only a slight exaggeration.

"Aye, child," the Tibetan said in a throaty baritone. "The neat, compartmentalized, and ultimately dissatisfying world you have constructed is being razed. The disorientation you feel is the experience of your old gridpatterns being blown to pieces."

"I can see the wrecking ball now!" I wailed comically.

The Tibetan joined me in laughter.

"Yes, it is funny," he agreed, "especially if you choose to see it that way! That is a quality I like very much in you, and you should develop it further. You are not aware as of yet how great a survival factor humor is for anyone. Humor dissolves resistance, heals breaches, discovers new approaches and avenues for growth. Humor can find the needle in the haystack and the silver lining in a cloud of gloom. With humor, you will find that the changes coming into your life will not be disasters, but gifts. Laugh, and you will maintain your balance even when things are particularly difficult. And, in times of change, difficulties are always inevitable."

A time of change. Yes, that was what I had been feeling! I was ready for it. Until now, way too much of my spiritual energies had been tied up with controlling a massive amount of negative thinking— frustration with the limitations of my abilities, confusion over my career direction, and a struggle with finances. It had sapped so much of my vitality that relatively little was left for creativity and new inspiration. The image that came to me now was of an automobile operating on two cylinders. The image suddenly reminded me of a dream I had had about two weeks earlier. I repeated it now to Haurvata.

I was a passenger of a car traveling along a busy freeway. Suddenly, I noticed all the heads of the people in passing autos turning to stare at something behind me. As I looked around, a white streamlined sportscar passed me to my left. I gazed at it in admiration. Never had I seen any car so beautiful, and yet so unique in design! I couldn't place its manufacturer, and decided at last that it must be a rare custom-built car or a prototype of a car of the future. As it drove away, its license plate declared in simple letters, "Honolulu."

"Honolulu," I thought to myself. "That's where I was born!" In a flash, I found myself in the driver's seat of the futuristic car. The car then revealed itself to be even odder. It had no engine, no control panel, nor any bit of mechanical equipment or parts. Despite this strange fact, the car drove itself remarkably smoothly, swiftly, and safely. For awhile, I sat in the car enjoying myself immensely. But soon I became restless and fearful—how can this be happening? How can any car drive itself?

Panicked, I quickly took control of the situation. Somehow, I gathered the tiny car in my arms like a hoopskirt and sprinted down the freeway. It was a ridiculous sight, and I woke up grinning and laughing!

Haurvata listened carefully to my dream and chuckled at the incongruous final image. Then he offered his interpretation of the odd dream.

"This dream is basically about the difference between the little self and the Soul self—the ego and the individuality. The white car is the symbol of Soul, the pure vehicle for Spirit which you, and any sincere seeker, may become. As you noticed, the car drove on its own power, which was non-mechanical and self-generated. This shows that the true source of all power is within Soul itself, and not anything less, such as the mind or the emotions.

"The little self, on the other hand, is the part of yourself that wants to control the vehicle. Through ignorance, it distrusts Spirit's ability to guide Soul through the challenges of life. It overrules

Spirit and tries to do things through personal effort and struggle. This makes the little self feel, and perhaps look, important. But, from the spiritual point of view, such efforts are merely ludicrous. Even worse, as you have discovered at first hand, personal effort and struggle will tire you. It will drain your energies and shut off the creative inflow of Spirit. In short, it will leave you 'high and dry' just when you need divine help the most.

"Now here is one more thing about the vehicle which you have overlooked! It is very important, so I will point it out to you. It has to do with the design of the car itself. The use of the car as a metaphor for Soul—a 'vehicle' for Spirit—as well as the car's white color as a representation of purity, are conventional and thus easily recognizable spiritual symbols. However, the rest of the car is very individualized and original! I believe you used the words 'futuristic' and 'unique.' The passengers of the surrounding cars on the freeway admired the white car, but not because it moved without mechanical means. Indeed, they could not have known that from the outside! They admired the car because of its great originality, power, and beauty!

"Soul also has its own originality and unique beauty. Each Soul is unlike any other. By the time Soul reaches the point of being a seeker of self-realization and god-awareness, it is utterly itself! The dream was thus pointing out to you the level of spiritual individuality you have reached. This individuality is entirely different from personality, which is associated with the ego. This individuality of which I am speaking is the fruit of spiritual development over lifetimes of experience and training. It is an individuality built upon choices made, a particular interest and style developed, and a specific spiritual mission taking shape.

"Thus, the dream is telling you that you must cease pursuing self-improvement in the human consciousness, and surrender instead to the perfection of Spirit! Simply allow Soul to express itself by following the inner direction along the lines of your natural interests and abilities. Then life will be as effortless as the ride down the freeway in the vehicle you just described!"

This information stunned me in its clarity and simplicity. As a friend of mine would have joked, Haurvata's advice was a real B.F.O.—that is, a "blinding flash of the obvious." I would never have described what I had been doing in his terms. But, thinking

22

about it, I found that it was accurate. My line of reasoning was this: in order to have greater results in life, I had to work harder, be more clever, and forcefully conquer all obstacles in my way. When I tried this approach, however, I found a ghostlike obstinacy to my problems. What Haurvata was suggesting was nothing short of revolutionary: stop struggling and Be.

"I think I get it!" I whispered excitedly. "At least, I understand it mentally. Now if I can just do it! Do you think it will work for me?"

"Of course," replied the Tibetan matter-of-factly. "It will work for anyone. The principle I've been describing to you is called the Law of Unity. This law is essential to any Soul who wishes to grow into the full expression of its true individuality. Male or female, adult or child, the law operates in the same way for all.

"The essence of this law is that all ego-limited efforts dissipate your spiritual power. And any effort that has at its core a sense of lack, fear, or self-serving need is an ego-limited effort. When your personal power is dissipated, naturally your ability to accomplish great things will be limited, despite what might be exceptional innate abilities. Now the only way to regroup your spiritual forces, and thus unify your life, is to serve God through the higher self, or Soul. For in serving God, you are serving the whole, including yourself. Therefore, serving God is the more universal attitude. It results in increase for both oneself and others, on levels of creativity that the personal self could not possibly match!

"Two metaphors come to mind to explain this to you. First is a team of horses with the personal self holding the reins. The horses are all lined up in a row facing forward. But their stances are not quite parallel to each other. So if one were to project their line of travel in space, you would see that the horses' directions would soon diverge. In other words, they would fan out the way the spokes of a wheel do from a central hub."

"Interesting. Go on," I commented encouragingly.

"That is what your life has been like up until now. Your efforts have been multiple energies projected in diverging directions. Your writing, teaching, spiritual life, family life, and friendships—they all seem to start from your center, yet when they go forth from you, they begin to pull in different directions. When your efforts start out, this divergence is not apparent. But by the time your efforts have been out there a while in time and space, they are as clearly separate as the individual spokes of a wheel are separate from each other!"

"Extremely interesting!" I said. "Don't stop now!"

"All right," Haurvata continued. "Now to the second image. The second image is simple. It is a big white horse, with you riding bareback on it. You are holding onto its mane—no saddle, no bridle, no reins. The horse and you are one Soul. It moves and you are right there with it. Its direction is straight ahead. No deviations, no obstacles. Just straight ahead. The white horse is a symbol of yourself as Soul. The power of that horse is your own purified spiritual power. As in your dream of the white car, you do not have to make any effort to control or direct the horse, for its nature is of God.

"You have come to the point of unifying your desires and efforts in this life. This has been made possible through the inner work you have done to clear the way for this unification to occur. All your fears and limitations have been sapping your confidence and making you afraid to live such a unified existence. It was as if you were afraid to put all your eggs in one basket, in case you might fail. So you split up your efforts to placate the damaged and frightened ego. But none of your partial victories have been satisfying to you because they were not generated from the depth of your Soul, from a unity of spirit, heart, and mind. If you had trusted God more, you would have learned sooner how to live in order to be truly happy."

I felt strangely at peace. I compared this feeling to the utter exhaustion and relief one feels after an emotional outburst, or after the sudden consummation of a long and arduous physical struggle. I was coming out of a gnawing restriction in my life and sensing the possibilities hitherto unseen.

"You know," I began brightly, "it occurs to me that dragons have colors, too. Is that significant?"

"For our purposes," he answered, "only one color is important—the gold dragon."

"And why is that?" I asked.

"Gold is the color of highest material value," he replied. "It represents what is most precious, the ultimate alchemical transformation of consciousness from dross into Soul. Therefore, the golden dragon should be for you a symbol of the highest you can achieve in this lifetime—the refinement of self into Soul in order to

24

act with courage and love for all life. You see this now?"

I looked at the wall to the decorative dragon poised above us. Its body undulated like waves upon a storm-tossed sea, and its eyes were distant and unfathomable as stars.

CHAPTER THREE
Call of the Unknown

We stood at the top of the world, numberless snow-covered mountains surrounding us in every direction. Below us were more crags and peaks tinged with a soft blue light. At my feet, the snow melting in patches revealed the dark soil, the granite rocks and pebbles. Soon there would be spring flowers—perhaps lupines, violet-blue like the light in this strange and lonely part of the world. I took a deep breath. No other air was quite like this—thin and light, like a rare elixir.

I looked happily at Haurvata Sampa, the man who had brought me here. His back was to me. It was broad and square, covered with a roughly woven garment of natural-colored wool. In this environment, my teacher looked like a shepherd, except that his expression was not particularly pastoral. It was, instead, direct, forceful, penetrating. Foremost in his order of teaching masters, the Unmani Dhun, Sampa often resided in a small hut in the recesses of the Hindu Kush Mountains along the border between Kashmir and Afghanistan. His job was to guide the fortunate individuals chosen to receive direct training in his ancient system of expanded awareness.

Now Haurvata turned and rested his attention on me.

"Do you know why you are here today?" he asked. "Here" meant present in the spiritual body, rather than the physical. The latter was occupied with the daily tasks of a writer, wife, and mother while the subjective self was free to travel the inner worlds at will. "No. Not really," I said truthfully.

It had been a few weeks since our last, fateful meeting in the bookstore and restaurant. I had made use of the intervening time to contemplate upon the concept of integrating my life on a higher level. I had even tried to begin my day on an earlier schedule. However, it was fair to say that I hadn't gotten far on any of my projects. My efforts were, as usual, rather more inconclusive than the Tibetan liked.

Thus, I felt uncomfortable as the purposefulness of his thought was directed at me. It was probing into me, searching for something . . . I didn't know what. But as quickly as it began, it stopped. He turned away again and lightly slapped his thigh. When he faced me the second time his expression was completely different. He laughed softly.

"Well then, God's lion, since you don't know, I will tell you!" he said in a low rumble.

I stood quietly, expectantly. I had learned long ago in my relationship with this particular Adept to only say what was necessary, and no more. If I chattered, as I tried to do in the early years of our relationship, he only frowned and fell silent. At times, before I had learned better, he would stop me with a wave or a look and dismiss me abruptly. Before I knew it, I would be back in my physical body with a sense of disappointment and loss. So now I merely waited, my mind and emotions quiet, waiting for Haurvata to speak.

"The Unmani Dhun have invested a certain amount of training in you," he began seriously. "Now it is time for you to do something for us. We cannot wait any longer for you to be readier for the task. You have the necessary skill with words, which we believe can be used to do a service for God. Are you willing?"

"Why, yes, I guess so!" I answered, surprised.

Since my first awkward attempts as a girl of seven or eight, I had written every kind of communication imaginable. I had authored news articles, stories, essays, literary criticism, educational curricula, poems, fiction, and even brochures and press releases. I had logged

27

my share of hours as a reluctant editor to other people's efforts. Now, as the wife of an attorney and mother of a teenaged boy, I split my time between domestic duties, my writing aspirations, and educational consulting. For the last eight years, I had been teaching as a writer-in-residence in California public schools.

I had always been driven from one kind of writing to another, never settling down to pursue any field with commitment. This pattern of my career frustrated me, and left me with a strange sense of being able to do everything, and yet nothing. In the many years of my relationship with the Tibetan, he had never once mentioned anything about my writing efforts. I thought with a start: I had also never mentioned anything about my writing to him!

I looked at him now, completely attentive and full of curiosity.

The Adept continued in a calm, matter-of-fact voice.

"The Unmani Dhun have in mind certain books which will reveal the timeless truths, but in a different way than we have put them forth in the past. You see, few people desire truth and few can grasp it, but of those few, fewer still are able to apply truth correctly and naturally in their lives. Are you beginning to see?"

"I think so," I answered. "It's similar to what happens when I try to teach something new to my students. At first, only a portion of them really pay attention. Of that portion, a handful understand it correctly. Then, of that handful, a few actually take the ideas into themselves and have the experience I am trying to pass on. After a time, more and more catch on and the ideas spread. But it takes a surprising amount of effort. Is this something like what you meant?"

"Yes, that is the general idea," replied Haurvata, nodding his short-cropped head. "Of course, as you know, we can do little for those who are not interested in what we have to teach them. They are not ready for the knowledge, for as yet, they have little need of it. It is need which stimulates a subconscious receptivity to new information. Need creates receptivity. This is the principle that the advertisers in your world know by heart!"

"I never thought of it that way," I said, surprised by this unexpected connection between spiritual principles, my everyday problems with teaching, and modern consumerism.

"But there is much we can do," he continued, "for those who sincerely desire the knowledge but need assistance in applying it to themselves. It is for the sake of these Souls that the Unmani Dhun exist. For them we are guides—no more and no less. We bring them slowly out of the body consciousness into the awareness of the universe! Because we come and go between this world and the invisible ones, we are also called spiritual travelers. This, my friend, you already know.

"But to accomplish our work, we also need the assistance of individuals like yourself. We cannot succeed without you. Some assist through their jobs, some through their families and personal relationships, others just by being. Whether a teacher, writer, businessman or mother, each of you can function as a 'vehicle' for Spirit in this world through your knowledge of truth. The negative force also has its vehicles. So we need you for balance as much as for forward movement! Do you see the picture now?"

"I do," I replied. "But how do I fit into your plans?"

"It is simple," he said, turning away from me to gaze into the blue-white distance. "You have a talent for applying truth. Look into yourself, and you will understand what I am saying."

He paused for a moment, allowing me to do as he had suggested.

After a minute of self-contemplation, I shifted about uncomfortably.

"I am getting a vague idea," I finally answered. "I have always been rather pragmatic-minded about spirituality. I always ask myself, 'How does this work?' I guess I am skeptical without being closed-minded. But is this the sort of thing you mean by the term 'applying truth'? I take it that I'm going to be writing some books. What is it exactly that I'm supposed to write about?"

"Ah," Haurvata smiled, pointing a brown, big-knuckled finger at me. "We needn't be concerned with 'books'—for now, just 'book.' One book—the first. It will be an unusual task, an unusual sort of book. Not merely a novel, not exactly psychology, but something like a combination of the two. This book is already inside yourself! The subject will be nothing less than a revelation of an ancient mystery—the mystery of the sexes."

My eyebrows arched upward for a second, but the teacher plunged on.

"We have placed this knowledge inside you on an unknown basis. That is, we have taught it to you over the many lifetimes of your physical existence. We have watched you grow, much as the gardener watches the garden under his care—planting the seed, watering and fertilizing the ground, providing sun and shade, and waiting patiently for the rich harvest that lies dormant in the germ! "Now comes the time of harvest. The fruit hangs ripe on the vine, and the bee comes humming to the pollen. It must be gathered now or wasted. It must be gathered and shared for the celebration of life that depends on the personal creativity of each Soul. This is the spiritual creativity of living to the highest degree of awareness you have earned. This creativity brings the complete transformation of self, the dying to be reborn as the earth does in her cycle of seasons."

He paused for breath and looked into me with warm eyes.

"This planet is preparing for a Great Death. No, not a war, my child," he said, sensing my thoughts, "though it can be so if enough of you fear, wish, or imagine it this way. The kind of death of which I speak is different. The history of the world has seen many ages, and this, as you know, is the last. However, it is many hundreds of thousands of years long in physical terms—long enough for a million Souls to achieve immortality.

"The process is generally a slow one. It takes billions of years in the so-called natural process of hit-and-miss for Soul to wake from its dreams, seek, then find the true life of Spirit waiting like the germinal seed inside itself. But the path of the Unmani Dhun has always been available to speed up the process for individuals who show special promise and the required amount of motivation. Our work, however, is harder in ages of greater illusion. Though in truth, all ages of man are steeped in illusion!"

The Adept chuckled to himself, as if laughing at a private joke between himself and the world he had chosen to serve, out of compassion and love.

"Shall we go inside and take some tea?"

The light on the mountain tops was clear and intense as it reflected off the white expanses of snow. The teacher's face, however, shone with an inner light that was brighter than any physical sun. I squinted into his face and nodded happily.

The Tibetan bent his back as he entered the hut. I followed after him and sat cross-legged on a clean, worn cushion that had once been brightly dyed. The hut was carefully, though simply, built with large wooden beams and a thickly thatched roof. A small fire lay guttering in the central hearth, the smoke lazily rising and disappearing mysteriously in the air.

The snapping of twigs was sharply defined in the silence. The Adept seemed to be humming a tune—something which I had never heard him do before. I glanced at him in surprise. He took no notice, but deftly built up a small mound of wood, upon which he blew until he had aroused the fire into a cheerful, crackling blaze. From a hook he hung a blackened cast-iron kettle, brimful of snow melt. It was a familiar and beloved sight: plain but for two dragons curving serpentine necks around the bases of the handle.

Soon the kettle was sending up a plume of steam. He flung a handful of herbs into the bubbling pot with a flourish and placed two cups in front of him in readiness. Then he faced me seriously again, taking up where he had left off.

"Do you have any questions so far?"

"No questions," I gulped. What was true was that I had so many questions, they crowded into each other, obscuring their outlines until I could not pick out a single one to verbalize.

His expression was mildly approving. "I see you have learned a few things since you first came here. You intuit correctly. The mind cannot grasp what is being said, but will only get in the way. Do not engage it. Leave it aside to chew on its bone while we do the work of Souls!"

He poured the tea into the rude porcelain cups and handed me one. Several small twigs still swirled in the greenish-brown water, and the steam from the cup felt good as it caressed my face.

"It's good! Thanks," I said. In this small room, with the pale lances of sunlight slanting in, I felt as if I could dwell forever. A lonely kind of joy, like the cry of a wild bird, rose out of my heart and filled me with a deep longing.

"What is it you feel, my lion? Tell me," said the Adept.

"I feel . . . I feel . . . happy," I replied, embarrassed by my lack of a greater concept than this overused one. "And yet . . . strangely sad, too. Can you explain what I feel?"

"I can," he nodded, setting down his now-empty cup. "It is the joy of Soul—Soul who knows and revels in its own freedom. It is also the loneliness of Soul, because freedom means the lack of the very illusions that give comfort and security to so many. It is the paradox of the individual spark of God who, in the awareness of its total freedom, is stunned by the enormity of its responsibility to give and receive love.

"Can you understand this, my child?"

"Yes, Haurvata," I replied. It was what my heart, without words, was feeling.

"It is a familiar feeling, no?" he asked, smiling.

"Why, yes," I replied, surprised at the sudden thought. "So it is. It's as if I just remembered something, and all the emotions associated with it came rushing in!"

"Well put," he responded, filling our cups again with the steaming brew. "You remember because you have come to this point before. Again and again, you have been carefully guided to this crossroads inside yourself. But again and again, you have turned back. Do you know why?"

"Yes," I admitted.

"Tell me then," the Adept commanded softly.

"Well," I took a deep breath and began, "it's . . . it's because I have been afraid of the unknown."

"I see," the Adept said softly. "The unknown. And what of it?"

I was silent. I considered carefully what I had just said. "I . . . I don't know," I finally answered, shaking my head in frustration. "I can't see any more."

"You can see it," the Adept said quietly. "I will help you."

I looked into his eyes and felt myself being lifted gently above the level of awareness at which I was presently blocked. It happened so quickly, I felt no resistance to the movement. Then, from somewhere, came the sound of a distant wind, at first gentle, then thin and biting.

"What do you perceive?" urged the Adept's voice.

At that moment, I saw a wall. It was extremely high, crudely though strongly built, and very old. I described to the teacher what I had seen.

"You have built that wall stone by stone," Haurvata commented.

"Me? Why?" I queried.

"Perhaps you're afraid of King Kong?" offered the Adept, his voice amused.

I chuckled, too. "Be serious," I admonished. "This is my state of consciousness you're making light of."

"I am being serious," the Adept insisted. "Wasn't the story of the giant ape made into one of your favorite old-time movies?"

"Yes," I replied. "I loved it! The wall was built by natives on a tropical island. They wanted to keep this gigantic ape out of their hair. They built a village on a small strip of land on the outside of the wall, by the water. They even performed exotic rituals and sacrificed screaming native girls to Kong. Whether Kong was going to eat them or make love to them, I could never decide which!"

"Do you remember what it was like on the other side of the wall?" Haurvata chuckled.

"Sure," I replied. "A prehistoric jungle filled with dinosaurs and other oversized beasts."

"Well, now," continued Haurvata, "do you think what the natives did was right? In other words, would you have built the wall? Would you have sacrificed screaming girls?"

"I think I'd have built a fleet of canoes and searched for a more civilized piece of real estate," I ventured. "No. Just kidding. I suppose, being in their frame of mind, I'd have done whatever seemed to work at the time. But the virgin sacrifice bit seemed unnecessary. The wall . . . hey, wait! Are you saying that the wall I saw inwardly is like the wall the natives built to keep out King Kong?"

"A metaphor," the Adept apologized. "I am fond of them, as you know. They work so much faster and better than logical explanations! But here are the aspects of the comparison you need to consider. People build walls inwardly for the same reason the natives in the movie did: to protect themselves from something that threatens them.

"But the unfortunate thing about a wall is that it not only keeps unwanted things out; it also keeps you in. A wall, in spiritual terms at least, is thus a trap for Soul. When you put up a wall inside yourself, the tendency is for whatever is walled out to become more and more fearsome over time. It can even become a jungle where whatever is most archaic in you can survive in all of its prehistoric splendor."

"Oh! I get it," I mused. "Man feels overwhelmed by a much greater force and wants to do something to placate it. The virgin sacrifice is a ritual surrender to a greater power, I suppose. Like a dog who bares his belly to a stronger dog so that the latter will leave him alone. But why a female, I wonder? Is that significant?"

"Surely," said the Adept. "It is the feminine element within man that surrenders to the higher power. But there is a darker meaning here as well. When there is fear, the feminine element is generally what is sacrificed for the sake of a defensive stance. In other words, fear hardens people. It makes weapons and walls.

"This walled-out area is what psychologists call the subconscious and unconscious part of man. What exists here are personal memories and collective genetic memories, biological instincts, and the abstract language of human spiritual evolution stored as symbols. Exploring these areas of consciousness is like opening up the electronic circuitry of a sophisticated machine. You become aware of both the simplicity and complexity of what you see. The human dimension is just that simple, and that complex."

"I see," I ventured. "This makes me think of why surrealism is so weird. It's all that primitive, unconscious stuff spewed out as art."

"Correct," nodded Haurvata. "Art is always a good escape valve for these pressures, and literature has always been an excellent repository for subconscious material. Haven't you ever wondered why the Grimm fairytales are so 'grim'?"

"Sure," I admitted. "To our modern sensibilities, they seem pretty primitive and violent. It's hard to understand how the authors could have had children in mind when they wrote them."

The Adept shook his head. "These stories were not 'written' in the usual sense of individual authors, nor are they particularly for children. They developed over time as popular folktales in the oral tradition. The Grimm brothers, Jakob and Wilhelm, merely collected the tales and set them down in books. But the reason for the tales' powerful strangeness is the concentrated symbolism that comes from the German culture's repressions of human needs, desires, and fears. As I have suggested, the higher the wall, the more exotic the creatures that lurk on the other side."

"That's fascinating," I exclaimed. "So there's a lot of subconscious material in these tales, right?"

"Yes," said Haurvata. "But I do not want to give you the idea that sweet, innocuous stories about harmless rabbits are always preferable, either. After all, the subconscious exists in children, as it does in adults. Children are often invigorated by hearing stories that acknowledge the subconscious power, especially if these stories suggest how to harness or reclaim this power for themselves.

"The spiritual guides work to make you aware of these hidden areas of your consciousness. They want to give you freedom from the control these areas can exert over you when allowed to function on a mechanical basis. Whether they are fears, prejudices, or past conditioning, destructive tendencies or driving ambitions, sexual aberrations or past failures, these 'problems' constitute sources of potential spiritual energy.

"The ordinary man is ordinary because his spiritual energies are locked up in these ways. His inner consciousness is an impenetrable jungle. When he gets into trouble, his only recourse is to pray for divine intervention. He imagines help as coming from an outside source simply because he feels so powerless himself. But the answers are never outside him; they are within."

"But how?" I interjected. "I mean, how can someone who has never done inner work start?"

"How did you start?" asked the Tibetan.

"Well . . . by getting to know myself better," I began.

"Exactly," said Haurvata. "And that is where we must all begin, and continue working throughout our spiritual evolution. The answers are within the Self. One must push back the wall and reclaim more and more of the inner life for oneself. Then, finally, the wall itself must be dismantled and the great unknown confronted face to face."

"About my wall . . . " I began.

"Yes?"

"How does it relate to my inability to get beyond this point in the past?"

"You must dismantle the wall. It is time," he said quietly. "Otherwise you may revert back to a previous cycle and miss your opportunity for freedom. You see, it takes time for any Soul to become aware of the contradictions of material life. When the individual is sufficiently dissatisfied, he or she can discover the inner life and begin to make rapid progress.

"However, it can also happen that the individual finds a way of sedating himself against this harsh revelation. He can take refuge in materialistic solutions with a vengeance. All addictions, whether to alcohol, money or human relationships, bears some similarity to this syndrome. The individual realizes that there is no security in human life, and grabs at whatever he is most attached to in hopes that it will be the answer to his needs. This choice plunges him into a cycle of sowing and reaping further negative effects, and the window to freedom closes once again."

I contemplated upon all the Adept had said. Yet I felt only affection for my wall, for its venerable age and the hard labor which had created it. I even felt a surge of pride thinking about how tall and wide it was, how sturdy and solid. I had made it. It was mine. Could I really give it up?

That was when I began to hear the wind again. I looked about, trying to determine whether it was an inner sound I was perceiving, or an outer sound. The wind grew in volume and gathered around me in white shapes, like wolves around their intended victim. Then it howled in a voice supremely lonely and majestic. I had heard the call of the unknown, and the longing inside me to go one step further won out over my fears.

It was then that I was above the wall, looking out over the world as far my eyes could see. But that was not very far. Beyond the wall lay a wide expanse of luminous emptiness. It contained either everything I'd ever hoped for, or perhaps absolutely nothing at all. Whichever it was, I couldn't yet tell.

CHAPTER FOUR
A Journey in Time

After seeing over my "wall," I expected to find myself at home once again, an hour mysteriously vanished from the clock, but everything otherwise normal. This was the usual thing, but today was not usual in any way. What happened instead was that I found myself in a garden in back of a small clapboard house that I vaguely recognized. Pungent vegetation smells drifted in the humid air, which was stirred by cool breezes.

To one side stood a shaded wooden table made of pine planks nailed together. It was grey with age and exposure to the elements. Upon it were stumps of dried fern bark and clay pots. Garden tools were put away neatly under the table. A few orchids, staked to supports, rose from the pots. A bank of blue and white irises overflowed from the yard to the right. In a shaded spot under a tree, an orange-and-white cat lounged, its eyes two slits against the sunlight.

I stood there orienting myself to this place. My awareness grew that this was my home in Honolulu. Or rather, had been my home. The house had been razed to make way for a subdivision over thirty years ago. The memories I had of it were dim, but I estimated that this was around the year 1954. I caught my breath, for suddenly in the distance a figure unbent itself out of the bushes. It was my grandmother, a white cotton cloth over her head under a battered straw hat.

"Do you know where you are now?" I heard a voice say.

I turned around with a start. Haurvata Sampa was about five feet behind me. He was wearing a blue cotton shirt and a pair of bermuda shorts. He smiled amiably at me and continued watching the woman work in the garden.

"Shhh," I hushed. "That's my grandmother! Can't she hear us?"

"Of course not," he laughed. "We're not 'here' in the usual sense. We've gone back in time. We can observe but we cannot be perceived."

"What's the point?" I asked nervously. "Why are we here anyway?"

"Funny how uncomfortable people get when meeting up with their own past," the Adept chuckled. "It never fails. Why, I wonder? Do you really think the past has gone somewhere? That it has vanished because time 'marches on,' as you put it?"

"Well, do you mean it hasn't?" I asked crossly. "I thought Soul only lived in the present moment. Eternity is the single moment of nowness! You've taught that to me yourself."

"Calm yourself," the Adept cautioned, putting his hand on my shoulder. "What I said was true. But did I not also mention that 'now' contains both past and future? No? Well, I have neglected your education, then. Which we will correct presently! Look around you. What do you see?"

With that, Sampa swept his arm around with a grand gesture. I took a deep breath and let my gaze absorb the full measure of this experience. It was eerie. But now that I knew we could not be seen or heard, I felt a little safer. The knot in my left shoulder undid itself and I was able to finally relax.

"It's my house," I answered, heaving a sigh. "I must have been around five or six then . . . now . . . whichever. I remember very little of it, really. It was before most of my memories began."

"Correct," nodded the Adept. "Do you know why you do not remember this period very well?"

"No," I said, shaking my head. "Do you?"

The Adept smiled broadly. "I do! Come with me."

He led the way to the entrance of a hothouse in which an

assortment of succulents and flowering plants grew on tables under the filtered light. Silently, we walked down the length of one of the aisles. There, at the end, played a little girl around six years old. The girl was thin and brown with short, black hair. On her feet were a pair of oversized straw slippers. She had mixed soft mud into jar lids and placed flower petals and tiny leaves on the surfaces in deliberate designs. The lids had been placed in rows on a bench. The child was humming as she worked.

"Lion," called the Adept, his tone friendly.

The girl looked up quickly and joy spread across her serious features. She ran into his arms.

"Teacher! You're back!" she cried, her dark eyes glowing.

"And I have brought a friend," he said, nodding in my direction. Chills ran through me. What was going on here?

"I thought you said . . . " I began.

"This one can see us," the Adept said soothingly to me. "Be at peace, child. There is something you can learn from this experience that is to our purpose. Listen and learn."

I smiled wanly at the child, who looked up at me for what seemed to be eternity. Then she broke her gaze and fixed it back on the Adept.

"How have you been, my friend?" asked the Adept charmingly. He had knelt down to her level and was now squatting agilely on the dirt floor.

"Fine," the child replied, shyly. Then, on a sudden thought, she piped, "I can move the pies away for you. Here. It's not dirty, see?" She brushed the bench with a small hand and offered it to Haurvata as if it were a velvet throne.

"Ah, thank you," smiled the Adept. "And what manner of pies are you making today?"

"Oh, mostly apple, some banana, and . . . I don't know. What kinds are there?" she frowned, tilting her head like a sparrow.

"Cherry, lemon, many, many kinds!" laughed the Adept, catching her on his lap. "What does it matter? You make them all look so good, I will take one of each!"

"They're not done yet!" giggled the child. "You have to wait."

"All right, I will," said Haurvata. Then he glanced at me and back at the little girl.

"Do you know who this is?" asked the Adept casually.

The child looked at me once again, considering. "No," she finally said, shaking her head slightly.

"Well, my dear," explained the Adept, "she is my student. She is one of us, you see. I am teaching her something about time."

"Time?" asked the child brightly. "Oh. Do you have a watch, then? My grandpa has one. It is silver and has a long chain. I wish I had one."

"No," laughed the Adept. "I do not have a watch. I have something better!"

"What's that?" asked the child, full of curiosity. "I want to see it!"

"You are already seeing it, my child," answered the Adept. "This woman is from the future. Your future. As you are from the past. Her past."

"I don't understand," protested the child, shaking her head. "This is not the past. This is now. The past happened already. It's gone." She waved her hands around to show the emptiness in them, which was all that remained of yesterday.

The Tibetan looked at me and winked sardonically.

"Ah, but lion," crooned the Tibetan, more patient than I'd seen him, "how have you come into the present moment? How did your body grow from a tiny baby into a six-year old girl? Did it happen just today?" He gave an exaggeratedly astonished look that set both the girl and myself laughing.

"You're silly," giggled the child, pushing on his nose affectionately. "I GREW up! That's how we all do it."

"So it is," nodded Haurvata seriously. "You do not have some old, outgrown baby's body lying around somewhere, then?"

The child shrieked with laughter and tumbled out of his arms. "NOOO!" she tittered. "I GREWED up! Don't you know?" she teased.

"Well," smiled the man, "I am just trying to make a point, you see. The baby you once were is now you. The you as you are now will one day be a grown woman. Everyone carries around her own past and future. It does not go anywhere. It is always present, always here, now. Do you see?"

"That's hard," frowned the girl, resting her cheek gently on his arm. "Let's play something now."

"Tonight we will play," he reassured her. "We will go

40

somewhere fun. And I will teach you more about time. It is not hard when I show you, you will see."

"All right," she relented. The girl turned to look at me and smiled. Her eyes were deep brown pools that drew me down into them. Sighing, I smiled back, feeling as trapped by these events as a bug in a jar.

Suddenly, a flicker passed in her eyes. Something had caught between us. What was it? Some invisible, unspeakable flash of recognition. It felt like . . . love. Was it really love? Could the woman I was now give and receive love from the child of her past? Could love heal the distance between us, and sustain the younger self through the long and lonely future she had yet to traverse?

The cooing of mourning doves in nearby trees drifted into my awareness. My teacher had come to stand by me, his hand gripping my arm. The scene before us dissolved and we were once again "between" one time and place and another. Generally, this kind of experience was momentary, transitional. It was the "white space" that constituted the flow of life, the energy upon which we traveled when moving our awareness between any point in, or outside of, time and space. Religion called it the Holy Spirit.

"We seem to be nowhere, and yet everywhere," I remarked, sending a thought gently to my teacher.

"Yes," he answered. "It is the larger reality in which time and space exist as smaller dimensions."

"Uh, what are we doing here?" I asked, a little uncomfortably.

"Is this disturbing you?" the Adept asked. "Is there some place you would rather be instead?"

"Well," I admitted, "formlessness bothers me. I'm not used to it. At first, I feel free and wonderful. Then I feel totally lost. Take me somewhere concrete, would you?"

"Fine," said Haurvata. Instantly, we found ourselves seated in an old-fashioned train, moving noisily along iron rails. The smell of wood, leather, and dust pervaded my nostrils. I sneezed. The motion of the train was jarring, but surprisingly calming, too. It was earthy and rhythmic, like a mother's rocking, or a boat swaying on its moorings with the tide. I felt better immediately.

The Tibetan and I were dressed in traveling clothes of cotton and light wool. He was wearing a dark suit and a hat, while I was clothed in a sky-blue skirt and jacket with a white blouse underneath.

41

I looked down at my hands. They were immaculate in white silk gloves.

"This isn't one of my past lives, I hope," I said fretfully, admiring the beaded handbag on my lap.

"No," laughed the Adept, "merely a mock-up to soothe your jangled nerves and satisfy your desire for a more structured experience. Is it satisfactory?"

"Very," I sighed, settling happily into this pleasant illusion. "Now, if you can keep the Indians from attacking, I might be able to really enjoy myself."

"Hmm," he grunted. "A pleasant excursion is hardly a good enough reason to drag you out of the body for, do you think? Or have you forgotten what our purpose in this experience is?"

"Oh," I replied, surprised. "I guess I did forget. What was it I was supposed to be learning?"

The Adept sighed. "It's very simple, dear one. You are tasting what experience could be like beyond the wall of your fears. To begin with, I am trying to break up the hard concrete of your mental concepts about time and space. This is very important to you, and I would advise you to pay attention instead of drifting off like you are now considering doing.

I straightened up immediately and put on an attentive face.

"That's a little better. Keep it up," he encouraged. "The Unmani Dhun are entrusting you with an important 'job.' As you may remember, this is the task of writing about the male and female spiritual currents at work within individuals and the world. To do this, you must be able to tap into your bank of memories, for much of this knowledge is already stored there.

"However, you must try not to think of what you are doing as 'remembering,' for in reality, the concept of 'remembering' is clumsy. Or, to put it in another, more neutral, way, remembering is going back into time in order to play out experiences. A faster and more accurate method is to simply allow relevant data to come to the surface of your awareness as needed.

"It's like the difference, say, between the pony express and the modern computer modem to transfer information between two points. Both work, of course. But who would want to use the former, if the 'technology' to use the latter is available? The 'technology' of which I am speaking, of course, is expanded awareness. Are you following me so far?"

"Right," I replied. "So what you're trying to do here is to show me how illusory time is, is that right? By taking me back and forth into and between times?"

"Correct," nodded the Adept, an amused twinkle in his eyes. "Is it working?"

"Apparently," I laughed. "I certainly don't have the, uh, respect for time that I've had before. Why, you seemed to be able to cut through it like margarine."

"Don't get overconfident," cautioned the Adept. "In the first place, it is not that time is 'unreal.' In its own way, time is very real indeed. In fact, without it, experience would be one big pot of stew instead of a sequence of logically connected events. The mind, which is linear in nature, would not be able to make any sense of it. Time exists as a response to the natural structure of our minds. It is not so much a fact as a perception. Do you see what I mean?"

"I think so," I answered. "In other words, if the mind were different, if it were capable of perceiving simultaneous experiences, then our idea of reality would be drastically different. Am I on the right track?"

"Very much," agreed the Adept. "But that's a terrible pun."

As he said this, the door swung open and a mustachioed man with a cap and an officious air began his way down the aisle. The other passengers in the sparsely inhabited car handed him tickets as he walked by. He gave the tickets cursory glances and pocketed them. I looked questioningly at Haurvata, who merely smiled politely and held out a pair of tickets on our behalf. The train employee peered once at us over his glasses, then lurched on his way.

"The mind, dear one," continued Haurvata, "is like an early version of the modern computer—limited in its capability to store, access, and transfer information between its data bases. Even in the most intelligent of people, the mind becomes easily confused. The clearer the anchor points of physical reality are to it, the less it is able to imagine and postulate a reality different from what it knows.

"That is why intellectuals are hardly ever candidates for the expanded awareness," he said. "They have too much invested in a materialistic viewpoint which, as far as they can measure it, validates their assumptions. They fail to consider that their very beliefs

43

predispose them toward certain experiences and deny them others. What they cannot understand, they dismiss as error or chance. Their more subtle human gifts of intuition, imagination, and spiritual insight have atrophied from disuse. Thus, their minds can encompass matter, but never Soul. But this is merely intellectual arrogance at its most common. It is a description as accurate for the man in the street as it is for the so-called person of science."

"But what would it be like if our minds could conceive of simultaneous realities, of time within time, and so forth? Would the world be better for it?" I asked skeptically.

"I do not mean to suggest that it should be otherwise for the majority of people, daughter," said Haurvata. "This discussion is mostly for your benefit. I want you to realize that you must go beyond the conventional in gathering the material for your book. Go beyond time. Go beyond the mind. And most of all, go beyond the limited concept of yourself which time and mind is conspiring to trap you within. The world has its standards, of course. You are aware of what they are. But are these standards yours?"

"That's difficult," I said, fidgeting with my gloves. They had become warm and I removed them, wiggling my fingers gratefully.

"First of all, I've obviously had enough inner experiences to know that life is more than what the mind and the senses report to me. For example, I've come to realize that I don't remember much of my early childhood because I was outside my body so much! You were with me even then. You called me 'lion' like you do now. How could I have forgotten that?

"Still, it makes me uncomfortable to appear obviously different from other people. If I went around talking publicly about other planes, traveling into the past, and so forth, I'd be labeled as either a fool or a charlatan. I don't much relish ridicule. Is this what you're leading up to? Am I committing myself to public notoriety by taking on this 'job' you're offering me?"

"All right," Haurvata began. "First of all, you did not 'forget.' A curtain was drawn over your early experiences outside the body so that you would adjust to the physical world and live a constructive life within it. This is no different from the reason people are unaware of their dreams. Science has proven that we all dream. Moreover, we know that the activity of dreaming is absolutely essential to our well-being. However, many people do not recall their lives in the dream state. Have they really 'forgotten'? No. They have simply chosen to pull a curtain over their experiences because they are not yet prepared to deal consciously with their dream content.

"You are wondering why this is. I shall tell you. There is always a danger that the dream material will be disturbing and disruptive to the daily life of the dreamer. Recall what I have said to you earlier about the subconscious and unconscious life that lies hidden behind each person's 'wall.' If a person has no tools with which to decipher the dream content and organize it into a useful pattern within his overall life, it can become a source of anarchy instead of wisdom.

"In the same way, other kinds of inner experience such as out-of-the-body travel, which I prefer to call expanded awareness, can also be disruptive to normal living. The difference between the 'sane' and the 'insane' is really very simple and can be viewed along these lines. The sane person can deal with the complexity of human experience. He understands that both the subjective and objective have standards of reality and does not confuse the two.

"The insane person, on the other hand, is incapable of making that distinction. He tries to live out his subjective realities on the objective level. He might jump off buildings believing he can really fly. He could kill his mother because the 'devil'—the personification of his own evil drives—told him to do it. The point is, the subjective content has overwhelmed his ability to deal constructively with it. The wall has cracked open and all the fearsome monsters are pouring through!"

"But what about me?" I persisted. "Why was it better for me to have the curtain drawn over my earliest spiritual experiences?"

"You needed time to establish yourself on the physical plane," Harvata replied. "You had to accept your path in life, no matter how difficult it was, and decide to stick it through. You could not be allowed to withdraw into your inner life as an escape from the loneliness and boredom of your youth. I needed to close off your options temporarily to force you to grow stronger. But I never left you, my dear one. Never."

I did not look at the Adept. I kept the tears from spilling over by an effort of will and fixed my eyes on a woman's hat five rows down.

"Now, as to your fears of notoriety," continued the Tibetan blandly, "You can look at it that way if you choose to. It is a rather small sacrifice compared to, say, burning at the stake or being fed to the lions. You will not lose your family, your home, or your real friends. But of course, what you do is entirely up to you. You can back out if you wish. It is not too late."

"Look," I pleaded, "I'm not saying I won't do it. And I am truly grateful for all your guidance and support over the years. But I still need to contemplate on this, Haurvata. What you're asking isn't going to be easy to do. I need to think about the consequences to my life if I go ahead with it. Maybe nothing will be different. Maybe it will all be different. I just don't know."

"Well, take your time," he replied neutrally. "We've waited this long. A little while longer will not matter."

"You know, the thing that bothers me most is this," I added. "Why me? Surely there must be someone more qualified than me. I can't be the only candidate for the task."

"No, you are not," sighed the Adept, removing his hat to his lap. "But you have the most to gain, as well as the most to give in this matter. It would be an even exchange of the spiritual coin. Thus, you are our first choice. But you are by no means the only choice. As a matter of fact, the same information has been given out, and will continue to be given out, through the inner channels. It is already 'in the air' as you say.

"Similar books have been, and will be, written about this subject. However, these will be filtered through the lenses of each writer's particular mental structures, which at the present time is mostly interpretations and applications of psychology. In your case, it is felt that you could add the spiritual dimension for those who are ready for this viewpoint. There are truly more people ready for this than you currently believe. Trust me."

"I do trust you," I insisted. "I still have doubts about myself, though. I'll see what comes through. If I'm the right person, I suppose the material will come together. But now I have a question for you before this strange experience ends."

"And what is that?" the Adept asked.

"Did we change my history by going back into time?"

"No, dear one," Haurvata assured me. "We did not touch the 'solid' core of physical reality, which is rigid and unbending. What we affected was the inner, subjective state of the girl who needed to know that she would survive to be herself, and make a significant contribution to life. And we affected the life of the adult woman who is still unsure of her past and her future."

"Yes," I answered softly. "I see what you mean. I guess I'm still anxious about the same things as when I was a little girl. I'm still a little afraid that my life will amount to nothing in the end."

"Well, then, think about what you can do to serve the whole," replied Haurvata. "What YOU can do. Others may pass legislation, mold public opinion, amass wealth. But I see you as a potential Adept. This is your training period. Do not waste it."

The rocking motion of the train filled my mind as Haurvata fell silent and appeared to doze, his chin upon his chest. I turned to see the countryside speed by. It was lovely, though a little dry and desolate, as if waiting for a purpose to do more than just exist as it had for a hundred thousand years. But this, of course, was after all an illusion. I shook my head, wondering what in life was not an illusion. Was abandoning my own anchor points of reality truly a safe and sane thing to do when so much was unknown about the present, the past, and the future, crowded into the pregnant moment called "now"?

CHAPTER FIVE
For Once, Then, Something

Winter was passing. Despite the occasional fog-shrouded day and the chilly mornings, the trees seemed to know. Their bare branches exploded into pink and white blossoms which floated gracefully in the sky like foam on the waves. Hedges, clipped radically in the fall, now boasted tender twigs festooned with new leaves, pale green and pale red. Spring bulbs peeked above the soil in my garden, and forgotten pansies, left for dead in last summer's heat, now resuscitated themselves in patches of dark green, ruffled leaves.

Everywhere, restless stirrings from soil, limb, and branch sent out a subtle vibration of hope and promise. I set aside a day for contemplation upon the new season. The morning would be devoted to spiritual reading and thought, and the afternoon for planting the garden seeds I had received from a mail-order catalogue.

The contemplation went well. Recurring thoughts popped up unbidden about the male and female embodiments of Soul. Memories of my lessons about "the wall" and my remarkable journey through time with Haurvata Sampa washed back over my awareness. Though I had accomplished relatively little since those experiences, I struggled to believe that I was doing as much as I could. I attributed the vague restlessness I felt to the coming of spring.

After lunch I gathered the egg cartons I had saved over the winter and cut off the lids, counting and stacking them on the floor of the enclosed patio. I counted eight. I walked out to the toolshed and dragged out a bag of potting soil and a large bucket. Then I chose my seeds and carefully snipped open the hermetic seals enclosing them. I planted orange zinnias, mixed carnations, forget-me-nots, bells of Ireland, geraniums, and ranunculus.

I was excited, and slightly uneasy at the same time. As a novice gardener, I was anxious for the seeds. I worried that I would either not water them enough, water them too much, or that the temperature of the patio would be too warm or too cold for the seeds to germinate. Nervously, I covered them all with plastic wrap and put them where the light would be brightest.

After a quick clean-up of the area, I slipped on a pair of canvas shoes to take a stroll around the garden. Last year's daffodils were already in bloom, snail bait ringing each cluster to safeguard it. A patch of white alyssum had reseeded itself and was coming back strong around the border of rosemary which was speckled now with pale blue flowers. I noted the progress of the tulips I had planted two months before. Then I turned the corner toward the backyard pool and felt a shock for which I was completely unprepared.

Two people were lounging in chairs by the water. In the moment of surprise and confusion that followed, I remembered thinking that they looked like hippies from the sixties. On the other hand, their floor-length clothes were clean and their expressions were far from "spaced out." One of them, the man, reclined with his knees bent, showing bare, spatulate brown feet. His head was tilted back as if to absorb all he could of the sun's rays, and he sported dark sunglasses.

The woman was small and also darkhaired, with a simple, long blue and white dress. Her perfect heart-shaped face and pale, creamy-yellow skin made her look like someone from a Persian miniature or a Chinese painting. I realized she was Asian.

The woman looked up calmly and smiled at me like a gracious guest at her host. The man sat abruptly erect in the chair and swept off the glasses in one dramatic flourish. It was my teacher, Haurvata Sampa!

"Ho ho ho!" His laughter boomed out at me with the complete enjoyment and abandon he was capable of when pleased or amused. The woman laughed too, but I could not hear her voice amidst the rumble of my teacher's merriment. Her small nose crinkled up and her eyes sparkled kindly at me. I noticed that she wore cloth shoes like the kind we call "mary janes." Her delicate arms and hands folded like white wings in her lap.

"You gave me quite a scare," I said, my adrenaline still pumping from my momentary fright. "I should have recognized you, Haurvata—but the second person's presence confused me."

"I apologize, dear one," the Tibetan said. "But it was you who called out for me, was it not? So here I am, your teacher, with an honored guest!"

He had stood up, his swarthy face beaming. He bowed slightly to his right and gestured to the pretty woman still seated in the redwood chair.

"The Unmani Dhun Adept, Kyari Hota," he pronounced clearly.

Haurvata had told me once that the term "Unmani Dhun" meant "the tenth door," sometimes known as the "spiritual eye" or the eye of Soul. When I looked into Kyari Hota's delicate hands and face, I could not help wondering how she had come to earn her admittance into this powerful group.

The female Adept beamed back and her face broke into a gentle smile. As she stood, I saw that she was petite, no more than five-feet-two inches tall. I walked slowly up to the two, awed by the presence of a spiritual teacher I had not yet met—a female one, at that! I was, for the moment, speechless. I did, however, reach out my hand tentatively, as one might reach to touch a beautiful but delicate sea anemone in a tide pool.

She looked deeply into my eyes and took my hand. Hers was light and cool.

"I am delighted to greet you."

Her voice was unexpectedly firm, and the resonance from it rang musically in my head like Tibetan bells.

"It is always a special pleasure to be asked by my revered brother, Haurvata Sampa, to assist in the education of a pupil. I understand you have undertaken a mission for the greater unfoldment of the human race. A worthy, if difficult, goal! Your area of interest is one of my 'specialties,' as you might say. I am to be your 'consultant' in this endeavor. To sum up, we shall work together on this book, the three of us. That is, if you are in agreement?"

She lifted up an eyebrow and smiled pleasantly at me. A hundred unformed questions about this female Adept jostled for attention in my head. I pushed them all back with difficulty and answered as simply and to-the-point as I could.

"I would be grateful," I said. "I don't know much about this book yet. I have a few things written down in notes. But other aspects are still mysterious to me. For example, I was told that this knowledge exists within me already on 'an unknown basis.' I have been trying to figure that one out for many weeks! I have my doubts that I will have enough on the subject to fill a book. I guess I'm also having questions in some other areas as well . . . "

Kyari Hota smiled reassuringly. "My friend Haurvata Sampa has reviewed with me your training to date. Never fear. We will guide you safely out of your little harbor into the open ocean! Soon you will become accustomed to the vastness and freedom of the cosmic seas."

Her words had a strangely bracing effect on me. They struck me as more than a prophecy of the future. They were declaring a new reality in the present. I felt the power of this reality giving me a new and unfamiliar energy. I shivered all over. Was this what a tree felt like when spring urged it into a sudden profusion of blossoms? I felt myself brimming over with happiness and confidence.

"May I offer you something to drink?" I asked brightly.

"I would like that," the woman smiled, showing small, ivory teeth. She turned sweetly to Haurvata, who answered with a short nod. "One for him, too, if you please."

I ran as swiftly as I could without tripping back to the kitchen. I brought out a pitcher of herbal iced tea, a container of apple juice, three glasses, and a plastic bowl full of ice cubes. I set the tray down near them and pulled up another chair. They had been in animated conversation while I was away. The part I overheard as I approached centered on the recent change in the weather. I was amused at how ordinary this all seemed! And yet here they were, two Adepts, sitting for all appearances like a suburban couple relaxing at the edge of their backyard pool. The thought made me chuckle despite my nervousness. Haurvata caught my mood and responded to it.

"Ah! Finally we have succeeded in making you see the

51

humorous side of things, dear one. I was truly worried there for awhile. I thought that you might break out in hives or something worse. Are two Adepts too much for you? Are we overdoing things a bit? If so, I'll leave immediately!"

He rose abruptly as if to go.

"No. Don't go!" I exclaimed. I was half afraid he would really disappear, as he always did when he was finished with our lessons. Then again, I was amused by his theatrics. I laughed out loud and felt an enormous tension leave the muscles of my chest.

"Ah! She laughs. Now perhaps we can get down to some serious business." With that he donned his dark glasses with an exaggerated gesture and reached out to pour the iced tea.

I giggled and held back a wave of hysteria that I felt approaching.

Haurvata handed the glass he had filled to Kyari.

"Thank you," she said, taking the drink from him.

"Now sit and listen," Haurvata told me. He nodded to the female Adept, who took one sip from her glass, then set her drink down on the tray. During a brief pause, she looked thoughtfully at me. Then she began to speak.

"Today we would like to discuss the evolution of the sexes from the spiritual angle. Call it 'spiritual chemistry,' if you will, or perhaps even 'sexual evolution.' It is a subject that has confused people over the years, even the spiritually progressive. Many false concepts cloud the issue. These concepts are embedded in the race consciousness and within the collective-unconscious memory bank of mankind.

"Of course, it is also true that the correct concepts reside in the collective bank as well. However, these correct concepts exist deeper down than the false ones. They have been pushed deeper by the accumulation of ideas built up over time like layers of sediment. If you could excavate through these layers, you might see the concepts lying in strata much like the remains of ancient fish and prehistoric crustaceans.

"The truth about man and woman, however, is even more ancient than the dinosaurs. It is the original creative impulse from God which divided Soul's embodiments into male and female on all the lower planes of creation. To the male embodiment God gave its qualities of activity and aggressiveness, the drive for expansion, experience, and mastery. To the female embodiment God gave its qualities of rest and passivity, the instinct for withdrawal, self-contemplation, and love.

"The male embodiment held the key to spiritual transformation, while the female embodiment knew the secret of physical manifestation. To every Soul taking a form in the lower worlds, God gave these two matched parts in the hope that, over the many centuries of its existence, each would realize both these aspects of the God state and return perfected into the higher worlds.

"In the beginning, during the Golden Ages of the lower worlds, this solution worked well. The knowledge of the source and purpose of this division was conscious in the minds of all sentient beings. Man and woman respected the divine plan and nurtured the balance between male and female qualities within each individual, and indeed within the animal forms of life as well.

"Though the pull toward the male half was always stronger for men, and toward the female half for women, this attraction never broke the bonds of love and trust between them. They correctly saw in each other the embodiment of their less developed side, and sought to bring their own God qualities into balance through the other's example. But over time, this original idea changed and began degenerating into what it has become in present times. In fact, once the degeneration of the idea began, sometime around the end of the Silver Age, it went very quickly. Of course, I am speaking about several hundred million years. The central theme of the myth of Arthur tells about this process of degeneration."

"Really? I've always been interested in Arthurian legends! So much fiction and fantasy has used the raw material of those legends. Was Arthur real, then? And the knights of the Round Table, too?"

"Yes and no," the diminutive Adept answered.

The afternoon light illuminated her dark hair and a slight breeze seemed to play with her as it gently blew her dress and soft filaments of loose hair that framed her face. Haurvata sat as if he were as completely absorbed in the discourse as I.

"But in the main, the answer is certainly yes," she continued. "The biggest mistake scholars make is in placing the legends too near to the present, where they are mixed with the trappings of chivalric traditions. The original story is far, far older than that!

"Now the legend of Arthur is an archetype which has become

such by entering into the race memory of the people who inhabited the region which is now Great Britain. As Souls reincarnated in new bodies, they solidified and spread this archetype among the peoples of Europe. The archetype carries a high etheric vibration. In other words, it is a seed story imbued with an important spiritual lesson. Many old tales are like that. This is the reason for their survival and undying popularity over time.

"You will find that the Arthurian legend appeals most to certain people, and these will be in the following categories: Souls who had incarnated during the times described by the Arthurian legends, and those for whom the lessons inherent in the tale are necessary for further spiritual growth."

"Do I fit into either of these categories?" I asked.

"You fit into both," came the mild answer. "Now to go on. If you remember the tale, one of its central features is the betrayal of King Arthur by Queen Guinevere and the Knight Lancelot through an extramarital affair. They are found out and she is tried and sentenced to death. At the last minute, she is rescued by Lancelot and lives out her life as a religious recluse. At least, that's one well-known version."

"How does this fit into our discussion about the change in viewpoints about male and female?" I couldn't help asking.

"Camelot is a race memory of a time of transition between two of the ages of man: the Silver Age and the coming Bronze Age—a change from a relatively peaceful and positive era to one of greatly increased bloodshed and negativity. From our point of view, at the beginning of the current age—the Iron Age—Camelot appears like a shining vision in a mist. It calls up all our nostalgia for a better time on earth, a time which will never come again!"

Kyari Hota stood up and walked abstractedly to the geraniums which eagerly reached toward the sunshine with simple white buds. A small white butterfly, a sight I hadn't seen all winter, fluttered around her head and landed on the flowers, gently fanning its wings. White on white, they existed for a moment out of time.

Then the butterfly rose from the flower, circled Kyari Hota's head once more, and zigzagged away in an erratic course across the garden. The Adept regarded the sight and turned a brilliant smile on both Haurvata and myself. Then her eyes rested on mine.

"What did you see, my daughter? Tell me."

"A white butterfly. It landed on that geranium and then flew away," I answered.

"Is that all?" she asked.

"Well . . . ," I hesitated. "It seemed so special, you know. As if time had stood still. It had to do with the butterfly being white and the flower being white. When the butterfly landed on the flower, just fanning its wings so peacefully, and the flower just . . . being a flower, it was . . . hey! I've got it! It reminded me somehow of Soul being divided into the active and passive principles, like you just described. Soul at rest and Soul in action. And both being part of one thing—the whole!"

I was excited by my discovery, probably overexcited. I nearly spilled my iced tea, but caught the glass before it dumped its contents on my lap.

I heard the sound of tinkling laughter. It was the lady, my new teacher. We all laughed together.

"Well-perceived," murmured Haurvata when we had all enjoyed our hilarity.

Kyari Hota said, "You have just had an example of the expression you questioned earlier—'on an unknown basis.' It refers to hidden knowledge. You see, when you looked at the butterfly landing on the white flower, you felt something vibrate within. Like a bell being struck, the feeling echoed in Soul, its ripples moving outward to the conscious mind and physical senses. But until you struggled for it, searched for it inside yourself, you understood little beyond the first mundane interpretation you originally gave it."

"Is this what they call a waking dream?" I queried, using a term I had heard from someone else.

"Yes, something like that," she agreed, "though life is generally what it is on face value, daughter. That is to say, if your grocery sack breaks because of a leaky milk carton, normally it just means you have to buy more milk! But every once in a while life gives you back a deeper, clearer picture of itself, or of yourself. Do you understand this?"

"Yes, I do," I replied. "Robert Frost had a poem to that effect. It's one of my favorites. I believe its title is 'For Once, Then, Something.' It's about someone who looks into wells, always searching for something, but always getting back only a reflection of himself. Then one day he thinks he spots something white at the bottom, but a drop of water from a fern falls to the surface and blots out his vision. He says, 'What was that whiteness? Truth? A pebble? For once, then, something.'

I sighed. "Now I understand why I loved that poem so much. It reminded me of my own condition. Everyone's. Trying to see beyond the surface appearance of things, trying to see beyond oneself. A glimpse, then the vision closes!"

"Yes," replied the Adept with feeling. "And so it is with all Souls who, as you have found, attempt to move beyond the appearances of the world. For what lies at the bottom of all things is nothing less than truth itself!"

"But can we know truth? Can our minds even perceive it?" I asked.

"Yes, surely," Kyari nodded. "As I have been trying to point out, it is already inside you—inside everyone. First it must be recognized, then lived. But mainly, it must be lived. And the way to live truth is by applying love to every situation that confronts you in family, work, and play. Love will bring truth into your life; it will make truth as tangible as a white pebble is tangible! Truth remains out of reach only for those who deny themselves the experience of love. You see?"

She reminded me so much of Haurvata Sampa. I had a fleeting thought that they could be brother and sister, or even a male and female version of the same self. It was a striking idea, and I tucked it away to return to later.

"We have gotten far afield of poor King Arthur I'm afraid, ladies." There was a tone of amusement in Haurvata's husky voice.

I had almost forgotten his presence, if that can be believed. Kyari Hota tilted back her tiny head and laughed.

"That is true, my friend. But please don't say it is because we are women and can't keep a thought going in a straight line!"

"Never crossed my mind," Haurvata protested. "But now that you bring it up . . . "

Kyari Hota silenced him with a smile and a dismissing gesture. "All right," she said laughingly, "on with poor Arthur. Poor only in material terms, however, for though he lost the battle to establish his ideal on earth, he won a further step along the spiritual path. Camelot had to fail because the times were against it. The negative force was gathering in strength for a push into the next lower cycle on Earth. His goal was noble, but hopeless. Yet it was his mission to make the attempt, and he did so with a good heart. That, dear one, is all that really matters in the end."

She said the last remark in a low, soft voice and her gentle look sank into my most secret heart. I realized how tense I had become about so many things. I was especially overwhelmed by the largeness of the endeavor I'd been asked to take on: to write about the male and female spiritual forces. Inwardly I said "thank you." Kyari looked kindly at me and went on with her discourse.

"The betrayal of Guinevere and Lancelot was the betrayal of the spiritual ideal of true love between man and woman. The love of Arthur and Guinevere was not a romantic or sexual love, though it contained elements of both in balance. Because it was accepted as marriage always can be—a spiritual opportunity for mutual growth and companionship, while being of assistance to others—it was successful for awhile.

"However, when Guinevere met Lancelot, the lesser ideal became stimulated. When the pair gave in to their temptation, the poison infected everyone around them, and created the rift which eventually brought down the kingdom of Camelot."

"I thought it had something to do with Mordred, too," I piped up.

"Ah, yes, Mordred. An interesting symbolic aspect of the story. Mordred stood for Arthur's baser sexual instinct. That Mordred was sired out of an unnatural alliance between Arthur and his sister is our clue that the problem is in fact internal to Arthur himself. The sorcery that surrounds both mother and son points to the destructive potential of undisciplined sexual energy. For the sex urge, when indulged in without discrimination and spiritual love, can be as negative as sorcery. For instance, don't you use expressions like 'that old black magic' when referring to sex?"

"Yes, we do," I agreed. "It's a common metaphor for sexual attraction—lust, actually. Lust is like black magic because it can take you over, almost hypnotize you with its power."

Kyari nodded in agreement. "Now all debts must be paid by the debtor, and Arthur's spiritual debt was incurred by giving in to sexual excess. Arthur's debt thus came back to him in the form of Mordred, his son. But Arthur refused to take responsibility for his act of lust. He rejected Mordred, who grew up twisted with bitterness and anger, dreaming of revenge."

"Hmm," I mused. "I never saw it that way. The onus of lust always falls on Guinevere and Lancelot, which seems to deflect attention away from Arthur's own mistake. Now I can see his part in the drama much more clearly. He wasn't just an innocent victim!"

"That's right," Kyari nodded. "The original cause was Arthur's, as he was the most aware Soul within his sphere of influence. But notice, too, that Arthur had several chances to forestall the tragedy of his life: first, by accepting responsibility for his mistake through acknowledging Mordred as his own; and second, by taking a firmer hand in separating Guinevere and Lancelot, for the good of the whole, once the danger became present. Arthur did not do the first because fear and self-loathing overwhelmed his compassionate nature. He did not do the second because his spiritual blindness left him weakened and unalert. Arthur thus turned his back to his responsibility not once, but two times. So his fate, and everyone else's, was sealed."

"So what about Guinevere and Lancelot? How were they related to Arthur's spiritual debt?" I asked.

The Adept replied, "Arthur had to learn the hard way—the only way—the value of a spiritually balanced love over the black magic of possessiveness and lust. He did this by continuing to love Guinevere and Lancelot even though they had given in to desire and betrayed his trust. By forgiving them, Arthur began the process of learning to forgive himself for his similar weakness.

"The two lovers learned something, too, of course. But they were inexperienced Souls compared to the more spiritually complicated Arthur. As symbols, Lancelot and Guinevere represent the dangers inherent in a purely romantic love: They became so wrapped up in themselves that they failed to see where their actions were leading."

"I understand something now," I said slowly. "I remember my reaction when I saw a movie about Arthur and Guinevere, years ago. I was a teenager then. I felt such a sadness, watching everything precious crumble, feeling pity for Guinevere, Lancelot, and Arthur. Perhaps I was thinking of the lessons I had already learned, and would learn again, on this subject."

"True," she said shortly. "What you need to understand, my daughter, is that the original ideal of man and woman is constructive,

58

while the ideal that has since replaced it is brutally destructive. It may be the negative force's greatest invention, even greater than the nuclear bomb! For a bomb merely destroys the body, whereas this insidious mutual tearing-down that is going on between the sexes is keeping both men and women chained to a world of death and shadows. Unless we return to this golden ideal once again, the potential for spiritual evolution that is now before us may be utterly lost!"

Her face was suddenly serious, with no trace of humor or lightness in it. During the seconds it took for this statement to sink in, I could hear the chirping of a bird and my own breathing. I thought about the world—the possibility of large-scale annihilation juxtaposed against this vision of a Golden Age reborn. I wondered how this tremendous change would be able to take place, and what the Unmani Dhun Adepts were doing now to prepare the way for it.

CHAPTER SIX
Inner Man, Inner Woman

The next few weeks went by very quickly. I began researching the library and bookstore shelves for anything resembling the book I was determined now to write. An older friend, Ruth, a bright and talented woman sculptor in her early sixties, loaned me about seven volumes from her private collection of spiritual and metaphysical literature. One of these books in particular caught my fancy. It was a very thorough and thoughtful explication and reinterpretation of the anima-animus concept. To the average reader, it might have sounded dryly academic or heavily psychological. But to me, it was gold! I couldn't wait to meet with my spiritual teachers again and ask them for their insights on the same topic.

Though I didn't see either teacher, they were very much on my mind. I felt their invisible presence often, and sometimes, when my inner questions were answered especially swiftly, it was clear to me that they were carefully guiding my search. I was aware that through the Soul-faculty of knowing and being, I could commune in this way with the higher consciousness. I was happy, sensing that I was growing spiritually and learning to tune in with precision and feeling to Spirit.

I noticed during this period that I was more tuned in than usual to my inner world. Small hunches and intuitions saved me time and trouble in both my domestic and career responsibilities, making all of my efforts more efficient and pleasant. I perceived how subtle these inner "messages" were, however, because so often in the past I had not heeded them. One time, for example, I had been gardening and my hands were covered with dirt. As I began washing them with a garden hose, I noticed that I had forgotten to take off an expensive wristwatch which had been a birthday gift from my husband. I stopped to take it off and placed it in my pocket for the time being.

A small voice said to me, "Just remember that you put it there." It was so quiet that I did not listen. Soon afterwards, I threw my muddy clothes into the washing machine. A quarter of a cycle later, I realized with horror what I had done and ran to save the watch! Of course, it was no longer ticking. That very night, a friend called and I mentioned my sad story to him. "Coincidentally," he had done a similar thing himself. He advised me to get the watch professionally cleaned in order to prevent internal corrosion. When I got it back, the watch was fine. But I had gained something even more precious: a real appreciation for the small guidances that come from Soul!

Finally, after the third week of being "on my own," I asked for a "face-to-face" meeting with one of my teachers. I contemplated before retiring to bed, putting my attention gently on the Unmani Adept Kyari Hota. However, that evening I could not get to sleep. I was literally charged with energy and rose after forty-five abortive minutes to sit quietly in the living room and read. I switched on a lamp and bent to pick up a magazine. I quickly jumped back and gasped, for there on the couch was the female Unmani Dhun Adept.

"You should be used to this by now," she teased.

I was definitely pleased to see her.

"Well, I did call you," I said cheerfully. "I thought I'd see you in the dream state, though. I couldn't sleep, so I came out here to read."

"You have something special to discuss with me?" she asked rather abruptly. The Adept stood up and walked several feet away from me. An inner light poured out of her, illuminating everything around with a special glow.

"Yes, as a matter of fact," I replied, "I'd like to ask you about the concept I've just been researching. It's called the animus and the anima. I first read about it a long time ago in the writings of Carl

Jung. It seemed true, but then again, somehow incomplete. The book I've just finished reading, written around 1980, is much more penetrating. Its viewpoint is not as hung-up with Victorian notions about women. What I wanted to know is, is this theory basically correct? Can it help me to understand more about the male and female? Would it be useful to others?"

Kyari Hota nodded her head thoughtfully. "It would be a very useful concept for others. There is a great deal to this subject, however, so let's begin immediately. You have made good progress on your research, by the way. I have been watching you and helping where I could. You are doing an excellent job of following your intuitive hunches, and the positive attitude you've adopted is helping you to be more productive.

"Now to the anima and the animus. First, let us define the terms. The anima is the female principle within the male, while the animus is the male principle within the female. Both the anima and animus are spiritual currents. They are like the alternating currents of electricity. In the male, one current is more dominant, and in the female the opposite is more dominant. But both sexes have the two currents circulating through their bodies. Look over here! It's easier if I show you."

Kyari gently cupped my face with both her hands and tilted it slightly upward. As she removed her hands, she raised them slowly in front of my face. Between them a ball of soft light began to spin and glow. Soon, the light resolved into a figure of a man and a woman whose very atoms seemed to tremble with the radiance of stars. After a minute of observation, two energy patterns became apparent to me. One pattern twisted like a figure eight, while the other spiraled around the body like a cocoon.

"What do you see?" Kyari asked.

After I told her, she explained. "The figure eight motion represents the physical flow of energy through the body. This energy is electric, and feeds the body through its system of nerves. When this energy pattern breaks down for whatever reason, the body isn't properly nourished and will eventually die. Organ by organ, everything will simply quit, like rooms with the light switches turned off one by one. Are you following me?"

"Uh huh," I said, with a look that was often on my face when I was concentrating hard on something not within the physical realm.

"Good," she said, then continued briskly. "The spiral motion you described represents the psychic flow pattern of energy. This energy is not physical, and cannot be detected by mechanical means. However, this system carries the basic life force of the individual—his or her drive for survival and growth. Now, the psychic provides nourishment for the physical. Therefore, if an individual's life force is lowered, support is withdrawn from the electrical system of the body. The relationship between the psychic and the physical energies is the basis of psychosomatic illness: real illness which is brought on by emotional or mental causes.

"The physical and psychic energies of both men and women contain male and female elements. To put it more concretely, every woman has some male hormones and every man has some female hormones. On the psychic level, men and women contain active-passive, intuitive-logical, and other types of dynamic oppositions that constitute an individual's emotional and mental tone."

"Like in the Tao te Ching?" I asked, citing the book of Chinese philosophy that was a favorite of mine from many years ago.

"Yes, precisely," she smiled. "But do you remember the objective of this philosophy of yin and yang?"

"To follow the Tao?" I offered.

"Yes, to follow the Tao," she answered, pleased. "The Tao is neither male nor female. It is neither active nor passive. It is the middle or neutral current. Following that current is the way of the Unmani Dhun Adepts—and their students!

"Now Jung had his hands on the correct concept, but like a fish, it slipped out of his grasp and splashed back into the waters of the pure consciousness. Jung was, as you observed correctly, too saddled with his cultural teachings to see the truth. Jung believed in the basic inferiority of the female current in general, and saw only its negative effects. He also thought that the animus in women and the anima in men were somewhat stunted by nature, and had no possibility for contributing anything truly important to the overall being. Today, this general attitude is still held by the majority of educated people. But it is not truth."

The Unmani Adept walked slowly towards me. The silk folds of her long dress rubbed against each other and made a curious soft squeal that was both pleasant and disturbing. I looked into the depths of her eyes and felt my awareness expanding to contain whatever she was going to tell me next.

"The truth, daughter, is simply that both the male and female currents—the animus and the anima—are gifts from God. And as gifts from God, they are a holy trust placed in the hands of the human race for its eventual unfoldment. The female current in men will unfold them to their higher selves, while the male current in women will generally do the same for them. I must explain this, however.

"Most men and women do not develop their opposite sides to any degree of spiritual usefulness. So they exist simply as sexually polarized beings. A sexually polarized being is incomplete. Yin or yang, by itself, is incomplete. It takes the unification of the two polar principles, merging with the neutral flow of Spirit, to put back Soul back in its original form. This constitutes the true spiritual marriage: the transformation of the self into a spiritual whole!"

"But what about the more 'ordinary' kind of marriage?" I asked, puzzled. "What about the 'soul mates' theory? I don't believe in it, but others seem to. Or at least they seem to want to believe in it."

"Ah, soul mates," she sighed, slowly pacing the rug in front of the fireplace. "May I build us a fire?"

"Oh, sure! Let me do it," I said.

"Don't bother," she answered. "I'm an expert. Just listen." She bent down to open the doors to the fireplace, wadded up newspaper, stacked sticks and small branches, then deftly held a match to several places to make the whole catch in a sudden blaze. Soon she balanced a choice log on the top of the pile and carefully closed the doors. She was talking all the while.

"At the heart of the soul mate theory is the belief that people, as individuals, are irremediably incomplete. In fact, some occultists still speak of 'male souls' and 'female souls.' In other words, you cannot be fulfilled until you find your 'other half,' in the form of an ideal mate. This is sheer nonsense! Soul mate theorists do not realize that maleness and femaleness, yin and yang, do not exist as separate halves in the world. They are constantly interacting and perpetually self-transforming polar aspects of the same force."

She wrinkled her nose in mild disgust at the concept of soul mates. Then she seemed to completely release her reaction, and her expression was radiant once more.

"Soul is an atom of God, therefore complete," Kyari smiled. "If mankind is made in the image of God, how could one be anything but whole? If soul mates exist, then they exist as the male and female currents in each individual which, when united, restores him or her to a balanced spiritual awareness. This finishes soul mates. There is nothing more to say about them."

She swept out her arms with a flourish and dismissed the topic in no uncertain terms. I was just getting into the discussion myself and felt caught short by this abrupt ending.

"Now, to your other question!" She sat down beside me and patted a cushion on her lap.

"What?" I asked. I had forgotten what the other question was.

"Your question about marriage between men and women—ah, now there is a more fruitful avenue for discussion! One might, through close contact with a loved one of the opposite sex, so transcend the normal human boundaries of ego that a glimpse into the higher world is actually achieved. What happens when any individual truly loves another is that his or her sense of self expands to encompass the other. In other words, what was hitherto a narrow 'me' now becomes a much bigger 'we.'

"Remember when Jesus Christ said, 'I and the Father are one'? He was speaking as a self-realized Soul with an expanded sense of 'I.' This oneness is the merging of the individual with the spiritual life stream. One never becomes one with God, but one with Spirit. He might more accurately have said, 'I and the Holy Spirit are one.' He could have actually said that, of course, but we must accept what is handed down through the recorders of the Christian Bible.

"All right, how are we doing so far?" she paused, giving me a chance to catch my breath and sort out the previous ideas. I felt we were going awfully fast, much faster than usual, and my mind was puffing to keep up.

"Fine, I think," I said optimistically. "I'm following you, as far as I know."

Kyari Hota laughed. "That's what I like in a person—complete confidence! You know, we'll have to work on that sometime."

"Yes," I grinned sheepishly. "I guess I can get pretty tentative sometimes. Now, I am really curious. With all this potential for spiritual growth in male and female relationships, what always goes wrong? Why isn't the potential fulfilled more often?"

"Ha!" she spat, sounding a lot like the Tibetan at that moment.

"Have you ever heard of the concept, 'projection'?"

"I'm not sure. Will you explain it to me?" I asked.

She nodded and went quickly on. "Projection is what happens through the imaginative faculty of any human being . . . in other words, the thought and feeling functions combined. In general terms it means that we throw out a creative energy whose nature it is to manifest what we have imaged inwardly. Do you understand this basic idea?"

"I think so," I said. "You mean, the way our ideas and expectations about life shape what we experience?"

"Precisely," she affirmed. "In fact, the process works very much like a movie projector, with the film being the images stored in the inner bodies and the screen being life itself. Thought is really either abstract perception or feeling perception. And of the two, it is feeling perception which is the more powerful in the lower worlds. Thought, furthermore, being an inner action, has a spiritual responsibility attached to its use. Thus, one is accountable for whatever one thinks and projects outwardly, for it is bound to return to him or her fulfilled in a direct, or somewhat roundabout, way.

"Men and women have come so far from their original vision of Soul that their imaginations cannot conceive of the wholeness of this marvelous entity! Instead, they 'project' outwardly the very aspects of themselves with which they are least comfortable and experience it as an 'other.' Now this seems complicated, so I will go over it in various ways until you understand. It is really simple, once you get the basic idea and start recognizing instances when it is happening.

"All right, now listen. Men and women tend to be least comfortable with aspects they perceive to be extremely male or extremely female. For example, women may fear appearing aggressive or taking leadership, particularly when it entails the harder sides of leadership such as disciplining others. This is because women are taught to be nurturing and to please. Men, on the other hand, may reject gentleness, unassertivenes, and so forth, for fear of appearing 'weak.'

"People who cannot accept their anima or animus, or some portion of their inner male or female selves, tend to deny the existence of these aspects. Of course, these male and female selves are still there, but buried. Nevertheless, the tendency of any organism is to seek wholeness. As you have seen through the picture

I have given you tonight, this wholeness of male and female exists on the physical and psychic levels in both sexes.

"The instinctual drive for wholeness takes place on an automatic basis, since wholeness is the template from which all individuals are cast. When any individual rejects a portion of himself, the rejected aspect is thrown outward or projected, and manifests in the outer world somewhere. The instinctual drive for wholeness manifests as sexual desire on the physical level and affectional response on the psychic.

"Now it stands to reason that these rejected portions of ourselves are probably going to be crippled, stunted, twisted, or otherwise distorted from a lack of fulfillment and integration within the whole self. So it's no surprise, then, when the projections come to life in the form of grotesques in the projectionist's experiences. The portions of yourself which you do not acknowledge have an uncanny ability to knock at your door and enter your life anyway. But they are never completely satisfactory, to understate the case.

"Examples of anima and animus projection abound. For example, women who long for a romantic lover project this ideal into a 'Prince Charming' fantasy, or some more modern version of it. What is funny about this, however, is that the image is completely unrealistic. Most men, for whom the male aspect is dominant, do not tend to be romantic.

"The romantic male ideal is simply a projection from the female of her own ego-centered emotionalism. This sounds unkind, so I will be more specific. The romantic urge in women is really the female ego which wants to be the center of attention, the center of a man's world. She wants to be the object of someone's love or someone's passion, but this is simply a role she wants to play, irrespective of the real men involved. To put it in its most negative light, women 'use' men to fulfill their romantic vision of themselves."

"This is fascinating!" I exclaimed thumping a cushion and jumping to my feet. "Women always complain about men using them, so this certainly puts the problem in a different light!"

"Hmm!" she murmured, carefully slipping off her shoes and tucking her tiny feet under her legs. "Another way women try to use men is by manipulating them through their sexuality. The image here is the temptress, the vamp, the sexpot. The scenario is this: Women arouse sexual desire in men, which is naturally then directed to the source of its possible fulfillment. Women bask in the sexual attention, and most ultimately give in to the demands of their men.

"However, sooner than later it usually happens that a man, once satisfied, loses the intensity of his attraction. His ardor cools, and the woman suddenly sees herself as one who has been 'had.' In fact, both have been 'had'—the woman through her own self-centered manipulations, and the man through ignorance of his spiritual responsibility for his own sexuality."

"You know," I interjected, "this reminds me of something I heard once: Men play at love to get sex; women play at sex to get love."

"Yes, that's the idea exactly," she laughed. "I want to make it clear that in both of the cases I've described, the woman is projecting her masculine aspect onto a man who will pursue and conquer her, whether romantically or sexually. There is a real need here for the woman to accept more of these masculine impulses within herself. She must be her own Prince Charming, and come to her own rescue from the dragons of her submerged inner power. Strength, courage, dignity, nobility—these qualities are latent within every woman just as they are within every man."

The fire, which had burned perfectly for a long time in a cheerful blaze, was now slowly flickering out in the fireplace. I looked at the clock and the LCD readout flashed 2:30. I did a few neck rolls and stifled a yawn. I was finally getting sleepy.

"I see it is time to stop for tonight, dear one. You have been a patient listener. Tonight in your dreams I will give you more to put in your book on this subject. You will not remember the information precisely, but when you sit down to type on your computer, it will all come back to you. I am always with you. We are preparing you to be of greater service to God, and the process takes time and effort on all of our parts. Sleep well now, and farewell."

That night, I dreamed I was a princess in a shimmering castle that rose high above the clouds. From my towers and battlements, I could see for miles and miles across my kingdom, which was laid out in neat farmsteads and cozy villages. The land was fertile and the people content. But a sad event had lately taken place. The prince, my husband, had gone to fight a battle with fearsome monsters that had been terrorizing the border people of my kingdom. The monsters were unknown in my peaceful region, but by their reputation, I knew them to be merciless in victory and vengeful in defeat. Weeks had passed and the prince had not returned from his battle. Though my heart told me differently, everyone else presumed him to be dead. Our only hope seemed to lay in the baby I was carrying, which was now close to term. I knew he would be a healthy son, an heir to his father's throne. One morning I began my labor. From my bed, I could feel the ground tremble violently as if from an earthquake. But it was not an earthquake. The monsters had made their way across my kingdom to the very walls of the castle. The smoke billowing in the distance told me that many villages had burned that day to mark the progress of the fearsome creatures. At the very moment that the doors of my castle gave way, my son came into the world. He cried no tears, but looked at me with cool, keen eyes before rising to pick up a sword and shield of blue light that had appeared at my bedside.

At my doorway stood the intruder: about ten feet tall and repulsive—an enormous serpent-like creature covered in armour, dripping with slime and decayed vegetable matter, as if it had been under water for years. The creature had many arms, each one ending in pincers. I looked with terror into its face. I was surprised at how oddly intelligent it seemed, especially around its sad-looking eyes, which were ringed with scales. My son leaped up to do battle. Without hesitation, he hurled his sword directly into the creature's throat. With a grotesque cry, it convulsed and died on the spot. Then, out of the bloody carcass emerged the form of my husband, the prince, unharmed.

The child ran into the arms of his father in joyful reunion. Somewhere in the distance, a bell pealed as if for a wedding, and rejoicing broke out everywhere in the land. My husband came toward me with our son in his arms. The blue sword and the shield had lost their brilliance and were ordinary once more. I looked into my husband's eyes and saw the light there instead, softly glowing.

CHAPTER SEVEN
The Paradox of Love

I saw the monster of my dream as my own fears and self-loathing, and the scales that surrounded its eyes as my resulting inability to see truth. But the blue sword and shield were mysterious and powerful symbols. I could not fix their meanings, and concluded only that powerful forces would come to my aid when needed. This idea pushed my inner confidence to a higher level and I slowly began to see my life through a different perspective. To my chagrin, I discovered many areas where I had become passive, allowing myself to be victimized by other people, circumstances, and most frequently, by my own laziness.

These areas formed "dead zones" of unawareness, areas where my consciousness had a tendency to "fall asleep," as Haurvata liked to say. This lack of awareness affected me in two ways. First, it formed psychic "sink holes" where the spiritual energies drained away and were wasted. Second, it created openings for negative energies to come into my life, following the vibratory law of like attracting like. I knew my passivity was endangering me, and had to stop.

I began several disciplines at once. First, I inaugurated the use of a dream diary. A tiny book lamp, clipped to an open page of a three-ring binder, allowed me to write down my dreams at any time of the night without waking my husband, nor myself up too fully. Ever since childhood, my dreams had always been vivid and memorable. But lately, I had grown complacent about them. If I could not interpret a dream immediately, or if a dream did not form a sensible narrative, I tended to shrug it off as of no value. Now I started to write down fragments of dreams, snatches of dialogue, and even isolated words and impressions. I had collected several weeks' worth of these dream "shards" before they yielded a coherent shape and purpose. But the value of this exercise was clear. Somebody was trying to tell me something, and that somebody was me! The least I could do was to learn the language of my dream-self and listen carefully whenever she tried to speak.

The second discipline I began was harder. I stopped eating refined sugar. It happened this way: Several days of steady writing had been yielding surprisingly good results. I had been waking up earlier and putting in four to six solid hours worth of work on the manuscript. At the same time, I had begun mild stretching and toning exercises which invigorated me in an unexpected way. One day, however, after a morning of productive work, I took a break and ate a few cookies.

Soon afterwards, a strange lassitude came over me. I felt like I weighed 200 pounds and had been deprived of sleep for several days. After a half-hour of struggling to form complete thoughts, I stumbled to my bed and collapsed into a deep sleep. An hour later I woke up, refreshed and ready to return to work. But I was jolted by the realization of what had just taken place. It was so subtle, I nearly missed it. I was no longer able to tolerate refined sugar with impunity. It had become for me a powerful soporific.

The third discipline was neither spiritual nor physical, but structural. Here was the key to the success or failure of my efforts to manifest in a practical way the spiritual insights I had received. I had to get myself organized! As an independent contractor, I found this aspect of my life to be the most difficult. Unlike those who worked for an employer, I had nobody standing between myself and the results of my efforts. If I slacked off, or lost my enthusiasm for my work, I simply didn't bring home a paycheck.

In many respects, I realized that my lifestyle was a blessing rather than the curse it sometimes seemed to be. My finances constantly gave me the mirror image of the kind and quality of attention I had been giving to my occupation. Most of my friends, on the other hand, like Jean, a bank loan officer, could put themselves on automatic pilot at their jobs. But their very ability to rely on an outer authority and structure caused many of these same people to flounder where such outer authorities and structures did not exist.

Whether they wanted to lose weight, exercise, read, or improve themselves in any other way, their good intentions did not often result in the fulfillment of their goals. If I wanted to be different, I knew I needed to discover ways of managing myself, including motivation, goal-setting, time-management, and rewards for success. I also knew that the "management methods" I chose had to be in line with my own individuality.

Since I abhorred clock-watching and record keeping, for example, I bypassed those hyper-methodical daily diaries which allowed you to mark down every detail, including how many miles you traveled that day and what you spent on gas to get there. I bought instead a "Sniglets" "coined-words" calendar that motivated me to use the pages by coaxing out a chuckle. I set long-range goals through creative thought and contemplation, and immediately began to work on the small steps that were needed to achieve them.

Finally, I discovered the secret beauty of lists! I simply jotted down the things I had to do as I thought of them and worked at completing each item until I cleared my list. Sometimes I transferred a few remaining items to a new page, and worked on these first before they got "old" and "spoiled." If something remained on my list for too long, I realized that I was subconsciously avoiding it. There were two reasons why this might be so.

First, the item I had written down might be inappropriate or require further scrutiny. If so, I would take a closer look at it inwardly to see where the problem lay. Second, it might also be that my entire spiritual "tone" was going toward, or was already in, a down-cycle. The latter reason was especially interesting. I had discovered that maintaining a neutral, detached attitude toward the small steps I was taking made me faster and more efficient in completing the items on my list. When I slipped into reacting to, and holding opinions about, these items, work became as smooth as dragging a dead carcass across a desert. My shorthand formula for this awareness was: Neutrality equals energy; opinions equal resistance.

As I began to make significant progress toward my goals, my confidence soared. My love quotient toward my work also increased, and from it came more contracts and fruitful experiences in the teaching field. I was learning about the relationship between my inner and outer worlds, and how the right effort in one area generated valuable growth in the other. Then one night, I had a curious dream. In the dream, I was about to enroll in a strenuous exercise class. The required clothing consisted of two pairs of tights, to be worn one underneath the other. The inner pair was white and sheer, while the outer pair was heavy and black. I found out that the white pair was going to cost me only about one dollar, but the black pair would cost nearly ten times more. I was baffled by the necessity of buying both pairs, and seriously considered ignoring regulations by purchasing only one. In the end, however, I decided to follow the requirements and pay for both.

My husband helped me interpret the dream. We had recently been discussing the idea of the inner and outer worlds and the need for balancing both. When I recounted the dream to him in the morning, he quickly saw that the two pairs of tights referred to this concept. Once this central symbol was deciphered, the rest of the dream's meaning fell into place. The exercise class meant that I was embarking on a project which would require effort on both the inner and outer levels. The inner work, consisting of thought, feeling, imagination, and planning, would be relatively effortless. But the physical effort of putting in the time and labor to bring the vision into reality would cost a great deal more.

The dream reinforced the importance of what I had learned recently about the practical ways to keep myself in peak inner and outer condition. I had to keep my connection to the inner worlds clear and pure; yet I also had to put in a great deal of physical effort if ever I were to see the results of my dreams. How willing was I to do all of this? A few lines of a Langston Hughes poem came to mind in answer to the question: "Hold fast to dreams/for if dreams die/life is a broken-winged bird/that cannot fly." I wanted to fly.

The next few weeks were spent in a whirl of activities that kept me running, if not actually flying. As a writer-in-residence at a local high school, I taught four classes of poetry writing one day a week.

This commitment yielded 130 student poems which had to be read, annotated, recorded, and the best of the lot carefully edited, typed up, and duplicated. On top of that, I had begun a special family writing class on Monday nights for parents and children. It was a private class, and I was excited to see how it would unfold. Several birthdays loomed up ahead—my husband's and son's. The volunteer work I was doing in the community needed attention this week, as well. I spent all my spare time composing, typing up and duplicating memos. Then my computer broke down. Birthday presents needed to be bought and a cake made. I wondered when the next time I could take a breath would finally come.

On Sunday, I spent some time with my friend, Polly. We talked about male-female relationships, and I spoke in a general way about some of the ideas I was getting on the subject from my spiritual teachers. Polly was a tall, rather athletic girl with brown hair and a cheerful smile for everyone. She was eight years my junior. We seemed not to notice the age difference because our points of view tended toward a similar philosophy. Polly had been a psych major in college. Now she was doing temporary work while trying to sort out her life after her recent divorce.

I had met her ex-husband several times, and marveled inwardly at the complete incompatibility in the match. Today I decided to be franker with her than I had been in the past.

"Look," I began, as we sat in her car, our respective sacks of groceries jostling as we went over the supermarket speedbumps, "just tell me one thing, O.K.? Why did you marry Jesse in the first place?"

Polly laughed, though there was an edge to her laughter.

"Good question. Well, he was cute. He had a killer of a smile—just dazzling! You have to admit he has a good smile!"

She looked at me and I reluctantly agreed. "He has a great smile. And?"

"Uh, well . . . " she struggled to continue, "I guess I was just lonely, and there was Jesse. We had a great time at first. I was crazy about him. But then he changed, or maybe we both changed."

"Polly, did he really change?" I asked, seriously.

My friend turned the corner sharply, sending a sack of cat food sliding across the trunk.

"No," she admitted gloomily, "he didn't change. It was just me who couldn't see. I saw what I wanted to, what existed inside my own head in my fantasies about love. I never really 'saw' Jesse at all. That's the truth."

Her mouth was trembling, and I could tell that tears were welling up in her eyes. The divorce had been two years ago, but Polly was still working through the disillusionment of six years of marriage. Jesse had a girlfriend now, and seemed quite content with his job, his boat, and the absence of a mismatched relationship.

Jesse and Polly's two young children went back and forth, since their parents lived only a few miles apart. So far, Polly noted that the children didn't seem to be showing signs of "emotional trauma," as she put it. But it was clear that she was looking for signs of damage every day, like the fearful owner of a brand new, precious car.

That evening, after the dinner dishes were stacked in the dishwasher, I looked around and realized with some surprise that there was nothing more I had to do. I tapped on my son's door and requested a lower decibel on his stereo and hastily retreated to my office to sit in my contemplation chair and simply relax. I noticed my husband had put a fresh pink-orange rose in my crystal bud vase next to my computer printer . I thought about him now with affection. What had I done to deserve such a considerate, faithful, intelligent man?

I closed my eyes and let my body sink into the chair, my muscles releasing and my breath becoming deeper and slower. I noticed a sore place near my left shoulder blade, my usual "holding area," and reached awkwardly behind me to try to press into it.

Just then a familiar low voice from behind me said, "Don't strain yourself. I can fix it for you in an easier way."

I swiveled around. It was Haurvata Sampa.

"Haurvata! I'm so glad to see you," I said happily. "It's been such a hectic week. The computer is in the shop, but before it broke down I actually got a lot done. The book is going well—I've got plenty of notes and I know I can do it after all!"

"There was never any doubt in my mind," he countered, "though I wondered if you would ever get off the fence and get on with it."

I laughed. He was blunt as usual, and accurate.

"Well, are you ready for your next lesson?" He spread open his hands toward me. They were large, square, and brown. They seemed capable of anything, yet they were as gentle as any mother's.

"Am I!" I sighed. "I'm all ears."

"No, not here," Haurvata frowned slightly. "I feel a disturbance in the atmosphere."

My walls were vibrating from the bass of the rock selection that my son was blasting on his stereo.

"I know what you mean," I agreed. "So where do we go? For a walk?"

His eyebrows raised. "In this rain?"

"What rain?" I asked, surprised. I hadn't noticed rain, and the sunset just an hour ago was beautiful and clear. But just then a rumble of thunder rolled across the sky. I gave Haurvata a startled look.

He laughed quietly. "No, child, I did not make the thunder happen. But a storm is on its way. So we will make a different kind of journey this time. Somewhere where we will not get wet!"

A murmur swept through the air, and I knew that it was beginning to rain indeed. Soon the sound of the drops were clearly pattering on the driveway and upon the hedges that fronted my window.

"I'm ready," I grinned. "Tell me what to do."

"Just sit as you were, close your eyes, and relax. Look for me in the inner vision. When you see me, you will get up and walk towards me. I will take you from there."

I did as I was told, this old routine a familiar one from many years of training in inner travel. Like a child, however, I was always interested in whatever he had to show me that was "new." His patience with me always struck me as remarkable. I had learned from his example how to deal with my son, who was now a teenager, and had always been from infancy a particularly strong-willed child.

I had once asked Haurvata about my son. He had answered, "The only way to commune with a stone is by becoming water. The only way to commune with water is to contain it in a vessel or a channel. To love your son, you must flow around him and show him how to soften naturally to Spirit. To love your husband, you must help him give shape and form to his inner life so that he will become more consciously aware of himself as a spiritual being."

I had told Haurvata it was working, as our family life had unfolded steadily over the last few years, and now seemed capable of even greater things. I thought about the greatness of love as I went deeper into myself. I began to tune into the heavenly music that tonight was like a musical jangle of bells and other instruments I couldn't name. I wondered what experience I would have tonight. But just as I was speculating on this, I felt a slight sucking feeling from the top of my head. Instantly I was out of my physical body and in a world of great beauty.

I seemed to be in a lush tropical garden. The sweet, slightly heavy scent of flowers permeated the air. It reminded me of floral "potpourris" which women liked to steep in hot water in their homes. I wondered if the idea for this practice came from experiences Souls had on this particular region of the higher worlds. The paths were perfectly groomed, and every square inch was filled with something interesting and lovely.

Then I saw the Tibetan Adept sitting crosslegged under a flowering tree. He looked up at me as if greeting me for the first time that day.

"Ah!" he said, with satisfaction. "You're here. Now we can begin."

He led me along the paths, past clear streams of strange translucent water the color of sunsets, and onward to a pagodalike structure I began to make out in the distance. A short walk brought us to the steps. It was an extremely simple building made of what looked to be a pale whitish stone and plain birch-colored wood. The wood gave off a subtle, pleasant odor, very fresh and neutral. We walked quietly up the stairs. In the central courtyard, a man was giving a lecture.

He was of medium height, thin, and looked to be in his late forties. He was bald, and wore a simple tunic and leggings the same color as the building. The class he was leading consisted of about twenty-five or so men and women sitting on the ground. The man sat as well, not upon a raised dias, but on the same level as his pupils. Outside the inner courtyard, a wide wooden walkway with a low railing wrapped around. A few scattered people sat there, listening intently and looking on.

I whispered to my teacher. "Why are these people sitting up here rather than in the central courtyard?"

Haurvata replied, "They wish to be accepted as students by the teacher of this House of Wisdom. They come here every day in hopes he will turn to them and say, 'Come with me.' But every day he does not say this, one eventually becomes discouraged and drops away. If you come here often, you will see what happens."

I looked now with interest at the aspiring students sitting reverently on the hard floor, wondering which ones would leave and which would remain. I followed the Adept silently as we descended the few steps to the lecture area. The teacher who was speaking stopped and looked at Haurvata. He folded his hands and bowed low.

"Greetings, my brother. Students, you are fortunate today to be in the presence of the great Unmani Dhun Adept, Haurvata Sampa."

His words were mild, but filled with a quality of beauty and strength. The students obviously knew of Haurvata. Their faces were suffused with admiration as they looked respectfully in his direction.

"Many thanks for allowing us to join your gathering, Vahira Manu, my brother. I am here only for a short while. This is my student," said Haurvata in his deep voice.

The teacher nodded, looking at me with mild interest. I bowed to him and then to the rest of the assembled group. Haurvata motioned to me and we sat down to the side, near Vahira Manu. I noticed then for the first time the special quality of light that fell in a broad column through the open roof to the area where we were sitting. It was healing, yet energizing at the same time.

"I was speaking about love," said the teacher, picking up where he had left off. Then he resumed this discourse.

"There are many concepts about love. But love is not a concept. It is the heavenly music, the Voice of God echoing throughout the worlds. This is love, my friends. Nothing less is true love. The Voice of God creates the worlds and withdraws them back into Itself at the end of the Maha Kalpa, the Great Cycle. The Voice of God gives life to Soul and enables each to be a god unto itself, a god of its own universe. Yes, dear ones, this is love.

"But, what? You say there are other kinds of love? Ah, so there are! There is love of place, love of one's fellow man, love of man for a woman and vice-versa, and the love of parents for their child. There is even love of food and drink."

The students smiled, and some chuckled. It was a relaxed group, used to being together, and no longer in strict awe of their noble teacher.

"Well, then, are these things love as well? Tell us your opinion, Sampa. Speak to us."

There was a soft murmur in the crowd and a group of expectant faces turned toward the guest. Haurvata thought for a moment, then bowed respectfully to his spiritual brother.

"Ah, but tonight I wish to hear my brother Vahira Manu speak on this subject, and share his wisdom. But I will agree that it is necessary to rank love, if you will, in a scale from the highest to the lowest. One must discriminate between what has within it the required pull upward, and what will sink of its own heaviness."

"You give a good picture of it, my friend," smiled the slender man. "Yes, the pull upward is what distinguishes true love from the false. Does your love uplift? Does it draw you like flame draws a moth onward and upward to the Godhead? Ah, if so, it is good. If not, it is something else masquerading as love. See? It is simple. There is nothing more to say about love!"

It was clear that the students assembled today expected more than this brief lecture. Unspoken questions were clearly written on their faces. Haurvata looked at me, silently asking if I had a question as well.

"Master Manu," began one woman with a broad face and bright grey eyes, "if love is so simple, why do we have so many problems with it? Why is love not easy, as you describe?"

The small group nodded and murmured approval as one. I did as well. It was a good question.

"Simple? Easy? Are these the same things, then?" asked the teacher, flashing a sharp glance into the crowd. "I said it was simple. And so it is. But easy? No, dear ones, love is the most difficult thing in the world. Why? Because we mistake attachment for love. We mistake the desire to fulfill our own needs through another as love. Love is difficult because we need it too much!

"A spiritual poverty grips at the heart of the lower worlds, my children! It is a poverty of love. Materialism has been substituted for love, but all the money, power, and success in the world will not buy one moment of joy, or a minute of freedom. People cloaked in furs and brilliant with jewels are going to bed hungry tonight. And their hunger is something for which there is no earthly solace.

"Will you be one of these hungry ones? Or will you be fed? If you need love, then you must first find love within yourself. And to

79

find love within, you must give it out with no thought of reward. For love is only Spirit, and Spirit belongs to no one. It is God."

With that, the teacher rose and walked quietly away. The group of students sat for a moment, absorbed in contemplation of the teacher's words. Then, slowly, they began to file away as well. I looked up at the walkway where the aspiring students sat. Already, one had crept away. About six remained.

Sampa was on his feet. "Ho! What was your impression, child?" he asked me, grinning. "How do you take to our revered teacher, Vahira Manu?"

"I find him pleasant, with a subdued power," I replied thoughtfully. "He is a good speaker, too. What he said was very simple and to the point. He did not waste words, nor overfill the minds of the students with more than they could accept."

"You are a good observer," the Tibetan remarked approvingly. "He has that reputation! So you, in writing this book of yours, must learn to be. Not so complicated. Not so long. Do you see?"

"Yes," I laughed. I had learned to discipline myself over the years to be brief and accurate. But it was a continual struggle which I didn't always win. I appreciated the reminder.

Now we walked outside the temple into the gardens which surrounded it. I was surprised to find that it was rather bare. However, a large pond sparkled like a single jewel in the plain landscape, flowing with the same incredible water I had seen earlier. A few water lilies floated on the shimmering surface. Subtly glowing quartz sand filled the area, bordered with smooth stones. Small flowers grew up between the stones. Otherwise, all was extremely undecorated. I remarked upon the contrast between the plain temple grounds and the splendid garden through which we had passed earlier.

"It is Manu's way," Haurvata explained. "He dislikes clutter. This temple is one he built with his own hands."

We sat on a mound near one end of the pool. My mind was full of thoughts about my friend Polly. I decided to ask the Adept about her.

"Haurvata," I said, "I have a friend whose heart seems broken because of a failed marriage. Although her mate has gone on with his life, she is obviously still unable to let go of the past. She is a capable and attractive person. Still, she can't seem to find a new mate, and she worries constantly about her children."

"Your friend has become too materialized in consciousness," the Tibetan said without hesitation. "She wishes to fix things in an unchanging way, regardless of whether they are even working or not. She needs to develop her objective senses more. If she would learn to enlarge her awareness, her horizons would expand considerably as well!"

"I have told her about expanded consciousness, of course," I replied. In both the waking and dream state, this technique enabled one to perceive and explore the interrelationship between the inner and outer worlds. "But Polly is so caught up with her problems."

"There is little you can do directly, child," said my teacher, shaking his head. "But you have planted the seed. Perhaps when her tears have watered it enough, it will sprout into a new life, yes?"

"I hope so," I mumbled. A fish leaped out of the water and fell with a flash of silver scales into the pond.

"Let me explain to you one of the particular problems women in general have with love," offered the Unmani Dhun Adept.

I looked at him strangely, and he began to laugh deeply and softly in his chest. "Do you not think I am qualified to discuss such matters?"

"Oh, of course you're qualified," I said hastily. "I didn't mean to look at you strangely. It was just . . . unexpectedly put, is all."

"Well, then." He furrowed his heavy brows and got down to business. "Women in general are too much concerned with relationships. They cannot let things be, but must always be 'working' on this one, and 'salvaging' that one, and 'understanding' that one over there. They try to understand feelings through their feelings, and that cannot be done any more than one can understand the mind through the mind."

"Men do that," I countered.

Haurvata chuckled. "Are you taking this personally? Of course, if you are, that's your business. Anyway, a woman solves nothing, understands nothing, if her perspective is too narrow. A woman must learn the technique of going about things obliquely to resolve a problem. When she attacks directly at her or another person's emotions, she only finds the walls getting higher and wider. Women must use creativity and logic more instead, balancing the overcharge of feeling with other spiritual currents! This will make her outflow far healthier and more constructive for human relationships.

"An individual cannot live mainly on emotions, but needs more which is solid and nurturing to his spirit. Sustain and strengthen a person's spirit, and the rest will follow, including emotional love. For a man, a little emotional love received goes a long way. Children need more, particularly as infants. And women who have not developed their spiritual sides seem to need it most of all."

"Haurvata, why do women seem to fall into this emotional trap so often? What is wrong with us?" I was disturbed by this tendency in women and wondered if it pointed to some irremediable flaw.

"Nay, dear one," Sampa reassured me. "Sincerely, I say no. When I speak this way, I am merely focusing for the moment on the particular errors of the one sex. That is not to say that the other commits no errors as serious as this."

"What of men's shortcomings, then?" I asked.

"Ah, I was coming directly to that," he smiled. "Men fall into the trap of feeding on this emotional love in a way that isn't respectful or just to the women in their lives. They fill up on it in much the same way as they'd put gasoline in their tanks. Often they think that if they bring home a paycheck every month, kiss the wife on the cheek, and take her out to dinner once in awhile, they are giving an adequate return. But what they have not done is to reach into their inner resources to make a true gift of themselves. By this refusal, they lose the opportunity for intimacy, friendship, and self-sacrifice. They also do not discover much of their own spiritual natures. In short, they have failed the spiritual potential of marriage, if not the material one."

I was deeply interested in the conversation taking place. I said, "O.K. You've given me a good idea of what men and women can do to correct their errors. But what perspective can both sexes take to enable them to fulfill the potential of marriage?"

"Men and women can be examples of love. They can transform their materialistic notion of love from 'having' to 'being.' They must love themselves and fulfill themselves and be as complete as possible unto themselves. They must stop playing the tug-of-war game of emotional giving and taking. You see, child, giving and taking is still on the emotional level. What is needed is for men and women to see themselves simply as vehicles for the God force which gives through them. They must impersonalize their love. Only then will their Souls shine and awaken the sleeping divinity in themselves and their mates as well."

I thought of all that I heard this night, in the company of my teacher and the subtle teacher, Vahira Manu. I stored this inside my heart and found myself once more in the physical body. Outside, the thunder had abated, but rain was pouring down, giving the earth one last blast of chilly winds and rain before the inevitable spring.

CHAPTER EIGHT
Relationships

I was bending over the rim of the toilet bowl when the telephone rang that morning. It rang loudly six or seven times before I realized, to my consternation, that the answering machine had been turned off. Slowly and heavily, I made my way to the phone and picked it up.

"Hello?" I answered, trying to sound as normal as possible.

"Hi!" replied the caller. It was Kyari Hota, the Unmani Dhun Adept. "I thought I'd come by and take you to breakfast. I'll be there in a half-hour, if that's all right with you. I've got something to show you!"

"Wait!" I groaned. "Not so fast. I appreciate the offer, really, but there's some things you don't know."

"Like what?" asked the other voice.

"Like I have to teach this afternoon," I whispered.

"Oh, that's all right," Kyari replied. "This won't take that long. Maybe an hour or two. When are the classes?"

"12:30 until 3:00," I said. "But I need . . . "

"It's just 8:30 now," she broke in. "I'll have you back home by 10:30 at the very latest. That gives you two whole hours to get ready. Isn't that enough time?"

"Oh, all right," I moaned. "I've got a hang-over! I don't feel well. So now you know."

"Well, why didn't you say so?" she responded. "What did you do, anyway? You're not much of a drinker."

I laughed bitterly. "That's the problem."

"How much did you have?" Kyari asked.

"One glass of wine," I stated in a flat voice.

"One glass?" repeated Kyari. "One? Oh. Well . . . it stands to reason, I guess. Certain adjustments have been made on your physical body in the last few weeks. To put it simply, we 'upped' the vibrations a little. Nothing major—just clearing away a few of your most troublesome energy blockages so you can finish your work! We thought you noticed."

I groaned and sank down resignedly into a kitchen chair. "I did notice," I replied. "I chose to ignore it just this one time. We went to a big, fancy party with a bunch of legal beagles. The food was great. I should have stuck with the diet Pepsi. When you 'upped' the vibrations, you 'downed' the poison tolerance threshold. Now, my question is, why can't spiritual people eat junk? Now just tell me that. Where's the justice?"

"Well, look," she cajoled, "you're not as badly off as you think. The worst is over, and nothing much can be gained by lurching around the house feeling sorry for yourself. I'll be there in a half an hour. It's important. You'll see."

"O.K.," I relented. "But make that 45 minutes."

It took me that long to make myself presentable, as I was moving rather slowly. By the time I put on my shoes, I heard a car pull up the driveway and honk its horn. I stared curiously out the window. It was Kyari Hota, wearing slacks and a pullover, emerging from a sporty candy-apple-red car.

I came to the door, shaking my head in wonderment. "Wherever did you get that car?"

"Come on," she urged. "Get in. It rides as smooth as a cloud!"

I walked once around the vehicle to admire its sleek lines. The car was brand new, sporting only the name of a dealership where the license plate should have been. I sank into the seat, which closed around me like a leather glove around a baseball.

"Well!" I breathed. "I'm impressed. Now tell me how you got this machine."

Kyari opened up the glove compartment and took out what seemed to be a brand new wallet. She flipped it open and showed me a new credit card. "Pre-approved," she smiled. "I can test drive it for two days or 200 miles, whichever comes first. And I won't even need it for that long!"

Then she put the car into reverse. We drove two miles to a coffee shop and found a booth by the window. Kyari ordered a cup of herb tea and some fruit salad. I ordered a cup of decaffeinated coffee and whole wheat toast, well done.

The waitress, who called us "honey," brought our hot drinks immediately. As the steam rose from our cups, the Adept reached into the large vinyl bag she was carrying and brought out what looked to be a photograph album.

"Guess what I've got here!" she said pleasantly.

"Looks like a photograph album," I said. "Whose is it?"

"Yours," she answered.

I stared at the covers for a full minute, then shook my head. "No, it isn't," I said. "I've never seen it before."

"Oh, well, it's not exactly one of yours in that sense of the word," she corrected herself. "It's a collection I put together for you from different periods of your life. The pictures are from your spiritual 'records' which, as you know, are filed away in the inner worlds. As your teacher, I've got access to them. I hope you don't mind."

"Oh, God," I groaned, my head in my hands. "I don't believe this is happening to me. What are we doing this for?"

"Ah," sighed the Adept. "I was getting to that next. You see, it's time you got more from the experiences you've had as a female in this lifetime. That way, you can better consider your options for the present and the future. You have had a tendency to repress unpleasant memories."

"Am I going to have reason to repress this one?" I asked.

". . . and because of this tendency, you haven't gotten as much conscious awareness out of your experiences as you could. Difficult experiences should be remembered, my friend—not the emotion in them, but the objective lessons inherent in the challenges."

"O.K.," I sighed, finally accepting the direction of this conversation. "You're right, of course. I'm feeling a little grumpy, that's all. Don't pay me any mind."

The Adept patted my hand and flipped open the covers. I supposed I expected to find baby pictures, but what I saw instead was a black and white photo of myself with a bouffant hairdo, a tight, thigh-high skirt, and spike heels. The amount of eye make-up shown in the photo would have lasted me a week under my present levels of use.

"Do you think she might be my evil twin?" I proposed.

She chuckled and turned several more pages. I cringed to see more ghastly photos of myself in the sex-kitten stages. It was clear from the evidence how absolutely I had accepted the need to be attractive and passive, an adornment to men. A few more pictures showed me in the hippie stage: long straight hair, almost no makeup, and almost no clothes. I was going 'natural.' Next came a marriage picture, then me in an advanced state of pregnancy, waddling around with a big belly and a Peter Pan haircut. This was the turning point! I was beginning to resemble the current me, minus the belly. I flipped through the later pictures quickly, since they were more familiar.

"You'll see the purpose of this presently. Now take a look at these." Kyari flipped quickly past several pages until she came to a rogues' gallery of old boyfriends.

I looked at the Adept darkly and said in a quiet voice, "I hope I get a great deal out of this experience."

"That depends on you," she countered. "There are patterns in these relationships I don't believe you see. That's what we're here this morning to correct, for you must be able to apply the spiritual concepts about the male and female to your own life before you can explain them to others."

"This is fascinating," I said, bravely. "Go on!"

"I will! Recall, then, that the last time we were together we discussed the concept of the anima and the animus. This is the male principle within the female, and the female principle within the male. Personally, I prefer to call them 'inner man' and 'inner woman.' The existence of these two principles within humanity provides balance, and gives each person the potential to become God-like.

"Now, the problem is that most people have difficulty making good use of these opposite sex qualities in themselves. Instead, they prefer to act out their dominant side and find mates to act out their less developed traits. By doing this, they cut themselves off from their spiritual potential. Furthermore, their incompleteness makes it likely that they will attract other incomplete people to themselves. Unlike mathematics, two halves in this case do not make a whole! Incomplete people tend to be dissatisfied with each other, because each reflects what the other is lacking within himself.

"For example, when we left off the last time, we had been discussing how women often project their animus because of their inability to accept and act out male qualities in themselves. Their tendency to repress and deny these assertive qualities results in their taking a rather complicated stance vis-a-vis men. It is complicated because they can never be direct and open, but always indirect, round-about, and calculating. An example is the expression, 'a man chases a woman until she catches him.' This accounts for woman's reputation as a manipulator. Men think of women as devious, or at best, paradoxical. But insofar as they act this way at all, it is out of a perceived necessity!

"Now this phenomenon of calculation and indirection is not limited to women. Men who have strong feminine sides can also act in similar ways. They try to draw people and opportunities to themselves rather than to charge out and create something. They hide their motives and are frequently secretive because they are subconsciously fearful of not getting what they want. The passive techniques they use are calculated to get what they want without an open battle. They fear they might lose an open battle, and they believe their chances are better through manipulation. They may become so good at hiding their motives that their motives finally become hidden from themselves."

I was surprised to hear this. But inside myself, something clicked. A perception slowly began to form, and I started to sense how this discussion applied to my own previous male-female relationships.

"I'm beginning to recognize this description," I interjected, as the waitress came by and poured some coffee into my cup. "Not all of my old boyfriends fit this pattern, of course. But surprisingly, many of them do. I'm amazed."

"Don't be," smiled the Adept. "The situation is not unique to you. Many people's selections of mates fit into patterns. That's because many people are functioning out of unconscious projections in this area of their lives."

"I hadn't fully realized that," I mused. "But now that you put it that way, the shoe certainly fits a lot of people's feet."

"Now, to continue," said the Adept, taking a sip of lukewarm mint tea. "The underlying cause of the aberration I've just described is introversion. The forces of Soul, which should flow naturally through the individual and out to the objective world, become locked inside the ego. This is the danger for the minority of men who fit this description. Sadly, it is the normal scenario for many women, since the healthy expression of desire and personal will is often denied or repressed in them. That is, until now. That's what we of the Unmani Dhun hope to change.

"In your case, you have been attracted to a series of men who basically fall into the spiritual pattern we have just described. They were men who expressed feminine traits more than the masculine. Can you see this?"

"Yes! Most definitely," I agreed excitedly. "I never understood it, though."

"These men radiate a kind of feminine energy that many people—both men and women—find irresistible. A word that is often used to describe them is 'boyish.' Now boys can be attractive because of the mixture of the feminine and masculine, the child and adult, in them. They are, by turns, playful and assertive, then moody and imaginative. But men who are like boys also tend to be rather self-centered, irresponsible, and immature, like real-life boys. Then why are women attracted to them in the first place? The reasons are complex.

"One type of woman who is attracted to feminine men has a fondness for playing the 'mother' role. Such women feel more comfortable being maternal and nurturing than in being equal partners with men. They like the sense of control and authority they get from having a man dependent on them. In a way, however, this is an evasion of a hidden issue. The issue is, why is it necessary to get a sense of control and authority from emotionally dependent people? A similar but more constructive experience might be, for example, to become a corporate manager in charge of hired subordinates. But this would require a willingness to work for a position of authority in the objective world. The 'super mother' is seldom willing to do this.

"On the other hand, some women like feminine men because

they offer a reinforcement to their own femaleness, including the qualities of feeling, imagination, and inner vision. These women may have weak female self-images and seek men who demonstrate the very qualities they think they lack. Or, these women may simply have highly developed masculine sides and need a feminine man around to keep their lives in balance. Relationships between feminine men and the type of women I'm describing here are less destructive than those between feminine men and the controlling 'super mother.' In fact, some of these relationships might even turn out to be mutually constructive for both parties.

"However, the key here is awareness. One must be aware of the proper relationship between the masculine and feminine currents and strive to keep as much of a balance as possible within oneself. So what is the proper relationship between these currents? To put it briefly, the role of the feminine is to provide inspiration and feeling to the masculine. The role of the masculine is to be attentive to these inner currents and act upon them in responsible ways.

"All right," I said. "I think I get it. The bottom line is: We have to be balanced, or our relationships won't be. So, in my case, what did I do, exactly, that was wrong?"

"I wouldn't call it 'wrong,'" the Adept said, charitably. "I would call it . . . a 'hands-on' approach to learning through experience."

"Oh, you mean like clobbering your thumb with a hammer?" I joked.

"It's amazing how well pain works to get one's attention, isn't it?" she smiled back. "You chose feminine, anima-driven men to push yourself to accept responsibility for the masculine qualities dormant in yourself, and to value and utilize better the resources of the feminine. By seeing through these men's convoluted inner processes and manipulative outer actions, you saw the consequences of introverting the masculine current within yourself. By experiencing the frustration of their failure to materialize their ambitions, you realized the importance of not denying dreams and aspirations of your own. When you finally came to these conclusions and began to assert your own masculine and feminine sides consciously and constructively, this pattern in your life completely disappeared."

"That's right," I said happily. "I finally saw it clearly. And I knew what I had to do."

The waitress came back with another refill of hot water and coffee. She was pleasant, making small talk and finally asking us if we were sisters. At the same time that I said "no," Kyari answered "yes." The woman looked strangely at us, and I controlled the urge to roll my eyes upward in despair. Kyari, however, was unruffled.

"We're actually relatives," she confided seriously. "We're from northern China."

This news had an interesting effect on the woman. She seemed to perk up, and began to comment about how she'd always wanted to go to China, but everyone always told her she was crazy. Finally, she complimented us on how very, very slight our accents were, and how well we spoke English.

Kyari smiled and said that China was a fascinating place, and that if our waitress wanted to go there, she should read some books and look at some pictures and go there first in her imagination. Kyari said that no dream was impossible, and suggested casually that perhaps the waitress had had a past life in China. The woman thought about that for a few seconds, then laughed and shook her head.

"Oh, I don't believe in things like that," she said, waving her hand as if to dispel the suggestion.

"Well, it's an interesting idea, anyway," smiled Kyari as the woman walked away, carrying her pots of beverages.

"If we're relatives, I'm Ling-Ling-the-Panda's aunt," I hissed. "How can you say those things! I thought Adepts were supposed to be . . . to be . . . dignified. Or at least honest."

Kyari's dark eyes twinkled at me in amusement. "What do you know about it?" she asked bluntly. "Honestly, you did have a lifetime in China as a distant relative of mine. Maybe there's even some panda blood in you as well. Anyway, I think you missed the whole point of the exchange."

"I hate bamboo shoots," I groused.

"The waitress was responding to the spiritual current coming through us," she continued. "Mentioning China was simply the trigger for her to open to Spirit, to her own dreams and aspirations which she has allowed to slip away from her. Many men and women are like her, my dear. They have given up their personal fulfillment too easily for the sake of material security, or simply for a lack of courage or commitment to their own cause. Now a seed is planted.

It is up to her to do something with it."

"I had no idea," I replied contritely. "I thought you were playing with her."

The Adept shook her head. "Frankly, the image you have of what to expect from a spiritually evolved Soul is appalling. We will do anything—I repeat, anything—that does not harm Soul in order to bring an individual to a higher level of life. The conventional image of the saint does not fit the spiritual Adepts. We are not without joy and a sense of humor!

"Self-denial is fine for the beginning student who needs to discipline the mental passions such as anger, lust, greed, and vanity. But the Adepts are beyond such temptations. Therefore, we can have anything we want. Even red sports cars! If we do not use all of our freedom, it is only because we do not need it. Now, you are much too tense these days. If you would stop trying to be such a block of wood, you'd relax into something more like yourself. You might discover who you really are. You might even like it."

"All right. I asked for that," I sighed. "But lay off the 'block of wood' stuff, O.K.? Haurvata has come very close to calling me 'Pinocchio' already. No, don't ask me to explain. Anyway, since you're in cahoots with each other, you probably know."

"Well, soon you'll have to start thinking about teaching those classes, dear one," Kyari smiled, changing her tone. "So I wanted to speak to you about the men in your life who didn't fit into the pattern I've just described. A number of them were very traditionally masculine people."

Kyari turned the pages of the photo album and pointed out some of the people she was referring to. Then she began her explanation.

"Up until the present, you've had difficulty pursuing your dreams with confidence, and many of your choices in males reflected this problem within yourself. Yet, in general, your past life records show a distinct preference for a life of change and action. Your leadership experience in former incarnations has been extensive, and you naturally gravitate to positions of responsibility.

"The truth is, you've been somewhat hobbled in this lifetime in order to prevent you from doing, through reflex, what you've done so many times in the past. The limitations of your childhood were useful to curb your natural aggressiveness and self-centeredness, and cultivate in you some much needed humility and compassion for the

92

average person. It also forced you to turn inward to have a place to direct your energies, since expressing yourself on the physical plane was so difficult.

"So naturally, you have attracted the more aggressive and successful type of males into your life as well. They were the healthy expressions of your already well-developed masculine nature. But you didn't fully acknowledge this masculine part of you in the old days. Conflicts arose which you never understood to be the result of two strong egos jockeying for position. This is a difference you value so highly in your relationship with your husband today. He is a strong man, yet secure enough in himself not to have to be bossy. He is a true friend and companion in your life, plus the supportive male you never had in a father."

I smiled at this description of my husband. It was very accurate, and I knew how lucky I was. "I really appreciate everything you've shared with me. Relationships are really quite simple, once you understand yourself better."

"Yes," nodded Kyari. "But understanding your own projections is not enough to survive. One must also understand what kind of projections the opposite sex often places upon you. I'd like to talk about that now. Just as women traditionally tend to project their undeveloped masculine qualities onto men, men do the same to women. These feminine traits include the qualities of physical nurturing, warm affection, intuition, and feeling.

"Some men are suspicious of women for having these aforementioned qualities. But the truth is, men need very much to develop them. Men who have projected out their female qualities have a difficult time establishing and maintaining relationships, and are cut off from discovering and exploring their inner worlds. They live superficial lives, never opening their hearts to others in the true spiritual sense, and never allowing love to reach upward to the divine.

"Now here's a key difference that you may have noticed between men and women. Whereas women generally admire feminine qualities in men, men do not normally feel the same way about masculine qualities in women. This is because feminine qualities are by nature cooperative. Masculine qualities are competitive. Thus, many men feel instinctively threatened by women who demonstrate these masculine qualities too obviously—particularly in the fields of their own interests and endeavors.

"The instinctual urge of the primitive male principle is to assert dominance. The reason for this instinct is the preservation of the species through the Darwinian principle of survival of the fittest. This instinct to dominate is of course kept in check by the social need to interact and cooperate in a civilized environment. But men are often confused when they find themselves competing with a female. It goes against their primitive programming. It is all too archaic!

"A man who demands that a woman be feminine in a rigidly traditional sense is one who is terribly protective of, and fearful for, his own dominance. He needs his mate to be beautiful, subservient, and anything else he values in order to feed his image of himself. Because his own well-being is connected somehow with how the woman functions in his life, he is particular about how she must behave, look, speak, or be. Generally, he is a man who thinks of a woman as an extension of his self-image because his own ego is too fragile to stand alone. Being in a relationship with a man like this is bound to be dissatisfying because he will never accept and support a woman for the inner being she is. He cannot, because he isn't doing the same for himself.

"Some men are narcissistic romantics with visions of how dashing and strong they might be if only their women were more attractive or feminine! This falls roughly into the age-old category of 'If only you were this way, I could be that way.' It puts the responsibility for our inability to realize some desired quality upon another person. Of course, this is partly true, but in the long run not a helpful way to view the situation. Even if other people's behavior and attitudes play an important part in one's reality, the only real power we have for sure is the right and ability to change ourselves.

"Now to sum up, my daughter. The choices everyone makes of a mate always mirror the spiritual unfoldment he or she has attained at that time. If your mate does not treat you with kindness and consideration, it may be that you do not treat yourself that way. If a man does not communicate with you, it is likely that your inner male and inner female are not communicating, either. Your critical spouse mirrors back your own self-criticism and perfectionism. And on it goes. Once you see this, you will realize that marital unhappiness is just a symptom of an inner dis-ease. Before you try to change the other person, decide first to work on yourself. The results will be greater, and the changes will be real.

"Do you have any questions so far?" asked Kyari, taking a deep breath.

I was about to shake my head "no" when I was suddenly struck by a thought I was eager to express. "I'd like to ask a question about my marriage, if you don't mind."

"Of course," answered Kyari. "What could be more relevant?"

I had been married to my husband for several years now. We had been married once before, but our marriage had broken up when my son was just four years old. An incompatible second marriage intervened for me, whereas my first husband stayed single and finally went to law school to better his life.

A brilliant but reserved man, he had not been able to understand or sympathize with my need for affection and interaction. While he was patient and slow-moving, I was intense and desired change. When we broke up, we agreed to disagree and parted amicably. Then, five years later, with my painful second marriage behind me, we got back together. This time it proved resoundingly successful.

"Well, what I want to know is," I began, taking a deep breath, "why has my marriage worked this time, when it failed so miserably before? Have we changed? Or did we not know each other in the first place? Or were we just too young?"

"Slow down," said Kyari, chuckling. "But yes, I'll answer this for you. To simplify a rather complex story, your marriage is working the second time because you are now on much higher levels of consciousness than you were when you made your first attempt. In the old days, both of you were very unbalanced and, lacking wholeness, could not sustain your responsibility for creating the life you both wanted. Nor had you enough spiritual insight to avoid the pitfalls along the way. You projected onto each other many hopes and expectations which were your own responsibilities to be and do.

"Because you were inadequate, you found each other inadequate. Because you did not love yourselves spiritually, you could not love each other. Your need for each other was for self-gratification, not for giving. The reason your marriage failed is typical of why most marriages, whether they end in divorce or not, fail. You did not know what marriage was for, and you did not know yourselves."

"Oh," I grinned. "I'm glad I asked."

Kyari gave a hearty laugh. "Daughter, now you see your husband as a great and shining Soul. And this is the same vision he holds of you. You see yourselves reflected back in each other's eyes, and neither will betray the other's love and trust! You are indeed fortunate, yet this gift is one you have both earned out of the difficult struggles of your emerging spiritual selves."

We left a large tip for the waitress. Kyari winked and called it the "China fund." I learned something more about compassion that day. I realized that the greatest gift one could give another is the power to believe in oneself—the power to dream a life, whether it took you to China or the inner worlds.

96

CHAPTER NINE
The Active and
Passive Paths to God

The adjustments the Unmani Dhun had made on my vibratory rate gave me a greatly increased level of energy that lasted for many weeks. After my lesson at the cocktail party, I carefully avoided any food or drink that might trigger a negative reaction. During that time I charged ahead on many projects I had begun months before. I wrote proposals, letters, memos, grants, and spoke on the telephone to many people about my work in the schools.

Inevitably, the easy flow of energy that been such a gift began to wind down. I did not heed this change, however, and kept pushing myself for a few extra days, which stretched into a week. Then one day, completely exhausted from several full days and nights of work and little sleep, I lay down in bed to take a short nap. Hours later I awoke. My physical body felt like lead and I grimly realized that I was sick. A tightness in my chest showed me that my lungs, always the weakest point in my body, were infected. I began to cough. I had depleted my body's resources and ignored its warning. Now I would have to pay the price.

Luckily, it was a rather modest price this time. A common sense regimen of light, healthful eating, adequate sleep, and a modest work load brought me back into balance. Acupressure treatments, which worked so well on my body, cleared the lung problems and spurred the healing process on. I breathed a sigh of relief, chastened by this close call!

This mild physical collapse was but a shadow of the chronic respiratory problems I had begun to experience at age ten, when I came down with pleurisy. In my adult years, this ongoing series of lung-related illnesses began to take an increasingly long time to heal. Constant, high fevers wracked my body for weeks. I coughed up phlegm until my chest was sore and I lost my voice to laryngitis. Antibiotics did not seem to make any kind of impression on the mysterious organism causing these episodes. I used to imagine it laughing every time I tried a new drug to expunge it.

During the early years of my formal spiritual training, these illnesses were particularly bad. I had been undergoing some trying emotional times in my personal life. As my spiritual growth progressed, however, my emotional life also improved, as did my general health. My lung illnesses became shorter, less frequent, and less serious. However, like a recovered alcoholic, I knew I would never be able to forget that this condition was serious, and could threaten my life.

One day, after I had recovered sufficiently from my illness, I drove to downtown Sacramento to meet my husband for lunch. After a pleasant meal at a Mexican restaurant, we parted company. I parked my car nearby at tree-shaded Capitol Park and began to stroll. The day was pleasant and mild, though not particularly warm. Few people were lounging outdoors at this time of the year, but the park was busy anyway with office workers and joggers rushing to and fro. An empty bench appeared in a spot of sunshine. I made for it, then closed my eyes and relaxed. Kyari Hota's voice broke in presently.

"It's good to see you," she said cheerfully. "There is much I want to discuss with you today. Are you feeling better now?"

"Yes, thanks," I answered happily, opening my eyes. The Adept was standing before me in a blue business suit. "I am definitely better. So what's this all about anyway?"

"I would like to discuss with you the active and passive paths to God," Kyari replied, sitting down beside me. "You see, daughter, there is only one path to God. Yet creation, being dual, is made of two aspects: the positive and negative polarities, or the male and female currents, as you know. The existence of these currents in turn creates two conflicting and complementary approaches to spiritual unfoldment—the active and the passive. The active and passive approaches are two distinct ways to link yourself up with the God Force. Bring these two approaches into balance within yourself, and you can step through the narrow door into the heavenly worlds!"

"Your timing is perfect," I yawned, as the sun moved behind some clouds. "Balance is precisely what I've been lacking lately. I think pushing myself too much is what got me sick as a dog."

The Adept nodded. "You've ignored a primary fact of life. The lower worlds operate within natural cycles. These cycles come from the pulsing of spiritual energy in the universe and the rest points between them. Spiritual energy, once emitted, travels as waves in time and space. Individuals experience these waves and pulses of energy in all the things they do, from their jobs, to creative endeavors, to human relationships.

"In practical terms, this means that you go through periods of energy and boredom, inspiration and discouragement, harmony and disagreement. Become alert to such cycles and you can intuitively ride the waves as they peak, while gathering strength during the lulls in between. Ignore these cycles, and you fall prey to many errors in judgment, leading to small and large losses. For example, someone may give up on a project or a relationship just before it becomes successful by mistaking a rest point for total failure. On the other hand, one might inaugurate a big push for a business after a positive cycle has expended its energies, and wind up losing everything."

Two squirrels ran chittering across the lawn in front of us and up an enormous oak tree. They looked down at us, scolding noisily.

"I get it," I interjected. "In my case, I didn't realize that the new spiritual energy I had been given was a wave. I guess I expected it to continue indefinitely. When I pushed it, I crashed!"

"The only mistake you made was in not easing your efforts when the spiritual currents were no longer supporting you," said Kyari. "The stress upon you caused a lowering of your physical stamina, and your illness-pattern set in."

"Yes," I admitted. "Pushing Spirit is a lot like doing the backstroke on dry land!"

Kyari chuckled. "Well, at least you've learned a lesson you will be unlikely to repeat soon. Balance, you see, is a result of being alert in your relationship with the spiritual forces. A good analogy might be the actions of a surfer in the ocean. First, a surfer has to position himself for a wave. Then he has to approach it correctly, keep his balance, and maneuver through the tube created by the breaking wave. Then, when the wave is dying, he has to withdraw from it gracefully, so he won't end up falling and losing his board. The surfer has to maintain a healthy respect for his element. The sea is beautiful, but it can also be dangerous to one ignorant of its ways!"

"Good comparison," I said appreciatively. "Awareness, attitude, balance, right action, and discrimination—I didn't realize surfing was so spiritual!"

"Well, perhaps not all surfers look at it that way," Kyari smiled. "But I suppose the very best of them learn the principles to apply later when they are consciously interested in spiritual things."

The Adept rose from the bench and stretched. "Well! We've been sitting for long enough, don't you think? Let's walk some."

I was grateful that I had listened to an inner nudge and had worn comfortable, flat shoes that day. Kyari liked to walk, and her stride was surprisingly strong and tireless. We strolled across the lawns where spring flowers had been planted. Above us a line of royal palms rustled gently in the breeze. The Adept was talking all the while.

"Now, the error you made that caused your illness was the overuse of the active principle. The active principle is the masculine polarity. It asserts itself in striving and aggression. The active principle is the force we use to move through experiences on the wheel of life, throwing out causes and reaping their effects over and over. By sowing causes and reaping effects, we learn to discriminate between alternatives, perceive the relationship between our actions and their effects, and refine our fields of action to ever higher levels of endeavor.

"The active principle in individuals gives them the drive and confidence to pursue a goal, and to continue their quest in the face of obstacles. Without a strong aggressive side, no spiritual seeker could attain the heavenly worlds. He would have given up long ago, having given ear to the passive forces of the world that whisper constantly against the struggle and loneliness of the spiritual life!

"The passive principle counterbalances the active through its qualities of negation and rest. The passive expresses itself through the feminine polarity in the tendency of all matter to wind down and dissolve. The passive is the force of automatic, cyclic change—the natural ebb and flow of the physical universe. The passive principle in Soul works toward harmony and balance with all other forces of natural life.

"When faced with obstacles, the passive principle, unlike the active, will give way. It does so not out of weakness, but out of its own inner instinct for self-preservation and survival! The passive side in the individual will say, 'Do not expend your energies in futile efforts. Save yourself.' The passive instinct makes us keenly aware that life is not merely a pawn in the hands of our will, but a flow of forces greater than ourselves!

"Do you understand this so far, dear one?"

"Sure," I answered. "It makes perfect sense."

The Adept smiled and continued.

"Both active and passive currents, by themselves, are incomplete. Both are necessary to create balance and stability for one's movement toward the Supreme One. Used together, active and passive function as counterpoints, creating a dynamically balanced tension between opposites which can lead to the higher wisdom. However, as you've pointed out, it is indeed rare for this balance to occur. Now I'll describe the reasons for this.

"Cultures frequently favor one mode over the other, creating negative attitudes against the one less accepted. For example, an aggressive culture such as yours tends to value conquest, achievement, and expansion. A civilization which elevates the active principle at the expense of the passive can flourish for a while. But eventually it will self-destruct due to its ignorance of the forces outside the sphere of its will, which will bring it toppling down! This is, in a sense, retribution from the passive side, which always wins out in the end when it is abused or ignored.

"A culture which is dominantly passive frequently worships the natural world, its forces and cycles, at the expense of individual development and achievement. Passive cultures look back more than forward, and their deepest desire is to keep things stable and unchanging. A passive culture is ever the victim of more aggressive cultures for the obvious reason that its nature is to give way, while the nature of the aggressive is to expand.

"The contribution of passive cultures lies frequently within religion and philosophy, and sometimes art and music. This is because the passive mode makes a study of tuning in to what already is, on the many levels of the invisible worlds which your people call 'heaven.' Active cultures contribute most frequently in the areas of material invention, and spread these contributions through its third gift, conquest. Yes, you heard right. I said conquest. It is through conquest that valuable ideas have spread, both within a planet and through solar systems. It is a time-honored, though generally violent, way of breaking up the static resistance of minds to change!

"How does the individual figure in this cultural and planetary drama of warring forces?" she ended dramatically. "The individual is himself a battleground of these contending forces! The individual's challenge is to understand and thus bring these forces into balance within himself. If he does not, he faces at best a stalemate in his spiritual development, and at worst, a disintegration of his personality and the structure of his ego!

We had come to an intersection where the park ended. From where we stood, we could look back and see the Capitol dome rising above the tree line into the sky. Ahead of us, a new luxury hotel covered a whole city block, looking richly casual in its sand-pink exterior and ironwork balconies. Slow-moving traffic clogged the three-lane one-way street. A vendor conducted a thriving business selling hot dogs and soft pretzels from his tiny cart.

As we approached the street corner, we observed an old woman in a shabby sweater trying to decide whether or not to cross the street. As the signal for crossing came on and the crowd automatically surged forward, the woman put a foot tentatively out into the street and drew it back, as if mortally afraid of something. This happened over and over, through several changes of light, as we stood watching in fascination and pity. Finally, the woman launched herself forward when the light was against her, and scurried with terror across the street.

I sighed and looked at Kyari.

"Well, what do you think?" asked the Adept neutrally.

"The woman has some kind of mental disturbance," I speculated. "Somehow, she's become so passive that she can't make the simplest of decisions, like whether or not to cross a street."

Kyari nodded in agreement. "At times, all normal individuals come to some conflict in one or another area of their lives, and this makes it difficult to make a decision. However, most trivial questions are dealt with automatically and do not require attentive decision-making. This frees the individual to focus on the important issues of his life with the required energy and stamina to emerge victorious.

"When the individual becomes too passive, however, this distinction between large and small matters disappears. Even the smallest decision becomes weighty. Too much conscious attention devoted to trivia scatters and squanders the aggressive impulses of Soul and depletes its power to make progress in its life. Thus, it is vital that the passive instincts are not allowed to dominate, and that the basic 'stance' the individual takes toward life is an active and vigorous one."

At the next light change, Kyari stepped lightly off the curb and I followed. We strolled through the lobby of the hotel, decorated in pale pink, maroon, and teal blue. We admired the dramatic flower arrangements of anthuriums and bird-of-paradise, and discussed the modern art sculptures which gave the hotel environment an atmosphere of creativity and expression. Finally, I picked up the conversation where we had left off.

"I really understand what you're telling me about the problem of passivity," I said. "But what happens when the opposite dominates? I mean, when someone is too aggressive instead?"

Kyari slowed her walk and answered me. A few of the hotel guests gazed at us with mild curiosity, overhearing a part of our serious conversation as they walked past. "Basically, it becomes a problem of the overdevelopment and overuse of will—the aspect of the ego which is the channel for the aggressive instinct in the individual. The individual with an overdeveloped will thinks he or she can get a desired objective simply through setting up certain causes. This can include a baby who cries for milk to a spiritual student who believes he can win God through mental postulates or sheer personal effort!

"This actually works to a certain extent, since Spirit is responsive to thought, and projected thought is one of the results of an active will. Nevertheless, many negative possibilities exist: The individual can demand something for which he or she is not yet ready. Results can come with some unexpected and unpleasant consequences. Most common of all, the individual can become tense and frantic in his or her desire to reach a goal. Tension, however, closes down the individual's ability to receive. Therefore, the irony is that the overuse of will can result in complete failure where a less aggressive approach would have succeeded better."

"Well, obviously then," I concluded, "the balanced approach is best. But how do you recommend we achieve this?"

"Through the thoughtful use of both approaches," Kyari answered softly. "The proper use of the feminine principle is to be humble before one's fellow Souls, including our spiritual teachers, our loved ones, and life itself. For they are all simply various faces of God. To remain humble is to be receptive to the guidance of God, who will show you when to give way in any matter, and when to stand firm, when to show your mind, and when to conceal it. This receptivity, combined with good discrimination resulting from a life of action, will be all you need to progress on the path of God. Remember, too, that 'action' in the spiritual sense goes beyond the physical level to include whatever one sets into motion through thought and feeling."

Soon we left the hotel and walked west for four or five city blocks. The stained and weatherbeaten exteriors of several nearby buildings contrasted surreally with the elegance of the more modern downtown structures. The older buildings were targeted for demolition as part of a redevelopment plan for the area in the near future. Currently, however, they continued to house run-down pawn shops, seedy taverns, and "hotel" apartments with rickety fire escapes suspended precariously outside. The smell of urine and vomit permeated the air.

As we walked slowly past one of the buildings, the blank stares of the street people haunting the sidewalks and alleys penetrated right through us. I remarked uncomfortably to Kyari that I felt as if we were walking among ghosts. The extremes of consciousness I was experiencing triggered an awareness I had not clearly held before. I was beginning to feel that whatever was not right with these people included more than their material condition. Something was amiss on the inner level as well.

"Poverty and wealth are also functions of the active and passive currents," Kyari noted, sensing my thoughts. "On this particular city block, they exist side by side, as they do within the consciousness of every individual. In other words, poverty and wealth are states of mind and ways of being. A man born in a ghetto could become mayor of a city, while another person raised with every privilege might descend into the life of a transient. Poverty can never be entirely wiped out because it is a result of spiritual choice rather than entirely the outcome of social forces."

By now we had arrived at the entrance to the Greyhound bus station. Kyari stopped and motioned me inside. We walked through, observing the line of people waiting at a numbered gate, and the small crowd in the waiting area which had now become accessible only by token. The sign read, "Ticketed Passengers Only." I glanced at Kyari and said, "I guess that's to keep the transients from using this place as their living room, huh?"

The Adept nodded. I gratefully noticed that she was heading in the direction of a fast-food restaurant that adjoined the bus depot. There, at least, we could sit down. "Come on," she winked. "I'll buy you a cup of tea." When we were settled, drinks in hand, I presented her with my first question.

"You know, I agree that people aren't just the victims of society. We all have a great deal of potential control over our lives. But why would anyone choose poverty over wealth?" I asked, frowning.

Kyari replied, "Choices are made from various levels of awareness. Choices made out of ignorance of the spiritual laws are bound to be flawed. But this is the only way Soul learns—through direct experience. The fact that Soul has a choice at all is fairly revolutionary in itself. After all, it wasn't too long ago that the class system determined the economic experiences of all people. Individuals were cast into lives of poverty and wealth, opportunity and limitation, with much of their experiences already determined by the 'accident' of their birth. This kept people passive, for the social forces were overwhelming to them.

"Democracy, however, has quickened the spiritual opportunity of all people during the closing years of the current age. Democracy enables individuals to make choices based on their spiritual awareness, without being utterly blocked by circumstances of birth. Still, as you can see, many do not take advantage of this freedom. They are not yet on the level of unfoldment to be able to create a better life through the active force—the creative power of Soul."

The loudspeaker called out a bus that was ready to board its passengers. In a few minutes, the shiny vehicle pulled out from the garage and merged with the traffic on the street.

"This is really fascinating," I sighed, thinking about all I was hearing. "I want you to talk about wealth and poverty some more. I don't think I understand it well enough yet. How does it relate to the active and passive forces?"

"Basically, poverty is the result of the passive force gaining dominance over the individual," she began. "Passivity is a weakened life force, and a lack of material things is only the outward symptom of a more serious inner problem. Of course, I am not speaking of frugality by choice, but true poverty, as in not having enough to live decently and contribute something creative to life. Passivity is at the low end of the survival scale. Its close cousins are fear, dependence, isolation, and self-destruction."

"Didn't the Calvinists believe that poverty was a sign of God's disfavor?" I interjected, catching at a stray thought wandering around in my mind.

"Yes," the Adept nodded. "But this only demonstrates the fallacy in man's common way of thinking about himself, which is to accept a passive position in relationship to God. To put this bluntly, God has nothing to do with whether you are rich or poor. Wealth and poverty are self-created, and depends on the individual's readiness to be active in shaping his own material experiences. So how do you shape your material experiences? The same way God does it—through the life force, or Spirit. Soul can thus create and sustain a family, a job, hobbies, artistic expression, community service, and the like, as it wishes. But first Soul must open itself to Spirit, which is the God force within."

"Well, are you saying, then, that wealth is a sign that a person is spiritually evolved? If so, what about women? I read in the newspapers that they tend to be more pessimistic about the economy. They tend to be poorer than men, too."

"Women as a whole are poorer than men because they have had less experience in material manifestation than men. Their normal sphere of activity until modern times has been confined to cycles of the natural world, such as childrearing and agriculture, which are parts of the passive side of life. Today, however, they must expand their ability to be productive and creative in every field. This means that women as a group must learn to unleash the active forces of Soul—to begin, sustain, and end cycles of individual creativity—in order to grow, learn, and contribute something valuable to life."

"You mean, something other than childrearing," I said.

"Yes," the Adept replied, "although I don't mean to imply that childrearing is not important or valuable. Raising a child with spiritual love and awareness is one of the most vital contributions any man or woman can make, my dear. However, it is not creative in the sense I am talking about. To raise a child, a person is basically responding to another's needs during biological and psychological cycles of growth and change.

"To write a novel, on the other hand, one must take the initiative onself. Furthermore, this initiative must be sustained. Cycles occur here, too, except that creative cycles are very different from the 'naturalistic' ones of the physical world. Instead, creative cycles are spiritual experiences that lead to a change in the consciousness of the creator. Through experiences in creative cycles, individuals come to know more about Spirit and their relationship with it. Do you understand this?"

"Yes," I said, seriously. "I can also see why women are having a difficult time now. They are being torn between their comfortable patterns of passive creativity in motherhood and domestic life and the challenge of individual creativity through jobs, artistic pursuits, and the like. But I believe that there is no turning back now. Everything that has happened to break down the family has cut women's traditional supports from under them. They are being forced to become individually creative just to survive!"

"Right," agreed Kyari. "And while the situation is fraught with tension, it is also a part of the enormous spiritual opportunity of these times. When women find ways to contribute their individual creativity to the present and future, everyone will benefit."

"That's really inspiring, Kyari," I sighed. "But I'm dying for you to answer my other question, too. I mean, if wealth is better than poverty, is being very rich the answer?"

"Absolutely not," Kyari smiled, shaking her head. "Extremes of poverty and wealth indicate a lack of balance in the individual's experiences. Soul's goal is not the accumulation of wealth, but simply the ability to live a complete and responsible life. Furthermore, daughter, the lesson Soul is learning through being able to manifest material things does not lie in 'having' at all! It lies in 'being.' In other words, Soul learns the principles of creativity which allow it to manifest whatever it needs, in harmony with the good of the whole! This creativity is the essence of Soul, for through it, one can become a God of his own universe in any plane or planet in eternity."

"O.K. So what are these principles? Are they a secret?" I whispered excitedly.

Kyari laughed and shook her head vigorously. "No. They aren't secrets! I'll describe them to you and you can share them with whomever you like. But remember, each will receive according to his or her own level of ethics!"

"What exactly do you mean?" I asked, curious.

"Just that while the laws of manifestation will work for anyone, the purity of one's purpose will determine whether the results will be positive or not. Anyone who uses these laws with a selfish motive will create a debt which he must pay, if not in this lifetime, then in another.

"So, to go on—here are the laws of manifestation! First, step one: Have a clear, singular goal in mind. By goal I mean the end result of whatever you desire in your life. Your goal must be clear because clarity creates an inner picture which serves as a mold for Spirit to fill with life. It must be singular because unity of purpose gathers the forces of Soul, including the will and the imagination. Do not clutter this step by picturing the myriad details necessary to the process of achieving your goal. This will scatter the aggressive forces and create conditions that can limit Spirit. Leave the details to unfold naturally through the creative process.

"Now, here are some cautions to keep in mind during step one: You cannot choose a goal that doesn't have your complete love and sincere interest. You cannot choose a goal to fulfill another person's image of you, or your fantasy of yourself. These mental constructs lack the attracting force which comes, not from the mind, but from the heart. The only goals worthy of your creative efforts of manifestation are those which reflect your true inner being—goals that are part of your natural mission in life!"

"Hmm! I see a problem right there. A lot of us don't know ourselves enough to even select the right goals. I suspect it's because we don't accept ourselves as we are, so we don't like to look inside."

"You're correct," affirmed the Adept. "It all stems from a lack of self-acceptance, a sense of unworthiness. People look everywhere else but inside themselves for their true goals. Therefore, even when they put all the right kinds of effort into manifesting their aims, something always goes wrong. They need to stop, work on loving themselves more, then proceed from there."

"This is great!" I exclaimed. "Go on."

"All right. Now the second law of manifestation is the easy part," she continued. "It involves putting in the physical and mental effort to make the goal a reality. This means, for a writer, learning your craft, reading, writing, and so on. The higher your goal, the more years of effort you must spend to achieve it. There are no shortcuts, and you should be suspicious if any are offered. During this period, you must make sacrifices in your immediate comfort for a long-term benefit. It's a time of disciplining yourself from doing anything that will take you away from your goal. It's a time for gaining strength, courage, and humility as your sincerity is tested by the negative forces of the world which will attempt to turn you from your goal."

"Easy? Did I hear you say easy?" I asked in mock dismay.

The Adept chuckled. "Well, perhaps easy is not the correct word. Straightforward may be more accurate."

"I'll accept that," I sighed. "So what's the third step?"

"The third step is simple. Not easy. Actually, it isn't even straightforward. But it is simple."

"O.K. O.K. Tell me."

"The third step is getting out of the way."

"What? Say that again?"

"In other words, after you select the proper goal and make the appropriate efforts, you must simply relax and allow God to do its part in the creative process of manifestation. For in truth, you do not work alone, but in partnership with Spirit. This should fill you with confidence, gratitude, and joy, knowing that God loves you and is constantly leading you into a greater awareness and experience of life. Getting out of the way, then, is not passivity, but simply the common sense action of a person who holds the door open for someone else to walk through!

"Many people do not realize the importance of this step. They hold the door open but block the entrance! Then they are puzzled as to why their human efforts are not matched by God's grace. The answer is clear. They are too anxious, fearful, or attached to the outcome to let Spirit do its part. The worst ones are those who think they know better than Spirit. They try to direct it, but this can't be done. If these anxious ones would only relax, they'd find that Spirit can be trusted! In fact, the results will be greater, more surprising and original than anything the human consciousness alone could ever have achieved."

"O.K.," I said, taking a deep breath. "I've got a question. What about positive thinking and visualization? How do those approaches fit into what you are saying?"

"Positive thinking and visualization are fragments of the whole," she said quickly. "They are parts of the way manifestation works. The problem is that people have adopted these fragments without the knowledge of how they work within the entire creative process. For example, visualization is important, but it will not work without a singular, clear goal in mind, and one which is suited to your own beingness. When people first discover visualization, they act like children in a candy store, mocking up fantasies left and right without considering the consequences. Does it ever work? Hardly ever! Soul could care less, and does not cooperate in these childish escapades.

"Furthermore, visualization is not, as many people believe, mostly a matter of visual pictures. Pictures help, but it is really the emotional attraction we have toward those pictures that imbue them with vitality. You may have a clear picture of something, but if you do not have any deep emotional attraction toward it, you still will not get it. Emotional attraction works to draw to us both positive and negative experiences. A great fear of poverty, for example, naturally results in poverty. Do you see now what I mean?"

"I sure do. I guess it's the same thing, then, with positive thinking?"

"Correct," she nodded. "Too often positive thinking is arbitrary and willful. It bears little relation to Soul's true purpose and may be entirely selfish as well. Also, positive thinking can never stand alone. The correct efforts must still be made. But now I'd like to conclude by saying a few additional things about the laws of manifestation. They are subtler points, and I want to make sure you understand them."

"I'm all ears," I said. The loudspeaker announced an arrival. A family with three pigtailed girls went up to the fast-food counter to

110

get drinks.

Kyari began speaking. "Once you have chosen a singular, clear goal that is correct for you, have made the required efforts, and surrendered the result to God, you must have absolute faith that your goal will be accomplished. I repeat, you must have absolute faith! Doubt is destructive to the inner image—to the feeling you have of it. It shuts off the current of emotion that gives your inner image its vital, attracting force. So never doubt. After all, if you have done all as I have instructed, it is not reasonable to doubt. But doubt can become a mental habit, and those who are addicted to doubt are doomed to failure! What shall a doubter do? Quit doubting! Or live a life of disappointment and regret. The choice is his.

"Finally, you must not make an exception of yourself in how the laws of manifestation work! These laws are universal and unchanging. They will work for anyone, without exception. They will work for you. No one is so special, so exceptional, so vile, so bad that these laws will fail him. If you feel you are the one exception in the universe, then hang onto this distinction. It's the only one you will ever have. It's a fool's title, and dearly won."

The Adept winked at me and rose unexpectedly from her seat. She reached into her pocket and drew out something which she deposited into my hand. I stared down at it. After a moment of baffled silence, I spoke.

"A chocolate truffle?" I asked, incredulously.

"Didn't you want one?" she asked, raising her eyebrows in feigned surprise.

"Well, I guess so," I sighed. "I've been thinking about one all day. But I didn't think . . . "

"Tsk, tsk," she clucked. "You manifested it and you might as well enjoy it. Just think, if you had only been thinking about a white Porsche instead . . . "

She chuckled, then rose from her seat. I remained where I was, staring at the mound of brown chocolate nestled in ruffled paper. Suddenly, my eye caught one of the pigtailed girls—the smallest one—looking at me with interest. Her eyes were dark brown like the Adept's, fringed with thick lashes. I did not think at all, but acted on the moment's impulse.

"Here," I said, getting up. "I guess you must have wanted this, right?" I smiled a little and put the candy gently into her hand. A

111

look of surprise and recognition flared up briefly in her face. It was Soul recognizing its own power to manifest whatever it wants and needs in life—whether a piece of candy or the realization of God.

CHAPTER TEN
The Dream of the Bear

The information about the active and passive paths to God helped me to clarify the problems I'd experienced in my own life with both passivity and overuse of will. I had the bad feeling that both attitudes were buried at a deeply unconscious level in me. I feared that it would take great effort to ferret out these negative mechanisms and to establish a balanced approach. A premonition of defeat crept into my thinking, warning me that even as I sought to change my behavior, the passive side was marshalling its forces to win the war by attrition. Meanwhile, I also began to experience a series of nightmares for which I could find no logical explanation. Each one of these nightmares was completely different from every other one, except for one thing: I woke up terrified and screaming after each.

Tonight was no different. Just before morning, I had the following dream. I was living in a two-story house into which a large female black bear with a small cub had somehow entered. I was hysterical with terror. What was strange was that, as the observer of the dream, I clearly saw that the bear intended no harm to me. While not particularly tame, it had no desire to cause destruction, either. In a calmer frame of mind, I could have simply left the house to get help, or somehow led the bear outside.

Instead, I enticed the mother bear upstairs into one of the bedrooms and closed the door. Then I led the cub outside of the house. That was the end of the dream, as I woke up in terror. But I remembered the ominous feeling that I had made a mistake by what I'd chosen to do. Soon the she-bear would be aroused into the very rage I had feared, and then created, by locking her in the bedroom. I had done the very thing calculated to threaten her—separate her from her precious cub.

That morning, I ruminated a long time about my series of nightmares, and particularly about the dream of the bear. I wrote it down in my dream log for future reference and went on with my duties of the day. However, that afternoon, just before I usually began my preparations for dinner, I had an unexpected visit from the Tibetan.

"Good afternoon," he said, his smile flashing.

"Oh! I didn't think I'd see you so soon," I exclaimed happily. "I've been thinking of talking to you about my nightmares. They seem to be getting more frightening by the week! I nearly didn't make it last night!"

"You will elaborate, no doubt," the Adept stated.

I summarized the highlights from my series of nightmares and ended with the story of the bear.

"Ah, I will speak to you of this dream, dear one," said the Tibetan. "It is significant to the subject of our on-going discussions. It is also a power dream for you, in a spiritual sense. But first I would like to comment on this general program of nightmares which you have briefly described.

"These nightmares are actually part of the spiritual cleansing you are undergoing in order to take this next step in your personal evolution. With every level of unfoldment, and each further degree of surrender, a greater requirement is placed upon the student. The requirement is to be filled with the ideals and life of God, and not with the junk and sludge of the materialistic worlds!

"I speak metaphorically, yet the mind-stuff and emotional baggage we carry is truly nothing but weight and pollution compared to the reality of love and service. Now, what you are experiencing is the cleansing of the mental and emotional garbage that has hindered you for lifetimes. If you would look without faltering into the faces of these dreams, you will see what I mean! Now, to assist you on your way, I will interpret for you this dream of the bear. Listen closely and you will 'catch' the sense of how to do this for yourself.

"The house in your dream represents your consciousness. The fact that it had two floors indicates that the dream was concerned with two levels—the emotions and the mind. The clue to unraveling the symbolism lies in your strong response of terror when the bear entered your house. The she-bear in your dream represents your own deeply repressed aggressive instincts. A bear is a good symbol for this since it hibernates during part of the natural cycles of its life, yet when aroused, can wreak great damage.

"The dream indicates that by denying this aggressive instinct, instead of incorporating it into your nature, you may unleash the very harm you wish to avoid. Locking the bear in the upper floor means that you are trying to confine this aggressive urge within the mental sphere. However, suppressed aggression is always dangerous, for aggression is a form of spiritual energy that must be released for the sake of physical, emotional, mental, and spiritual good health.

"The cub is the offspring of its mother, therefore the cub represents the results of your repressed aggressive instincts. By placing the cub outside your house, you wish to separate the cause from its effect, but this cannot be done. Cause and effect exist in and through each other. You must accept responsibility for the masculine in yourself. Then you must allow Spirit to transmute and use it for a spiritual purpose.

"Your strong masculine side has been bred from lives of ambitious striving. Many times, you have been involved in political or military leadership, often as a ruler or a soldier, not infrequently provoking bloodshed. Through these experiences, you developed a taste for exerting your will over the masses of people. You have been both fair and ruthless, open-handed and cunning, while Spirit has guided you closer and closer to the middle path of self-mastery. This pattern of evolution is part of your individuality, for you have chosen an active role in life and all that goes with it, including responsibility for the causes you set in motion.

"In your present life, you have set about the task of balancing your aggressive, willful side with the qualities of love, humility, and service. However, you will not succeed by denying what you have been until now. Your past is neither bad nor good, but the price of growth. It has brought you to this moment. You can still serve God as a warrior, if not as a saint. And believe me, God has more need for warriors than for saints in this age! I can see that you are surprised and concerned by my interpretation. Do not put such a negative light on it, my friend. Your past life experiences have bred a strong will, discipline, and determination which, turned now to the things of God, will serve you well."

I was silent for awhile, recovering from the shock created by all the Adept had said. It was true that I did not expect such an interpretation. In fact, I had been completely mystified by the dream. If it hadn't been for Haurvata Sampa, I would probably never have understood it at all. Certainly, I would never have understood how it fit into my overall unfoldment over many lifetimes. I expressed my gratitude, as well as my admiration, for such spiritual insight. Inwardly, I also vowed to follow the Tibetan's advice and incorporate the aggressive side of myself in some way. But how?

"Now," he continued, "know that the purpose of this dream is to point out your need to integrate and spiritualize the aggressive, masculine side in you, which you have so long denied. Your childhood problem with anger is due to the blockage of this tremendous energy inside yourself. All anger has its roots in a lack of outflow of the aggressive force, caused by introverting the naturally free, creative expression of Soul. Your tendency toward self-criticism is part of this introversion, while the tendency to criticize others is a projection of this same introversion.

"It is true that you need to learn to adopt a humble, passive stance to certain obstacles and give way to opposition when necessary. But you need to go forth with confidence and courage, as well. When to give way and when to forge ahead will be clearer to you when you no longer feel compelled to repress one side of you. Remember, though you are female, and must necessarily conform to certain norms of society, your inner freedom is absolute. Do not shortchange yourself through a misunderstanding of your own unique, individual nature!

"Well then, lion," said he, suddenly smiling, "have you the stamina to travel beyond the body to meet a teacher who is perhaps greater than any you have visited thus far?"

"Greater than Vahira Manu? . . . than you or Kyari Hota? I don't think I'm quite ready for . . . for God, do you?"

The Tibetan threw back his massive head and laughed uproariously.

"No, child! Never fear. Your time to see the face of God is yet before you. Now we must make another kind of journey. Will you trust me to take you there without further explanation?"

"Of course," I said enthusiastically. "I'm ready! What shall I do?"

"Nothing," he said softly.

I gazed into his eyes and felt myself falling into a tunnel of darkness. Down, down, down, I fell, finally shooting through into a world of golden-orange light. Colored globes appeared all around me. Then, in the distance, I perceived the form of the teacher in a body which sparkled like a million stars.

For a moment, the scene before me seemed to shift and waver. I was adjusting to a level of perception more refined than the senses to which I was so accustomed in the physical body. When I gathered my poise, the Tibetan was before me.

"Where are we, Haurvata?" I asked.

"The second of the inner worlds," he replied. "You may recognize it in a moment. Do you see those mountains over there?"

He gestured his arm behind him. I looked, and for a second could see no mountains, until I realized I was already staring at them! They were so large that I had to strain my neck to try for the peaks.

"Tir, Geza, and Kamshar," informed Sampa. "And at the foot of those, our destination—the throne of the Shangra Raj, Lord of the Lower Worlds!"

"Oh!" I exclaimed involuntarily. The Shangra Raj was the ruler and distributor of the negative force within the dimensions of the lower worlds. I had had several run-ins with him personally before. I was not eager to see him again, even in the company of a great Unmani Dhun Adept. My expression must have shown my feelings.

Haurvata laughed mildly.

"So you are not eager to pay this visit, my child! Sometimes a lion, and occasionally a rabbit—and today is a day for the rabbit! Shall we go back to the body with our cotton tails bounding in the air?"

He laughed merrily at his own joke, until finally I smiled too, albeit unwillingly.

"The Shangra Raj is not exactly a favorite teacher of mine," I grumbled testily. "He's cruel, treacherous, and dangerous! He'd use any means at all to keep Souls in the lower worlds, and he deals in fear and lies. You said I was going to meet a greater teacher than any I'd met before. You tricked me!"

Haurvata's merriment could not have been greater. He threw back his head and laughed again, and this time I did not join him. I thought of the times Shangra Raj almost annihilated me through various ploys. Especially in the early years of my training, he was constantly at my heels, hounding me to turn back to my familiar traps of fear and isolation. Once, I nearly committed suicide. Slowly, I had fought my way back to sanity handhold by handhold.

"Are you sulking?" grinned Haurvata, catching my mood. "It seems the negative force may still hold a small part of you, my friend. It can prove to be a costly piece. Shall we not take it back?"

"O.K. You're right," I shot back. "But I don't see what can be gained by going to see this lord."

"Your fear and loathing is misplaced," counseled Haurvata. "Of course I knew this was your attitude. It is why I have brought you—to face what you fear and dissolve this tie once and for all. For as you know, you are linked through vibrations with anything for which you have a strong emotion, whether good or bad.

"Now, you are in my company and under my protection," he continued. "No harm can come to you here. The Lord Raj is expecting us, and his discourse will be one of the most interesting you have heard so far. Are you ready to go on?"

"Yes," I said reluctantly. I knew what he said was true, but I was still less than anxious to face this great negative entity.

We walked for a short distance through a populated area which appeared to be a suburb of the great city of Kamshar, home of the Shangra Raj. Colorfully dressed people were busy at their occupations of tending gardens and various arts and crafts. They were a handsome race, of medium height, dark-skinned with a strange tint of blue.

Many of the people stared at us, and some of them bowed low before Sampa. I wondered if he was well known here as well. He seemed to hold an open passport to every land.

After we had walked what seemed half a mile, we stopped to drink water at a bubbling spring set off by attractive pastel-colored rocks. A drinking ladle had been set among the stones for those who stopped to quench their thirst.

"The waters from the frozen peaks of the Three Mountains," Haurvata mentioned reportorially.

We both drank. I was not thirsty, but the water was so strangely sweet and refreshing that I had three ladlesful before we went on. Then from the sky, a hovercraft descended, circled us twice, and sank gracefully a few hundred feet in front of us. Sampa had halted as he first saw it in the sky, and now he motioned me to wait also. The driver of the vehicle, a smartly dressed woman in a purple and red uniform, got out and marched over to us.

"Greetings from our lord, the Shangra Raj," she called, saluting Haurvata with a formal gesture.

"Greetings," said the Adept quietly. Then to me, "Come, daughter. We go to the palace."

We climbed into the craft which lifted rapidly into the air and sped off in the direction of the towering peaks. I glanced apprehensively at Sampa, and he winked back at me. Though he said nothing, I could read his projected thoughts.

"Never fear, my child. Your motion sickness does not exist in this world, where the law of gravity is different. You will feel no discomfort."

I breathed a sigh of immense relief and settled down to enjoy what was possible of this unexpected adventure.

As we approached closer to the mountains, I gasped at the beauty of its surface, which gleamed like crystals in its many-faceted ridges and chasms. The peaks themselves were shrouded in clouds, but from the faces of the sheer cliffs, breathtaking rivers of clear water plunged down. The water—or perhaps it was the mountains—made a music all its own, like a female voice singing a tuneless song which was oddly stirring and hypnotizing.

Soon we disembarked. The Shangra Raj's residence was a brilliantly decorated palace held up by tall columns encrusted with semi-precious stones. The interior exuded a lush, oriental feeling, like a sultan's palace in long-ago Arabia. Only a short time passed before we were gazing up at the visage of the Lord Raj himself, seated on a rather plain golden throne draped with the skins of wild animals.

"Ah, so you have arrived! Welcome to my home, honored

guests," the great lord said. His eyes greeted the Unmani Dhun Adept respectfully and then rested on me with frank appraisal. I began to feel like a mouse being sized up by a cat.

Then the lord laughed. "I see you have brought one whom I dimly recognize! She served me once, and has since seen fit to leave my household. Normally I do not grant favors to those who are disloyal! But in this case, since an Unmani Dhun Adept has asked, I make this exception."

He glared down at me, his face stern and arrogant, but admittedly handsome in its masculine features. I was fascinated with the swiftly changing expressions on his face. First the kind and gracious host, then the cold monarch, then back to gracious host again. I wondered if the Tibetan was noticing.

But the Adept bowed low and respectfully where he stood, remaining in this position as he spoke. I was completely taken aback at this display of humility.

"We have come here, my lord," said Haurvata, "to ask your favor. We are here to learn from your wisdom, which is the greatest in the three worlds of your domain. My student here most humbly wishes your indulgence so that she might learn from your own lips the great laws of your land regarding the sexes. Will you speak to her, sire?"

"You call me 'sire'?" Shangra Raj sneered derisively. "You, the great Unmani Dhun Adept to whom my own people bow as if you were lord here instead of me!"

I trembled despite my bold front. I decided the best tactic at this point was to follow the example of my teacher. I sank slowly to my knees and bent my head.

Then suddenly, as if a fresh wind had just blown in, Shangra Raj changed his tone.

"Ah, but come, my friends. Rise, rise! Do not bow before me. Sit here with me as my colleagues and equals."

He motioned us with his hand and as if on cue, servants padded on silent feet to place two gaudily upholstered chairs near us.

"Yes, I will speak to this one . . . your student," he continued, his voice lightly mocking. "There is in truth much I can teach her, though she has come to believe there are others with greater wisdom than I. But now she will see what she has forfeited by choosing another path. My worlds are vast and filled with the nectar of knowledge sweet beyond measure! Knowledge which offers the promise of power over the hearts and minds of Souls. And I myself am the source of the power! It flows out of my body into all the worlds below."

"Look, and you will behold the truth of what I speak!" He motioned us to the great window to our right. As we walked over to it, I held my breath at the sight which confronted me. The palace of the Shangra Raj perched near the base of the massive three mountains. From this spot, a stream of lights poured down into the lands below, filling it with color and music. Our spiritual senses also perceived these same lights descending in successively stepped-down currents into the planes below.

We turned to acknowledge our admiration, which was clearly visible on our faces.

"So! Now you have seen!" barked the lord. "I will speak to you then about the sexes." Thus began the following discourse from the Lord of the Three Worlds, the Shangra Raj.

"Male and female are two parts of the whole which you call Soul. The nature of these two parts is divine and unchangeable. Their workings comprise one of the greatest mysteries ever confronting man today! He will never unravel it, and it is useless for him to try. The one part is ever contending against the other, and now the war between the two is at its greatest, despite the efforts of the Unmani Dhun to improve relations.

"Man despises woman and fears her hold on him through sex and the constraints of the family. Woman, in her timidity and ignorance, believes that the love of a man is her greatest necessity and becomes a slave to this illusion. Man uses woman for his sexual plaything, housekeeper, and caretaker of his offspring, while woman uses man to provide for her material necessities and buffer her from the realities of the objective world.

"Ah, my friends, man and woman use each other as mere tools to satisfy their selfish desires and avoid responsibilities. Yet they cry and complain that they are not understood, not appreciated! Hah! This self-kissing fools only themselves, but will not prevent them from reaping what they have sown through such lives of miserable self-serving.

"Your teacher Haurvata Sampa has taught you that I, the Shangra Raj, mean to keep Souls in these lower worlds like trapped

121

animals. Against their will, I enslave them and blind them to the higher realities which the Unmani Dhun Adepts offer. But these are lies! Men and women cling to their blindness with all their might, which makes my work simple. All I must do is sit back and stir the pot once in a great while! The rest goes on automatically, as does everything in my kingdom.

"Now is a time of great change upon the earth plane. Woman is beginning to glimpse her own potential as a free spiritual being. This is causing tremendous disruption in the family and society. But even with these great outer changes, nothing has changed. Yes, I say, it is still unchanged and will remain so!

"For the human consciousness is a fixed web of archaic conceptions which condition man's view of the world and all he experiences. Though the spiritual planes lie at man and woman's fingertips—nay, in their very heartbeats—they deny their own natures because it is not what they have been taught. Surely if you teach man that he is a rock for a long enough time, he will eventually start mineralizing his body. And this is precisely what has happened!

"Nothing will change until men and women change their basic ideas about who they are and where their responsibilities lie to themselves and to others. They must learn to fulfill their own needs, then in goodwill and unselfish love join with another for companionship and helpmeet. But will this ever happen, I ask you? And would you be here today, asking for my wisdom if you thought so?"

The lord of the negative worlds laughed quietly. He looked at us with hard eyes, full of certainty and world-weariness. I realized with a shock that this was no different from the way I had felt many times before. I saw my own cynicism mirrored in his face.

CHAPTER ELEVEN
The Shangra Raj

The great lord rose from his throne, his opulent garments rustling as they dragged on the smooth, polished floors of rare woods set with semiprecious stones. A look from Haurvata bade me rise also, and I did so. The Shangra Raj approached me and looked closely and disconcertingly into my eyes.

"Ah, it comes back to me now," he hissed slowly. "To fall so far from my grasp. More is my pity for you! So you think you will achieve the last? You believe you will see God?"

His laughter was contemptuous and rang like hammer blows throughout the vast room. I looked quickly at the Adept, but the Tibetan's eyes were on the Shangra Raj, and they were cool and mild.

"It will be more difficult than you can possibly believe!" the Lord of the Three Worlds continued, his eyes flashing. "Let me remind you how difficult!"

All at once, his arms opened wide with a bold gesture. I felt struck by something, but there was no physical pain. I was being sucked into another reality, helpless against the force which was dragging me down into a heavy whirlpool of blackness.

The only way to describe my experience is that it was something like watching a film, with me as the audience and an actor in the drama as well. At first, countless tiny pictures flashed before me, flipping by like the pages of a calendar to depict the passage of time in old movies. Then the pictures slowed down and one of them seemed to grow and grow until it became a full-fledged reality, and I was in it!

I saw myself as a young woman in a dry, dusty place. The sun scorched my face, and my feet were hardened through the thin sandals I wore to protect them from the rocky ground. I seemed to be the youngest daughter here, a position that made me practically a servant. I carried a jar of dirty water from the house. The jar was heavy, so I stopped to rest. I happened to glance at the horizon, from which rose a small cloud of dust. Horsemen were coming. I was afraid. I ran inside.

The next thing I saw was the horsemen, dirty soldiers armed with swords and leather armor, rampaging through the house. They grabbed what food they could find, destroying what they could not take. My two older sisters and me they raped. One of my sisters was badly beaten. An old man in a striped robe lay bloodied on the ground. Though as the observer I felt little emotion, I knew somehow he was my father. The sound of weeping and lamentation filled the air. A dark seed of fear and hatred grew in my mind.

The picture faded.

Now there were flames. I felt the scorching heat. I thought perhaps my house was now on fire, set by the soldiers. But it was not a house. It was myself who was on fire. In a small village somewhere, I was being burned as a witch. The pain was tremendous as the flames caught the hem of my dress and ignited my body. I screamed.

In the crowd was the single face that meant something to me. As the observer, I found it. He was a dark-haired married man in middle age. He had made me pregnant, and had betrayed me to the authorities of the village to save himself. I was condemned to death for the crime of casting a love spell on him. He looked at me in terror and guilt. His wife, a haggard and hard-faced woman, her face contorted with hatred, shouted over and over again, "Burn the witch!" I felt my face sear. The pain was so intense that I left my body.

As I floated away from the charred corpse that was once my

physical shell, I felt the joy of release from the horror of my torturous death. I floated peacefully for what seemed like an eternity, among endless regions of light. But this joy and peace was not to last!

Soon I saw myself as the daughter of a French aristocrat. The poverty and plainness of our home was puzzling. I saw my beloved mother, a beautiful, delicate woman, on her deathbed. Her face, turned up to me for the last time, was as pale as a camellia, and her heart was broken from grief. Her husband, a profligate with some mental instability, had lost the entire family wealth. We were penniless.

My father's sanity completely unraveled. My sister married a man who loved her despite our social shame. But I was not so lucky. Confused and unhappy, I found myself, a small, fearful chestnut-haired young woman, on a boat to Tahiti. I was contracted to be married to a planter, an older man whom I had never met before. Then I, as the watcher of the dream, saw this planter as he stood waiting on the dock. He searched for the face of his bride with an oddly familiar mannerism.

This planter was the same man who had once betrayed me to a witch's pyre! The young girl saw him, and her heart fell. What was this foreboding she felt? Swiftly, so swiftly, the pictures sped by: a life of hard work, discord, financial reverses, marital infidelity, and in the end, suicide by drowning.

Now I was seeing a lifetime in China. I was richy arrayed, beautiful and young. My feet were bound, and jade and gold bracelets hung from my pale arms. A disgustingly fat man was making love to me. I felt nothing. I was a concubine, completely taken over by opium addiction. I died a painful and degraded death, my mind filled with visions of demons, choking on my own vomit.

Now something even stranger was happening. The visions of the opium took over what I was experiencing. Rooms upon rooms with low ceilings, all separated by thin partitions, came into view. In each room, men and women were having sexual intercourse. From my vantage point above the scene, I could see into each room. All the acts of sex were characterized by a mindless frenzy, a degraded lust which hung like a palpable stench over the whole environment. Men and men, women and women, men and animals, people in groups—every possible combination in every possible variation of sex was here taking place.

I felt terrified and disgusted! But still I remained, fascinated, the pull of the strong sexual current beginning to beat inside my own sexual center, stirring in me similarly exaggerated desires. Suddenly I found myself in one of the rooms. I was engaged in the sex act with a man whose lower half seemed to be that of a bull with an enormous, erect organ. Several women with voluptuous bodies and eager, laughing faces joined the orgy. The pounding of the male organ resolved into the sound of a drum beating insistently in my head, my body, everywhere! Soon I was just a point of terrified awareness with the drumbeat pressing on me, suffocating me. I became fearful of my survival. I cried out!

The scene changed abruptly, as if torn from existence by the extremity of my fear. This was a rural scene in India. From close by, I began to hear the sound of chanting. Then I saw them: a line of perhaps seven wandering Hindu monks clothed in identical robes of saffron cloth. I felt a sudden, overwhelming sense of dread. I didn't wish to be found by them. A well stood before me. I dived into the well. Down, down, down I fell into the cloudy water.

I swam near the bottom, pleased with myself for having avoided the chanting monks. Then suddenly before me was a strange sight: a frog with a golden crown. Stranger still, he was singing a song! The song was familiar, so I joined in, supplying the lyrics as he stopped singing. Then I noticed the eyes in this frog's head. Beneath the small gold crown, in his slick green and slightly comical face, were hard, cynical eyes. The Frog King began to stimulate me sexually. I felt myself responding, enjoying his caresses. I lapsed into a coma of sexual lassitude, all alertness vanished. Then my lover halted, looking at me with a contemptuous knowing in his hard eyes.

"So," he sneered softly, "who do we have here? Is it the she-goat? Is it the betrayer?"

The Frog King faced me with menace in his eyes. I knew he was someone powerful, dangerous! I had jumped out of the proverbial "frying pan" into the "fire"! I swam like a streak of lightning up to the surface of the water, with the Frog King in hot pursuit!

Immediately, I found myself back in the palace of the Shangra Raj, collapsed in my chair. My heart was beating fast, my adrenalin pumping through my body as from any physical danger.

The eyes of the Tibetan were kind as he peered into my face. "How do you fare?" he asked quietly.

"O.K." I said meekly. The shock of plunging back to this reality after the terror of the moment had temporarily disoriented me. Behind Haurvata, however, I caught the unmistakable sound of the Lord Raj chuckling. Suddenly, a goblet of water appeared under my nose.

"Drink!" came the gruff voice of our lord and host.

I looked up and saw the face of the Frog King for the briefest moment superimposed upon the face of the Shangra Raj. It was the same cynical eyes, the same hard smile! It had been he!

Nevertheless, I accepted the water with unsteady hands and drank my fill.

"Well, child, what do you think now of your chances of showing men and women a better way to live with each other?" His voice was mocking. "I have given you back your own memories from a fraction of the lives you have led. A small sample of man's inhumanity to man and woman! The briefest of glances at the depths to which mankind will descend in the pursuit of lust, self-will, and power!"

"Sire," I said weakly, "I believe a better way is possible. Perhaps not for the masses of mankind, but for the individual who desires a higher path. Can this not be?"

"That is not for me to determine," said the lord darkly. "It is my responsibility to make Souls desire to stay in the lower worlds, where they belong. And if a few of you escape—why, what do I care, since countless more will remain, reincarnating into bodies over and over again, creating new debts as fast as they can repay old ones, with only the slightest gain at most in their understanding of the laws of life!

"And of all laws, one they understand least of all and betray over and over again, life after life, is the law of love. Ah, you look surprised? Do you think that I, Shangra Raj, am ignorant of the high laws that govern the spiritual hierarchy, of which I am a lowly part? You are ignorant like the rest of the sniveling fools who cower before me, fearing and loathing me as if I were the cause of their own weaknesses!

"No, foolish one, I am not the cause of man's undoing," he said

127

slowly. "Man himself is. Sex is a tool for procreation, and little else. It gives man and woman pleasure because it serves my purpose— the perpetuation of physical life. No matter how wonderful it may seem, sex is only a shadowy reflection of a more arcane joy—the union of Soul with the heavenly Sound. This is an ecstasy that you earthlings have neither the imagination nor the courage to pursue!

"Man is Soul but believes that he is an animal. At best, he believes he is the mind or emotions. But because he has forgotten his true nature, nothing else fits into place. It is like trying to make a puzzle without first knowing what it is supposed to look like when it is put back together. Man has lost his image of wholeness.

"And to complicate matters, his fragmented image of himself has caused him to misunderstand the other half of his being. In sex, man's instinct is for a simple release of his seed into woman, for it is his nature to provide this for procreation. More than this, sex is a form of ego-gratification! Woman's instinct, however, is more complex. Because she must nurture the seed to bear the fruit of the union, and care for the child into adulthood, her response is emotional as well as physical. For her, sex is a form of affection!

"When a woman opens her physical body to a man, she also opens her emotions. This is unavoidable, for it is an essential mechanism for the survival of the child-to-be. Though contraception has changed the physical result of sex, it has not changed this emotional mechanism. And woe to woman who believes she can be liberated from her nature through promiscuity. And more woe to man, who believes he can use her for his pleasure without responsibility to her feelings!

"Souls are at various levels of maturity regarding sex because they are at different levels of spiritual unfoldment. It is that simple! When an immature woman opens herself to a man through sex, her feelings are likely to be vulnerability and dependence. When an immature man engages in sex, his response will probably be power and dominance. Sex abuse and domestic violence, which are so rampant in the modern societies of your planet today, are the syphilitic children of this hopelessly circular tangle of immature sexual responses!

"Woman has found herself at a low place in life because she naively looks to love, sex, and family as the trinity of her adoration instead of to God, the Holy Spirit, and Soul. She wishes to float off

128

in a dream of love rather than to face the harsh realities of her own state of consciousness and work for spiritual responsibility and wholeness! She is unhappy and needy because she is incomplete. Yet she drags man down to her own level and makes him believe he is inadequate because he cannot give her what she lacks.

"In truth, men are also shallow creatures, a mechanism of sleeping, eating, fornication, and daily labor, not too dissimilar to a dinosaur in the smouldering youthful ages of your planet! Men's total lack of imagination and the shapelessness of their emotions make them helpless to reach the heavenly worlds without assistance. Without women, men would be content to fight each other in displays of aggression and self-strutting until the end of the worlds!

"Today, in your western countries, women and men are trading and mixing roles. Can this work? Only with understanding of what it is they are doing! It cannot be done blindly. Children growing up without the constant nurturing from the mother or father become stunted both emotionally and mentally. Women who find themselves successful in what were traditionally men's roles may discover that they are unaccountably dissatisfied. Men who try to respond emotionally in the way women demand may find their lives becoming no longer understandable. Why?

"Consciousness is a fixed pattern built on countless impressions, decisions, and experiences from many lives. It cannot be changed so quickly! Man and woman must both carefully study the situation before them and sort out what can be changed, what should be changed, and what kept stable. Since they do not, their children suffer from a miserable uprootedness of spiritual values—an uprootedness that makes the modern cities of your world like vast spiritual ghost towns where people wander in a howling loneliness!

"Ah, you are wondering at my words. You, child, do not know what I am—I, the Shangra Raj, Lord of the Negative Worlds! I am not the cruel monster you have created in your imagination. The force I wield is impersonal. It is governed by laws established with the beginning of your worlds! I merely oversee these laws. And if I seem cruel, the cruelty is merely the power of this current of itself, nothing more nor less! I serve the spiritual hierarchy just as the Adept here with you serves in his own way.

"You see me as you see yourself in a rippling pond, distorted but familiar! Yes, my child, I say when you look into my eyes, you see yourself as in your worst fears. I am not evil, but only your concept of evil. Just as the Adept is your concept of good!

"You see, when the Soul is born in a body, it takes on the genetic entity and its programming. Soul does not enter the body in the womb as so many of the religionists claim, but only after birth. Between physical lives, it dwells in the worlds some call heaven to learn better what it failed to learn in its corporeal experiences. The womb 'memories' some claim to have do not indicate the existence of Soul in the prenatal state, but only the completeness of Soul's identification with the body once it has adopted it and called it 'home.'

"Your genetic programming emphasizes the characteristics of your sex, and due to this imbalance, you seek both those experiences which will express this emphasis and those which will balance it with its opposite. Is this clear? In other words, men will generally seek experiences which go along with their innate masculine tendencies, at the same time seeking to correct these tendencies with feminine experiences. The first kind of seeking is conscious, but the second kind of seeking is often unconscious.

"The most obvious way of balancing one's masculine or feminine tendencies is to look for a mate of the opposite sex. But more interestingly, it can also take the form of Soul mocking up experiences which will require the uncovering of opposite qualities in itself in order to succeed at mastering these experiences.

"To give an example, a Soul in a male form who is at a fairly high spiritual level may be seeking to balance aggressive tendencies with greater compassion for all life. He may find himself choosing a mate who has some disability requiring his compassionate care. Or, he himself may choose a disability which enables him to finally identify with and understand the position of the downtrodden and helpless. Either way is good if it brings about the change desired!

"Yes, this is the way it can be! But the process of change is a slow one in the billions-of-years duration of my worlds! Only now the Unmani Dhun Adepts are making much ado about carrying off a paltry few of you with such illusions as the promise of seeing God! Ha! Who has seen God? Has he? If he says yes, then he dissembles! For there is no God, foolish one, only the raw force of life itself, and myself, the lord of it all!"

The face that said this was contorted with a power that broke out of it in harsh, glaring lights that blinded me!

"Cover your eyes," warned Haurvata, and touched my hand where it lay cold on the arm of my chair.

I did so, stifling a desire to cry out. Then, with a sudden but gentle pull, I found myself floating through a tunnel with colored lights all about me again. I reached out in consciousness for Haurvata and he was there. Shortly, I found myself back in my body and in my office, where this wonderful and terrifying adventure all began.

I opened my eyes to find my teacher sitting there on his chair smiling absently at me as if nothing out of the ordinary had taken place. I laughed out loud.

"What do you find amusing, my lion—or is it my rabbit today?" he responded, winking.

I guffawed loudly.

"Probably a combination of both," I joked. "Maybe we can call it a ralion . . . or a libbit?"

"I like libbit," he said mildly. "Ralion sounds like a vegetable. Well, libbit, how did you like your adventure? Was your trust in me misplaced?"

"It was terrifying, wonderful, and . . . and . . . I guess mostly surprising!" I stammered. "There was so much he told me that I didn't know! And other things surprised me, too. It's true I never understood the negative force before. I always thought of it as evil! But never again! And I did get a glimpse of my own negative tendencies in his eyes."

"What did you see?" asked Haurvata.

"Oh, cynicism, contempt, pride . . . and something else, too," I answered, struggling.

"Keep trying," urged Haurvata. "What is this something else?"

"I don't know. A kind of weariness, I guess. I could call it boredom, but that isn't quite it. Do you know what it is, Haurvata?"

"Yes, my friend," he said seriously. "And because you have it already, but merely need me to clarify it for you, I shall tell you. It is a heaviness of heart. It is the price the Lord of the Three Worlds pays for the privilege of distributing the negative current. It is this heaviness that enters into every Soul who allows itself to be used as the negative force's tool, knowingly or unknowingly. Do you understand this?"

"I do understand!" I said, releasing a breath that came from deep inside. "It is how I have felt for so many lifetimes. It is what made me almost take my own life years ago. It is a feeling more powerful than any concept of evil that we know!"

"Truly said," the Unmani Adept replied in his resonant voice. "The negative force in its pure form can crush a person like a clod of dirt! In smaller doses, the negative force is like a drug, giving man a sense of power, pleasure, and even an illusion of freedom. Then, when man is hooked, the negative force is stepped up even more through him! Eventually, this negative force flowing through its channels destroys its own channels. That is why the negative force is constantly seeking new avenues for its distribution throughout the lower worlds! No, it is not evil, but it is the closest thing to it!

"You are exceptional, my child, because you are one of the handful who has dwelt in the center of this negative power without being completely crushed or corrupted by it! Though mocked, degraded, tormented and enslaved, still you were not beaten. You survived, somehow, in a way unique to yourself. But mostly you did it through mocking up huge reserves of the same qualities as the Shangra Raj himself!"

"What?" I asked, astounded.

"In other words, you mocked up pride, cynicism, contempt, and anger. Having lived so closely in tune with the negative power that you learned many of its secrets, you correctly intuited that the Shangra Raj himself survived through a mock-up of attitudes. You copied him and survived his worst assaults until they subsided in intensity. Your worst run-ins, however, have been with the pure essence of the negative force itself. This is the heaviness you speak of!

"The pure negative force directed at any person, or flowing through any person, is totally destructive. It can drive someone insane, or chase them out of the body and precipitate death! But the negative force also risks something when it attempts to annihilate a Soul in this manner.

"You see, because Soul is a spark of God, and a pure positive atom of its creator, it can never truly be destroyed. It can only be wounded and gravely set back in its spiritual unfoldment—which is certainly more than a slap on the wrist! But the ego self does not know this. Much of the power which the negative force wields over people comes from their erroneous belief that the negative force can destroy them.

"Thus, when the Shangra Raj directs the full force of its pure negative current at anyone, it has used its greatest weapon. It has stepped out in the open and revealed exactly what it is to its intended victim! It did this to you, my child, fully expecting to defeat you and send you plummeting down the spiritual ladder which you have struggled so hard and long to climb. But instead you saw and understood the greatest secret of all: You could not be destroyed by anything! Thus, you won your way into immortality and the Shangra Raj suffered a costly defeat!

"Why costly? Because now you know his deepest secret—his hidden weakness! And because you have the courage and the words to tell the world about it! That is why!"

With that, the Tibetan laughed so hard that his body shook and the air within the room seemed to reverberate as if a jet were flying overhead. I did not laugh. But deep in my heart, I felt a joy that was as strong as his laughter.

CHAPTER TWELVE
On the Breath of the Gods

Several weeks later, I narrowly avoided coming to blows with three bullies at a street corner on the way back from the dentist. I was driving home, my face and mouth still numb with novocaine from a new filling. At a four-way intersection, I waited for a green arrow to indicate permission to make a left turn onto the main road. Suddenly, I heard men's voices calling out from my left.

"Yaaaa," they laughed, sneering and pointing. "Oh, look! It's a chink, one of dose gooks. Hey, flat face. Hey, you over there! Hey, doncha hear me? Hey, chink! You deaf or what? Hey, chink lady! Over here!"

Of course, I looked at them. They were three unkempt and slovenly dressed men who, from their appearance and manners, I assumed were either drunk or terminally stupid. Generally, I have not had a great deal of trouble with ethnic slurs, jokes, or innuendos. What I heard, I ignored. After all, what would be the sense of reacting to ignorant and hateful people? I proceeded to disregard the men. Still, the taunting kept on.

"Hey, chink lady," they all yelled. "Hey, you over there! Gook face, hey, come on!"

The green arrow was taking forever to appear. While I waited, a small slice of life passed before my eyes: Here were three pitiful specimens of manhood who needed desperately to feel "big." Today they decided to torment a helpless female, too scared and powerless to defend herself. Probably they'd done it before. Probably they'd do it again. I must have looked like a perfect victim.

Except that today, I wasn't in the mood to be a victim. I'd had my share of that under the dentist's drill just a few minutes ago. I turned to stare at the men square in the face. Then I made a motion universally understood by slimeballs everywhere—I "flipped them the bird."

It was amazing what a transformation occurred in the men with that one magic gesture. They stood dead in their tracks, momentarily stunned into silence, followed by a barrage of four-letter words that made up in sputtering rage what it lacked in variety. They were bulls goaded into action by the sight of a red flag! One of them started boldly out into the intersection toward me. But then, as luck would have it, the light turned green. I waved pleasantly and turned left.

Later on, I wondered if I had done the right thing. Would God strike me down for descending to the level of fools? I didn't think so, and besides, some part of me decided it was worth whatever I had to pay. Whoever said that spiritual people had to be victims, too?

That evening, I was full of energy and alertness. I realized that the incident of the day invigorated me because it forced me to act in an uncharacteristic way. It broke down some molds in my own self-image, and gave me access to reserves of energy previously locked away behind my "nice person" veneer. I thought perhaps Spirit was using this incident to goad me to be more assertive, a quality I had denied myself in the dream of the bear.

Suddenly, I felt a gentle presence beside me. It was Kyari Hota. I kept my emotions in check so that my spiritual senses would not be overwhelmed and could maintain the special awareness necessary for these meetings to take place. But it was not easy to remain neutral.

"You're back!" I exclaimed. "I'm so glad. Why did you take such a long time?"

"It will be easier on you if you are more detached about these things," she said humorously.

"I am detached," I insisted. "You think this isn't detached?" I mugged a grotesque, cross-eyed face and set her laughing with me.

"Well, it's acceptable for a start," she joked. "We have a lot of work to do, so let's not waste any time."

I grinned and hugged my knees. Then I told her about the incident with the men at the street corner. I was full of curiosity about what she would think.

"You have a good insight into it without me," she chuckled, shaking her head. "No one can survive spiritually very long while accepting the role of a passive victim. In this particular case, they had it coming, and it is something they'll think about before they assume a superior position with a weak-looking person again. Also, you're correct about the freedom you gain when stepping out of restrictive social molds. You must be free to act spontaneously in the moment, and too many 'shoulds' and 'shouldn'ts' cuts down on your valuable inner freedom."

"I thought you would be shocked," I confessed.

Kyari laughed. "Well, another Adept might not agree with me. But, goodness, it's not as if you kicked them in their groins, you know! Look, it's a beautiful night. Let's take a brisk walk, shall we?"

"What? Right now?" I asked, surprised.

She nodded and dematerialized into the atoms of the air. After a momentary retake, I went out of the room and changed my clothes into a warm-up suit and jogging shoes. I tied an extra sweatshirt around my waist and came out into the living room where my husband was watching a miniseries which had been on all week.

"How's it going?" I asked, watching the set for a moment.

"Hmmm, pretty boring, actually. I keep hoping this is going to get better. But it never does. What a total waste of time."

He pointed the channel changer at the set and instantly dismissed the unsatisfying program. On the screen a raisin was singing a popular tune from the 'sixties.

"You're going outside?" he asked, eyeing my clothing.

"Uh huh! I'm going for a walk. I won't be long."

"Well, have a nice time," he mumbled. After awhile, he called, "Want me to come along?"

"That's O.K. I'll be fine," I returned, heading for the door. It shut quietly and put me outside in the crisp night air.

Outside the moon was completely full and almost directly overhead. It played in and out of the clouds which flowed over its face in fantastic shapes. The neighborhood took on a strange appearance, the houses looking oddly vulnerable as the reality of invisible presences filled the air.

The sylphs, wind elementals, were busy at work tonight in the upper regions where the clouds were scudding across the moon. As I thought of them, a dust-devil swirled around on the street and crossed my path, whipping up a dervish dance of leaf debris. I began to walk toward the main street. A meow behind me made me turn around. It was my cat, Mitzi. A white long-hair with calico markings and a bushy tail held up like a flag, Mitzi had seen me leave the house. No doubt she came to check whether food was in the offing, though dinner had been only two hours ago.

"No, Mitzi," I called, "no food this time. You've had your dinner. I'm just going for a walk!"

I strode jauntily away. Looking back, I saw the cat get up and begin to trot after me. She kept her own pace, however. I knew that she would leave off as soon as I turned the corner. Mitzi was no dog.

I started to wonder where Kyari Hota had disappeared to. Would she show up? I frowned. The night was absolutely beautiful. Still, I didn't like walking alone. I decided to walk to the corner and wait there. Then, in the distance, I saw someone walk toward me. It was she!

"Thank goodness! I thought you had left!" I complained.

"I had to get my running shoes on," she grinned.

Sure enough, on those tiny feet, previously clad in yellow silk slippers, were a pair of white leather Adidas. I laughed. A spiritual master in jogging shoes. This was too much!

"So you think I can't run?" she asked, lifting a tiny eyebrow. In sweatpants, she looked even smaller. But remembering the last kung fu master I had seen demolishing bigger and younger opponents, I decided to cut the laughing.

"Oh, no!" I said amiably. "I don't think anything like that."

We walked companionably for five minutes or so without talking. The street was quiet, except for an occasional car or two going by. At night, with the junior high school closed, Birch was not a busy street. I kept thinking how happy I was, just walking with a friend. And then I realized with a start who that "friend" was. I looked at her from the corner of my eye. Just then, she looked at me, too. We both began to laugh.

"Look," I began impulsively, wishing the street lights were less bright so that the stars could be seen. "I know this is pretty blunt. But I've been doing some thinking, and the question occurs to me. Are women spiritually inferior to men?"

"Now that is an interesting question!" she remarked in her lilting voice. "Well, I'll tell you, since you ask."

We had stopped at a crosswalk and waited for a truck to barrel past. Then we padded across and turned toward the park. She seemed to know where I wanted to go. Or perhaps she had her own plans. I couldn't decide who was leading whom, but I knew we were in perfect harmony. I waited for her to continue.

"In order to answer your questions, it is useful to distinguish between what simply exists, on a spiritual level, and what is merely symptomatic of one's race or culture at a particular stage of development. The idea of male superiority is a cultural legacy of the last several thousand years. But it wasn't always that way. Long ago, the Earth Mother, whether she was called Isis or Ishtar or Demeter, was the supreme goddess of your cultures. The Earth Mother represented nature, and since women were closely associated with nature, they shared the goddess's prestige.

"The status of women fell as mankind's way of life changed from nature-dependent to nature-controlling. The first people were hunters and gatherers. Next came agricultural groups, followed by pastoral and nomadic societies. With every change, people disassociated themselves more and more from the Earth Mother and became oriented to conquering nature rather than revering and preserving it.

"As time went by, the more aggressive nomadic groups that worshipped male gods overran the more peaceful societies. They established their male gods as the highest ranking, and placed the female goddesses in subservient positions. This general pattern of male-dominant societies overrunning female-oriented societies has continued to the present day in Africa, Asia, and the Americas. The source of the most recent changes has been European civilization, which, as you know, is extremely patriarchal.

"Whenever a society underwent a conversion in male or female orientation, its members changed their belief patterns. Female sexuality, once honored, became suspect. Decision-making became a man's job. And so it went. But no one should take any of this personally, my dear. It is a matter of politics and economics, not

138

Spirit. Social organization upon earth continues to change, and though the changes seem slow to you, they are constantly tipping the scales in favor of one sex, then the other. During this current post-industrial, electronic age, women again have access to economic power, and thus the means to perhaps balance the scales. I expect this will happen."

"Hmmm," I mused. "I certainly hope so. But you mentioned something that I'd like to ask you more about."

"Ask away," said Kyari Hota.

"Well, it's what you said about women being associated with nature. I've always heard that, but why? Why are women and nature linked? It doesn't seem all that logical on the surface. Is it just because women bear children the way nature bears whatever it bears?"

The Adept answered, "There is more to the 'Earth-mother' cliche than the average person knows! For example, your scientists have discovered that life forms on all levels of evolution have as their foundation a female genetic structure. Only with the addition of the male chromosome does life become male. But remove the necessary male component and life reverts to its female form. It does not work the other way, however. You cannot take away a female chromosome from a fertilized cell without the cell dying. Nature also shows that female life forms can sometimes reproduce without males. But of course, males cannot reproduce without females.

"What this leads to is that the female of the species is much better adapted to life on this plane. The female genetic structure is more harmonious with physical plane laws than the male genetic structure. Her reproductive ability mirrors nature's. Women, for example, are known to menstruate according to individual cyclic patterns associated with the moon's phases, and groups of females living together have been known to menstruate together as well.

"Male activity, on the other hand, is generally not characterized by this cyclic quality. Lacking this instinctive sense of the ebb and flow of the natural world, men fall prey more easily to certain kinds of mistakes. They tend to assert themselves when they should give way, and senselessly expose themselves to risk during times when withdrawing and gathering strength is the wiser decision. Like it or not, men must harmonize themselves to a great extent with the rules of a basically feminine environment. If they do not, they will suffer from many diseases and setbacks in their personal lives. Nor will they ever fully understand the reasons behind their troubles."

"This is fascinating," I exclaimed, enjoying the coolness of the night air and the refreshing candor of Kyari's discourse. "I've never heard it put this way before. You make it sound like men have a lot to learn from women!"

"Yes, dear one," agreed Kyari. "Certainly, women are just as spiritual as men. In some ways they are more spiritual, since they are generally in greater touch with their inner worlds. That is to say, women feel, imagine, and intuit with less inhibition than men. They are more open-minded and curious about spiritual matters. The advancing frontiers of science will one day catch up with them and provide an intellectually acceptable language for what these intrepid Souls already know exists. Men demand outer proofs, while women's standards of reality are more internal."

"That's true," I nodded, easily keeping up with her slow stride.

The Adept turned the corner as a thick-coated dog trotted up and looked at us with bright eyes. He was obviously well cared-for and probably out for his nighttime stroll. Kyari and I stopped to pet and talk with him. After a few friendly sniffs and wags, the dog left us and we walked on.

The park was before us now and I could see the tops of the trees rustle gently in the wind. A bench appeared in the moonlight. We headed for it and sat down. As we sat, we fell silent for a short time, enjoying the night sounds, the delicate murmur of wind and leaves.

"I'm really grateful for what you've told me," I said hesitantly. "It makes a lot of sense. But if women are the spiritual equal of men, as you seem to be saying, why aren't there more female spiritual masters? I don't understand all the implications here."

The Adept smiled patiently. "Let me say it this way, daughter. Soul incarnating in any sex or race is the equal of any other Soul in its worth to God. Even the men who insulted you are loved by God, and therefore you owe them God's love, if not your personal affection. But the female and male embodiments are made for different purposes and different experiences, so it stands to reason that some major distinctions will exist.

"The female genetic structure, being similar to the natural cycles of the physical plane, has the advantage of physical stamina and intuitive body wisdom. However, for this same reason, it has less spiritual stamina than the male. To achieve self-mastery, women must rise above the instincts of the body which drive them to fulfill their reproductive and nurturing functions and keep their attention centered on physical concerns. They must become more detached from their need for material security and emotional relationships, and dare to risk all for the sake of higher rewards!

"They can do this, of course. Nevertheless, due to the disadvantages I've just described, most Souls choose the male form for those lifetimes in which they are in line for mastership. After all, it takes many lifetimes before anyone achieves the level of candidacy for mastership. Furthermore, it is common to fail the tests, which are very difficult. Therefore, it generally takes several additional lifetimes before one achieves this ultimate goal. The female genetic structure simply presents additional obstacles which most prefer to avoid.

"Still, for individual reasons, some Unmani Dhun Adepts have chosen to take their final tests in female lifetimes. In my case, the spiritual challenges I needed to face for mastership were best attempted as a woman. I passed my tests and chose to use this form when appearing to those in a body consciousness.

"You are living in an interesting time. Right now, many highly developed Souls have taken female embodiments in order to bring civilization back from the brink of ecological disaster, social anarchy, and war. The female's greater concern for the family and her sensitivity to the spiritual and emotional side of life are being used to bring a greater stability to society. But in order to make their influence felt, women must learn to uncover their masculine qualities. They must take the bold step outside of their traditional roles and work openly for spiritual and social change. A great many of these Souls can achieve self-mastery while living in the female form if they truly desire to."

"Well, that's good news!" I said happily. "The bottom line is, Soul itself isn't limited by the body's limitations! Of course, some feminists are going to get upset with any talk of differences at all! They don't realize that the true self is neither male nor female, and exists independently of the body. They're defensive about their femaleness because they believe that their sex greatly defines who they are. Once you remember having lived as a man and as a woman

141

over and over again, it's impossible to think about it like that again!"

"That's it exactly," the Adept agreed. "Without that awareness, women are bound to feel shortchanged with this explanation."

"I don't blame them, really," I commented. "Growing up female, I couldn't help but wonder why there were such a paltry number of dynamic female role models in leadership positions within society. I mean, despite the fact that women are commonly depicted as the more sensitive and inward-turning sex, there certainly hasn't been an excess of female Beethovens and Shakespeares in the creative fields, either."

"The limitations society has placed on women's creativity are greatly responsible for these shortages," said the Adept. "These limitations are now rapidly dissolving. But whether male or female, successful creative people have one important quality in common. They have opposite-sex qualities highly developed in them. If they are men, they are likely to be unusually sensitive, emotional, and imaginative. If they are women, they are probably more aggressive, confident, and independent than most of their gender. This happens because creative people must have both strongly introvertive and strongly extrovertive qualities to manifest their visions.

"Strong opposite sex qualities in creative men and women, however, make them always unusual, often misunderstood, and sometimes even disliked or feared. It takes a high degree of self-assurance and inner balance to go through life with such inner gifts and outer conflicts. Some do not have such balance and self-assurance, and these unfortunate ones suffer greatly."

"I haven't thought of creative people in this way before!" I exclaimed enthusiastically. "It helps me understand myself better, too. Thank you."

"Just doing my job," winked the Adept. "But I haven't given you a very balanced picture of the spiritual capabilities of men and women yet."

"You haven't?" I puzzled. "Seems to me like you've done a great job!"

"No," she said. "I haven't. It's partly because I had to tell you what you needed to hear first—that there is nothing wrong with women. But the difference between male and female spiritual currents is easiest to understand in another way. For you, it may be a matter of survival to know."

"O.K. Let's hear it," I said gamely.

"It has little to do with talk," Kyari replied, and gripped me lightly on the arm. The scene around me dissolved and transformed itself into a vast rolling plain of browns and golds. A few scrawny trees dotted the landscape, and herds of graceful elands grazed in the light of a fading day. I sensed that it was late afternoon, with dusk perhaps only a few hours hence. Then, from the right side of my field of vision came a dark figure running as gracefully as any beast.

I turned to find the Adept and saw that she was sitting on the ground about ten feet behind me on a slight rise. She was dressed in roughly textured natural fabric of browns and greys, and her feet were bound in thin leather sandals. On her head a curious cloth hood hung around her ears in soft coils. She smiled and pointed to the figure. Her gesture made me turn my attention back to it.

It was a man, way over six feet tall and and very black. His body was spare, and his legs looked like they were made for speed. His right hand hefted a spear from which hung blond grasses or the mane hair of some animal. He was nearly naked, except for a cloth around his private parts, and his feet were bare.

The man stopped about three hundred yards from us and watched the herd graze for a few minutes. Then he began a rhythmic singing or chanting that started low and slowly rose in pitch and strength to float in the air currents to our ears. He held his spear above his head, his face raised to the sky.

"What is he doing?" I hissed.

"Go and see," smiled the Adept. She pointed at me with her finger. I felt a force pulling me under as sleep pulls one into a dream. Immediately I was no longer an observer of the man. I was the man himself.

I was Masai.

"Prophet!" I called, my voice a dark river through which moved a strong current of pride.

"I am here, son," replied Kyari Hota, rising to greet me.

I walked slowly up to the small woman with pale skin. She was my teacher and guide. A Wise One.

"How do you like my prayer song?" I asked, grinning broadly. "I have made it with many power words from my dreams. I think you have sent them to me. They are like a necklace for the Gods to wear. Do you think they will like it?"

143

"They will," Kyari nodded. "It is a beautiful song, full of the longing of Soul for God. But there is something more in you, as well. I can see it in your eyes. What is it, my son?"

"You see everything," I laughed. "Yi! There is to be a war. Many warriors will go to fight with the Ajemubu along the river. I am of age. I go too."

"Mkhuto," the Adept sighed, "you are not entirely unhappy about this."

"No, teacher," I said, a little abashed. "I am a warrior. I was born to fight. Does that make me a bad pupil? Can I not fly in my dreams? Can I not see the future? All of these powers you have taught me will make me a greater warrior than any of my enemies. I will be safe from harm, never fear. My legs are swift and my arm is sure!"

I flashed a confident smile as I ended my boasting. The Adept nodded and asked me to sit down.

"I hurt my neck looking up at you, Mkhuto," she said affectionately. "You have grown so tall so fast. Only yesterday you were a stalk of grass, easily bent by a stronger wind. Now you are a bull elephant trumpeting your prowess to the sky."

"And here is my tusk!" I laughed heartily, thrusting my spear into the air.

The Adept shook her head. "There is still some boy in you yet, Mkhuto. Do you not think it may be too early to tell whether you will be a great warrior like your father, or perhaps someone even greater? Someone who will not bring bloodshed, but wisdom to your people?"

"What can be greater than a warrior, Wise One?" I asked, puzzled. "My father is a great warrior, and he is also King. I am the eldest. I will be king, too. And a warrior. I cannot be a great wizard like you, who travels on the breath of the Gods. But if you will stay with me as my advisor, come and live in my house as my chief minister, then I will have power and wisdom, besides! Stay, teacher. I will make my people accept you. At first they will fear you, but soon they will come to love you. You will see!"

"No, Mkhuto," Kyari said softly, touching my shoulder, which was now close to hers. She looked into my eager face and love sank down deep, deep into the rich soil of my heart like winter rain. "I am but a guest on this earth. I live with the Gods, and the Gods as you know do not take the side of one man over another. I have taught you this! But one day your people will need wisdom more than power. They will need to use their minds above their spears, and their hearts more than their childish magic. And I will not be there. Only you will."

"But teacher," I began.

"No, hush," the Adept said. "Close your eyes and I will give you the Sight. It will be the last one from me. But when I am no longer here with you in the body, I will still be with you watching over you from the Land of the Gods. You can travel there to see me if you wish. I have taught you. Remember. Now look."

Her hand came up to my forehead and gave me a vision. It was not as clear as usual, but more like dreams when you lay burning with fever. It was full and busy, and later I could not remember anything but a few pictures: a war, my coronation as king to succeed my dead father, another war, many dead. But then I remember also seeing one more thing. I saw myself as an old man walking away from my village, carrying only a water gourd, a pouch of meat, and my spear.

Suddenly, I was back in my female body. The Masai stood where he had first stopped and waved his spear in the air, singing his prayer song. He looked slowly around as if sensing something, but did not seem to perceive us. Then he ran swifty to the east, his strides casting long shadows before him in the dying sun.

After a long time, the man disappeared from my view. I felt a loss, as for something precious that was mine, which had been taken from me.

"Kyari?" I said.

"Yes, daughter?" she answered, squinting.

"What was all that about?"

"You can answer that for yourself," she said. "How did you feel? What were you thinking?"

I shook my head violently. "I don't know. Unusual stuff. I felt young, confident, eager for the coming battle, ready to prove myself. There was not a shadow of a doubt in my mind that I would win many battles and become a great King. I assumed that I could have power and wisdom, too. Like Solomon, I guess. There was nothing that could stop me."

The Adept nodded. "Yes. And how do you feel now? I mean,

as yourself?"

"What?" I frowned. "As myself? Oh, I get it. As a female. Well . . . I don't know. Different from him, I can tell you. But what does that prove? I'm not a Masai in this lifetime. What does it tell me about men and women?"

"If you can remember the feeling of being 'him,' you have a better way of understanding than anything I can logically say to you. He was connected with the life force very directly. He was filled with it. He did become, by the way, a great warrior. And a good king. But what he saw and did on the battlefield chastened him. Ruling his people mellowed him.

"Then one day, after his sons were grown, he did an unheard of thing: He abdicated in favor of his eldest son and left his village, much to the sorrow and lamentation of his wives and children, and the people who had begun with admiration of him, and had grown to love him. He spent six months wandering happily all over his kingdom, and into the outlands of another tribe with whom the Masai had a treaty. But one day they found him and slew him as he slept."

I nodded, watching the drama unfold on my inner vision as the Adept told it. "The murderers were a pack of scoundrels from the neighboring tribe, paid assassins. But they were really employed by . . . my son, the new king. Why, Kyari?"

"Because he feared you," she said simply. "Remember that you had sowed the seeds of your own masculine reputation in your early teens. You were larger than life for many people by the time you left your family and began to wander. Though you avoided the company of men, the very fact that you were alive and at liberty was a threat to your son and his family. What if you changed your mind and came back, demanding the throne? What if, denied the return of your status, you enlisted your old allies and waged a war on your son? Who would the people support?

"Actually, it was your son's wife who instigated the plot. She was consumed with jealousy because she knew her own husband would always live in your shadow. The poison attempt that killed your favorite wife was by her hand. Your son was always weak. He listened to her and the venom penetrated his own heart. You know this man today. And there is something in you that wants to reach out and put a spear into him before he can do it to you.

"But it's too late, lion. You died then. But you were not

blameless yourself. You never taught him as you should have. You were too busy being the powerful ruler, the wise statesman, the father of your people. But never, never the father of your own children. In this, you failed."

The Adept got up and turned her back to me. She walked slowly away as I stared at her disappearing back. After many minutes I realized where I was, and how I had gotten there.

"Hey!" I shouted, running frantically after her. "You can't leave me here!" My lungs seemed about to collapse, and my head near bursting from the blood pounding in it. I knew I was going to fall with the next step and die there, my body carrion for the vultures of another time. Then suddenly, everything changed. My legs were black pistons carrying me lightly, effortlessly across the ground. My lungs were white sails that caught the air. And my heart was as strong as the sun beating down on my dark skin!

"Lion!" sighed the Adept, opening her arms to me as I quickly closed the distance between us. "Come back then, my son . . . my daughter. Let's go home now."

She placed me gently back on the park bench. I sat there awhile, staring at my feet, which looked strange to me for some reason I couldn't quite fathom. Then the memories flooded back to my mind, and I jerked my head up, staring at the Adept standing above me.

"Wait a minute!" I gasped. "What just happened?"

The Adept laughed heartily. "Survival. Yours. I wouldn't have left you. It can't be done, anyway. Your body belongs here where it will live out its alloted span of life. I hope you learned something from the experience, though."

"I'll say," I murmured. "I can't begin to describe everything I'm thinking and realizing. About that lifetime, and the lessons I did—and didn't—learn. Also the difference of being male. It's not just a matter of physical strength. As Mkhuto, I had a sense of power I don't have in this lifetime. Could that be the connection with the spiritual current, like you say?"

"Yes," answered the Adept. "But let me explain further. Men have this connection, but it doesn't mean they necessarily use it for anything spiritual. Just as in Mkhuto's life, they often use it for conquest and domination. They do this because they do not know any better. Even today, whether in the corporate world, the stockmarket, or in the sports arena, it is the same aggressive use of the God current. In balance, it is fine, but most of it is a sheer waste!

"Now women can get this current, too, but since they do not have a direct link-up, many look to get it from men—generally either their mates or their sons. Failing this, they may resort to reliance on religious, psychic, or occult practices which give them a feeling of security and power over their lives. However, the long-term effect of such a reliance is to trap them into even greater dependency. The tool becomes the crutch, as it were. If you do not believe me, research the area and find out how many true believers in these fields are men and how many are women. You will find that the majority of followers are female.

"But here is a secret women do not know. They do not need men or magical practices for this link-up with the spiritual forces. They can get it through opening themselves to the Holy Spirit through contemplation and cultivating the state of spiritual surrender. If a woman knew and trusted this, she would be taken care of by the best possible agent, God itself! She can be a complete spiritual being within herself!"

"I see," I sighed thoughtfully. "You were right. It is a matter of my survival. I was confused about this, and sometimes I do feel like I'll never succeed in getting this book written, or getting my consulting work to flow on a regular basis. Like I'm missing a synapse somewhere inside me. I've been frantic looking for it. But what you're saying is that all I have to do is learn to surrender my life to Spirit. Then I'll have all the energy and power I need."

"Exactly so," the Adept said firmly. "Confidence, opportunity, the right tools to do your job—all are waiting for you to establish the proper relationship with Spirit. Well then, if you like, I will lead you to some resources for further research. But now I would like to conclude this discussion by returning to the topic of mastership, particularly as it pertains to women."

"Please," I smiled. "That's exactly what I'd like to hear."

The Adept nodded, her face pale against the night.

"The most revered feminine image in the religious field is obviously that of the Virgin Mary. Not the real woman, of course, but the idealized Mother of Christ. The Virgin Mary is really the Earth Mother rehabilitated, via the Greeks, into the Christian mythology. We find variations of the Earth Mother incorporated into every religion. Other goddesses exist, as well. For example, the Hellinistic mythologies contain many feminine dieties such as Hera, Athena, Aphrodite, and Demeter. They represent various aspects of the polarized female current, including more masculine personas such as Athena and Artemis, the goddesses of wisdom and hunting, respectively.

"These goddess images are useful to acknowledge and understand the personalities of women and how they express themselves in society: virgin, lover, wife, mother, wise woman, and career person. Most women are likely to identify with one or two images more than the others. And a well-balanced woman will have some characteristics of each! Still, we must distinguish between idealized male or female 'types' and the possibility of mastership.

"Mythological and religious archetypes are not real gods and goddesses, but simply projections of our fragmented understanding of the Divine. As such, they are not incorrect, just incomplete. Mastership, on the other hand, is the total unfoldment of the self, including both male and female qualities and the unique individuality of the unfolded Soul. Your goal must be self-mastery, and nothing short of it! Do not look for this outside yourself, as your society has no image for it at all."

With that she got up and walked into the night. I blinked twice and she was gone.

The spot on the bench was empty without her. I put out my hand to touch it, and it was still warm. I glanced around, wondering if anybody could have overheard us or seen her disappear. The moon emerged from a pocket of clouds and spread its pearled light upon the grass. Finally, I got up and walked home.

Somewhere, from the Land of the Gods, her voice came back to me. It was soft and clear.

"Lion," she said, "I gave this name to you in that African lifetime. Live long and be mighty. This time for God."

149

CHAPTER THIRTEEN
The Power of Sex

Sex was on my mind today. The headlines of the morning paper had placed still another sex crime case before the public's attention. The story was accompanied by a photograph of the victim, a pretty girl whose smiling face made an incongruous counterpoint to the printed story. So often, in today's society, sex was surrounded by aberration and violence. Even in some of my own past lifetimes, this was true as well. How could a normal bodily function become so negative? Perhaps I was missing some crucial awareness, I wondered. How important was sex, anyway, to the spiritual study of the male and female?

I wrote down a number of questions and tacked the list up on a bulletin board above my computer desk. I was determined to get the answers to these questions one way or another, whether through contemplation, reading, or asking one of my teachers, Kyari Hota or Haurvata Sampa. Toward that purpose, I went to the local bookstore and bought a few titles that sounded promising. But reading them in the weeks that followed disturbed more than illuminated me. Something was missing, but I could not put my finger on what it was.

One day, as I was annotating student papers at the desk in my office, a gentle voice interrupted my thoughts. I put the pen down and looked up. It was Kyari Hota.

"Good morning," she said. "I thought I'd come along and see how you are doing. I had a feeling you wanted to see me."

"That's an understatement! I've got a lot of questions I want to ask you," I began, stacking the papers neatly to one side.

"I know," the Adept said matter-of-factly. "I believe you wanted to discuss the subject of sex?"

"Right," I nodded. "I've been reading some books about sexual practices that are supposed to lead to spiritual illumination. Frankly, though, I'm getting more confused than ever about this sex thing. May we talk about it now?"

"Certainly," Kyari nodded. "It's an issue charged with a great deal of human feeling. But really, it is very simple in its essential facts."

She collected her thoughts for a moment, then turned to me.

"It may be helpful, however, to take a journey into the inner worlds. There I could show you, as well as tell you, some of the important realities in this field of study. Are you feeling up to an adventure today?"

"Sure," I said, stifling a yawn. "I'd love to! I was nearly falling asleep at my papers anyway."

"Then we shall try something different," suggested the Adept. "I want you to chant this sound over and over again, rolling it around in your mind until it fills all of space. Let yourself fall into it, deeper and deeper. I will be with you shortly in the inner worlds."

I closed my eyes and began chanting the syllable she gave me. At first it was just a thin thread of sound, a word like any other, though without any apparent meaning. But soon the sound changed. It seemed to resonate in the brain, expanding my center of awareness outward. Within this expanded center, I could see colors and shapes take form. Soon a world appeared out of the mist and in it was the Unmani Dhun Adept.

"Greetings," said the female Adept, wearing light-weight clothing and sandals. "Welcome to the Museum of the Kali-Ra."

As I adjusted myself to the vibrations of this place, I perceived that she was standing in front of a modernistic building whose surface resembled greenish-blue glass. A fountain of sparkling water splashed down from a large sculpture whose shape suggested to me

151

an abstract woman's figure, interpenetrated by the figure of a male.

"Whew!" I exclaimed, craning my neck to see the sculpture's full height. "This is a new one on me. What is this place exactly?"

"The Museum of the Kali-Ra," Kyari repeated, gesturing widely with her hand. "You asked about sex, and this is the best place to research it. The Kali-Ra is the sex force of the lower worlds, the governing power of the procreative current operating in material bodies. In this building you can find out more than you need to or probably want to know about the sex force. As your guide, I will select a few experiences for you that will be most valuable, however."

As she explained, she walked slowly toward the building. I followed. There seemed at first to be no door, but as we neared the structure, I could see that one of the glass panels was sliding open. Before we went in, Kyari snapped her fingers at my ear. I started, and suddenly became aware of a crowd of people in garments similar to the Adept's walking in and out of the building, talking and laughing all around us. The transformation was so startling, I gave Kyari an alarmed look. She laughed merrily.

"I could see that you had not fully turned on your inner senses, my dear. That will not do. You must use all of your awareness to get the full impact of your subjective experiences. Otherwise, they will not be able to register on that primitive machine you call a mind! Since you are to be writing about this, we cannot bypass that particular organ. Do you understand?"

"Uh huh," I agreed, grinning. "Thanks."

We had walked in by now, into what seemed like a lobby of a grand hotel. The Adept and I stood in a short line, and when we reached the desk, an attractive male, his brown hair curling at the temples, asked our names and places of origin. Kyari gave her name and for her place of origin, the Unmani Dhun. The man flashed her a bright smile and gave her a thin, transparent disk that stated this information. I gave him my name and place of origin as well, and received a similar disk. I looked questioningly at Kyari who, in answer, placed the disk on her chest. I followed suit. Somehow, the disk stuck fast. I asked the Adept how the device worked.

"It works on a principle similar to the way static electricity works on earth," she said.

"You mean the way my skirt sometimes clings to my nylons?" I giggled.

"Essentially," she replied. "Now, shall we begin our tour?"

We passed the first part in silence, as I waited for the Adept to speak. Since she did not, I took the time to take in the art work, which depicted in mural form the creation of male and female embodiments from the single atom of Soul. Beautiful sculptures flanked us on both sides, luminous in the pale blue-green light that fell in streams through the walls of the museum.

"What do you see?" asked Kyari finally.

"The creation of male and female," I answered. "I believe the sculptures are all sexual in nature, too. Although I confess I can't make heads or tails out of a good many of them."

She laughed. "You cannot understand all of them because the sculptures are from various planets on the physical plane. Differences in bodies and artistic imaginations account for the confusion."

"Oh," I said, raising my eyebrows. I looked at a strange shape and wondered whether it represented a difference in body or imagination, but did not really feel like asking.

"We have gone ahead of the scheduled tour," Kyari mentioned. "At some point, I'll allow it to catch up with us so you can hear something of what they say here. But for now, I would like to take the time to lecture to you and answer any questions you have on the subject of sex."

"I'm ready," I piped up.

The Adept nodded and went ahead immediately.

"The sex drive is the body's instinctual desire to unite with the 'other' and thereby make oneself complete," she said. "It is based on the male-female polarity of the lower worlds, and Soul's innate wish to be the whole instead of a part. The afterglow associated with the period after coitus is actually very similar to the blisslike state sought by many meditators. It is a loosening of attachments and a sense of well-being that comes from the expansion of self which sexual consummation can temporarily create. But the key word here is temporary. Sexual union is not a viable path to the higher consciousness."

"Ah hah!" I exclaimed. "That's the key all right. I felt there was some truth to what the authors I've been reading were saying in their books. Yet there was also something that didn't ring true in the idea that sex could be used to get to God."

"That's true," the Adept nodded. "The problem is this: No phenomenal experience, whether physical or subtle, can substitute for the hard work Soul must perform in order to earn its right to be a vehicle for God. This includes facing and paying off its spiritual debts, developing the qualities of love and service, and learning to live in the higher worlds as a citizen, not just a visitor.

"The idea that sex can open the gates of heaven for one is simply the attempt to substitute the feeling of heaven for the experience of heaven. It is a romantic illusion, like the belief that speeding down the freeway in a fast car can make one free! Alcoholics and drug users have similar motivations, and their efforts are equally unsuccessful. Sooner or later, the pursuit of spiritual expansion is set aside for the more reliable goal of immediate sensual pleasure. This pleasure, however, is a mechanical one, and like anything mechanical, it tends towards repetition. Then sex becomes simply an addiction, a reflexive habit of the body, and a stumbling block to Soul."

We were walking through a gallery which displayed a collection of drawings and paintings depicting lovemaking in various forms. In the serene atmosphere of the museum, the works took on an almost clinical interest. I detected many specimens from the earth, but was especially fascinated with those from other worlds. All, however, seemed to have one thing in common: the act of intimate touching and coupling.

"O.K.," I nodded, sighing. "So you're saying that sex does not work as a spiritual path. But if this is true, why has this theory survived for so long?"

"Because," continued Kyari, her eyes merry with humor, "people would like to believe it is true!"

I laughed. "No! Be fair. Is that it, really?"

"All right," she relented. "In all fairness, the practice has some historical basis. The so-called spiritual practice of sex is a remnant of an ancient system to systematically open up the sexual center in man, gather its energy, and move it up to each higher spiritual center in succession."

"And can it work?" I asked, perking up.

"Only in theory," she responded blandly. "In reality, there are some real problems with the practice. First, there is the difficulty of obtaining adequate spiritual guidance to accomplish this. The knowledge has been mostly lost, and the practice itself has not kept up a line of living masters. Second, it is a slow and inefficient method at best. It is too easy to lose a student to the minor power currents of the lower spiritual centers. Thus, completing the process would take lifetimes and lifetimes, if one succeeded at all. The practice survives, but with few serious adherents."

"Well!" I sighed. "This has been a real revelation. I'm really glad I got this clarified. Can we keep going on this topic, though?"

"Certainly," replied the Adept. "But first I want to show you something over here. I think you'll be interested in this."

She took me by the shoulder and pointed down a pale-pink corridor that glowed softly. At the end of the corridor was a room with chairs for perhaps a hundred people. We entered and sat down. Puzzled, I looked questioningly at the Adept, but she only fixed her gaze in front of her. I followed suit. Soon strains of music filled the room and a fully dimensional image materialized in front of us.

"Holograph?" I queried in a low voice.

The Adept nodded.

The image depicted a man and a woman in the act of lovemaking. As the physical touching created sexual response, colorful emanations began to rise from the bodies of both participants. At first the colors were pale, then vivid, almost electric in hue. A deep red color began to grow from the sexual centers, then spread everywhere, tinging the other colors with a crimson glow.

At the culmination of orgasm, there was another burst of energy. Surprisingly, this was yellow-white in color, stronger and brighter than the rest. The light suffused the body and spread everywhere, seeming to radiate from the heart center in ever-widening circles. The two circles interpenetrated and their atoms mingled. Soon a vast orb was formed from what was once two, and the visual effect was like a womb of light in which the two lovers floated in perfect peace.

After the image disappeared, I remained seated in my chair. "Wow. That's the dream all right," I remarked.

"That's the potential," the Adept said. "Most of your people are too self-centered to ever achieve this. With all the attention you place on sex, you do not have enough detached awareness and concern for the other to complete this circuit. This little 'show' you saw had less to do with sex than with love."

155

We left the room and retraced our steps to the main area, where Kyari pointed out the libraries and historical displays of different races' depictions of sex, including gods and goddesses whose primary attributes or functions had to do with female or male sexual energy. I recognized some from the earth world, including the eight-armed Kali from India and a graceful marble figure of Aphrodite.

"I notice that most of these artifacts depict females," I stated. "Why is it that women are associated with sex more than men? I mean, where are the male sexual counterparts of Kali and Aphrodite?"

"Well, Aphrodite had her Adonis," said Kyari. "But it was his physical beauty that attracted her, and beauty that attracts sensual or emotional love is part of the female current. This is all connected with the procreative function of the female. As for the Kali, she is an interesting construct containing both creative and destructive functions, the two faces of the feminine, as it were."

"What do you mean by 'two faces'?" I queried.

"It is a metaphor for the mother who brings forth children but can also devour them," Kyari answered. "In other words, what 'mother nature' gives in bounty, she can also take away in capricious destruction. It is an image calculated to arouse fear and respect for the diety specifically, but also for females in general. In the broadest sense, however, it also means that the feminine current can lift individuals up in their aspirations toward God, or plunge them into the maw of sex and materialism."

"I see," I mused.

We had walked into an area where representative processes of sexual reproduction in various life forms were being simultaneously shown in separate viewing and listening areas. Standing back from these areas, we could look around and see several at once. I was surprised to notice groups of children with adult leaders, as if on field trips. I questioned the Adept about it.

She replied, "It is the usual thing. Preadolescent children are brought to this museum to learn about the spiritual and material aspects of procreation. Unlike in your world, sex is considered a basic subject here, and no one is considered educated without a thorough foundation in the facts and responsibilities of handling this powerful current!"

"It sounds like a great idea to me," I agreed. "It's no wonder people in our world grow up so mixed up about sex. We're totally ignorant compared to the people of this world! Is this why we have so many sexual aberrations like violent sex? It may seem morbid of me, but I've been wondering about the reason for it."

The Adept tilted her head thoughtfully and continued speaking.

"The sex-violence angle can be understood better in the context of the spiritual ideal we have just seen," Kyari said slowly. "Generally, of course, it is the man who victimizes the woman in a violent sexual encounter. What is happening here is that the giving of self has become introverted into a 'taking' from the other. And what greater thing is there to take from another than life?

"Mixed up with this mode is often anger toward, and fear of, the female current itself. The violence is an effort to assert power over what is feared. At the heart of this aberration is a person with a severe split between his inner male and female selves, the one fearing and loathing the other. This inner scenario projects itself into violent anti-female social behavior. The fact that there is so much of this anti-female violence in your culture shows the need for greater integration of the masculine and feminine forces on the individual level. It also points out the fact that sex is a powerful force that can be used for good or ill."

"That helps," I nodded. "But you brought up something interesting. Why do men fear women, and through them, sex?"

The Adept had stopped walking and took a seat at the foot of a serenely smiling female diety, her features oriental like a statue I had once seen of the Chinese Goddess of Mercy, Kuan Yin.

"Well, there are basically two reasons," the Adept replied. "First, sexual difficulties exist for the male embodiment that most women do not experience. You see, the vibrations produced by male and female chromosomes in one body can be quite confusing to some males, especially since men are raised by women, and all small boys identify with their mothers at first.

"This explains the need for male tribal rituals and the whole turbulence, and sometimes even violence, of male adolescence. It also explains the prevalence of homosexual fears among many men. Boys feel a need to sever their inner and outer dependency upon the female in order to take on male identities in society. Grown men often feel they must continue to affirm their distinctness from women in order not to slip back into that old dependency, or into a confusion

157

of sexual identities."

"Is this why there are so many more sexual deviations among males than among females?" I queried.

"Precisely," she nodded.

"All right," I said. "So what about the second reason that men fear women?"

"The second reason is the desire for power," continued Kyari. "People in general, and men in particular, strive to be in control. But during sexual arousal and sexual consummation, they are certainly not in control at all! The ability of women to arouse the irrational in men scares them. Furthermore, the temporary suspension of ego-definition in the giving of oneself to another during sex is frightening to anyone whose ego-structure is weak.

"Moreover, sexual intercourse opens up each person's emotional body to his or her partner. Not through the sheer act of penetration and orgasm, of course, but through the changed awareness that can result from the sex act. Actually, what I am describing is very similar to the process of spiritual surrender which is so crucial to every true seeker of God.

"Surrendering to God results in a relaxation of the will, a purification of the personality through selflessness, and a sense of expanded awareness in which one feels a kinship with all of God's creations. This is a 'sharing of self' at the highest level, my daughter. For when you surrender your little self to God, God also shares something of its own qualities with you!"

I shook my head. "The comparison astounds me. But it makes perfect sense! Is that what the Song of Solomon was all about?"

"Yes," replied the Adept. "I believe a line from it goes, 'Let him kiss me with the kisses of his mouth, for his love is better than wine.' He's referring, of course, to God's love. Sexual imagery is simply the closest metaphor available on earth for this experience of uniting with the Holy Spirit. A related metaphor is becoming 'drunk' on the liquor of Spirit, generally called 'wine.' Get the picture?"

"Yes," I sighed. "And all this time people are going around talking about sex as 'chemistry' and all that. This conversation makes that stuff seem pretty inane."

"Not inane," chuckled the Adept, "just limited. 'Chemistry,' as you call it, is just sexual 'taste,' similar to a taste for certain kinds of foods, whether spicy or bland or fried. It has as much to do with love as flavor has to do with nutrition! In other words, it is not a reliable indicator of what will help you to grow and thrive as Soul. Part of maturity is discovering that while carrots aren't ice cream, they are nevertheless sweet, and have the benefit of being constructive, rather than destructive, to your body. In the same way, the individual discovers that love is preferable to pure sexual attraction, and gives more happiness and pleasure in the short and in the long run, too."

"We seem to be obsessed with sex these days, though," I commented. "For example, it used to be that sexual desire was considered sinful and shameful. But nowadays, we are made to feel guilty if our sex drives aren't strong enough!"

"Yes," nodded the Adept. "The old notions about sex as sin were wrong and had to be corrected. But as usual, the reaction was to swing the pendulum to the extreme opposite end. Given complete freedom of expression, people's sex drives will always differ. But in general, sex drives are greatest in youth, when sexual polarization is strongest. Later, when the experiences of adulthood, such as marriage and parenthood, bring the individual more into an inner male-female balance, the sex drive also comes into balance."

We had made our way through much of the museum. The Adept stopped occasionally to point out a feature or discuss some of the curious lore of this world. Then we came into a room hung with paintings and other forms of art work depicting famous lovers in history and literature. The shelves were lined with books with gilt edges. I walked up to peer at the titles and found one that read Romeo and Juliet.

"It is time for you to learn about romantic love," the Adept said in her musical voice.

She gestured to a chair in a corner, and we both sat down. After a period of silence, a small group appeared at the doorway and soon filled the chairs of the room. A man who was obviously their leader kept standing. After glancing in our direction, he smiled an acknowledgment and began his discourse in a friendly tone.

"As we were discussing, romantic love is a projection of our own idealized masculine or feminine qualities to a person of the opposite sex. A woman sees the man as a hero of her fantasies and a man sees the woman as the princess of his dreams. Idealization of the other and intensity of feeling are primary characteristics of romantic love. The idealization comes from powerful masculine and feminine archetypes being triggered in the individual's subconscious. The intensity stems from the strong desire to unite with the 'other' and fulfill the longing every person has to be whole as Soul.

"Because romantic love is essentially a projection of a part of ourselves, it includes both pain and happiness. When we are with the one we love, we feel whole and exalted. When we are apart, we feel incomplete and dejected. But even our dejection can seem wonderful when we are in the throes of romantic love because our emotional state has expanded so far beyond the normal. The expansion of positive emotions is the greatest benefit of romantic love. It gives us the experience of being more connected to life. Cords of love radiate from us to touch everything and everyone around.

"The flaw in romantic love is that it idealizes the 'other.' This keeps reality from setting in for a while, but eventually the mundane breaks through. When the spell is broken, the lover may see the other's flaws and think he has made a mistake in his choice. He may even decide that he has been fooled or betrayed. It is more likely that he has only fooled himself. On the other hand, a romantic's vision of his beloved may not be so far from the truth. In this case, the match may be a good one, and the couple can shift relatively smoothly into a day-to-day relationship after the intensity of the romance has dissipated."

"Now, do you have any questions or comments so far?" the guide asked, his eyes momentarily resting on the individuals in this group.

"Well, could you say that romantic love is the religious ecstasy of the common person?" offered a silver-haired man ironically.

The group laughed a little at this joke, and the leader smiled. "Yes, I suppose so. Romantic love is really a desire to embrace life, but focused on a single person. Underneath all people's urges to find this love is the need to give of themselves and open their hearts to a more complete spiritual experience. As a first step, romantic love shows the individual that he cannot isolate himself in life; he needs people. An occasional loss or rejection teaches him compassion for another person's pain. Vulnerability and passion are the trademarks of romantic love. But they are the marks of the God-seeker as well!"

The Adept winked at me and I smiled back. The group stayed

on to hear more about some of the lower worlds' romantic heroes and heroines, and the spiritual lessons hidden in their stories. However, Kyari motioned me to follow her, and we left quietly through another door. Soon we entered an enclosed garden almost suffocatingly beautiful with singing birds and fragrant crimson flowers. In the distance I could see the blue-green walls of the building shining in the light of this world.

"O.K.," I began, "I can accept what I've heard about romantic love with no problem. It fits my experience and observation. But people are not going to give up their attachment to romantic love so easily. And I don't know if I believe it's all that bad. After all, isn't romantic love a step above what we had before, at least on earth? You know, arranged marriages and all that."

"That's true," conceded Kyari. "Defined as the personal choice of one's mate, romantic love is certainly an advance over past practice. The freedom to select a mate enables you to learn discrimination from making conscious choices. Eventually, each of us learns from our decisions. We seek to balance the male and female forces within ourselves so that we can better answer our own needs. We stop seeking idealized qualities in others. We can understand each other's strengths and weaknesses, and go beyond that to appreciate the divine Soul within.

"But love must progress beyond the romantic if it is ever to realize its potential. This happens in stages, and a relationship may stop at any of these levels. For example, an individual's 'first love' is generally remembered as a golden experience because it is frozen forever at the romantic stage. Furthermore, it benefits from its complete newness and the vividness of its emotional and physical sensations. Many people are addicted to romantic love because of the 'high' it provides, and more is written about it than about any other kind of male-female love. But if you are interested, I can tell you more about the growth of love."

"Please do," I urged.

"To repeat, then, the first stage is romantic love. The lover idealizes the beloved, centering his attention on the 'other' as something to be attained or won, and united with himself. A heightened sense of 'I' results as love temporarily expands the boundaries of the ego. The second stage finds the lover's attention drawing back into himself. This is a natural reaction to the extreme other-centeredness of the first stage. In the second stage, the lover begins to become more objective about the good and bad points of the beloved in relationship to himself. He asks himself, 'What can this person do for me?'

"Often, relationships end with this stage. One lover, if not both, recognizes a mismatch and backs away from an unwanted commitment. However, if there is a real thread of love here, the relationship can rise to another level: stage three. Stage three is the period of adjustment that two people undergo when they confront the reality of personal differences. The lovers discover the truth beneath the idealized images they once cherished and shift their expectations to reflect the new reality. They begin to make compromises for the sake of the other. For example, one party might have to relax his standards as he sees that the other person isn't as orderly as himself. During stage one, such details don't seem important, if they are noticed at all. But now, small things take on new meaning as the attention shifts from the ideal to the practical.

"It takes a great deal of flexibility and inner stability to give another the space to be himself, while remaining true to ourselves. Many relationships flounder at this level, unable to make either the adjustment or a clean break. However, assuming the relationship realizes the potential of this stage, it can go on to a still higher level. The fourth level is an other-centered level again. However, it is radically different from the other-centeredness of stage one. In stage four, love blooms into a willingness to make sacrifices for the other. The question that is asked is, 'How can we help each other? What can we do to make each other happy?' With this kind of selfless giving, the couple can truly function as a unit, making mutual effort toward mutual goals. This is important, for a couple must have similar goals for their relationship to work in the long run.

"Finally, through a life of mutual effort toward mutual goals, love can ripen into true companionship, divine good will, affection, and complete acceptance. Time is essential to achieve this fifth stage, just as it is important to aging a good wine! The stresses of life are always going to be present, but for those who can survive them, the rewards of a lasting relationship are great. The individuals learn loyalty, perseverance, and understanding. In return, they find that they have also earned friendship and intimacy. Death is never frightening to those who have truly loved and been loved. For death

162

is a kind of surrender to something greater, which they have already experienced in the arms of their beloved.

"Do you have anything to add, my dear?"

"I do," I nodded, taking a seat on a garden bench. "In my country, we have so many divorces. Getting to stage five of your description would take several lifetimes for most couples!"

"That's a truer statement than you imagine," laughed Kyari. "Many people do indeed take several lifetimes."

"Well, what I'm getting at is this. What can you tell me about divorce? Is it always a bad thing? Should people generally try to stay together and work things out?"

"That is a simple question with a complex answer," smiled the Adept, sitting down beside me. "People part or stay together for many reasons. Some are good reasons, some are not. Divorce is more common now because you are free from social and legal sanctions against it. The pressures that keep a marriage intact are equalized by forces that wear away at it. Thus, individuals have to make individual choices about what they will do. To state the obvious, people must use common sense and do what seems best for all parties. When there are children involved, this is especially critical. Children can be harmed by either a bad marriage or a bad divorce. You must determine the real needs people have and try to meet the most essential ones—for example, stability of home for children, a source of income for a divorced mother, and so on.

"The real trauma of a divorce doesn't come from just the sudden separation. It comes from the emotional wrenching that usually accompanies the separation. People feel let down by a divorce. They expect to feel bad, so they do. They tend to affix blame, either upon themselves or upon their former spouses. The emotional atmosphere becomes polluted with many negative feelings, and this prevents the healing and spiritual growth that a new cycle could bring. Often, the divorce becomes the couple's final chance to lash out at each other, to inflict a parting injury, to have the last say! Children who get caught up in the crossfire are doomed to sustain some injuries of their own as well.

"Generally, people divorce because of a discord of personalities and values, or insoluble material problems. However, a more positive reason for divorce is the need for each person in the marriage to grow spiritually beyond what the marriage can allow due to its natural limitations. Under the latter conditions, parting need not be a source of sadness or anger. The individuals may even remain good friends due to the bond of affection and understanding that has been established between them. Good will can always exist even when relationships end or change. Remember that we are dealing with Soul. The most important thing we can ever give another is good will, which is another name for divine love, the true energy of the universe!"

Then, very purposefully, the Adept stepped toward me with open arms. I felt myself being suddenly lifted out of this reality. When I next became aware of my surroundings, I found myself in the chair of my office. A stack of student papers sat neatly to one side. On it was a dark red flower which filled the room with a fragrance from another world.

CHAPTER FOURTEEN
The Way Home

The daffodils began to bloom in rapid succession. Bursts of yellow and white with orange, trumpet-shaped crowns shouted up and down my garden path. In the midst of them all, a few blue irises reached upward, stately and peaceful on their long stalks. March was changing its garment of grey rain and chilly winds into April's colorful wardrobe. The snails knew this, too. They appeared from their winter hibernation, or from whatever subphysical dimension they inhabited, to leave sticky trails along my wooden walkways.

It was time to "harden" the seedlings, now sporting the required four leaves, in the mild outdoor spring air. I set them on a square wooden area used in the summer to hold our outdoor barbeque grill. As I carried the last egg carton out of the enclosed patio, I saw her—Kyari Hota, bending gracefully over an uptilting blue iris, as much a beautiful flower as the one she was now admiring.

"Hello, Kyari," I said quietly, trying to avoid disrupting the calm mood of this scene.

"Good morning, daughter," she returned, straightening and turning to face me. Her almond eyes were like dark ponds in which colorful fish of the inner worlds might swim in eternity.

"I'm putting out my seedlings to harden them in the outdoor air," I offered, pointing to the egg cartons lined up like regiments of soldiers. "I wonder if they'll survive. I hope so."

"Do not hope, my daughter," smiled my teacher. "Intend. Then intention will magnetize the desired result toward you, and all the necessary steps along the way will be made clear."

I thought about this, then tried out the corrected attitude inside myself.

"I see what you mean," I said shortly. "It feels very different. It feels like a powerful connection between this moment and the future I've imagined—a connection between these seedlings and the mature plants full of flowers!"

"Yes," Kyari replied. "This connection you sense is Spirit itself, which is the binding force connecting all living things. But the connection is activated through intention. Spirit is like the wires strung all over your city to carry electricity to homes and businesses, and Spirit is also the electricity itself. But intention is like the switch at the power plant which sends the energy through the wires which connect the city. Without intention, dreams remain only potentials. With intention, they become realities!"

"Yes, I see!" I agreed. "Hoping for something to happen and creating it through intention is miles apart, isn't it?"

"It is," the Adept smiled.

"But Kyari, is creating through intention always best?" I queried, feeling for something that was vaguely forming in my mind. "What I mean is, can someone project an intention too aggressively?"

"Very good, daughter," the Adept said approvingly. "You are thinking ahead! The aggressive and the receptive both have their place, as well as their time, as you have seen through our previous discussions and experiences. Furthermore, there is always the issue of ethics—that is, whether your intentions would be ultimately harmful or beneficial to the whole. If, however, your ethics are good, you are free to use the spiritual forces to achieve your goals without concern. The description I will give you may be similar in some ways to the laws of manifestation. Yet the viewpoint I am presenting today is aimed at a higher spiritual level.

"First, you must begin with an intention toward a specific purpose. This activates the flow of Spirit, vitalizing the connection between you and whatever you desire in life. Since Spirit is intelligent, it will also connect you with all the large and small objects, incidents, people, and experiences which you need to reach your goal. Chances are that you will be able to consciously predict very few of these necessary intermediary steps. Logic and reason will not suffice. So it is here that the passive mode comes in handy. Intuition is the passive or receptive side which is a general openness to information coming straight from the higher awareness, or Soul.

"Intuition is passive because it involves the relaxing of the will, and an attitude of humility, love, and trust in a higher power to guide and care for your welfare. Look at the most intuitive people you know, and chances are you'll find people who have strong beliefs in God or a higher power, whether this belief is traditional or simply personal to themselves.

"Intuition comes from Soul, because Soul is that which has the three-hundred-sixty degree viewpoint—the awareness of the totality! With this awareness, Soul can know where you and your goals are in relation to the whole, and thus how best to navigate your way toward the desired end. It knows what obstacles lie in your path, and how to avoid or surmount them. It knows the easy route, and it knows the tools along the way which can help.

"To understand intuition, consider the example of migratory and other homing birds. Your scientists have experimented with taking these birds from their homes and releasing them thousands of miles away in strange lands. Somehow they return to their place of departure within a few short weeks of their release. The internal homing devices these birds have are genetic. That is, they are born with them fully functioning and do not need to learn the homing and navigating behavior.

"Scientists realize that these birds must be relating factors of time and space to achieve their navigational feats. However, the scientists do not understand the mechanism of this ability, since our own brains, which have billions of cells more than those simple animals, do not come close to being able to function in this way. Nor are our most sophisticated computers able to duplicate this instinctive ability."

"So what is their secret?" I asked, interested.

"What is their secret?" Kyari repeated. "It is simple. These birds' survival depends on their ability to navigate their way across vast distances. Thus, they are imbued with a kind of internal map in which they can locate both their present place and time, as well as the place and time of their destination, relative to the present. The migratory birds' sense of the whole allows them to travel to their goals, no matter how you attempt to dislocate them.

"Now a sense of the whole is a very important feature of the ability we are describing. Birds are thought to navigate via the stable features of the physical world such as the position of the stars and the planets, including our sun. These positions are changing, of course, but relative to each other they remain the same. These positions of space and time form patterns which become coded knowledge the birds inherit as their genetic heritage.

"Man's experience is both like and unlike these birds' experience in important ways. First, modern man is faced with so many distractors and superficially changing events that the eternal nature of the universe is often obscured. But like these migratory birds, man also has a home, a destination. This destination is the heart of God. Though man has come a long way from his true home, he can still return if he gives ear to his spiritual instincts, his inner heritage as a spiritual being.

"Man can navigate his way back home, just like the migrating birds, through his innate sense of the whole. To do this, he must listen for the heavenly music, the Voice of God. It will tell him where he is and when he is, relative to his goals. It will adjust automatically for every factor, both known and unknown, present, past, and future. The Voice of God is constant, changeless, and unerring, and if man would listen to it, ignoring the phantoms of the senses, mind, and emotions, he would eventually achieve his goal.

"Have you ever gazed in awe as a flock of migrating geese cuts through the sky? Did you look up with a strange longing welling up in you, a lonely restlessness which you could not name? If so, you have felt this call, the call to Soul. It can be perceived as a feeling, sensed as an idea, imagined as a picture, or simply heard as a sound. In all of these forms, it is still the Voice of God."

I could not say exactly what happened just then. To describe it in words gives it more reasonableness than it actually had when it happened. I was still standing there, listening to the Adept speak. She was looking at me, those brown eyes swimming with a life force which drew Soul deeper and deeper into itself.

Suddenly, and yet ever so slowly, the Unmani Dhun Adept appeared to change before my eyes. She became a beautiful swan with outspread wings. The swan was luminous. Light poured from its every feather more brightly than the sun or moon, but without the harsh glare of either. This vision filled my sight until it seemed as if my heart would burst from the agony of love and joy it inspired in me.

Then came the silent impression which spoke deep, deep in Soul.

"I am the Voice of God," it whispered. "I am the holy sound and the pure Soul who listens to its call. I am the teacher, and I am you."

With the last words echoing through my awareness, the vision faded away. Again, Kyari Hota stood there, smiling deeply into my eyes. Some moments passed which seemed like a long time.

"I . . . " I tried to explain what I saw, but the Adept stopped me.

"Hush, daughter," she said patiently. "There is no need to explain to me everything you have experienced—or to anyone else, either. Some things just are. They are gifts. A kiss from the Lord of Lords. Take it."

Then she turned away and sat down in a chair at the edge of the swimming pool.

"The weather has taken a decided turn toward warmth," she said, smiling. "It will be summer sooner than you think!"

"Oh, yes," I said, shaking off the strange feelings the vision had generated in me, and tucking its memory away in a safe place like a beloved treasure. I came to her and plopped myself on a cushion near her feet.

"Time itself seems to be moving faster than ever before," I murmured. "Is there some truth to this, or is it all subjective?"

"Time is not truly objective, my child. It can be measured and portioned, and that is objective enough. But the experience of time is a phenomenon which is relative, and therefore changeable. What is creating the speed-up you sense is that the anchor points of modern reality have shifted radically in recent times. Man is playing catch-up with these shifts, and so it always feels to him as if he were racing.

"A more dynamic life, fraught with more variables and thus more choices, is the fate of man today. The more man's inner nature is engaged and challenged, the faster time seems to pass, for his attention is not on the slow movement of physical changes, but on the lightning fast reflexes of thought, imagination, and emotion. Of course, in addition to greatly increased inner freedom, modern life has also picked up the pace of change in the physical world as well. Not all of these changes are positive. All in all, the result is a much different sense of time than just fifty years ago."

I dipped a naked foot tentatively into the still-chilly pool. I had worn garden sandals to bring the seedings briefly outside, so it was easy to slip the sandals off to explore the water.

"With all these changes and distractions," I began, stirring the water lazily, "isn't it harder for us to find our way back to God? I mean, spiritual students have the help of inner and outer teachers, but what about other people? I wonder, how do people who are not on a spiritual path begin to take the first small steps to their destination? How does Spirit reach them?"

"Every Soul has access to spiritual guidance," she answered, twirling the long stem of an oriental poppy she had plucked. "But I understand your question. How does Spirit reach people who are not yet ready to consciously choose spiritual goals?"

"Yes, exactly!" I said, pleased with this clarification of my less precise thoughts.

"Well, one way is through stories," she answered, her eyes twinkling mischievously.

"You mean like fairy tales and stuff like that?" I asked, already familiar with the concept of "teaching stories."

"Yes, daughter," Kyari replied mildly. "Stories are like dreams, and function similarly to reach Soul on an unknown basis. That is, Soul knows what the stories mean, but the mind with its censors does not. So the stories are accepted into the consciousness, where direct information about the spiritual laws would not be.

"These stories illuminate the spiritual anchor points by which Soul can navigate its way back home again. These anchor points are generally spiritual qualities such as love, faith, honesty, sacrifice, service, initiative, and so on. When enough of these anchor points are in place in an individual's life, he or she will begin consciously searching for the Teacher. The search always brings the Teacher, as it did for you."

"Yes, indeed," I agreed, delighted by the turn of this

conversation. "I remember how I loved to hear and read stories when I was little. Not all stories, just certain ones which seemed particularly powerful—ones that gave me a feeling that there was something noble and wonderful in the world after all. Something more than just eating, sleeping, and all those mundane things!"

"You learned from these stories quickly and easily, my child," said the Adept. "This is because you were ready for the Teacher, and only needed to have these anchor points restimulated, as it were. We were already with you, using every opportunity to bring you step by step into a conscious awareness of Soul! Do you remember the column of light in the woods by your house? You were six or seven."

"Yes, was that you?" I asked quietly, my eyes wide. It had been one of my most profound childhood spiritual exeriences, and one which I had not shared with anyone.

"That was Spirit," she replied softly, "the Master Power. Do you remember how the light of the sun at sunset slanted through the trees and fell in pools at your feet? You were terribly lonely. In your heart you felt abandoned, and your whole being cried out for love so that you might survive that painful existence."

"I remember," I replied. Even today, the loneliness of that time could still come back sharply as a physical pain in my chest.

"You walked aimlessly among the trees," she began speaking, as if telling me a story that began "once upon a time." "It was your favorite time of day and you were no lonelier there in the woods than in the house where you did not feel loved or understood. You listened to the birds singing in the trees, and crunched your bare feet on the sweet-smelling dried leaves.

"Then you saw the column of light—a strange, wide column that reached straight down from the skies! You thought, even then, that it was odd how it did not slant, as the other shafts of sunlight did. You stood staring up and into it. Somehow you found yourself inside its light. Do you remember?"

"Yes," I replied, quietly recalling the experience in its fullness. "I felt something wonderful."

"What was this you felt, dear one?" asked Kyari kindly.

"I felt the protection and unconditional love of God," I said without hesitation. "I didn't know this before! But now I realize that is indeed what I felt!"

171

"Yes, child," said the Adept. "That is what you felt. But until today you did not consciously know it. You see, through telling you this story again—your story—I have increased two-fold its power by changing it from an unknown to a known basis. Do you see this?"

"Yes!" I exclaimed, amazed and grateful. "The lonely child that I was knew and accepted God's love, but unknowingly. Now the sometimes insecure adult still does the same thing! But when I can understand my own stories, then I have both my experiences, and the power of my experiences, too!"

"Amazing!" Kyari grinned, affecting exaggerated surprise. "We'll make something out of you yet!"

I laughed in pure delight. "O.K., tell me some more stories then!"

"I will do that," she said, smiling obligingly. "I will select stories which I feel are most helpful for the purposes of illustrating the spiritual lessons of male and female. The first one I will give you is a familiar one—the story of Adam and Eve."

"Ugh," I grunted, but she ignored me and went on.

"I won't retell the story, never fear. The Western world knows it well enough. But the traditional interpretation of the church fathers is, of course, that man fell through Eve's sin. Eve disobeyed God's injunction not to eat the fruit from the Tree of Knowledge of Good and Evil. Man was the innocent, faithful servant of God, led astray by Eve. The serpent was the tempter, a representative of evil.

"But here is a different interpretation of the story from the eyes of the Unmani Dhun Adepts! The God of this story is not the true God, but only the Lord of the Negative Worlds, our friend the Shangra Raj! He reveals who he is by his very desire to keep man and woman in a state of ignorance of good and evil.

"After all, man in a state of ignorance is easily controlled. Obedience is his only response to authority, which he has no basis for questioning. Authoritarian figures have a vested interest in keeping people from experiences which can develop their individual faculties of discrimination. Good and evil are the polarities of all possibilities in the lower worlds, and thus another way of saying 'the experiences of life.'

"Eve's disobedience to God in accepting the apple shows the tendency of the female consciousness to reach out in blind faith and trust for new experiences which the more rational and cautious male consciousness normally avoids. It demonstrates the spiritual role of the female in opening up for the male inner doors to exploration and growth. The serpent is the symbol of the latent spiritual power that exists only at a raw level until transformed by experience and discrimination.

"Of course, religionists' attention on sex, which supposedly followed the eating of the apple, is a reflection of their particular hang-ups in this area. And their lamentation about the 'fall' that resulted from Eve's choice shows their lack of spiritual knowledge about the true purpose of this world of learning."

"Let me get this straight," I interjected. "You're saying the conventional idea that mankind 'fell from grace' is incorrect? That in fact the 'fall' was positive, not negative?"

"That's right," agreed Kyari. "But let me give you another example, and my point will be clearer later. Prometheus and Pandora is a Greek version of the Adam and Eve story. In this version, the initiative to make man more self-sufficient is taken by a male. Prometheus disobeys Zeus by giving mankind gifts such as fire, previously a selfishly guarded secret of the gods. Zeus punishes Prometheus by chaining him to a rock where a vulture eats his liver for eternity.

"Then, not satisfied with this revenge, Zeus creates Pandora, the first woman, and gives her as a gift to Prometheus' brother Epimethus. Zeus gives Pandora a jar, cautioning her not to open it. However, God has created Pandora with a strong sense of curiosity, so of course she disobeys and opens the jar. From the jar all the ills of the world fly out to plague mankind forever more!

"While Prometheus has come down to us as a benefactor of mankind, Pandora is generally regarded as a negative symbol for the female. She represents the dangers of idle curiosity and of rushing off blindly into the unknown. However sensible this might appear, it is wiser to take her character in the context of the whole story. This includes a selfish and vengeful god with the ultimate purpose of keeping man subservient to authority through ignorance.

"Both the Biblical and the Greek myths depict characters who plunge humanity into a world of experiences, tests, and trials which can raise man to the level of gods. The very crux of the problem in interpreting these stories is this last statement. Religions do not accept man's elevation to a god-like state as possible or desirable.

Thus, they perpetuate the position of Zeus and the Old Testament God, Yahweh, who wish to keep man safely 'in his place.'

"Perhaps woman is the figure used in these teaching stories, so badly misunderstood for centuries, because the female is the receptive consciousness. One of the hallmarks of a receptive consciousness is curiosity. Curiosity is in turn a sign of genius, which is the courage to go beyond what is already known or accepted, and almost always requires the breaking of mental taboos and fixed cultural patterns.

"On the other hand, another aspect of these stories is the sobering warning that the female receptive consciousness, if not balanced by judgment and discrimination, can lead the whole into error and setbacks. This can be forgotten only at the cost of great peril to us all!"

"I'm astonished," I huffed. "And to think all this time we women have accepted the 'bum rap' for causing all the woes of the world!"

The Adept laughed. "The 'woes of the world' cannot be hung on any one sex. Both men and women must bear responsibility for what they have created through either action or inaction, speech or silence. Simple people ask, 'Why does God allow evil in the world?' But a better question might be, 'Why does man allow evil?' A good parent maintains the order of his or her home, while giving children the freedom to make mistakes and grow. In the same way, God runs the universe according to spiritual laws, allowing Soul to learn by direct experience the ultimate value of love.

"So to sum up, my daughter, stories can tell you many spiritual truths when listened to with an ear that hears. Most interesting of all are stories of ordinary people who struggle with their own shortcomings, and who achieve wisdom through experience. After all, this is the continuing story of mankind. If we accept a vision of false heroism—the good man versus an evil outside power—we may never understand that the real 'battle' lies inside ourselves. We must, instead, acknowledge our own need for further development through the educative processes of life.

"Perhaps because woman knows that every joy on earth is a mixed blessing—that her beauty fades, that the promise of marriage becomes an everyday toil, and that children are gained only through pain and nourished at the cost of her body and her

174

independence—perhaps this is why she is more at home in the grey areas of life, and less likely to become a fanatic adherent to the illusion of good and evil, the hero and the villain.

"It is the feminine part which beckons you irresistibly to these grey areas, which constitute the threshold of the unknown. That movement is necessarily an ignorant one. To confront the unknown, it is not the rational, formularizing, systematizing viewpoint which is the best guide. Prior knowledge, as an accumulation of rational deductions and related facts, has limited relevance here. The only really helpful qualities are love and trust.

"Once the unknown is breached and the challenge begun, courage and perseverance through action, the male element, becomes the next important component. But most of our greatest gifts and triumphs begin with the one ignorant, trusting step we take into the unknown. Trust life, for life is only Spirit, and Spirit is love."

With that she disappeared into the mild daylight, her atoms mixing with the air.

CHAPTER FIFTEEN
The Eagle's Riddle

One day in mid-spring, the eagle came for me. It was there when I opened my eyes in the morning and did not leave my side. Its eyes followed me and under its constant, vigilant scrutiny, I felt a change in the tone of my inner life. What was this eagle, and where had it come from? Though I didn't fully know the answer, I guessed that it had been sent by the Unmani Dhun Adepts, who were sometimes called "the Eagles of Heaven."

I had not given much thought to this metaphoric title before. But now I discovered much similarity in the powerful gaze of this majestic creature of the air and the Unmani themselves. It was a look that penetrated and illuminated at the same time—a look both watchful and expectant. I found it impossible to think, imagine, or speak anything negative while I was in the eagle's company. It seemed to be the essence of the purity and greatness of Soul.

Days went by and still the eagle remained. Strangely enough, I soon began to feel more comfortable and relaxed in its presence. I began to feel as though we both inhabited some stronghold in a high place, a place both beautiful and lonely—an eagle's aerie of the spirit from which we could see for miles and miles. I no longer felt the old inner restlessness and impatience for change. Inside myself, I felt suddenly very solitary and far away, as if at the end of all change.

Then one day, after the eagle had been with me for a week, I closed my eyes for a short contemplation. I was expecting little more than a moment of relaxation, allowing Spirit to wash from me all the cares and tensions of a busy day. I focused inwardly on a blue light and visualized it flowing down from the God worlds, bathing my mind, emotions, and physical body.

Abruptly, however, another experience broke in—an unusual and startling one, even for the type of occurrences which had become routine for me lately. At first all I saw was the familiar head of an eagle staring at me with golden eyes. Then the scene expanded. I found myself standing somewhere in the inner worlds facing not one, but hundreds of eagles! Row upon row they ranged, in semicircles, as if perched in judgment of the Soul brought before them. I was that Soul, stunned by what I was seeing. What was the meaning of this experience? Why was I here?

Then a voice seemed to emerge from the majestic and frightening assembly. It was a strange voice, with a vibration oddly harsh, as if the speaker were unused to speaking.

"What is it that love and power have in common?" the voice asked, posing the question in the form of a riddle.

Despite my trepidation, I piped up confidently. I thought I knew the answer to this query.

"That is simple," I replied. "The thing that love and power have in common is detachment."

In the place where we were assembled, the atmosphere was charged with the stillness and silence of a powerful and restrained collective will. The golden-eyed creatures stared at me with something moving in their beautiful eyes. What was it? Compassion? Pity? Or was it simply their awareness of the truth?

The harsh voice rasped at me again.

"Yes, that is correct," it answered. "But knowledge is not enough. Now you must experience it."

That was all it said. As soon as the last sentence rang ominously in my mind, the scene vanished.

Something about this curious event and the riddle posed by the assembly of eagles made me vaguely uneasy. I went about my daily affairs, but always when I looked with the inner vision, the mysterious watcher was still with me. The feeling of elevation changed into a mood of foreboding. It soon spread into my daily patterns of work and thought. Under the relentless, clear eyes of my guardian, I began to question my life as a whole and ask myself if I had ever done anything which was not, at its heart, selfish.

Like a person stranded on some desert island, I was forced to face myself in painful, microscopic detail. I saw the festering sores of self-pity, sloth, vanity, and anger in the corners of my awareness where I never bothered to check. And the greatest humiliation of all was the realization that I was probably the only one who never noticed these things in myself.

Then one day, the weather became very warm. The sun was bright, and even a sweater over a long-sleeved shirt seemed almost too much to wear. I marveled how much like summer it felt, and determined that I would leave my unhappy self-recriminations behind in a carefree jaunt to the zoo. After a morning of teaching, I got in my car and drove the short distance to my destination. My spirits perked up immediately as I wandered among the snapdragons and pansies in full spring bloom, and the vivid flamingos with curved necks stalking through shallow water.

Here and there couples or single men or women with small children strolled, watching the animals. I sat on a bench, as captivated by the human variety as by the more exotic species behind moats and bars. Behind me, at the snack center, a father was buying his small daughter an ice cream. I observed his care in delineating her choices, and in unwrapping the frozen dessert after the choice was made.

After an hour's worth of strolling, past the jaguars restlessly pacing and the monkeys swinging from bamboo structures on man-made islands, I again sat on a bench to rest. In front of me was a large gorilla. It stared past me with tiny, human eyes. Its hair was black, and the hairless portions of its body were like thick leather.

"May I sit here?" asked a deep male voice above me.

I looked up, startled. It was a handsome, dark-haired man in sun glasses, with a closely trimmed, neat beard. He was wearing a white polo shirt and a pair of cotton khaki slacks. On his feet were a familiar pair of leather sandals. It was Haurvata Sampa!

"Why, certainly," I grinned. "Please sit down!" I could not have been happier if someone had told me I had just won a million dollars.

Haurvata took a seat and removed his glasses. We sat in silence for a moment. The Adept put his attention on the great ape before him and spoke low and soft. The beast looked quizzically at him at first, then settled into a profoundly attentive expression. Then, just as quickly as the ape responded, he stopped. Haurvata ceased speaking, and the beast lumbered off to pick at some leftover fruits attracting a bevy of flies.

"Well, dear one, I have been watching you," Haurvata began. "You seem disturbed of late, and yet you have not asked for assistance. I almost did not come, but there is much about which I must speak to you. The zoo was a good idea, and it has lifted your spirits."

"I hadn't noticed that I didn't call you," I answered, a little surprised. "I guess I had things on my mind. It's funny, but sometimes when problems start preying on me, I forget to ask for help. I know that's the worst thing to do—it's best to release the difficulty to Spirit. But I got to a low state so gradually, I just didn't see it, I guess."

"That is true," agreed the Tibetan. "But today you saw where you have put yourself, and determined to make a change for the better. So I have come to you."

"Thank you, Haurvata," I said, in sincere gratitude. Then I told him of my experience with the eagles.

"I will keep silent about what you are describing," he said. "It is an unusual experience, and one I do not wish to explain to you at this time. But do not fear it, my child. The eagles mean you no harm. You have intuited correctly much about them, and the rest must remain hidden until you can see the truth of it for yourself.

"Now the only thing I can add to what you already know is that you must surrender all areas of your consciousness to Spirit. It is trying to illuminate you as a whole person. In order to do this, it must bring to your attention all the darkest areas Spirit has not penetrated and purified as of yet. Your pride makes you unhappy at what you have found, yet your pride is the thing you must surrender most of all. Surrender pride, and the talons of the eagle will cause no pain, and leave no scars. Surrender to Spirit, my child! It is the only way!"

His words were warm with urgency, and yet this, too, he released at once. His next look was lighthearted, wrinkling the corners of his tremendous eyes like starpoints traveling off into

179

space.

"Today I would like to discuss with you something which has been on your mind to write for many years," he began, abruptly changing the subject. "It is about children."

"Children?" I asked, surprised. "Oh, but of course. I have always imagined writing a book about children. Did you know that? And lately, I have been wondering if this subject might have a place in this book about the sexes. Does it, Haurvata?"

"Aye," said Haurvata emphatically, nodding his great head.

I happened to glance at the ape, who was sitting in a pool of sunlight, delicately eating a banana. I smiled at this charming sight and Haurvata chuckled with me.

"The ape knows what is important," Haurvata said, smiling at his hairy friend. "It takes a little bit of Spirit, and a great deal of food to keep this one content in the physical body. And so it is with most people as well!"

I laughed out loud at this joke until beads of tears formed at the corners of my eyes. Haurvata waited until I had had my fill, and went on.

"Children, dear one, are the physical result of the sexual union of male and female. But they are more, too—they are the testing ground of our spiritual awareness. If we can learn truth, and apply it to ourselves, we should then be able to apply it to raising our children. This seems common sense, does it not?"

"Yet it doesn't work so smoothly in practice," I countered.

"True," nodded Haurvata. "The difficulty is that our children are spiritual beings with positive qualities, negative qualities, and needs created over lifetimes of sowing causes and reaping effects. It is difficult enough for adults to diagnose their own imbalances and administer its cures. But as parents, they must have insight into the spiritual needs of their offspring as well.

"Most of the time, parents treat their children as their parents have treated them. This is the reality behind the expression, 'The sins of the father are visited upon his sons.' It is not truly divine retribution in the Biblical sense, but simply the spiritual law of cause and effect at work. The spiritual consciousness of the family attracts Souls who are in harmony with it, or who can benefit in some way from experiences in that particular group. There is never any mistake where, when, and to whom one is born. All these factors are considered carefully when Soul chooses a body here in the lower worlds.

"However, as you know, cause and effect does not imply the idea of 'fate' as such. Even though a previously created cause might bring one to a particular experience, it is always possible and desirable to rise above the magnetic pull of any pattern. A Soul must have the strength of character to determine whether or not he or she will follow a given road, even one well-rutted by the wheelmarks of his or her forefathers. This struggle against the pull of negative patterns is what strengthens Soul for the upward flight into the heavenly worlds!"

"I know what you mean," I interjected. "Once, after trudging for miles with a heavy pack on my back, I reached my destination and put the pack down. Later on, I went exploring without the pack and literally bounded up the trails! I felt so light, I almost flew!"

"A good metaphor for negative patterns and the release from it," replied the Adept. He fished a bag of peanuts from a jacket slung over his shoulder and began to feed a small group of cooing pigeons.

"Now, child, it is possible for parents, if they work hard and sincerely at it, to rise above their previous conditioning and make a better life for themselves and their children. In your case, for example, you learned from the negative example of your parents who, unable to rise to their responsibility, abandoned you as an infant. You, in turn, fought the urge to abandon your own son as an infant when your marriage encountered difficulties. This urge in you was as strong as it was irrational because of this negative pattern in your family. Yet you fought it, and won!"

"Yes, Haurvata," I agreed. "It was difficult, but I made a conscious decision not to give in to that urge. I even remember the moment I realized what the pattern was! I was in a park riding a swing while my son played on a slide. I believe it was the motion of the swing that somehow jarred my realization loose. The motion was like a mother rocking a baby. I realized that I had never experienced this kind of nurturing. I never felt safe and secure. I felt incapable of giving my son something I never received myself."

"You analyzed the problem correctly," affirmed Haurvata. "Now whether or not a set of parents can rise above their respective patterns as you have done depends on their general spiritual development. But what they require, once they have determined to

181

make a change for the better, is some clear spiritual principles by which they can be guided. Here is where I believe we can be of some assistance!"

The Adept poked the air with his square finger to emphasize his point. Then, without a moment's hesitation, he launched into his description.

"The first idea parents must understand and accept is that their child is a spiritual being, Soul. It is neither male nor female. It is merely passing through a sexually polarized form to gather experiences and develop an awareness of, and commitment to, its own wholeness and divinity! Knowing this, parents must regard themselves as teachers first, and caretakers second. They must provide more of the spiritual food for their children, along with an adequate amount of shelter and material well-being.

"The oversupply of activities and material goods which characterizes the dream, if not the reality, of modern households does not replace what their children are lacking—spiritual training. I do not mean church service, my friend. I am speaking of passing on the eternal principles upon which life is founded—the reality of God's love, the survival of Soul, and the responsibility we have to all life as vehicles for Spirit.

"It is far easier for parents to fill their children's lives with things and events than with spiritual content. This is because parents themselves have not resolved their own unasked or unanswered questions about God and Soul, and are not prepared to teach their offspring.

"Ah, my friend," sighed Haurvata, "I have looked into the eyes of your children on earth and seen this spiritual hunger. They come into the physical world open to learning, but there is no one to teach them. Soon they harden, and a worldly look comes into their eyes. They close their hearts and minds to the heavenly worlds and cease to believe in anything but the cold realities of their physical senses."

"I've seen that look," I said, sighing with him. "It makes me sad."

"Ah, but it is all so unnecessary," Haurvata said, shaking his head. "And one does not even have to believe in the spiritual teachers to pass on these eternal truths!"

"What do you mean?" I asked.

"Everything that a child needs to learn to keep him or her open to Spirit can be taught through just these three things," Sampa replied. "They are: imagination, responsibility, and freedom. These are not metaphysical ideas, and anyone can apply them."

"Can you explain further?" I asked.

"I was about to," he smiled. "To teach a child imagination is simply to reinforce for him the reality of the inner worlds. A child comes into this world with his attention more inwardly directed than outwardly. He travels naturally back and forth between the heavenly worlds and the physical plane without any training. He perceives these inner regions through psychic and spiritual awareness. Then, slowly, he learns to adjust to the laws of this plane through his coarser physical senses.

"Imagination is not what the materialists believe," the Tibetan continued, brushing peanut shells from his pants with his wide hands. "It is not merely fantasy and wish fulfillment. Correctly used, it is a doorway into the inner reality. Therefore, by teaching a child that what goes on inside himself is real and valuable, you can preserve his link with the higher consciousness within him. All of your geniuses of the earth had this gift of imagination. From Beethoven to Albert Einstein, each knew that the key to all problem solving, all creativity, lay within the universe of the individual imagination."

"I see your point," I nodded, accepting a handful of peanuts from the Adept. "The creative people like the ones you mentioned all used day dreams and night dreams as ways of contacting the higher power. I read once that Elias Howe, the American inventor, was stuck on the design of the needle for his sewing machine. Manual sewing needles had the thread hole at the thick part, and Howe couldn't find a way of making this work on his machine.

"Then one night Howe dreamed that he had been captured by cannibals. They threatened to cook him if he couldn't solve the problem of his design. Then Howe saw the spears the natives were carrying. The spears looked like sewing needles, but with the thread hole at the pointed tips. He woke up and used this design to solve his problem!"

"Excellent example," nodded Haurvata. "It is a good story of how the expanded consciousness can assist man, if only man asks with humility for help!"

"Now what about freedom and responsibility?" I asked.

"Responsibility and freedom go hand in hand," said Haurvata. "It is impossible to talk about one without the other. Parents believe that a child will simply learn responsibility and freedom as part of the natural maturation process, much as they grow facial hair or breasts. But this is not so! Responsibility must be built up as carefully as one learns how to swing a bat correctly at a ball—step by step! Then freedom comes as a direct result of the conditioned ability of the individual to recognize and obey spiritual laws.

"The principle of personal responsibility begins with an awareness of attitude and attention. This awareness is established when the child realizes the significance of attitude and attention as inner actions. What do your Johnny and Mary spend their time thinking? What are their attitudes and beliefs about themselves and the rest of the world? Thoughts, attitudes, and beliefs are not idle soap bubbles that pop in the air. They are creative impulses that move out into the world and bring back tangible results!

"Now I will tell you how parents fail at teaching their children these three key principles!" said the Adept in a low voice. "First, they give their children attention for what they are doing wrong, instead of right. This focuses attention on problems and fixes them in place, instead of dissolving the problems by modeling for children the opposite and desirable virtues.

"Giving attention to problems also gives children a sense of failure early on. This sense of failure works, after a while, like the old idea of 'original sin.' It makes the child feel an innate sense of inadequacy and guilt which comes from seemingly nowhere, but which soon grows to permeate his whole life.

"The second error parents make with their children is telling them what to do instead of showing them! Everyone learns best by watching someone else do an action, then by trying to achieve the action himself. This is called mimicking or modeling by some, and works especially well with the addition of patient coaching.

"So if you would like your children to be polite and thoughtful, first you must be polite and thoughtful yourselves. Then you must put your children in situations where they can be polite and thoughtful, too. The occasion may be offering a guest something to drink, or writing a thank-you note for a gift. But it is not enough merely to give commands! You must put the tools in their hands and stand by ready with friendly assistance while these actions are being done.

"The last error I will describe is one most relevant to our ongoing discussion of the sexes. Parents fail by acting too much out of their sexually polarized biases! To cite the worst examples, men are too impersonal and uncommunicative. They model for their children a dangerous lack of self-knowledge and misunderstanding of subjective realities. Men also tend to be arbitrary with their discipline and decision-making. This communicates authoritarianism—might makes right. It perpetuates the idea of male dominance and promotes the idealization of power.

"Women, on the other hand, are too coddling and weak-willed when faced with the need for teaching and disciplining children with real spiritual needs. Drug problems, for example, do not suddenly appear when a child is an adolescent. Such serious negative choices have their roots in earlier neglects in a child's upbringing. Women must stop believing that a nutritious meal and a hug will cure most things. Since women are generally better attuned to their children's subjective states, they bear a great responsibility. This responsibility is to help their children correct their spiritual weaknesses to prevent them from later becoming the victims of their own defects!

"Parents who are dominated by the male ideal of the family generally feel that their proper role is control and authority. Parents who are influenced more by the female current tend to believe that their role is love. But neither will answer the needs of children as long as the real spiritual role of parents is not fulfilled. This role is to be spiritual guides and teachers. It is a role which requires patience and compassion. It is beyond control and authority. It is even beyond human love. Do you know what this role requires most, my child?"

"It is detachment?" I asked tentatively, suddenly recalling the eagles' riddle.

"Yes, my friend," replied Haurvata seriously. "You have the correct answer. Detachment is not a lack of concern or feeling for others, nor an intellectual kind of coldness. It is the ability to remain unmoved by outer events and conditions, while centered in Soul. Detachment results in the freedom to choose one's thoughts and actions in the moment, and the power to always see truth and act with love. Cultivate detachment and your path through life will be paved smooth, and laughter and understanding will be your

185

companions.

He peered at me keenly. "Do you grasp what I am saying?"

"I believe so," I said, sighing. "I knew the answer to the eagle's riddle, yet I lacked the experience of it. I attained a wonderful state of awareness but couldn't keep it because I was not detached. The increased spiritual current caused me to see many new truths, but these included faults I had, as well. This triggered the reaction that sent me spiraling downward in spirits. Now I know how great an impact a slight shift of attitude can make in one's spiritual growth. I don't pretend to understand detachment, Haurvata, but I think it had better be my next project, right?"

The Adept just winked. "Never fear. Your progress is good, despite an occasional regression. The only important fact is that you are learning. For example, you are handling things very well with your son's entry into his teen years—a trying time for most parents! The reason for the difficulty has greatly to do with the male and female currents."

"Oh! It hadn't occurred to me," I exclaimed.

"You see," he began, "the release of hormones during puberty does more than stimulate the development of secondary sex characteristics. These hormones also trigger—for the most part, anyway—a boy's or girl's inner identification with his or her sex. A boy starts to become aware of himself as a male, a girl of herself as a female. This is necessary, of course, but like most things on the physical plane, it often goes to extremes.

"The danger is that girls and boys will become too greatly polarized into female and male identifications and lose their wholeness. In fact, this is mostly what happens to a great number of youth, particularly in a culture where masculine and feminine extremes are often encouraged. Taking drugs or alcohol, speeding in cars, fighting, and other kinds of antisocial behavior by boys are symptoms of this polarization. They are simply asserting their male dominance over the civilizing, controlling tendencies of society, which is a feminine force."

"Oh, I get it," I interjected. "Girls, on the other hand, become obsessed with relationships, both female friendships and boy-girl romances. They tend to spend their lives daydreaming, fantasizing, talking on the telephone, and being beset by moods. But what's most interesting to me is the fact that girls at this stage often become very

186

self-conscious and even self-effacing about their abilities. They can start doing poorly in school. I even read that girls' math scores are on par with boys until this age. After that, they take a real nose dive!"

"Yes," agreed Haurvata. "This happens because girls instinctively begin to see their worth 'in relation' to another—be it friends or a boyfriend—and less in terms of what they achieve as a single individual. Their falling math scores indicate a withdrawal from competing with boys, a way of showing submission."

"But is this good?" I frowned.

"Natural, but perhaps unbalanced," smiled the Tibetan. "Male and female development during puberty is recognized by everyone as a charged period physically and psychologically. Yet few people think of this as a spiritual issue as well. It is a spiritual issue because up until now, the individual has been more balanced between his male and female currents. This is what makes the child under twelve so delightful to adults. The term 'childlike' was invented for this pre-adolescent group, not for teenagers!

"But during puberty, a split occurs in most individuals. Boys put aside their feminine aspects, while girls put aside their masculine aspects, some more decidedly than others. Eventually, some of the balance is restored, but few are anything like the free and complete people they used to be as children. Most think of this as an inevitable component of adulthood. But I say differently. For most of what is lost with childhood is lost because of this male-female fragmentation!"

"Wow!" I whistled. "That's a pretty serious statement. I'm really going to have to think about that."

"Do that," replied the Adept. "And while you're thinking about it, ask yourself the reason for the saying, 'Unless you become as little children, you will not enter into the kingdom of Heaven.'"

"You mean that children are whole," I said thoughtfully, "because their male and female aspects are in balance? So we must work toward that balance as adults if we want to experience the higher consciousness! Is that it?"

"Congratulations!" laughed the Adept. "Of course, this is not to say that balancing the male and female forces is all a person must do to enter the heavenly worlds. But it is certainly crucial to accessing the inner qualities to make the journey. To put it more concretely, an individual needs the receptive state of the female and the boldness of the male to accomplish this goal. Without both, one is bound to fail."

"O.K.," I said, "I believe you."

"Now," began Haurvata, taking a deep breath, "you passed through some perilous times with your son in the last few months. You asked for help and help came, as you remember. This was due to your trust in Spirit. As you've learned, one's relationship with Spirit is always reciprocal. Spirit gives as much as you expect to get. At any rate, you saw correctly that you must let go of your emotional identification with your son. It was difficult, but you did it. And your approach has worked well for you."

"You know," I commented, shaking my head, "I didn't even realize I was so attached to him. But I think I understand the experience now."

"Go ahead," smiled the Adept. "Tell me."

"Well," I said, "I believe I had been unconsciously identifying with my son as my male half. When he reached puberty, however, he suddenly began to assert himself negatively in an attempt get me out of his psychic space. It came as a shock to me. I blamed him, and he was, in fact, pretty awful! Nevertheless, I had to look past his superficial behavior, recognize him as a separate individual, and accept him on that basis. The old relationship was no longer appropriate. We needed a fresh start."

"Good work," said the Adept approvingly. "That's it exactly. By the way, the same kind of thing happens between fathers and daughters, too. The father has been identifying with his daughter, idealizing her as his female half. Then she turns from him to boys! The father feels spurned, rejected. He can react violently, trying harder to control her as she tries desperately to break free. Let me also say that a lot in parent-child opposite sex closeness is natural and healthy for children. But adolescents have mostly absorbed this closeness already, and now need the space to be themselves."

"Hmm," I mused. "So it's not as hard on mothers and daughters, or fathers and sons?"

"It can be hard," corrected the Adept, "but not in the same way. We are speaking here of a male-female pattern between parents and their children. Mothers and daughters, fathers and sons can develop ego-based, competitive problems. But they aren't characterized by a 'break,' and they don't generate the amount of emotion that mother-son and father-daughter relationships do.

"Now I want you to understand this: This 'break' is necessary, but can be constructive, not destructive, to a parent-child relationship. It is ideally the beginning of a new cycle, one based on a more peer level of communication and freedom. Thus, a parent accustomed to using authority as a way of controlling a child will have the most difficult time when that child hits adolescence. He or she must step back and recognize that the child must cultivate his or her inner authority and establish internal controls.

"This doesn't mean that limits can't be set," added Haurvata. "But even this should be done in an even-handed and reasonable manner. Arbitrariness is simply authoritarianism in one of its guises. Thinking one can control an adolescent by edicts and threats is absolute folly! It is a losing battle every time. Either you break their spirit, or you alienate them completely. If you alienate them during this period, you have declared a war which will not end until they move away. In their twenties or older, some children make peace with their parents, but for many the hard feelings linger on."

"It's a scary thought," I murmured.

"Indeed," agreed the Tibetan sympathetically. "That is why I am telling you. So that you can tell others. After all, people want to do the right thing, but sometimes they do not know what that right thing is. The spiritual solution is the last thing they seek! But it will do the trick every time, don't you agree?"

"I sure do," I grinned. "In my case, I've changed my old ways and opened myself to something new. Actually, I'm finding that I like my son even more than when he was a child!"

"Ah, that's the point, isn't it?" said the Adept. "Too many parents look back on childhood as the golden years. This shows that they are attached to their roles as parents even more than they love their children. Parenthood should be an investment, not in roles, but in people. When children mature into adults, parents receive a second gift in rediscovering their children as friends!"

He clasped his hands behind his head and closed his eyes, enjoying the sunlight that bathed his rugged face in warmth. "Thank you," I said, then rose from the bench and slowly walked away. He was still there, his long legs stretched out before him, when I turned to look for the last time.

CHAPTER SIXTEEN
The Blue Heron

Linda Morris had had a baby. He was a beauty—a lusty boy, nearly twelve pounds at birth. The child, named Benjamin after Linda's great-grandfather, was perfectly formed and alert. His round, grey eyes followed you everywhere, and his smile could light up a room. I had visited Linda and the baby in the hospital just two days after he had been born. Vic, Linda's husband, was also there. We had chatted amiably for an hour before I left, discussing parenthood and the miracle of birth. I held Benjamin for a moment, reminiscing over the precious time when my own son was also that small. It already seemed several lifetimes ago.

Today, three weeks later, I was getting ready to pay the Morrises another visit. Vic had taken his accumulated vacation time to stay at home with Linda and Benjamin. Over the phone they still sounded excited but exhausted as well from the regimen of nightly feedings, constant diaper changing, and the colicky discomfort that set their son to nonstop crying. I could tell, also, how surprised they were that dealing with an infant was such a challenge for them. They were both bright, well-educated people from loving families. Yet nothing in their backgrounds or their childbirth classes had prepared them for the realities of parenthood!

I grabbed my car keys and handbag. I gulped down the last drops of tea on my way out the door. Then, suddenly, there she was!

"May I come along?" she asked, her face lit up in a pleasant smile. It was Kyari Hota, her head peering around the corner of the family room near the front door.

Choking and trying to speak at the same time, I succeeded only in guttering words and coughing loudly.

"Oh! Sorry," she exclaimed, patting my back. "I didn't mean to startle you. I assume you're aware of me when I'm around. But it doesn't always work that way, apparently."

"No it doesn't," I replied, still coughing. "Of course, I am always happy to see you. But how am I supposed to predict when you'll go 'poof' and suddenly be here?"

I gestured wildly with my arms.

"Well," she said thoughtfully, "you could try paying closer attention to what's going on in here."

She tapped a spot on her forehead and smiled kindly.

"O.K.," I relented, finally taking good notice of her appearance. She was wearing a tan wool skirt, a red sweater, and looked a little like a perky high school cheerleader. All she needed was a letter emblazoned on her chest.

"You know where I'm going, I take it?" I asked, resigned to the prospect of bringing an Unmani Dhun Adept with me on a social call.

"To see Linda's baby," the Adept shrugged, rather nonchalantly. "And since you're going to ask me anyway, I'll tell you why I'd like to come along. First of all, I do like babies. But more importantly, I believe this experience might trigger some things to put in your book. Are you game?"

"Why not?" I replied. "But what shall I tell Linda and Vic about you?"

"Oh, I don't know," Kyari returned. "You'll think of something!"

We climbed into my car and headed out to the suburbs where the Morrises lived. It was a beautiful neighborhood, full of the remnants of orchards and undeveloped acreage. At this moment, the cherry trees were covered in delicate pink blossoms. A dappled grey, swaybacked horse tore at the grass in a nearby field.

Linda and Vic met us at the door. I decided to introduce Kyari

Hota as a friend from school, since passing her off as a relative could get complicated in the future. We had some drinks and snacks at the breakfast table and tiptoed in to see the sleeping infant. As soon as we walked in the door, however, Benjamin woke up with a loud wail.

"That's O.K., I'll hold him," I found myself saying.

We retired to the family room and chatted leisurely for about an hour. During that time, Benjamin was passed back and forth between the four of us, and he was changed twice by his mother. I noticed how easily Kyari harmonized with our little group, how naturally she talked and put everyone at ease with her presence. By the end of the visit she nearly had me convinced she was not the strange being called an Unmani Dhun Adept, but just a sweet, intelligent woman called Kari, my friend from college.

We drove home slowly. Kyari, clearly pleased with the day's events, told me to drive along the river. Then, at a spot offering a tremendous view encompassing several miles of flowing water, white sand, and rocks, she bade me to stop. I pulled over and got out of the car. A narrow trail led down to three large boulders and a stretch of sand. We both picked our way along the trail and sat on the boulders, silently enjoying the endless flow of water to the sea.

"Well, daughter, what did you learn today?" Kyari asked, her eyes squinting into the glare of the sun reflecting from the water.

"I don't know what you mean," I answered frankly. "I don't think I learned anything in particular. What did you have in mind?"

The Adept skipped a rock across the water. It bounced six times. I looked at her with new respect.

"What did you notice about the baby?" she asked.

"The baby?" I repeated, surprised. I hadn't noticed anything in particular about the baby. "Hmmm. He was cute. He was big . . . He was wet."

Kyari laughed. "I can see that I'm going to have to take the initiative today. So here goes. I'd like to bring up the subject of personal space and spiritual surrender. You see, a baby is a good example of both of these principles. I believe this discussion will tie in nicely with Haurvata's discourse on children from a week ago."

"I'm ready," I said neutrally. "But what's our definition of personal space?"

"Don't you know the answer to that yourself?" she chided.

"Personal space is our own individuality," I offered. "I've

always thought of it as my privacy as a person."

"Correct," she said. "Personal space is the individual's sense of 'I.' It can be physical, as when you touch someone who doesn't like it. When this happens, you can be said to be violating his physical space. On the other hand, personal space can mean something less material, as when you offer unwanted advice or tell someone how they should worship God. The latter is an example of an intrusion which is psychic."

"I understand," I responded. The concept was a familiar one.

"When an infant is born, its sense of 'I' develops slowly in relation to several factors. One of these factors is dependency versus independence. Obviously, a tiny infant is totally dependent on others. However, if the adults around him satisfy his needs, he learns to feel secure and comfortable in the physical body. He develops the sense that he has control over his environment. It is a false sense of control, in a way, but for the time being, it works.

"The tricky part of parenting is providing the child's needs for security while slowly teaching him to enlarge his sphere of real independence. It is easy to move too fast and force independence on a child before he is ready. This early forcing will generally backfire, and cause the child to cling even more fearfully to his previous sources of security. It is also easy to move too slowly and keep a child dependent long after he is capable of doing for himself.

"How do these states of dependence and independence affect the child's sense of 'I'? As the child's sphere of independence grows, he increases his confidence in being able to 'cause' his own life. Even within the parameters of his parents' and society's rules and structures, he sees that he can mostly get what he wants, and that situations mostly work out to his benefit.

"As an adult, such an individual has a healthy sense of 'I.' He accepts the idea that, generally speaking, life can be counted on to respond to his desires and his efforts. Therefore, when it does not happen in this way, it is relatively easy for him to make allowances for these exceptions. He has a realistic notion of what he can control and what he cannot, and is philosophical about situations beyond his influence.

"Now an adult who has been either catered to by his parents, or neglected by them, will often have problems with his sense of 'I.' He may have difficulty being confident of his ability to manifest life, or anxiously try to control life's events in an unrealistic manner. In either case, he will tend to view others as sources of satisfaction or obstructions to his desires, and treat them as such. His sense of 'I' will tend to remain at or revert back to his infantile stage—the state of dependency on other people.

"Of course, no child actually comes into a lifetime without some sense of 'I-ness.' Every individual has a particular 'I-ness' built up over the accumulation of lives he has lived, both male and female. But my point here is that physical experience can shape a Soul's sense of 'I' to a great extent. Only the strongest Souls can rise above the most negative of upbringings and assert their 'I-ness' in the face of opposing forces.

"Love, however, builds a strong aura around a Soul's sense of 'I,' " she said, standing up and moving toward the edge of the water. "It forms a shield which is the positive spiritual force. This shield of love repels the negatives of life from the individual. This, my daughter, is the reason for the absolute necessity of love in everyone's life! Without love, you are like a fish out of water. Just as a fish needs water to breathe, move and survive, so every living Soul needs love. Love protects, builds, and uplifts the individual. And we owe every single ensouled form on earth this unconditional love!"

"I see," I interjected. I was finally starting to get interested. "The way you put it, love is sort of like a spiritual immune system. A strong aura of love will help keep out most negative experiences, and neutralize any that manage to get in! Is that the idea?"

"That is right," the Adept nodded, turning to look at me with shining eyes.

"And so, in a way, love is as essential to everybody as air!" I exclaimed, tumbling down from my perch. "I never thought of love in that way before. It puts a different light on it altogether. I'll have to contemplate upon this some more."

Now my thoughts began to form quickly.

"Is I-ness the same as the ego?" I asked, trying to compare these statements to theories I'd learned from psychology.

"Yes, in a way," answered the Adept. She had smoothed a spot on the sand and had sat down.

"The ego is another name for the sense of 'I,' and every spiritual student needs to realize its importance for unfoldment. Some so-called spiritual people will tell you that ego is bad. But this is nonsense! Ego is Soul in the human consciousness being aware of itself as a separate entity in the world. Only through a healthy ego can any individual begin to become self-realized as a spiritual being, as Soul!"

"I think I know why that's so," I offered. "When your ego isn't strong enough, you let too many other people into your space. You get confused trying to please everybody and in the end, you wind up not really knowing how to please yourself. That's it, isn't it?"

"That's it," agreed Kyari. "I might also add that this description fits more women than it does men. And that is why women are more dissatisfied in this life than men. Women are taught to please others first, not themselves. Pleasing yourself entails first knowing yourself. So most women shortchange themselves spiritually as well as materially by their lack of strong egos. They do not protect and develop the integrity of their personal space.

"Women therefore fight a special battle with this factor of inner confidence. And all men who have the female aspect strongly developed in them do as well. Just think for a moment of the kind of topics that creep frequently into women's conversations, and you will find that a great deal of it centers around personal troubles. This kind of conversation makes women feel good temporarily, but they pay a price for this indulgence. Negative empathy places women's attention on their fears and limitations, and the spiritual power drains from them! Women may not wish to hear this, nevertheless it is true."

"But I've always thought that it's a good idea for women to talk to each other about their troubles," I interjected. "The fact that men generally don't seems to me a weakness, rather than a strength."

"Ah, yes," she said, nodding. "Men do not talk about personal problems because their 'masculine code' forbids it. And this 'code' is based on the intuitive knowledge that the indiscriminate airing of private difficulties only breeds more of the same. Men have been more familiar with personal power in the last thousand years. So they know that they can lose their edge when they reveal their weaknesses. Thus, men refrain from this practice because it could cost them their confidence and their livelihoods, too!

"Furthermore," she continued, "men are action-oriented. Therefore, when men discuss a problem, they are more likely to be doing so with the intention of finding and acting upon a solution. Of course, the proverbial complaining drunkard at the bar is an exception to this generalization! Women, on the other hand, can discuss their problems for years with no real intention of doing anything about them. They apparently get enough of a release just talking about their problems with their friends.

"A great number of both men and women who talk about problems are not sincerely searching for workable solutions. They are emotionally tangled up with others and find it hard to extricate themselves, despite the fact that these very people are causing them grief and pain. Many fear change too much to try to direct their own lives for the better! The talking only gives them the illusion of changing something without the responsibility for change through thought, planning, and action. Thus, negative talk is the sugar pill of the troubled."

"O.K. Sometimes discussing problems is pretty useless," I admitted. "But all of it can't be bad. Don't you believe that men would benefit from more openness about their inner states? It still seems to me that their emotional uncommunicativeness is sometimes a real straightjacket!"

I saw her nod. "Yes, men can be too closed to exposing their own vulnerabilities. Some admission of weakness and fear is healthy for everyone. Actually, though, women don't really want men to own up to being weak and fearful. It only makes them more afraid. This would destroy women's myth that others around them are stronger than they are, and can take care of them. What women are really saying when they complain about men not opening up is that they want men to need and appreciate them more, and express it more openly. This is a real, legitimate desire, and a constructive request. But if women want men to open up their feelings, it is only fair that they be prepared for all sides of it."

"Frankly, this discussion is making me uncomfortable," I complained. "I don't know what I'd do if I couldn't occasionally unload my problems into somebody's sympathetic ear. In fact, just the other day, I went to lunch with one of my girlfriends. We talked for two solid hours about various things, and sure, that included our problems. Was that so bad?"

"Did it help?" asked Kyari coolly.

"Sure," I shot back.

"How are you feeling now?" she asked gently.

"Now?" I repeated. Not too good, I thought. But this was not something I wanted to admit.

"Fine," I lied instead.

"All right," she smiled. "Then the only thing to add is this. Sharing one's thoughts and feelings is one strong basis for friendship and companionship in this world. Like all good things, however, it can be abused. The sharing can be based either on sympathy or on compassion. There is an important spiritual difference between the two. Talk that generates sympathy opens up the sympathizer to the emotional and mental state of the person with the problem. A harmony of vibrations is established between the two. So, if the problem is anger, it won't be long before the sympathizer finds himself acting out this emotion himself, or carrying around some vague and unexplainable feeling of upset with the world.

"Now compassion is very different from sympathy. Compassion is the aspect of the Holy Spirit referred to by the term 'the Comforter, the Prince of Peace.' Compassion contains within it wisdom, patience, humility, and kindness. The only way for compassion to exist, however, is for one to recognize all other people as spiritual beings. Then we will be able to see people's troubles in the context of their ultimate growth and give them the love and psychic space to go through their necessary lessons. Compassion, by the way, is a spiritual quality, and not particularly a trait of male or female. Sympathy or empathy—the emotional identification with other people's negative inner states—on the other hand, is typically feminine. That is, the feminine current in both sexes, not just females in particular."

"O.K.," I said grudgingly. "I understand what you're saying to me. I guess I needed to hear this. I've indulged in the very kind of negative talk you're describing, and I guess I'm paying the price. My friend was talking about her marriage. She doesn't really love her husband but is staying with him because she fears being out on her own. For his part, he puts up with her but, understandably, he isn't thriving. Personally, I think they are both spiritually suffocating, but neither feels free to leave."

"Everyone's first responsibility is to his own inner growth, my child," said the Adept softly. "That seems like a selfish ideal, but it is not, since each person's inner growth touches us all. This is the spiritual ideal, which conflicts with the social code planted in most people's consciences. In practice, the spiritual ideal means that we have an obligation to choose our friends and mates wisely before we link our lives with theirs. But if we make a mistake, we are free to change it, doing so with love and compassion. To put it in a nutshell, we have no right to hurt others deliberately; but we also have no right to prevent another's pain. Pain is not the worst evil, dear one, as you know! And pain is more often than not the precursor of enormous spiritual growth."

"I think I can explain why empathy is such a common trap for women," I offered.

"Go ahead," encouraged Kyari.

"I think . . . I think women put their attention on negative emotions out of habit," I began. "I believe this has its roots in the negative images we've stored about ourselves. We believe, consciously or subconsciously, that we may be limited, so we don't try very hard to achieve great things—especially anything outside women's traditional roles. Men, on the other hand, are taught from the cradle to believe that they can achieve anything. Until now, women haven't had the same privilege. We don't adopt stirring ambitions. Our goals are often small. Mostly, we want to avoid pain and suffering and have a modest kind of personal happiness."

"Exactly," the Adept agreed. "But avoiding pain and suffering is actually a negative goal. And one cannot be motivated to achieve a negative goal. This is why you can't break a habit by saying to yourself, 'DON'T SMOKE.' You'll just wind up smoking more. But say instead from Soul, 'Enjoy breathing freely. Appreciate the taste of food,' and the body, mind, and emotions will more likely cooperate with you.

"If women are to become fully realized, they must learn to take on greater ambitions than just interpersonal happiness and the avoidance of pain! It is not well known, yet the fact is that more people fail due to the smallness of their goals rather than to the grandiosity of their goals. Men have succeeded more than women up until now partly because they have been free within society to 'dream big.' 'Dreaming big' called up the full resources of their hearts, minds, and souls!

"Women must also contribute their dreams to a new and better vision of society. The value they place on interpersonal bonds, community, and cooperation is essential now to balance the tendency for the world to sink under the weight of competition and mutual suspicion. The female side must supply an alternate vision, and then work hard to make the male element in society take it seriously. If it does not succeed, your planet may simply not survive."

"You know," I mused, thinking about my own lifelong battle with self-confidence, "I grew up never knowing what I was going to do with my life, and nobody ever even asked me about it."

"Luckily you had some obvious, innate abilities which you pursued, leading to your becoming a teacher and a writer," said Kyari. "It is often even more obscure and unsatisfactory for others. Parents, of course, differentiate their efforts to shape their children's egos along sex lines. They consciously try to make their sons independent and to set and achieve goals. They put sons in challenging situations, whether it is a team sport or an accelerated academic program, and encourage their male children to face their fears and weaknesses.

"On the other hand, these aggressive skills are much less emphasized for girls. Instead, female children are given greater reinforcement for being helpful, neat, polite, attractive, and avoiding conflict. Notice that most of these virtues are oriented to pleasing others and maintaining the status quo. Challenge, risk-taking, and surmounting obstacles thus figure less in the upbringing of females than of males. Females are not encouraged to be heroic and face the dragons of their inner and outer lives.

"Because of this difference in their early conditioning, girls grow up 'other' oriented, whereas boys grow up 'self' oriented. In other words, girls think of themselves 'in relation to' others. Their sense of self includes others in their personal space. Thus, a woman's self-worth is often tied into intimacy with a man, or affiliation with her friends, family, or children. This is why women are so concerned with friendships, marriage, and family relationships! Relationships are tied in with their sense of 'I.'

"Men, on the other hand, have a more exclusive sense of self. They generally depend less on relationships with others for a sense of 'I.' Their egos are more involved with their jobs, careers, sports, hobbies, or other interests with which they have a direct cause and effect relationship. This is because men by and large build their egos upon setting and achieving goals."

I thoughtfully drizzled sand through my fingers.

"What are you thinking, dear one?" Kyari asked softly, gazing into the line of trees along the opposite shore.

"Oh, I guess I'm thinking that women have really been given the short end of it," I answered. "We've accepted it because it goes along with our basic empathetic, people-pleasing instincts. I don't want to sound like . . . like a neo-conservative or something . . . but what if all you're saying merely points out that our traditional sex roles are correct? I mean . . . well, what if this is the way it's supposed to be?"

Kyari laughed. "You aren't the first person to have considered such a thought! It is certainly true that, for the most part, traditional sex roles provide the path of least resistance for many men and women today. These traditional sex roles have their basis in history. Women, after all, have less muscle mass than men, and are especially vulnerable during pregnancy and childrearing. In the more brutal times of our ancestors, a woman had to be subservient to males to ensure that she and her offspring would survive, instead of being killed by the stronger males. Her very existence depended upon paying close attention to other people's needs! Today, most primate societies continue to function along these lines.

"However, mankind's evolutionary needs are changing. It is no longer biologically adaptive for men to be strong and dominant and women to be meek and subservient. In fact, quite the opposite is true! The human race has exhausted the productive potential of the male-dominant model of civilization, and even before that, of the female-dominant model. We have seen the excesses and failures of both. The modern world desperately needs a new paradigm from which to explore its expanding universe if civilization is to survive, and even evolve further. This is what our collaboration with you on the male and female forces is all about. Have you not understood this yet?"

I stared at her a long moment without speaking. Her words were sharp, and pointed out to me that something was indeed not getting through. True, some progress had been made. But for whatever reason, I had slipped into an attitude of emotional lassitude and defeatism. From this self-negating realm, it was difficult to fully accept the weighty role which I had been assigned. I felt confused and rather stupid. I was in way over my head!

The Adept saw my reaction and spoke quietly and soothingly. "Don't feel badly. Everything will be clear to you in time. I know this is all rather overwhelming."

I shrugged, trying to be nonchalant. "I'll be O.K. Just keep going."

But for the first time that day, I began to admit to myself how low I had been feeling. Tears filled my eyes and I let them roll down my cheeks. A slight breeze fanned my face and chilled the wet places where the tears had left their trails.

"Do you wish to speak of what you feel?" asked the Unmani Dhun Adept.

She had come up beside me and stood a few feet away. We were facing the water which was rushing soundlessly by.

"All right," I answered, wiping my face with my hand. "It's hard to even put it into words. It's like a feeling of hopelessness about my teaching, my writing, everything. Nothing's going that badly. But I start thinking really negative things anyway, like—What's all this for? It will never amount to anything! None of my efforts have ever amounted to a hill of beans! Why even try?"

Kyari was silent for awhile. I could see her looking across the water as if at something far away. When she finally spoke, her voice was soft and low.

"Surrender, my daughter," she said. "It is the only way."

Surrender? Then Haurvata's voice came into my mind, the same urgent phrase.

"Tell me about surrender, then," I said unhappily. "I can think about it, but I don't know how to do it. I just don't understand what it is."

"Very well," said the Adept. Her tone had a calming effect on my troubled spirit. "Spiritual surrender is loosening the hold of mind and emotions on the sense of 'I.' It means allowing Spirit to enter into your personal space and illuminate you as a whole being. Henceforth you will be a non-personal person. That is, your existence will be free of the limitations of a personal ego, and will be instead a center for the forces of God to flow out into the world. You will become like a magnifying glass focusing the rays of the sun. Like the glass, you of yourself will do nothing. But as a vehicle for Spirit, you will concentrate the spiritual forces through your individuality, which will be a creative center for manifesting positive action in the lower worlds.

"Surrender is all this, my child," said the Adept, "but I will also tell you what it is not. Surrender is not giving up the ego in its normal functioning. It is not becoming a medium for spirits or an empty conduit for a rag-bag crew of astral plane derelicts to use for mischievous purposes! It is not passivity to one's own welfare or the welfare of others. You do not surrender common sense and responsibility by surrendering to God. You only surrender that which is holding you back from your own divinity."

"Surrender is like detachment, isn't it?" I mused, recalling the eagles' riddle.

"That is correct," affirmed the Adept. "Surrender leads to detachment from the results of your actions, and thus gives you true freedom and the ability to wield both love and power. It is the highest of spiritual actions you can take. And it is the primary lesson you are back on this plane to learn.

"And now, dear one, this is as good a time as any for me to speak to you about the self-negating attitude which is causing you so much pain. I will tell you the plain truth. This attitude is not humility. It is ego. It is exaggerated attention upon yourself, overblown expectations, and constant critical evaluation. One day you're on top of the world, the next day you're on the bottom. Neither is objective.

"If you do not establish a better foundation for yourself, you will be too vulnerable to the vicissitudes of life. You will be too easily inflated by success, and crushed by defeats. Detach yourself from your fear of failure, and you will fall naturally into the very state you have struggled, without success, to earn. This is what we know as 'grace.' William Blake wrote, 'The fox provides for himself, but God provides for the lion.' The fox is full of his own cleverness and does not need God. So, my question is—are you a fox or a lion? Do you need God, or do you not?"

I sighed, "I'm obviously not clever enough to be a fox, so I guess that makes me a lion. A lion who's trying to be a fox. A real woodenhead, huh? But, yes—I guess I do need God. Some hard kernel of pride in me just doesn't want to admit it! I want to achieve everything for myself—I guess so I can take credit for it. But today when I held Benjamin, I felt how relaxed he was, how trusting. I envied him."

"Yes, child," Kyari murmured, smoothing the coarse sand with a foot. "This is what I wanted you to feel from the baby. It is the attitude of trust and relaxation. You can be like that baby, if you try. For you are indeed in the arms of God, and it will not let you down."

A strange cry pierced the air to my right. We both turned and looked. It was a great blue heron, flapping his tremendous wings skyward from the shore where he had been hunting. His long legs hung down like heavy streamers and his neck projected straight ahead, purposefully. He was beautiful, and completely unconscious of it! My Soul went out to him, became one with him. For a moment, we hovered above the watery blue world, a feather on the wind.

"Just be," said the Adept, as she strolled slowly away from me.

I watched her becoming a smaller and smaller figure along the edge of the gleaming water. Then I turned to go.

CHAPTER SEVENTEEN
Beauty and the Beast

The Tibetan was in my room when I woke up this morning. I had been exhausted from a late night of annotating student papers and had crawled back under the covers just as soon as my husband and son had left for work and school. I felt something shake me gently but unmistakably. Never a heavy sleeper anyway, I awoke immediately. Then I saw who it was.

"What's going on?" I complained, sitting bolt upright. "It's only 8:30 in the morning. Couldn't you let me sleep just a half-hour longer?"

"No!" growled the dark-haired Adept. "You must learn to manage your time better and get to bed earlier. You put things off until the last minute and then have to cram to finish your jobs! In the inner worlds, nothing would work with this kind of disorganized attitude. Now get up and get cleaned and changed. We've got work to do!"

I grumbled under my breath but dragged myself into the bathroom to make myself presentable. The Tibetan disappeared until this was accomplished and showed up again a half-hour later at my kitchen table, reading the morning paper.

"Hmph," he muttered, frowning at the headlines and front page accounts of crimes and tragedies. "What a wonderful way to begin a day! No wonder the negative is such a perpetual motion machine in this world."

I made two cups of tea and sat down with him. Outside a slight drizzle was promising a rather dreary day. The birds, who normally sang so beautifully at this midmorning hour, had certainly found a dry place to hide for the moment, and were silent.

"Why such a rush?" I asked, dipping my tea bag thoughtfully as the steam wove braids in the air. "I thought we were almost finished. I thought we were doing fine."

"We are," agreed Haurvata. "But that only means that we must work harder now than ever before. The end of things is always, like the beginning of things, a most troublesome and confusing juncture. Another way of saying this is—the end and the beginning are really the same thing. When something begins, necessarily something else must have ended. When something ends, a new beginning is also in the offing."

"And this means that something else is beginning for me?"

"Yes, of course," the Tibetan said in his resonant voice. "But the energy and momentum you have built up to negotiate the writing of this book must not be allowed to diminish. You must not rest, but push on to the next task I give you, and the next one after that!"

"Ohhhh," I groaned, letting my head drop heavily on the table with a dramatic thump. "I don't know if you should have told me. Ignorance is bliss, you know."

"No, I don't know," Haurvata smiled, playing along with me. "And anyway, you are now beyond being used as a vehicle on an unknown basis! We could make limited use of you then. Now there are no limits!"

I peered sideways at the Adept with interest. He seemed even more full of boundless confidence than usual, exuding a restless vitality like a stallion eager to leap over the walls of his narrow corral. I decided to ask him frankly the reason for this.

"Ha! You detect my mood, lion?" he replied. "Yes, I am happy. Oh, I am always content, strictly speaking. But even we of the inner worlds experience times of greater and lesser flows of Spirit. My projects on the physical plane are going well, and I have reason to celebrate. I feel a major victory over the Shangra Raj coming, and through it, a spiritual renaissance of sorts—at least for a short time on earth! We will reach many Souls during this period. It is a great achievement, my friend!"

"Congratulations!" I exclaimed, sincerely pleased with this news.

The Adept acknowledged me with a wink, then grinned expansively. "Today I thought we'd take an expedition of sorts. You deserve some fun, and this will combine business with pleasure in an interesting way."

"An expedition?" I asked cautiously. "Where to?"

"The astral plane," he announced cheerfully. "—the vast dimension of reality just beyond the physical. You have been there many times before, of course. But today you will go there in full consciousness, accompanied by your faithful guide!"

"Oh!" I said, with some surprise. "Is this going to take long? I need to be back in time to get some letters out and write up a lesson plan for tomorrow. Not to mention going to the grocery store and . . . "

The Tibetan shook his head. "That is what I like about you—always practical! No, my friend, this will not take 'long' in the physical sense. As time goes, we'll be back within the hour. Is that satisfactory?"

"Great," I grinned. "Let's go!"

The Tibetan whispered a word or sound that echoed in my head. The sound spiraled like the internal revolutions of a seashell, drawing me inward. Finally, I felt myself lifting gently out of my physical consciousness and traveling rapidly through realms of light. At the end of my travels, I found myself facing the Unmani Dhun Adept, Haurvata Sampa. He was leaning against a tree, waiting for me.

"We have arrived!" he gestured expansively. "Do you recognize this place?"

"Not really," I replied. "Should I?"

The Adept nodded. "You might have remembered it from your childhood. We spent quite a bit of time here. You liked to ride the flying horses and visit the palaces and flower gardens."

"Goodness!" I exclaimed, turning around to stare. "Was that real? I thought it was my imagination!"

"Not at all," Haurvata replied. "But as you grew up, and the curtain closed on your inner experiences, you discounted your adventures as childish fantasies. Come this way. I would like to show you more of the countryside. The city is in the distance. Do you see it?"

I did indeed. Pale crystal towers and spires rose in the air like fairy castles amidst clouds of pure pinks and peaches. A translucent glow that was brighter and yet softer than electricity emanated from the city's majestic skyline. The city nestled in a curve of blue-green hills and white-peaked mountains. A single waterfall plunged down from one of the taller mountains like a column of light.

"They call it the 'Jeweled City,'" reported the Adept, striding down a broad, stone-paved road. "It is the archetype of every fairytale kingdom known in literature. People who have seen it have difficulty forgetting its great visual beauty."

"I can see why," I sighed, falling into step with him. "Funny, but just looking at it seems to give me energy—like feasting on food."

"Beauty is indeed a kind of food," agreed Haurvata. "It is food for the higher senses. Souls come here after the death of the physical body to refine their characters through daily contact with the beauty, joy, and serenity of this place. The creative work they do furthers their growth even more."

We walked along for what seemed a half-hour or more. I never tired, for the heavy pull of gravity common to earth did not weigh me down, and the air itself was light and invigorating. The road began to curve slightly to the right. The Tibetan's step became noticeably quicker. As we rounded a grove of trees, I saw why. About a quarter of a mile from us, across grassy acres, a herd of perhaps 25 winged horses were grazing and watering near the edge of a blue lake.

I gasped in astonishment. "I've never seen anything so beautiful!" I whispered.

The Tibetan nodded and pointed into the sky. "Look up. There are three of them flying. Do you see?"

Two of the three appeared to be engaged in mock battle. Charging at each other, they reared up when they got close and struck at the air with their hooves. The third soared above them, as if refereeing their contest. The wind carried their neighing toward us.

The other horses seemed unconcerned with the battle raging overhead. Several bent their necks at the water. Their snowy white flanks against the deep blue-green of the lake was a sight to behold. One of the horses had swum out and was now floating swan-like in the distance. I beamed at the Adept. "Wish I could take a picture of this to bring back."

"You can," he said with amusement. "That is what words are for! Now let me say a little more about this plane in broad terms. The physical plane is greatly influenced by the astral, and is to some extent interpenetrated by it. Most people's inner lives—that is, their imaginative, fantasy, and dream lives—are lived out on this dimension of reality. It is also the dimension most inhabit after physical death.

"The creative products of artists, architects, writers, and inventors—to give a few examples—are often the result of astral travel. Of course, they do not know they are outside of the body, because the movement of consciousness is subtle and does not trigger their physical senses. They simply feel a heightened state of awareness, with a greatly increased flow of inspiration and a suspended time sense."

"I just had a funny thought," I chuckled, stretching myself out full-length on the meadow. "These people would really laugh if anyone suggested that out-of-body travel was responsible for their ideas!"

"True," smiled Haurvata, taking a seat next to me. "All creativity, however, comes directly from expanded awareness—which is a movement of consciousness into subjective realities. For most people, however, subjective experiences are, by definition, not 'real.' They are far too inconclusive and ephemeral to be given much credence. But reality is not as uniform as people believe. On the physical plane, 'real' means anything that is measurable or discernible through the senses. On the astral, however, 'real' means whatever is created through imagination, or pictured feeling.

"The difference between one reality and another is merely the difference in the vibrations of atoms. But now we are getting into some technical areas. Perhaps a metaphor would be useful here. Take the way water can change from a liquid into ice, and even into steam. Regardless of its form, it is still water, is it not?"

"Agreed," I answered, closing my eyes.

"Well, in the same way, life can take many forms, yet still retain its essence. When a Soul leaves the physical plane, either in death, the dream state, or out-of-body travel, it generally comes here to the astral world. It has changed, as it were, from a "solid" to a "liquid" state. It can even continue, transforming itself to ever higher states until it attains the pure form of itself in the worlds of God. Now, do you remember how it is that the transformation of water is accomplished?"

"Through heating and cooling it," I offered.

"Yes. Cooling causes the molecules of the liquid to vibrate more slowly, forming a solid. Heat causes the molecules to vibrate more rapidly, creating a vapor. When Soul is encased in a physical body, its vibrations are slowed down, resulting in the solidity of the human consciousness. But after death, during the dream state, or during any creative activity, one is liberated from these fetters, if only temporarily.

"The spiritual exercises of the Unmani Dhun are an additional means to release Soul from its imprisonment in the lower vibrations. These exercises cause the inner bodies to vibrate in a way that releases Soul from the solidity of material reality, including the negative patterns accumulated over past lives. As a result, the practitioner is able to travel into the higher worlds and know his own immortality firsthand.

"Do you have any questions?"

"No," I replied. "I understand this. But I am puzzled about how imagination is used here to create reality. I'm not really clear on how this works."

Without speaking, Haurvata stood up and offered me a hand. I took it and rose to my feet. Immediately, we were swept up in an inner movment that deposited us in a room full of heavy, ornate furniture and tables covered with rich food. In the middle of the scene sat a middle-aged man with thin hair, eating ravenously. A group of attractive serving girls kept his plate filled and his goblet brimming with drink. In a corner, seven musicians played on instruments which created a jangle of sounds that matched the frenzied eating.

"Who is that?" I asked, controlling a trace of revulsion.

"His name does not matter," replied the Tibetan. "In physical life, he is an office worker in a government bureau. He is diabetic, and must watch his food intake carefully. But here on the astral plane he can consume what he wants. Unfortunately, the whole point of his diabetes is to teach him moderation and discipline of his senses."

"It doesn't seem to be working," I noted.

"No," replied the Adept. "The point of such handicaps is educative, dear one. But many resist the lesson."

All at once, I found myself in a tunnel somewhat like an elevator shaft. We were traveling quickly upwards, flashes of scenery whizzing by at incredible speeds. Finally, the movement stopped. I found myself at a construction site, the Adept by my side.

"How did you like your ride?" Haurvata grinned.

"I loved it," I laughed. "How did you do that?"

"The astral world is vast, daughter," he explained, "both in breadth and in depth. This is the customary way to travel between sub-planes. It is like your freeway system, as it cuts across states to unify the nation!"

"So what's going on here?" I asked, pointing to about thirty men and women who were raising the walls of a dome-shaped building. Each wall was a curved triangle, like the outside skin of a slice of orange. Furthermore, the surfaces of the triangles were planed so that the final effect would be like a round, faceted jewel glistening in the light. I asked the Tibetan what material was being used.

"It is similar to glass," he replied, "but harder, as well as lighter in weight. Observe how they are moving the sections."

The movement was being accomplished by a group of singers harmonizing with notes struck on a series of bells. The sounds were eerie and yet strangely pleasant. The sections vibrated, and were gently guided upright by several workers who moved them into place. I didn't see the seams where the sections fitted together. I also wondered how the building managed to stay upright.

The Adept replied, "Principles of geometry and sound, which were known in the physical world during its Golden Age. Do you see the man standing there in the white shirt and pants? And the woman in the yellow dress?"

I nodded.

"The first is a Swiss architect. The woman is from the Southwestern United States. Both have been traveling here inwardly to work on this project. It fulfills their imaginative vision of a domed building which would reflect light, and create a particular atmosphere of sound. Later, in their physical lives, the things they have learned will surface in their projects. They will be unable to recreate the astral dome exactly, of course. But certain concepts will be applicable. This is how ideas filter down from the astral to the physical. Look around you at instances of creative innovation and you will find yourself face to face with many inner plane travelers!"

The Adept turned and started walking away. He glanced in my direction. After one last look at the structure, I turned to follow. This part of the world was busy, with many pedestrian pathways and people strolling in every direction. Overhead, about a dozen flying platforms sped by, though without the obnoxious noise characteristic of machines. The people of this land were robust-looking, with rosy cheeks and bright eyes. Their strides were energetic and purposeful. I questioned the Adept about the difference between the creative industry of this place and the self-absorption of the man at his dinner.

"The latter was a lower sub-plane of the astral," he explained. "It is inhabited by those who are more interested in pursuing their fantasies of life, rather than discovering and living out a real one! The man we observed, here through dream travel, is merely a typical example. Many departed Souls do the same with their time on the astral, weaving illusions of food, sex, money, fame, or power— whatever their hearts desire!"

"But how can they do that?" I asked, puzzled.

"They can do that because the astral plane operates, as I have said, on imagination rather than physical senses. On the physical plane all of these material desires would require effort to fulfill. But on the astral, all one has to do is imagine it. This changes the rules of the game entirely! Anyone who wants to drink French wines every night can do it. The sky is the limit!"

"Gosh. Then what happens to people? Don't they fall into a trap of fulfilling their greeds and lusts?"

"Yes and no," answered the Tibetan. "Typically, those who have such tendencies do that at first. But, eventually, even the most decadent see little satisfaction in living only to satisfy the pull of their senses. Life here is much longer than on earth. Time hangs heavily on one's hands without a creative goal of some kind. So after awhile, most leave this trap and go searching for a better kind of existence. When ready, each is taken to a higher level on the astral. There they learn additional laws of this world and begin to contribute something more usefully creative as citizens of this land."

Haurvata waved his hand in the air. Suddenly, a pastel-colored vehicle descended to the ground. "Our taxi has arrived," he winked. "Get inside. I will give you a tour of the city from above, as I continue my discourse for today."

I climbed into the vehicle, which contained cushioned seats for four people besides the driver. We lifted up into the air and were soon a half-mile above the city, traveling smoothly above the buildings, roads, parks, and people.

Haurvata began talking at once. "I have brought you to this plane for a reason, my friend. As I have mentioned, the astral influences the physical, and the way it does this is through the imagination. Imagination—true imagination, not merely the fantasy of wish fulfillment—is made of thought and feeling harnessed to a creative purpose. The spiritual centers which men and women use to manifest their creative purpose are the solar center and the inner eye.

"The inner eye and the solar center can be correlated to the male and female spiritual roles in the lower worlds. They are opposite and equal powers which balance man between two worlds, making him both material and spiritual, body and Soul, at the same time. To give a simplified sketch of their functions, let me say that the spiritual eye gathers the forces of Soul, while the solar center distributes it. Whether one's attention is upon traveling to the heavenly worlds, or manifesting one's desires upon earth, these two centers are needed to secure the correct results. To understand why, you will need a more complete explanation of these functions.

"The spiritual eye, sometimes called the 'tisra til' or the tenth door, is the pineal gland located at the center of the forehead just above the eyebrows. Scientists aren't sure exactly what function this particular organ has. This is because its function isn't primarily physical, but spiritual. The gland provides a bridge between the physical body and the subtle spiritual worlds.

"The activation of the spiritual eye opens the inner door into the dimensions beyond the body. It is one of the two openings a spiritual student is taught to use for expanded awareness. The other is at the top of the skull, where the soft spot in a baby's head is located. The spiritual eye enables man to make contact with the infinite. It is his inner airport from which he can journey at will into the other worlds, and return safely to the body.

212

"The spiritual eye is the ability to see, know, and be in the inner worlds as a conscious being. As such, this center is associated with insight, or 'inner seeing.' This is not the same as the fancies and illusions of the mind or emotions, but is rather true spiritual perception. The key words for the spiritual eye are 'conscious' and 'active.' In other words, when you use the spiritual eye, you are 'being' and 'doing' something in full awareness!"

"You mean, like traveling with you in this wonderful contraption?" I said.

"Right. To put it in terms of our previous study, the spiritual eye is the 'masculine' aspect of man's spiritual make-up here on earth. It is the executive power in charge of conscious thought. Through its connection with the infinite, the spiritual eye gives mankind the ability to discriminate based on inner wisdom—to judge correctly the difference between truth and lies, between what helps Soul and what is an obstacle to it.

"So, to apply it to your needs, the spiritual eye basically works like this. If you wish to raise your consciousness, you must gather your scattered attention at this door of Soul. This will unify and concentrate Soul's energies for the upward flight. If you wish to manifest physical goals, such as writing a book or getting a new job, you need the spiritual eye to see and know the best way to go about doing this. Now I'll say this once, and it is very important: Those who can utilize the spiritual eye are the creative geniuses of their worlds. Their powers are not measurable by I.Q., but are far greater than anything the mind can muster!

"Are you getting all this, my friend?" asked the Tibetan.

"Oh, yes," I said. "I've got it. I can retrieve what I missed later on. Keep going!"

The Adept smiled broadly and continued speaking.

"Now to the solar center. The solar center is the ganglion of nerves at the back of the stomach which constitutes the sympathetic nervous system. The solar center is the part of the body that controls the automatic functioning of the vital organs. Whereas the tisra til is the seat of conscious spiritual thought in man, the solar center is the source of the subconscious power.

"The subconscious is like the engine of a car, with the conscious mind as its driver. An engine would be useless without the intelligent handling of a driver. But the driver could go nowhere without the harnessed power of his engine. In the same way, conscious thought provides the solar center with a purpose and a direction. The subconscious contributes the necessary energy to arrive at the chosen destination.

"You and every other human being are a result of this lifetimes-long interaction between the conscious and subconscious. Superficial mental data are discarded between lifetimes. But strong conscious thoughts become patterns of belief that are stored on a subconscious basis. Beliefs are indisputable personal laws, and constitute the molds from which our particular lives are cast.

"The process of molding the infinite and formless power of Spirit into limited and particular realities is the job of the solar center. And this can result in the expansion or limitation of the individual, depending upon what beliefs are stored there. A person with many positive, constructive beliefs will have a healthy solar center. He or she will be able to use thought and imagination to create concrete realities, and to transform dreams into full-dimensional experiences. This constitutes the distributive, outward-manifesting function of the solar center, as contrasted with the gathering, inward-focused nature of the spiritual eye."

"Then what would an 'unhealthy' solar center be like?" I asked, out of curiosity.

"An 'unhealthy' solar center would be one dominated by negative beliefs—beliefs like 'I'm unworthy of love,' 'Life is unfair,' 'I will fail,' and so forth. Beliefs such as these stifle the free flow of Spirit through the individual, preventing him from accomplishing his conscious goals. Thus, one of the most rudimentary jobs of all true spiritual teachers is to uncover these painful negative attitudes and allow them to be replaced with more life-giving ones."

"That reminds me of some articles I've read about optimism and pessimism," I interjected. "Apparently, the results of studies show that optimists are healthier in every way than pessimists, as well as more productive and creative at work. Psychologists don't understand why this is true."

"They do not understand it because of a particular bias they have," responded Haurvata. "It is a bias toward the material world as the accepted standard of reality. It is expressed best in your saying, 'I'll believe it when I see it.' In other words, nothing is real until it has hardened into physical fact. But the spiritual law actually works in the reverse. To correct the expression, 'When I believe it, then I'll see it.'

"The sum total of all human experiences can be traced back to primal spiritual forces in action: thought and feeling. The physical world is the dead core within the living wood of the ever-expanding universal life. Psychologists, like all scientists, are now realizing that what we 'see' is only a small portion of all there is. And beyond what can be seen lies the boundless inner worlds and Soul itself! Aye, my friend. Everyone is more than meets the eye. Each of us is an evolving, unfinished microcosm of divine creation. We are wise to believe the best we can of ourselves and each other. It is the greatest gift we can give, and receive."

I was silent for awhile, considering the implications of all that my teacher said. Meanwhile, we seemed to have made our way back to the white mountains and blue-green hills that surrounded the Jeweled City, where Haurvata and I first embarked on our adventure. The driver looked into the mirror at Haurvata, who nodded slightly. The vehicle banked gently to the right and began heading straight for the tallest peak.

"This is wonderful information," I said, shaking my head. "I thought I'd understood these things, but you've made it much clearer yet. Now, just one more question! Can men and women help each other to use their inner eyes and solar centers in the right way?"

Haurvata answered.

"Both men and women can help each other by living out their own spiritual insights and not interfering with their partner's choices and states. The temptation is always to try to change the other, but this only opens you to the possibility that you will project upon the other what you aren't facing in yourself. If there is a problem, communicating your viewpoint and making suggestions is appropriate. But threatening, punishing, withdrawing, accusing, or criticizing is not.

"The latter point leads us to the next way men and women can help each other. This is by giving positive feedback on what the other is doing right, and constructive feedback on where he or she can improve. The message behind this feedback, however, must at all times be affirming and accepting. The other person must know that, despite any specific behaviors under dispute, you believe in his or her intrinsic worth and value as Soul.

"The male and the female elements contain the brains and the energy of all endeavors within the human sphere. They provide the rational plan and the enthusiasm to fulfill any dream. But in order for men and women to assist each other in ways I have outlined, each must actualize the potential of these two centers within themselves. Remember, too, that within a family, the woman is in a sense the most powerful. For just as the hearth was the physical center of family life in the old days, a confident, beloved woman is the spiritual fire which gives strength and nourishment to all who dwell within her home even today.

"Do you have any questions so far?" asked Haurvata.

"No," I said, shaking my head.

The Adept smiled. "Very well, then. I will conclude our discussion on the solar center and spiritual eye with a story! It is the story of Beauty and the Beast. As you know, Beauty's father goes on a journey. On his way home he picks a rose from a magic house and garden which turns out to be owned by a hideous and frightening beast. The rose is for his daughter Beauty, who has asked for it in contrast to the material gifts which her sisters have requested.

"Because he has violated the law of hospitality by taking what was not offered, Beauty's father must die unless his daughter comes to live with the Beast. Because of her great love for her father, Beauty goes to the Beast. The Beast falls in love with Beauty and asks her to marry him. Over and over, Beauty refuses. Although she has developed a deep affection for the gentle beast, she cannot bear the thought of marrying such a creature.

"Finally, Beauty receives permission to travel home to visit with her family. But the Beast warns her that if she does not return by a certain time, he will perish! Beauty tarries, forgetting her promise, then recalls remorsefully her broken vow. She rushes to the Beast's side, only to find that he is dying. She cradles his ugly head tenderly in her arms and tears of sorrow fall on his face. She declares her love for him, asking his forgiveness.

"Suddenly, the Beast revives, transformed into a handsome young man. He explains to Beauty that a witch had cast a spell on him—a spell that could only be broken through the love of a beautiful woman who accepted him in his beastly state. Beauty marries the Beast after all, except that now the beast is a prince, revealed as his true self!

"Now Beauty undergoes as great a transformation as does the Beast of the story, but her change is less obvious. So I shall explain it to you! Beauty is concerned at first with emotional love, symbolized by the rose she asked for as a gift. Also, at the start of the story, Beauty's greatest tie is with her father, showing her state of immaturity, that is, of being in a dependent role in relationship to the male.

"Later on, because of the plucking of the rose, Beauty is challenged to move beyond her superficial understanding of love and find its deeper meaning within herself. She is offered an opportunity to become a spiritual equal with a male partner, instead of continuing in a dependent position.

"In the same way, many people start their relationships with the ideal of emotional love. However, the trials of marriage push them to go beyond it. When Beauty returns to her father's home, it is a spiritual test. Will she move decisively onward to a higher love, or fall back into her former, comfortable, and immature state—the realm of the emotions and dependency? This is the test of every marriage, my friend.

"Now, the Beast was always a prince and his actions demonstrated his inner nobility. Despite his sexual desire and spiritual need for Beauty's love, he did not force himself upon her. This shows the importance of self-discipline in love, and the desirability of waiting until the gift of true love is offered before taking it. It was the Beast's test of the solar center—to treat Beauty justly as he would his own precious Soul.

"Beauty could not give her love at first because she was spiritually immature. To see past outer appearances to the Beast's inner nobility was Beauty's test of opening her spiritual eye. When she finally goes beyond her limited viewpoint, lo! the beast stands before her transformed by magic into a prince! Now both parts have met their challenges, and the divine marriage is complete.

"So you see, child, love is the creative and transforming alchemy of the universe. It uncovers the princely Soul behind our bestial surfaces. Love takes you from a dependent creature cowering before the negative power to a resplendent being and a co-worker with the Divine! To put it in more mundane terms, if you want someone to be lovable, first you should treat him as if he were lovable. And if you would be loved, first you must believe in and see the shining Soul within yourself! The mirror reflects the image before it. And we are mirrors unto each other, and mirrors of our own beliefs about ourselves!"

The mountain was straight ahead, and under us the waterfall plunged downward with a thunderous sound. Even from our height we could feel the spray of the mist on our arms and faces. I smiled happily at Haurvata, and he reflected back my delight. Little did I realize that the picturesque part of this trip was nearly over, and my adventure was about to turn more serious than I could have imagined.

CHAPTER EIGHTEEN
The Sword of Light

The waterfall roared so loudly now that the Adept's voice could not be heard above the din. The driver signaled to Haurvata and began his descent. I did not know where we could be going and began to feel concerned. Both men seemed perfectly relaxed, so despite my fear, I settled down to enjoy as much as possible the strange sensation of traveling alongside a great cascade of thundering water. The velocity and volume of the downpour created drafts which buffeted the small craft. I gripped my seat and waited for the vehicle to stabilize.

Finally, we started to move forward again, skirting right, away from the falls, and into an almost invisible passageway in the rock. I thought at first that we were going to smash into the cliff face, and heaved a grateful sigh when we entered smoothly and easily through the tunnel to the other side. There I saw a level space about one square mile in size, like a small crater. We landed smoothly and got out.

"So why didn't we just fly over the mountain and land here the easy way?" I asked.

"You cannot see this strip from above," explained Haurvata, pointing. "It is protected by a veil of illusion resembling sharp, jagged peaks. Not the sort of thing you'd want to land on."

"Oh, spy-stuff! Very exciting. But why?"

The Adept guffawed. "The reason for the secrecy is that the Unmani Dhun have a spiritual sanctuary here. It is for training, mostly, but also for rest and protection when necessary. This world looks peaceful and beautiful, my dear, but it is not. Individual violence is rare, and well policed. But the fight between the negative and positive forces is never ending.

"The battles are fought psychically, and involve no bloodshed. Still, our victories and losses are significant. When we lose on the astral, the physical is affected. Because we live in a negative age of man, we are rather the 'underdog' here. Making headway is an uphill battle every time. Our aim is only to preserve enough of a balance so that Souls who truly want to take the higher path can do so. That is why you have seen me so pleased lately! We have been winning our share of victories. And this is why you are here, as well."

"I don't get it," I said, my eyes wide. "Battles, victories, losses! What does this have to do with me? I'm no warrior."

"No, not in the conventional sense of a warrior," Haurvata conceded. "But warriors are made by character, not by sex or physique. Doing battle with the Shangra Raj in this world takes subtlety, not force. The plane of imagination is also the plane of illusion! There is only a hairsbreadth of difference between the two. That is where the attack will come, when it comes!"

I mused over these words in silence. An uneasy feeling gripped me, but I shook it off, wanting to believe that everything would be as it had been up until now—peaceful and beautiful. Anyway, the sanctuary was well secreted in the mountains, and I assumed its defenses would be more than adequate should an attack take place. I tried to imagine what it would be like: laser guns, super technology like in the movies, a lot of flashing lights and explosions. I hoped I'd be gone before then.

The Adept must have picked up my thoughts, for he turned toward me and laughed. "Are you imagining what a battle up here would be like? Do not trouble yourself over the idea! We have a positive energy field wrapped around this area for thirty miles in any direction—wide enough to make it difficult to pinpoint where we are, especially since we have a decoy outpost near the Jeweled City and agents moving around inside to create a diversion. No, dear one, there will be no physical attacks, as I have said. But it is the psychic attacks you must watch for!"

"Oh, terrific," I deadpanned. "That makes me feel lots better. So how do I watch for something when I don't know what it is?"

"That is what we are here to rectify," he assured me. "If you are to be an agent of ours on earth, we cannot very well leave you unprotected. Nor can we hover around you like mother birds as we are doing now! You must be given some survival skills or you will be useless to us. Not to mention a sitting duck for the negative forces."

"Thanks," I said. "That makes me feel really confident."

Haurvata returned sharply, "The truth is, you already have excellent skills as a warrior. You simply aren't used to thinking of yourself in that way. Again, this is due to your lack of acceptance of all that you are inwardly. The sleeping dragon is going to have a rude awakening if it doesn't come out of its cave very soon!"

The Tibetan turned away and started walking toward a solid wall of rock. I stood watching.

"Say, do you see something I don't?" I called.

"Oh, excuse me! I forgot." He came back and touched me lightly on the forehead. Suddenly, the place was bustling with activity. Startled, I took a step backwards and bumped into a handsome young man with odd-colored eyes. He said something pleasant to me in a language I didn't understand and walked away.

"Could you do that to my ears, too?" I asked.

Haurvata laughed. "He was speaking the language used on his planet. Apparently, he took you for one of his own people. A compliment, really, though you are a little short of stature to be typical there. You may meet him again inside. Come along now. They are waiting for us!"

We resumed walking in the direction Haurvata had set out for a minute earlier. Now I could see an archway clearly in the rock face. Haurvata's back disappeared through the entryway. I was close behind him.

The place was crisscrossed with endless corridors leading into mostly small, spartan rooms. Above us, the ceilings contained clear domes through which poured the light of the day. Finally, we arrived at a closed door and pushed a button. The door slid back and admitted us to a large, bare room. A group of about ten men and women were sparring with white wooden sticks about two-and-a-half feet in length. Their teacher, a small woman with a braid down her back, focused intently on the group, her back to us. Our entrance, if noted at all, was about as significant as a fly landing on a wall.

Haurvata and I found a bench at the near wall and placed ourselves on it. I thoroughly enjoyed the beauty and precision of the martial movements, which were similar to the routines I had seen on earth, but much more graceful and complex. After about ten more minutes, the teacher halted the exercise with a command.

"Well done," she said in a low voice. "We are finished for today."

Her pupils, who had arranged themselves into rows, bowed slightly and tucked their weapons at an angle into their belts. The individual members of the group regarded us with friendly eyes, then slowly filed away. The women, I noted, were robust and glowing with health. One of the men, a lanky blond, remained behind. The teacher turned toward us and her gaze fell familiarly on Haurvata, then on me. I felt a shock going through my body. It was Kyari Hota, the female Adept!

"Greetings, brother," the petite woman said in her musical voice. "It is good to see you again, my daughter."

"Greetings," Haurvata replied, a twinkle in his eyes. "Daughter, may I present Kyari Hota, the Unmani Dhun Adept in charge of warrior training for our sanctuary."

"My God!" I exclaimed. "In charge of warrior training? You?"

"It is my honor to be master of warrior arts here," said Kyari, with amusement. "Do you think it not an appropriate role for a female Adept?"

"Er, no. I'm just surprised. I hadn't considered . . . that is, I thought . . . oh, never mind. I'm showing my ignorance, as usual."

Haurvata and Kyari laughed. Kyari patted me on the shoulder and grinned at me in a sweet, inscrutable way. I took a deep breath, filled with growing consternation. "I'm getting a bad feeling right now. I hope you aren't intending to teach me that routine I just watched. You'd have better luck training a flea circus."

Kyari answered, "We train warriors in many different levels of defense. Physical defense here is mostly for recreation, since it is rarely used. In your case, what is more to the point is an awareness of the psychic currents and spiritual forces that affect the individu level of survival. This will be more useful to you than swordplay or lightning fast physical reflexes."

Thank goodness, I thought. Lightning fast reflexes were not in the realm of possibility for me, even on the astral plane. Haurvata could see my relief and chuckled silently. Kyari merely appraised me coolly with her dark eyes.

"We will begin your first lesson today," she continued, suddenly all seriousness. "The subject is 'perfection.' Do you have any questions before we start?"

I shook my head. The warrior-adept motioned to the pupil who had remained behind. "Ven," she commanded. "Begin the exercise."

Ven, the blond pupil, positioned himself in the center of the room and began to move, slowly at first, then progressing into moderately quick movements. Nothing I'd seen before could compare to the height of his leaps and the grace of his whole body as it flew through space. The dance was comprised of circular movements punctuated by angular ones in a 360-degree orientation. It seemed to paint a picture I could almost see, like horses galloping or lightning striking in a storm. When he was done, Ven came back to the simple standing position from which he had begun. His teacher nodded and the young man left wordlessly. Then Kyari turned her gaze upon me.

"Now. Describe to me what you have seen."

"Well, if that wasn't perfection, it was as close to it as anyone has a right to get," I replied thoughtfully. "That was beautiful and, I suppose, deadly, too, if used in combat."

"You are half correct," Kyari allowed. "The dance was beautifully done, and by one of my best pupils. And yes, it can also be very effective as a means of physical defense. But perfect it was not. The beauty of this exercise came not from how closely it matched an idealized form or pattern. The beauty of the dance comes from the disciplined and knowledgeable expression of Soul. Watch me now. I will perform the same dance."

Kyari moved into the center of the room and sprang into action. Her movements were recognizably like Ven's, except that they were also very different from his. For one thing, her rhythms were more precise and martial. Strictly speaking, Ven was more graceful. Yet another kind of strength and beauty was evident in Kyari's confident execution. I was surprised, because, if anything, I'd have expected her to be the more graceful one.

When she was finished, she asked me once more. "Again. Tell me what you saw."

"I can't tell which was right, or which I liked better," I said honestly. "If I judged your performance by the standards of the first, I'd say you made many errors. If I judged Ven's performance by yours, I'd say the same about him. But after seeing both, I'd have to conclude that both were wonderful, though different. It's as if the two ways you interpreted the movements suggested more about what you were both going after, then any single way of doing it."

Kyari nodded. "Excellent. That's exactly so. Most people do not reach their full potential at anything because they do not see this. They are stymied, instead, by a false standard. That standard is, paradoxically, perfection. 'Perfect,' you see, does not mean 'without flaw,' as most people believe. It means 'complete'—in other words, 'whole.' Therefore, nothing in the lower worlds is ever 'perfect' except the imperishable part of us, Soul. Soul is perfect because it contains all the attributes of God, which is our standard of wholeness.

"The lesser concept of perfection creates the illusion that it's possible to match, through material effort, what is really an inner, spiritual reality. That is never possible. Anything man can possibly create is always a part, a reflection, an echo, and an image of Soul, which is in turn an individualized atom of God. If anything can be considered flawless, it is a product made by a machine. This is possible because the standards of a machine are merely physical. You can make a perfect hammer or a perfect nail. But a perfect warrior? A perfect writer? Never.

"Therefore, perfection can be a deluding idea when applied to an individual's creative efforts. For example, it is common for a writer to judge himself by the standards of the marketplace: whatever wins prizes or sells the most books. If a person believes he can come close to such ideals, he is heartened. However, he also becomes trapped by the rigid standards he has adopted for himself. If he realizes, on the other hand, that he will fall short of this ideals, he becomes discouraged. He has failed before he has even begun.

"Either way, the individual has collided with a self-created obstacle, and one of the greatest of the Shangra Raj's inventions: the success-or-failure trap. The desire for success and the fear of failure go hand in hand. The greater the one is, the greater the other is as well. As Emily Dickinson wrote, 'Success is counted sweetest by those who ne'er succeed.' In other words, people who fail savor success more than those who succeed. However, this kind of savoring is like the panicked gasping of a drowning man for air: an act which only pushes the desired goal further out of reach.

"But the Unmani Dhun hold out a very different standard of perfection. It has nothing to do with material comparisons, with worldly 'success' or 'failure.' This standard is two-fold: to live by the laws of God, and to be a new center of creation within God's worlds. In essence, one becomes perfect by simply being Soul. Living by the laws of God requires awareness and willing obedience. Being a new center of creation requires individuality. The dances you've observed were the results of both.

"First, Ven and I applied our awareness of the laws of motion and body dynamics to learn the steps in the sequence provided. Second, we allowed our own individualities to shape what we expressed—in other words, to allow our personal experiences and inner wisdom to flow out through the established patterns and change them subtly. In the second step, we also used our discrimination to detect when our interpretations drew us toward the original creative impulse that manifested the dance, or led away from it.

"The warrior-adept is never wrong, never right. We do not seek to be flawless, or to achieve a material standard of greatness. We only desire a higher expression of the whole through ourselves as Soul. None of us can BE the whole. That is for God to do. So we content ourselves with portraying our unique and individual part in it. We contribute this as a service to God, while watching and learning from the contributions of others as well. It is in everyone's hands what this unique contribution will be."

"Well, I'm relieved that I don't have to be perfect," I allowed. "The whole idea of perfection makes me feel pretty tense anyway. That runs counter to being a good warrior, doesn't it?"

"Yes," Kyari agreed. "A warrior cannot survive without a relaxed and ready will. A relaxed warrior is more alert, because his attention is free to respond to whatever the Higher Self points out. A tense person is generally trapped in some problem which is occupying his awareness to the exclusion of Spirit. Tension stops motion. It wastes energy. It blocks the will. Now here is something many people do not seem to be aware of: Most of anyone's tension is internally generated. This tension, in turn, stems from a lack of acceptance of one's total self.

"When an individual feels that he falls short of some ideal or has less ability than another person, self-doubt keeps his energies from outflowing into the world. His energies then build up like water behind a dam, creating great internal pressure. In feminine-polarized people, the internal pressure usually results in passivity, illness, and other self-destructive tendencies. In male-oriented people, the same thing often results in anger and destructiveness directed at others.

"In either case, it is still perfectionism at work to waste one's potential for spiritual growth. Thus, we do not put our attention on our weaknesses; we put it on our strengths. This enables us to share our gifts with the world, and gives us the courage to face and deal with our weaknesses as well. Once we understand and accept even that which is imperfect in us, the natural healing process will make us whole."

"Do you understand how to apply this to yourself, dear one?" Haurvata put his hand on my shoulder and gazed directly into my eyes.

"I think I have to be less critical of myself," I admitted, "as well as less critical of others."

"Idle criticism is indeed negative," Haurvata replied in his deep voice. "It tears down carelessly, and is the tool of the petty mind. But not all criticism is idle. I want you to distinguish between destructive and constructive criticism, my friend. You have a talent for constructive criticism due to the sharp edge of your mind. But like all sharp edges, it can heal or harm, and it can draw your own blood, too, if you are not careful with it. This distinction between useful and harmful criticism is important for you to make. And it may be important to others as well. So I will take some time to elucidate the differences for you."

He spread his hands in the air, his fingers wide apart.

"First of all, let us make a distinction between the critical person and the critical faculty. The critical person is one who is constantly finding fault with everyone and anyone. His or her destructiveness does not seem to distinguish between total strangers and loved ones, glaring crimes and innocent oversights. In fact, the most common victim of the critical person is his or her closest friends, mates, and blood relatives. The critical person lacks a sense of proportion, which is the hallmark of any good leader.

"This type of person does not have a sharp mind or keen discrimination. The nature of this mental habit is so inwardly destructive that it prevents those individuals immersed in it from developing rational skills. They cannot think things through. Their anger is their shield from revealing their inadequacies to the world. Mostly, others are afraid of them, and so they do often appear forceful and strong. But this is an appearance only, because behind so much anger is a well of fear.

"Now the critical faculty is completely different from the critical person. A good critical faculty is not destructive inner or outer talk. It is the ability to make fine distinctions, to see cause and effect and other relationships clearly, to see the flaws or truths in a line of reasoning or a plan of action, and to pick out the important ideas in any question or event. To develop a good critical faculty, one must be free of anger, for anger blunts and dulls. Anger blinds, whereas the critical faculty is the light of intelligence which pours in through the open window of Soul."

"Thank you!" I exclaimed. "That really helps me. Now I may be able to tell when I've crossed the line from the positive use of the critical faculty into destructive criticism. You know, the drive for perfection is really at the bottom of a lot of misery. We want the perfect body, the perfect car, the perfect family, the perfect job! We even have contests so we can play around at choosing someone to represent our ideal of perfection. And we want our relationships to be perfect, too! They never are, of course, and we don't know a way to be happy outside of perfection."

Kyari had been standing and listening all this time. Her posture was relaxed, yet alert. "The desire to deny or eradicate weaknesses is one kind of perfectionism," she said softly. "But another kind of perfectionism is the desire to be and do all things. This is not possible for the majority of people. Being an individual implies specialization and uniqueness of some kind. This in turn means that one must narrow one's focus, decide to go in one direction instead of another. Individuality thus implies limitation."

"Limitation?" I asked, the connection only half-formed in my mind. "Explain, please."

Haurvata replied, "The principle is one with which you are already familiar. You have simply never applied it to yourself. Take roses, for example. As a gardener, you know that in order to grow a single full-petaled flower, many buds are pinched off. This means that the plant sacrifices many little possibilities for one big actuality. You do this, too. Soul chooses to deny itself certain channels of expression in any lifetime in order to open fully to one or two. There is great power in this, due to the concentration of spiritual forces.

"Through limitations, Soul specializes and individualizes itself as a part of the whole. Painters choose watercolors, oils, or acrylics, then their type of brushes, colors, and painting surface. In the same way, we must choose what we are and what we are not. Certain choices affirm a direction and eliminate others. This is healthy and part of maturity—the growth from the 'limitless possibilities' stage of childhood to the 'limited but actualized' stage of adulthood.

"If you are under the impression that creative people are blessed with limitless ability, and therefore your own meager talents cannot compare, think again! Think of Vincent Van Gogh. Many people in this artist's own time thought that he could not draw, much less paint! His work was not photographically perfect, not visually 'correct.' His work was, instead, better than correct—it was individually creative. Van Gogh used his limitations to give originality, flair, and style to his work. He added something new and unique to our visual and spiritual experiences of the world, and expressed an aspect of God that had not been communicated before."

"I can see that a drive for perfection—that is, putting attention on weaknesses and rebelling against natural limits—goes against the growth of creativity and individuality," I remarked enthusiastically. "It introverts people's spiritual energy. It makes them like dead people: rigid and predictable. Creativity and individuality, on the other hand, are free and unpredictable. No wonder rigid people are so disturbed by children! Children are the most individualistic and creative of all!"

"Yes," replied Kyari, "that is often true. Yet the drive for perfection is soon hammered into children by parents and teachers. Children accept the myth of perfection because they want to please others, and be loved in return. Unfortunately, some adults love children not for themselves, but for what they want children to be. And what these adults want children to be is the ideal of perfection they have failed to achieve for themselves! The negative result from this drive for perfection is that it prevents the real individuality of the child from emerging. It keeps whatever true talent and creativity there is from developing through experiment and expression. It is a recipe for disappointment every time.

"Once you cast aside the delusional pursuit of perfection, you are free of a major source of guilt and fear. You are free—for what? You are free to take the risk of discovering the wholeness and uniqueness of yourself! As you do this, you will recognize in many previously rejected and/or unvalued parts of yourself the missing ingredients of your own greatness. You will be able to see how both your gifts and your lacks, and even your chance circumstances, play essential roles in determining the topography of your path in life."

"Do men and women differ in the way they approach perfectionism?" I asked, addressing the question to both adepts.

"Basically it is the same, my dear," Kyari said. "But up until now it has been mainly the female—as well as the female side of the man—who struggles most with the need for perfection."

"Why is that?" I asked.

Kyari replied, "Because society has taught you to distrust the feminine, to undervalue and limit its contributions to the whole. Because of this sense of inferiority, many women—and some feminine men—believe that their contributions would fall short of a standard they imagine to be ridiculously high. They sincerely believe that the world functions along these high standards. They never find out differently because they retreat before they get very far. The truth is, there is more psychology than objective superiority to the victories of most successful people. Many people with only a modicum of talent achieve their goals because their overwhelming confidence and vision is something the world cannot resist!

"Parents distort their female children early by emphasizing such virtues as having an attractive appearance, following rules, and demonstrating social graces at the expense of exploration and self-discovery. Girls, because they are more emotionally sensitive and cooperative, fall prey more easily to these attempts than do boys. There is nothing wrong with attractiveness, obedience, and good manners. But these skills must be kept in balance with the need for creativity and initiative, which takes courage. To live and be happy in today's world, girls must be warriors too!"

I thought about this last comment and how little we knew about how to raise our female children to be creative and provide interesting lives for themselves. As a matter of fact, passivity and complacency was not an unfamiliar problem among boys as well. In times of relative peace and material stability, mankind simply lacked the motivation to keep alert to both opportunity and danger.

I fidgeted uncomfortably and said, "You know, I've spent most of my life tied up in knots inside myself. All the attention I've put on my faults has kept me from outflowing on the level you and Haurvata seem to think I'm capable of. It isn't that I'm afraid of anything in particular. I'm just not sure I'd know the first thing to do as a warrior! Sure, I can survive well enough in a negative world. But a warrior must do more than survive. He has to win more ground for the positive force as well! At least, that's how I see it."

"Spoken like a true warrior," chuckled Kyari, her arms folded across her chest. "Come on. I'd like to show you something."

The warrior-adept led the way out of the training room, down the corridor, and up an interminable flight of stairs that led us outside into the clear air of the mountain fortress. A short distance before us, the falls raced down in a veil of mist to a turbulent basin below.

"The Sword of Light," shouted Kyari, indicating the awe-inspiring cascade of water. "It gives its name to our little sanctuary as well, a reminder that spiritual freedom must always be won and held in the dual worlds, by force if necessary, but without the excess of hate. The Sword of Light is thus the symbol of the vigilance and purity of the warrior Soul!"

We stood there for several minutes enjoying the majesty of the waterfall. Then Kyari lifted off and flew through the air to a spot a few hundred yards above us. When she landed, she waved to us. My mouth hung open. Haurvata laughed. "Did you not realize that you can fly on this plane if you wish to?" he chided.

"No," I muttered. "I've always flown in my dreams, of course. But it never occurred to me . . . oh well, here I go again. I guess there's a lot I don't know about getting around in this world. But if everyone can fly, why doesn't everyone do it? I mean, why ever walk? Why use vehicles?"

Haurvata answered matter-of-factly, "We walk because we have legs and need to exercise them. We use vehicles because flying for long distances tires the astral body, just as walking for long distances tires the physical body. But when necessary or desirable, projecting through the air is as natural as both walking and driving a vehicle. Now you try it!"

"How do I start?" I asked nervously.

Haurvata said, "Just like in your contemplations: Imagine your goal clearly and then picture yourself moving through the air toward it. You'll be there is no time!"

I did as I was told and found it as easy as he described. Soon I was next to Kyari on a ledge, which was covered with sparkling snow. Haurvata arrived a second later.

"So, my dear, how did you like flying?" grinned Kyari, her eyes dancing with merriment.

"It was wonderful!" I cried. "Flying must be to moving what ice cream is to food!"

"Good. Remember to use it, when the occasion calls for it. Now, to change the subject . . . from this height the Sword of Light sings less loudly. We can speak without shouting and still hear each other. I have brought you here for another reason as well. Watch the sky as we talk, and you will see something worth waiting for."

I gazed into the sky, which in this part of the world was tinged with pastel colors at all times, like the sunset over a tropical island. I wondered what it would be like to be a citizen here and take the beauty of this world for granted.

"You mentioned some hesitancy about becoming a spiritual warrior," Kyari began. "In fact, I'd be suspicious of anyone too easily thrilled with the glory and glamour of the role. In truth, there is no glamour and little glory in being a warrior. It is simply a level of commitment requiring an unusual degree of vigilance, loyalty, and discrimination. It is not a path for the starry-eyed, but for the Soul who has experienced all that the worlds have to offer and thus cannot be swayed by them. It is a path for one who has done enough evil to know good, and done enough good to know that good alone is not the answer to the problems mankind faces in the lower worlds."

Just then, I spotted something moving in the sky. "Look!" I hissed. "Is that it?"

At first "it" was an indistinguishable mass of motion, but soon there appeared to be two parts to this strange vision: below, a group of perhaps a hundred men rode on pure white horses, while above, a flock of blue birds formed a moving canopy above the horsemen's heads. The horsemen galloped across the sky in complete silence, but before them a strange moaning wind rushed through the land as they passed. After a long while, the horsemen disappeared from view.

My emotions were strangely aroused by this sight. "Kyari," I said wonderingly, "what was that we just saw?"

"They are called the Warriors of the Blue Light. Have you never heard of them?"

"Never," I said, shaking my head. "Tell me about them."

"The Warriors of the Blue Light are Souls who have chosen and been chosen to render their services to the Holy Spirit in the lower worlds for eternity. Each carries a blue sword and shield. When they gallop across the sky on their white horses, they might be seen by the fortunate ones whose spiritual eyes are open. The power of God goes before them in the form of a mighty wind that bends down the worlds."

"I saw the wind," I exclaimed excitedly. "Was that the God power?"

"Yes," nodded Kyari. "The God power uproots what was once fixed and rearranges the anchor points of one's life. It brings chaos and change, but only for the purpose of bringing Soul to a higher level of life."

"Wow. Somehow that reminds me of odd dream images I've been having lately," I whispered.

"Describe them," said Haurvata.

"The first dream image was a field of wheat bent to the ground by a howling wind. In another part of the same dream, a snow-covered mountain thawed, creating avalanches that rolled down with a roar. Another image I dreamed lately was of a field of fat, bright-orange pumpkins ready for harvest. But the last image is the strangest of all. In it, enormous, frozen whales were thawing and flowing downstream. Their numbers seemed endless! That's all I recall. Are these strange images, or what? Do either of you know what they mean?"

The two Adepts looked at each other as if deciding who would speak. After a moment's hesitation, Haurvata replied, "I will tell you what these dreams signify, my friend. They indicate the release of powerful spiritual currents into your life. The wind is the God power that is causing this change. The mountain is a symbol of spiritual attainment, and its thawing shows the dissolving of previous restrictions to your full expression of self-mastery. The pumpkins are a feminine symbol of a spiritual harvest on the physical level—a promise of material plenty and prosperity. The whales are a masculine symbol of the higher mental powers associated with the subconscious plane. The thawing here shows that inspiration, clarity of thought, and truth will now be available to you without limit."

"Oh!" I said quietly in the pregnant moment that followed. The dreams had uplifted me, but I had no idea that they foretold so much. Now I wondered what these coming changes would mean to the practical side of living. Would my consulting work in the schools become steadier? Would I finally be able to write what was in my heart?

But these questions had to be set aside for the moment. Kyari had taken to pacing the ground in front of us like a panther. "Well!" she finally exclaimed. "Your dreams indicate that we are on the right track in bringing you here today. I believe it is time to coax our sleeping dragon—that's you—from her lair! It is no longer safe for you to remain there, for the negative power knows of your existence and the potential threat to itself. From this point on, 'sleeping' can only be done at great risk to yourself. You have no choice but to accept the challenge and take stock of your new powers. In short, God's lion, this is your draft notice. The battle has already begun."

CHAPTER NINETEEN
The Inner Warrior

Kyari turned toward me and with a force that was not physical, hurled me over the edge of the mountain. The movement was so swift and unexpected, I had no defense against it. Before a thought of terror could pass through my mind, I was falling over the edge to the turbulent basin below. The survival instinct, however, took over automatically, the mind rapidly processing my options until it chanced across a recent entry, which stated simply: "In this world, you can fly." Immediately, I reached out in my imagination and halted my head-down plunge into the blue-green water. I marked a place on the terrain and made for it, traveling easily and rapidly until I was above the spot. Coming down was interesting, as I had chosen to fly "Superman" style, and had to right my body for a feet-down descent. I accomplished this through mocking up a gymnast leaping from a high bar to the ground. I bent my legs and landed with a little bounce.

In a short while, Kyari and Haurvata flew over and landed next to me. Kyari had a wide grin on her face and the Tibetan was controlling his amusement.

"Go ahead, yuck it up!" I growled, my hands on my hips. "You nearly killed me. I guess that's pretty funny all right."

They laughed until they had to lean on each other for support. Tears rolled down Kyari's cheeks and Haurvata's booming laughter rang through the air. After a while I began to smile, too.

"O.K., you jokers. What's the big idea? Aren't you two a little old to be pushing your friends off ledges? Or am I about to have a lit firecracker thrown at my feet as well?"

Kyari sat down weakly and spoke through her still-effervescing giggles. "No, you're safe for the present. Anyway, there was never any danger to you. If you hadn't remembered to fly, I'd have rescued you."

"Oh, so this was a test, huh?" I grumbled. "To prove to you I could do it?"

"No, dear one," corrected Haurvata. "To us you need prove nothing. It is to yourself you have something to demonstrate!"

"I don't get it," I frowned.

"It's just that you are not fully awake yet," smiled Haurvata sympathetically. "You are a warrior dreaming that you are a weak woman living a rather limited existence on the planet earth. Your dragon-powers are sleeping within you still! There seems to be no way for you to recognize your true self and shatter this dream except through proof of your own abilities as a warrior. This apparently stems from your stubborn insistence on seeing concrete evidence before you will believe anything. This skepticism is both a helpful and a harmful quality in you. In this case, it is harmful.

"We really do not know what kind of proof you require. You have not only survived the challenges of your life, but have developed yourself along unusual lines at the same time. You have had the company of the spiritual guides since childhood, and can travel in the inner worlds with increasing ease and familiarity. You understand a fair amount about the spiritual laws that govern the universes and can explain them to others. You are strong in your loyalty to Spirit. What more do you need to accept what you are and begin the task of developing your mission further?"

I stared at the Tibetan with a turbulence of mixed feelings. I did not like hearing him talk this way. He seemed to me almost upset, as if at the end of his rope with me. A feeling of panic threatened to well up inside. It was an old engram in my memory banks: perhaps he'll be displeased with me and abandon me! I refused, however, to give in to this insidious image. But another thought crept in to disturb me almost as much as the first. Did the Adept really and truly not know what more to do for me? I couldn't accept this at all. Over the years, I had come to rely totally upon him. I had never considered that a time would come when he might fold his arms and say, "That's all I can do for you!"

Moreover, I realized with growing surprise, I had never fully embraced the idea of becoming an Adept like Haurvata—his equal, rather than his student. Or more correctly put, I had projected the possibility so remotely into the future that I had shut the door to becoming that in the present moment. A flush went through my body as Haurvata's words sunk in. I began to feel like a bridegroom moments before his wedding: excited, nervous, and plain scared! Was I really ready to do this? How did I get myself into this mess anyway? The prospect of giving up my life of little responsibility for one of great responsibility, of replacing personal concerns with universal goals, gave me the cold chills. Once taken, this step could prove irrevocable.

At last, I shook my head. "You're right. There isn't anything more you can do for me. You two have taught me so much. I didn't realize that I've been dragging my heels. I honestly never thought I was capable of being a warrior before. I don't even make enough money at my job, I lose my temper occasionally, and I forget to feed the cats!"

I threw up my hands in bafflement. "How can someone like that be a warrior?"

The two Adepts merely chuckled. "You're so busy counting up your faults that you've totally ignored your strengths," admonished Kyari. "Didn't anything we said about perfection sink in?"

"Well, yes, but it takes time to apply what you accept mentally," I replied. "I'm merely describing my underlying rationale for not seeing sooner what you've been leading me toward."

"All right," said Kyari. "But that was then. This is now. Anyway, the things you're saying about yourself are nothing but petty mental objections. It reminds me of the proverb that starts, 'For the want of a nail, a shoe was lost.' Are you going to give up your spiritual destiny for the sake of a few human flaws you are so vain about? Yes, I said 'vain.' It's self-consciousness that stops you from becoming a warrior! It is the little self strutting around, whimpering, 'How do I look? How do I look?' Being a warrior is not a 'performance'; it is a service. As long as you're human, you'll have flaws. But what does it matter if others see your flaws? You are not doing this to be praised—you're making use of your natural talents to be a vehicle for Spirit."

"O.K.," I relented. "You got me. Look, folks, I'm a warrior. Now what is a warrior supposed to do?"

"Be less sarcastic, to begin with," said Haurvata wryly. "Then, just look, listen, and remember. In time, your view of yourself will change. It will not happen overnight, nor do we expect it to. But you must begin sometime, and it might as well be now! As we have said, we cannot hover over you forever. You need skills to survive on your own against the Shangra Raj. If you think his attacks on you have been bad in the past, it will only worsen in the future if you remain unprepared. Of course, you have learned a great deal since your early years, so these attacks will be more subtle than before. But they will be no less dangerous."

"You've said that before," I sighed, "and it makes me nervous. What are these attacks going to be like and how can I deal with them?"

"Good question," interjected Kyari. "We are about to show you. Haurvata?"

The Tibetan stepped forward and threw a cloak of white light around us. Then the scene around us began to shift and waver. Soon it dissolved completely and was replaced by another reality: a place with people sitting around in the ruins of houses and walking in streets that reminded me of ghettos on earth. The globe of light protected us, however, and I felt little. Then the Tibetan withdrew the protective cloak. The vibrations closed in upon us, and they were heavy and dark. Fear and hopelessness crept around us like fog, seeping into and chilling us to the bone.

"Enough," whispered Kyari, and Haurvata replaced the light again. We moved within it along the bleak landscape, observing the kind of world these people lived in.

"Haurvata, where is this place, and why do the people here exist this way?" I asked finally. "I always thought the inner worlds were free from things like poverty. But the feeling I get here is worse than anything I've felt in the cities on earth—heavier and more hopeless! Why is that?"

"The astral plane is a world where imagination rules, as we've said before. But some people's imaginations are attached to images of poverty, illness, violence, and the like. So here, on the lower levels of the astral, they create their own environments to duplicate as closely as possible their inner images. In actual fact, the environmental conditions are better here than on earth. But the negative vibrations are stronger because the current isn't dissipated into solid matter as it is on the physical plane. The 'hell' of the Christian religion exists in an area of this plane as well. But we will not go there today."

"That's something to be thankful for," I muttered. "But you know, maybe this is obvious and I feel silly asking, but . . . what exactly is the negative current anyway? I mean, why does it have to exist at all?"

"The negative current exists to give form, structure, and limitation to Spirit, which in turn creates the lower world environments where inexperienced Souls can grow into maturity before earning their citizenship in the higher worlds. It is similar to a kindergarten where small children play and learn, well-supervised by caring adults."

"But kindergartens are safe places, and the earth isn't," I objected. "How can your comparison work?"

"It's true that Souls on earth face hardships and suffering," replied Kyari. "But these very experiences are intended to educate and strengthen. Furthermore, whatever dangers the lower worlds hold for Soul, the scope of the harm that can be done is pretty well confined to the physical level. Soul harms others when it lacks judgment and experience. But the freedom to harm others is also the freedom to do good for others as well. Soul has been given this freedom so that it can learn what it is and choose to serve God. The evil men do to each other is the price of that freedom."

I considered this while Haurvata led us away from this dark place to one that was considerably brighter. A building appeared, surrounded by a pleasant garden. It reminded me of a country club. I found out, however, that it was a place of healing, a "hospital," as Haurvata called it. Here, individuals who had earned their entrance into this facility got help for spiritual problems lodged in the astral body. Many came here, I was told, before going on to higher regions on the astral plane. Haurvata continued his line of talk while giving us a tour of the public areas in the facility.

238

"How is the healing done?" I inquired.

Kyari had gone off on her own and returned in time to hear my question. "We can show you," she smiled. "I've received permission for us to observe some of it. Come over here."

Kyari led us to a room with large windows looking into a smaller room in which a man and a woman worked with a female child of about ten years old.

"I was told that she was physically abused and killed," Kyari reported in a low voice. "This experience is part of a pattern of being a victim and victimizing others begun many lifetimes ago. The Soul has paid the debt it has incurred and has learned better, yet the inner pictures need to be erased so the pattern can be broken. Watch how this is done."

I observed in fascination as the girl imaginatively projected onto a screen image after image of abuse and violence, both done to and by herself in various incarnations. During and after this experience, the man and woman talked to her. I did not hear what was said, but I saw the girl nodding several times and even smiling. Then the ceiling of the room opened up like a camera eye and a column of light came down from it to the reclining girl. From what I could see, I concluded that the patient was being given breathing instruction while the light bathed her. Then the man and woman began doing something odd. Their mouths were open, but their lips were not moving very much.

"They are intoning a note, a sound," said Haurvata. "All healing takes place through the twin aspects of the Holy Spirit: the inner light and sound. It fills the individual with the positive current so that the negative has no place in him. Beyond that, it is necessary to correct or remove the stored images that are destructive to us and others. You see, Soul moves from point to point on its inner images. That is why some Souls circle around and around certain experiences like dogs chasing their tails: they have one or two dominant images that obsess them, preventing them from further progress.

"The negative images, by and large, lead more easily to repetition because of the overwhelming emotional charges that generally accompany them and hold them in place in the inner bodies. Therefore, if one wants to rid himself of a negative pattern, it is necessary to find the seed images and release the charges associated with them. Generally, the thing that works best here is blessing the images, giving them detached love."

"That's very useful, Haurvata," I said. "I think a lot of people could use this information."

"That is why we are here," affirmed the Adept. "—to be useful to you, so that you in turn can be useful to others."

We left the room and toured some of the other areas. We were not able to observe any more healing, but Kyari pointed out the use of color, music, and dance as we caught evidence of them here and there. Kyari said that the arts were very useful for healing because they brought individuals directly and personally in touch with Spirit. Moreover, it allowed them to outflow the influx of this positive energy through some form of creative expression.

"Our schools could use this awareness," I grumbled. "The problems we're having teaching children seem insurmountable, but I can't help thinking that it's simple: make learning personal and creative for teachers and students alike! It can't be done with the short attention spans we have today. In the old days, life wasn't any less difficult, but I feel it must have been more focused, more unified. People need a way to gather the shards of their attention and center it inside themselves. Then maybe they'll be able to get interested in something, set goals, and accomplish their dreams!"

"The danger here is that you are turning out thousands of young people who are inwardly disorganized," added Kyari. "They are less spiritual beings than grist for the mills of capitalism—mainly as consumers of products and man-made experiences. This may sound like an exaggeration to some, but it is not. Education today is a primary battleground between the negative and positive forces in your world. After all, your youth is your future. That is why you have been attracted to this field, my daughter. Do not give up. There is much that can be done yet.

"This scattering of attention is a psychic weapon of enormous destructive potential. This is because attention is the source of Soul's power to select its experiences. To use an analogy, attention is like the silk a spider flings out from its body and attaches to some distant point such as a ceiling or a branch. The spider moves along this filament to arrive at its destination. In the same way, Soul puts its attention on some experience it wants and then moves toward it within time and space. If, however, Soul's attention is scattered, it lacks enough power to travel to any particular point.

240

"Since you're going to ask anyway," Kyari smiled, "I'll also tell you how Soul's attention can be scattered. First, it is scattered through putting its attention on things. Things have no energy in them; they are like black holes that absorb energy. A person who puts his attention on things thus creates for himself a dearth of growth experiences. If, conversely, attention is placed on a growth experience one wants, such as learning something or serving others, Soul receives energy to accomplish its desire. This happens because images of learning and service generate a high degree of life force and Soul moves more easily along these lines of attraction to its goals.

"The second way attention can be scattered is by placing it superficially on too many things. The secrets of any area of study never reveal themselves to the superficial learner! The great fear every educator has, of course, is that students will be too bored to go into an in-depth study of any field. But the truth is, skimming the surface is much more boring, and pointless to the student as well. Of course, by an 'in-depth' study I mean a hands-on, personally creative approach to it, not merely a quantity of information. Today, however, students are so unused to in-depth study that they will generally balk at the suggestion at first. Their attention needs to be trained to greater stamina for learning."

"I will add some points, if I may," Haurvata broke in.

"Certainly," replied Kyari.

"First let us leave here," the Tibetan said. "I have another place in mind that might interest us. Follow me."

Haurvata took off into the air and Kyari after him. Neither looked back, so I had no choice but to follow as best I could. I found that it was easier than the first time. The two Adepts got far ahead of me, but I never lost sight of their glowing astral bodies. After a while, they both entered a strange area of heavy vibrations. I followed, and all three of us landed together. The people, many of them young, were standing and sitting around at tables and benches. Soon, a group arrived to play music, a hypnotic blend of loud, avant garde, percussive and electronic sounds. Some danced wildly, but the vast majority just sat, totally absorbed in the music.

"This is another good example of scattering attention," motioned Haurvata as he indicated the crowd. "Music is a powerful tool for inner travel. The mind has no resistance to it. It enters one's consciousness and allows the listener to move to its source. Music comes from many levels. The more complex music such as some jazz and classical come from the mental worlds. But the music with the heavy beats and piercing sounds generally leads the listener to some place like this.

"Now I am not suggesting that music such as this not exist," cautioned Haurvata, fixing me with his steely eyes. "I am merely pointing out again that everything you take into your consciousness leads you to some place in the inner worlds. It can be a world of beauty and creativity, or one of violence and degradation. The music students are listening to today pulls them toward the lower astral plane, which is, at best, a rather uncreative place. It gives its listeners the illusion of energy and action, but what it really does is introvert them. They express less and less of their energies on the physical plane and, instead, live in a fantasy world on the lower astral."

"O.K.," I nodded. "Got it. Can we get out of here now? This music is really getting to me."

Kyari laughed and pulled the cloak of light around us again. "You know," she said to Haurvata, "this has been rather a lot for one time, don't you think? If you haven't more to show her, perhaps we could return to the sanctuary again."

Haurvata agreed, and we faded from this area, reappearing at the edge of the stream fed by the waterfall, the Sword of Light. The emerald blue-green of the water soothed my jangled nerves immediately. Kyari left us for a few moments and returned later with a handful of delicious pink berries.

"We are showing you these things, dear one, in order to help you to understand the way the Shangra Raj operates," stated Haurvata, turning a berry over and over again between his large fingers. "The negative power will not come to attack you with a gun or a knife. These you can easily recognize as threats. But the real dangers are not to your body, but to your inner being. Now here is a secret about the negative power which will be valuable for you to know. The negative power is not a creative force in itself, but merely reactive. In other words, it cannot initiate anything, but can only respond to what the positive element does or does not do. Mainly, it fills the void that is created when the God power wanes or is shut off in any area, be it in an individual, an institution, or a culture. So, to put it very simply, fill yourself with the God power at every moment, and you will always be safe from harm!"

"That's easy to say," I agreed, licking my fingers as the last berry disappeared into my mouth. "But people choose to destroy themselves with drugs, alcohol, and suicide instead. Why is that? Here we are talking about spiritual survival, while a lot of people willingly choose death."

"Do you want to know why?" Kyari replied. "It's because many are seeking release from the responsibility of being an individual, or Soul. They miss the comfort and security of being part of a stable and homogeneous family, tribe, race, or other group. But life in the modern world is neither stable nor homogeneous. It is, rather, diverse and constantly changing. Drugs and alcohol provide a temporary release from self-consciousness and self-responsibility. Even war can be a way of escaping from the burden of being an individual. War is a primitive, cathartic experience that returns man to the tribal consciousness from which he has recently evolved.

"You mean 'return to the womb'—that sort of thing?" I queried.

"Something like that," smiled Kyari. "In other words, the tribal consciousness has made mankind's decisions for so long that many are not yet ready to be thrust out on their own. The strain is too great for them, and they try to obliterate their pain and fear by various means. Have you noticed how often the theme of the alienated individual appears in your literature, for example? This feeling is very descriptive of the spiritual condition of the average person in your society. He cannot go back to the old ways of life, but he is uncomfortable with the lack of structure of the world today. The individual is caught between two points in evolution, and vascillates unhappily between them."

"Wow, that makes a lot of sense to me," I responded. "I'll bet that's why some people love being in large crowds. They like the feeling of merging their identities with a group."

"Yes," replied Haurvata. "But some of this must exist for balance in the world. If people become too individualistic, they cannot function collectively. The intent of our discussion, however, is simply to point out why so many seek oblivion in a world with so many opportunities. It takes a great deal of inner strength to stand on your own and create the kind of life you'd like to have. Some simply do not feel up to it, and there is no one to teach them the skills!"

"Is teaching these skills something a warrior could do?" I wondered.

"Oh, yes," nodded Haurvata. "Surviving as you've learned to do, the hard way, you'd have credibility with others who have had to struggle to survive as well! That would be a very useful service."

"There is another thing about groups you should know," interjected Kyari. "Groups form their own consciousness, which is a thought-form or energy field of attitudes and intentions. This includes everything from a hobby club to an entire race. The group entity exists on a spiritual level and can be seen with the inner vision. Once formed, it acts to maintain its own survival on an instinctive level, like any human being. It tends to resist change, since change threatens its survival as a fixed thought-form.

"Group entities can be positive or negative, like any entity. A family with a positive consciousness, for instance, generally does a good job preparing its youth for life. A negative group entity, on the other hand, can form when individuals decide to do violence within the shelter of a mob consciousness. People tend to act out negative attitudes more freely in a group because they don't feel quite as responsible for their actions. But groups can also exert a good deal of control over individuals within them. A religion or race, for example, may penalize a person for marrying outside of its circle. The punishment is psychological. The offending person is ostracized or cast out from belonging to the group."

"This makes me think about racial intolerance," I added. "You know, stuff like 'America for Americans' and all that."

"Right," continued Kyari. "The people who use such slogans feel that their group entity is being broken up from without. They are generally people who are most comfortable in stable, unchanging patterns and cannot cope with individual differences. They greatly define who they are by their group affiliation, so threats to the group identity are taken very personally. Racism and nationalism aren't the only expressions of extreme group identification. Some people even get violent over rivalries between sports teams! Perhaps you can understand more about why this happens now.

"The most precarious time for individuals who depend on a group for identity is when the group entity breaks down suddenly and rapidly. This happened twice in your country's history: when the white man met the American Indians and the Polynesians. The massive and rapid extinction of these groups is generally attributed to disease and war. While this is true on the physical level, the spiritual cause lies in the breakdown of the group's inner consciousness. This disintegration weakened the indigenous groups and made them incapable of resisting the white man's advances. This inner war was not fought with spears or bullets. It was fought with inner images and postulates. The white man's images and postulates, filled with their conviction of cultural superiority, overwhelmed these relatively more receptive, peaceful cultures."

"This seems to suggest that change should ideally be gradual," I offered. "I mean, it would keep things more balanced."

"Correct," nodded Haurvata. "When change comes gradually, the inner consciousness is replaced piece by piece and the person's sense of wholeness is maintained. This applies to groups, but naturally it applies to individuals as well. That is why in relationships, it is important to accept and support each other's beingness. When overt or covert criticism takes hold, this constitutes an astral attack, and the negative flows generated can really harm the parties involved. Criticism directed at loved ones is an especially insidious form of black magic, since people who have opened themselves to you—children and spouses in particular—are very vulnerable to your projected attitudes. It should be considered an act of violence to enter another person's consciousness to change him against his will!"

"I've heard this term, 'astral attack' or 'psychic attack' before," I commented. "But I'm confused about what it means. Do you mean that we can actually hurt other people through currents of energy directed at them inwardly?"

"That's right," affirmed Kyari. "It is rare for people to realize that they are doing this, certainly. Most do not believe that thoughts can have any effect on others. But of course, they do. A powerful person, or a group with a strongly focused intention, can affect other people through directed thoughts. However, anyone can easily survive these attacks by simply centering himself within the positive current. In this way, negative flows with nowhere to go boomerang on the senders. I do not suggest, however, that anyone practice techniques of sending back these negative flows. This reduces you to the level of your attackers, and opens you to further problems.

"Now, I'd also like to point out that what most people call

'psychic attacks,' are merely their own problematic inner pictures being stimulated by negative forces around them. In other words, more often than not, the problem lies within the one who feels attacked. The 'victim' projects the cause of his troubles to an outside source because he is unwilling to take responsibility for what ails him. Where do you pick up these negative flows? If you aren't careful, from anywhere. You can pick them up from movies, television, news reports, even from supermarkets!

"Supermarkets?" I repeated, raising my eyebrows.

"Seems farfetched? All right. Imagine this scenario: You're angry with your husband about something that you haven't expressed. You wander into the supermarket to buy some groceries. While shopping, you observe a mother yelling angrily at her child. Later on at home, your husband does something that makes you mad. Soon, your attention is completely absorbed on a hundred things that bother you about him. Then, the next time the smallest thing triggers you, the lid blows off! Your reaction is totally out of proportion to the offense. Your spouse is astonished. What happened?"

"I can relate to that!" I laughed. "I guess the point is, first you have to be open to the negative current by some harmonic chord within yourself. But you can pick up these currents anywhere."

"Yes," smiled Kyari. "Anywhere. To not only survive, but to thrive spiritually in the lower worlds, one has to be alert and aware of what is happening within his inner space. This is difficult for most people, whose inner faculties are like muscles that are flabby from disuse. Psychology isn't much help, since it regards everything that happens inwardly as unreal mental phenomena. Dreams are also considered to be mental phenomena. The truth is, the inner worlds are real, and full of real events. Until mankind takes this statement seriously, his survival will be precarious at best."

"Look!" called Haurvata, pointing into the sky. We gazed upwards and saw the herd of winged horses flying overhead.

"They're so beautiful," I sighed. "Does anyone ever try to capture any?"

The two Adepts laughed. "Just try it," chuckled Haurvata. "No, my friend, it is impossible without force. But they have been known to befriend a few fortunate Souls. They cannot be tamed, but they can be persuaded to stay and serve man out of love. I know one or two of the gallant beasts myself. You've ridden them as a child.

Perhaps you will again."

"Well!" said Kyari, taking a deep breath. "I think we need to end this discussion soon. So I would like to mention something of utmost importance in the coming years. You see, daughter, there is another important reason we have taken so much time to educate you on the mysteries of the astral plane. Do you know, by any chance, about something your scientists are warning of—the creation of ozone holes in the earth's atmosphere?"

"Yes," I replied. "It's increasing everyone's risk of skin cancer and is due to the depletion of the ozone layer. It's caused by releasing polluting chemicals—I think mainly chlorofluorocarbons—into the air."

Kyari nodded. "The ozone is a thin shield of gas in the stratosphere, the upper region of the earth's atmosphere. The ozone protects your planet from the harmful ultraviolent rays of the sun. When chlorofluorocarbon floats up and comes into contact with ultraviolet rays, it breaks down into its components, which include chlorine. Eventually, through a chain reaction, chlorine changes the ozone into plain oxygen, which can't shield the earth from ultraviolet rays. Now, the thinning of your ozone layer isn't the only effect your technology is having upon the earth's atmosphere. Some of your supersonic jets and attempts at space exploration have also penetrated the atmosphere. Nothing is known about the physical effects from these activities yet. But my concern is not physical, but spiritual.

"You see, the surrounding layers of gases that protect the earth constitutes the spiritual body of the planet, similar to the emanation of light around the body that you call an 'aura.' When this aura is disturbed, it changes the experiences of the people who live within it. You can understand this if you simply extend the concept of a group 'consciousness' for every collective body of sentient beings to include planets and solar systems. Thus, if changing a nation's consciousness is fraught with certain tensions, then shifting the consciousness of a planet is bound to produce some upheavals as well.

"The advances of modern technology and space exploration are changing the collective consciousness of the earth at a pace unheard of in the history of this planet. The movement toward greater global awareness is slowly replacing the consciousness of races and nations.

Space is now certifiably man's new frontier. Most important of all has been the growth of objective exploration into previously unobservable realms such as the atomic and subatomic. As man moves further into the realms of the invisible, his imagination will be freed to explore the subjective worlds and discover its reality.

"Any questions so far?" asked Kyari, wading into the water at the stream's edge.

"Huh? . . . Oh! Sorry, I was just thinking about what you were saying! Yes. It occurs to me that since the astral and the physical planes are so close together, the weakening of the planetary aura might let in more of the astral currents to the earth."

"Very good!" beamed Kyari. "This has been happening already in some areas. For example, the higher tones of pastel colors, similar to what you'd see in the upper astral plane, have come into popularity. Movies and books which are entirely science fiction and fantasy, or contain some of these elements, are increasingly popular. Space has already replaced the 'Western' as the popular adventure genre, and for good reason. The Western looks back to the past, but space adventures call up the future. You can have more imagination and fun with the future!

"However, more serious influences from the astral include these: There is a possibility that you will see more charismatic people rising to the leadership of your planet. This is physically possible because of the global dimension of communications technology today. But it will be even more likely in the future because a psychically developed individual can tap into the astral currents and use them to capture the attention of the masses. Now there are two ways to look at this. First, there is the possibility of demagogues leading the world to disaster. Second, charismatic figures may appear who will inspire the masses to greater individual and collective growth. Obviously, it could go both ways, and probably will!"

"You will need some unity, however, since eventually, in the next century, you will be confronted with the reality of intelligent life on other planets. Although things could change, I predict that earth will have its visitors within your grandchildren's lifetime . . . granted that you have grandchildren! This contact with other planets will come as a shock to most people. They will need strong and able leaders to lead them peacefully and confidently into the new reality of the global and solar community.

248

"A good analogy to this situation is one you're already familiar with. Before Commodore Matthew Perry opened Japan to commerce in the mid-nineteenth century, the Japanese felt their nation to be the race favored by the 'kami'—the gods. All others were 'barbarians'—not even completely human. The Japanese were ignorant of the vastness of the world and their own relative backwardness in many areas. Although they were not aware of the outside world, the outside world was aware of them! Eventually, the two had to meet and interact. In the same way, your planet and the rest of your solar system are bound to bump into each other. The universe is getting too small to avoid this much longer."

"O.K." I said, joining Kyari in the shimmering stream. "If I am going to be in the middle of all of this, what should I do? How can I prepare myself better?"

"I can answer that," laughed Kyari, splashing water on my legs with her foot. "Maintain a close connection with Spirit at all times. Keep your outer and inner bodies in tone so that no blockages shut this contact off. Clear up any and all debris you're carrying from any past life or the present life. Maintain your independence from the mass consciousness of the planet that would open you to the psychic currents that affect groups. Be aware of these currents, but be apart from them. Most important of all, fill your life with people and activities that you love and make you feel good about yourself and the world. Since life is an extension of imagination, now more than ever before, you need to avoid fear, pessimism, and all negative emotions in favor of love, positive expectation, and creativity. This is what a warrior would do. And the time to do it is now."

Haurvata laughed uproariously as Kyari and I resorted to splashing water on each other. Finally, I slipped and fell and Kyari fell trying to lift me up. Somehow, Kyari and I both got the same idea and, after a sidelong glance at each other, rushed out of the stream to attempt to drag Haurvata into our watery playground. Our attempts proved futile, as he was too strong for us. So we sat on the grass, wet and happy, and talked together for a long time afterwards.

CHAPTER TWENTY
A Perfect One

I returned to my physical body in time to finish my preparations for teaching and to get my work done around the house. However, the adventures of the morning were so overwhelming that I was withdrawn and distracted for several days afterwards. During that time, I had several dreams on the lower astral plane. In one of these experiences, I helped a woman who had committed suicide by jumping from a building to realize she was dead, and escorted her to a place where she could get further assistance.

Angry and panic-stricken, the woman had attached herself to me like a drowning person and dragged me down to an area of heavy negative current. There I was attacked by an entity who tried to strangle me with an illusory necklace, which was really her psychic hands around my throat. I ripped the necklace off with some effort and flung it to the ground. I pointed a finger directly at my attacker and shouted a spiritually charged word I knew. With that, I was lifted out of the danger and back to my sleeping body.

In another experience, I found myself again on the lower astral plane guarding a group of people 'demonstrating,' for lack of a better word, for the rights of homosexuals. A man with enormous anger against homosexuals attacked me. He was not well-versed in the use of astral powers, however, and he merely resorted to striking at me with his fists. Defending myself was much easier in this case, and I was quickly able to remove him to another place before waking up in bed.

I wrote these dreams down and spent some time reviewing my dream patterns over the past two months. I was interested to see that lately my experiences during sleep had become less and less symbolic and more and more "real." Yet the kind of reality I was now facing was unpleasant at best and frightening at worst. I wondered how this turn of events could possibly signify progress in my spiritual life. Without the help of the Adepts, I was forced to contemplate on this question on my own for two weeks. At the end of that period, I began to worry. What if they were never going to come back? Did this mean that I was now completely on my own?

One day, late at night, my husband visited me in my office and dropped a brochure on my desk.

"What is this?" I asked blankly, picking up the paper.

"It's information on that inn I heard about at the office," he answered, yawning. "It's reasonably priced, especially during the off-season, and I hear it's pretty nice. Look, I think you should go. Just to relax. Take your computer and write if you like. Read, walk along the beach, that sort of thing."

I stared at him, then opened the brochure. On it were descriptions of various cottages and their prices. A map showed that it was about two hours drive north of San Francisco above Bodega Bay. I looked up at my husband and he smiled.

"I thought I heard you say that you don't have any teaching work for a week. Why don't you go for two or three days? We can manage without you for that long. I think it would do you good to get away. If you like the place, we can go there together some other time."

I threw my arms around my husband and gave him a long hug. It was the answer to a prayer. The next day I made a reservation and before long, I was on my way. The drive took nearly four hours, but I spent it well, listening to my favorite music and thinking. I had forgotten the way long drives in open countryside soothed my spirits and stimulated the formation of new connections in my brain. The rugged California coastline with its curving shores, mist, and seagulls flying was spectacular. The smell of the sea spray mingled with the fresh scent of spring flowers and nearly drove my senses wild.

By the time I reached the inn, I had surrendered much of what had been bothering me during the past two weeks. Although I still had many questions, my confidence in the future was renewed. I accepted that life would be somehow different for me from now on, and I would meet the challenges as they came up with a cheerful and trusting attitude. If I'd truly been dreaming in a cave for so long, I was now curious about what it would be like to soar on the wings of Soul.

I lugged my bags and groceries into my cottage and wandered outside. The manager had pointed across the street to a trail leading to a cliff overlooking the ocean. I walked along it, noticing the orange-poppy foliage that was beginning to spring up everywhere. In the summer, this area would be a mass of orange and green. At the cliff's edge, I sat on a rock and watched the whitecaps form and dissolve and the waves endlessly rolling to the shore. A group of pelicans flew by in formation, breaking up to dive for fish, then regrouping once more.

After nearly an hour, I stood up to walk back. Haurvata was standing behind me, his hands clasped behind his back.

"Aloha," he said, a tiny twinkle in his eyes.

"What?" I laughed, shaking my head. "This is California, not Hawaii."

"It is not significant," shrugged the Adept. "Aloha means 'with the breath of God.' Did you know that?"

"I do now," I grinned. "What are you hiding behind your back?"

"This," the Tibetan said, proffering a handful of red poppies on long, hairy stems.

"Oh, how beautiful!" I exclaimed, accepting the unexpected bouquet. "Where did you get them? It's too early for poppies yet!"

"Not in some parts of the world," smiled the Tibetan slyly. "Inner travel has its advantages!"

We walked along the cliff, enjoying the mild weather and the delicious smells of evergreens and wild grasses. Then Haurvata turned to me.

"We have left you alone to adjust to your new experiences," he began. "It takes time to digest things, and with spiritual growth, this

252

is especially so. But we wanted you to know that we have no intention of disappearing forever from your life. We are your friends. Our association has been long in the making. We simply wish to shift the nature of our relationship somewhat. To use a metaphor, you are no longer a 'child' in spiritual terms. You are an 'adolescent' who must begin to think about the eventuality of being on your own in the 'adult' world of the higher planes. What do you want to be when you grow up? How are you preparing for this ambition in the present? These are the kinds of questions you should be asking yourself now."

"I understand," I nodded. "I've been thinking a lot about this. I've decided that I would one day like to be an Unmani Dhun Adept like you and Kyari. Beyond that, I don't know. But it's a pretty good start, don't you think?"

Haurvata chuckled. "Yes, a pretty good start."

He led the way to a grassy area that was protected from the breezes by a buffer of low cypresses. I lay on my back squinting up into the sky.

"Look, I'm getting better at answering my own questions, Haurvata. But there is one thing I couldn't figure out myself. Can I ask you about it?"

"Certainly," replied the Adept.

I reported my recent dreams to Haurvata, who only listened and nodded. I added, "I've noticed that lately my dreams have been changing. They aren't so symbolic anymore. Why is that?"

The Tibetan answered, "Essentially, symbolic experiences come from the plane of the higher mind, which some call the 'etheric.' For example, your two dreams of the ripe pumpkins and the thawing whales were both pure etheric experiences. Other dreams may have some degree of symbolism, depending on how much of the etheric current is present in them. Stories, like dreams, also vary as to how much symbolism is present. Some are very naturalistic and straightforward, say like a modern murder mystery. Other stories, like fairytales, are generally very symbolic.

"You are having many straightforward experiences on the inner levels right now, especially on the astral. We want you to learn to operate with complete confidence there because of the increasing blending of the two worlds now and in the future. But you will soon have many more clear experiences on planes above the astral as well.

This will come in due time. For now, you are handling yourself well and doing a good job where you are. I know it is sometimes unpleasant, but think of it as 'basic training' for greater duties. At any rate, your help is needed and appreciated, believe me.

"Now, I want to bring something to your attention. You still have one troublesome area locked in the inner bodies that we have not been able to dislodge so far. It has caused you to stop short of mastership several times before. It is a pity, and we would not like to have this happen again. Do you remember the girl in the hospital who was healed by looking at and releasing those painful images from her past? Well, I propose we do something similar. No, we do not have to go there to accomplish this. If you are willing, just close your eyes and see me in your inner vision. I will take you from there."

I did as I was told. The Adept appeared inwardly and the next thing I knew, I was in the passenger car of a steam locomotive clicking along the tracks. Haurvata was sitting at my side. I relaxed at once, recognizing it from a previous experience "between" times. As usual, the physical surroundings were realistic down to the last detail. Even my clothing was beautifully authentic. I took time to admire the silver bracelet set with seed pearls on my wrist, and the needlepoint handbag decorated with red roses. I smiled at Haurvata, who looked formidably dignified with gold-rimmed spectacles perched on his broad nose.

Haurvata winked back. He pointed to the floor at my feet, and as I looked down I was startled to see a white rabbit in a wire cage. I threw a questioning glance at my teacher and scooped up the cage, placing it gingerly on my lap.

"I believe you already know our fellow-traveler," Haurvata said graciously, nodding to the white rabbit.

"I don't think so," I replied, raising my eyebrows. I peered curiously into the cage. At the same time, the rabbit stared back, his delicate nose pressing against the wire enclosure. Suddenly, a thought flashed through my mind. From some cob-webbed corner of my memories, it leaped out to startle me.

"Pinky!" I exclaimed. The rabbit, of course, merely wiggled his nose and stared straight ahead. I found the latch to the cage door and opened it, lifting the small animal onto my lap. I set the empty cage back down on the floor of the train.

"Is it really Pinky?" I asked Haurvata excitedly.

Haurvata chuckled and cleared his throat. "If I may speak for the rabbit—yes, it is truly Pinky, your long-eared friend from your childhood! I thought you might like his company for a brief time. Pinky is on his way to another incarnation, and this is your last chance to see him in his present form."

I thanked the Adept and proceeded to stroke Pinky. The rabbit seemed calm and used to being touched. Even the occasional lurch of the train did not seem to bother him as we sped onward along the rails. Finally, I asked the Adept what we were doing here.

The Adept smiled and reached over to scratch between the rabbit's ears. "We are, as it were, on the 'time track.' It is merely a way to concretize the travel back and forth between experiences in time and space. Since you dislike a lack of form, it is also a way to make you more comfortable with the process. It is also a rather pleasant way to travel, don't you think?"

I laughed and agreed. "I'm glad it's not a hang-glider!"

"Now," began Haurvata, "I am going to allow you to re-experience a small segment of your past. Are you ready for this?"

"I am."

"All right, then. Let's begin."

The sun was suddenly very bright and I held my hand up against the glare. However, no longer was it an impeccably-gloved hand with a silver bracelet. It was, instead, large and leathery-skinned. My awareness at this point was a confused mixture of who I was then and now. Finally, however, the reality of the present faded like a dream and I was once again only the man himself, filled with a deep hatred.

I looked back from where I had ridden. No dust in the distance meant no pursuers. Ahead of me the horizon was empty of life. I took a drink from the pouch hanging at my side and nudged my mount, a bay mare, forward. The sweat on her flanks would have made her shine, but for the thick coat of dust on her. I patted her on the neck and spoke to her soothingly, reassuringly. To my left some low hills offered promise of shade soon, as the sun, high overhead for several hours, was now lowering to the west. I thought briefly whether I wanted to take the chance of capture by resting now, but the weariness of my horse and my own exhaustion made my decision for me. Whether I died here this day, I had to stop.

I turned my mare's head to the furthest outcrop of rock and found a secure position from which I could survey the land around me for several miles. Several miles was, of course, hardly enough if anyone was in pursuit. But it would have to do. I unrolled my bedding, removed my sword, and lay down, clutching its hilt. Within seconds, I was asleep.

The release into sleep was also a release from the body. I was above everything now, and could see for many more miles than from my human vantage point. In the far distance I saw something that disturbed me—a small swirl of dust, maybe eight men in all, riding hard this way. I tried to get back into my body but found I could not. It was like trying to open a locked door. Banging and hollering didn't seem to work. Desperately, I called for the Adept, and he was there beside me again in the train rocking monotonously on its rails.

"Haurvata!" I sputtered. "You've got to do something. He doesn't know he'll be caught. They're gaining on him even now. Let me back inside!" In my excitement, I jumped to my feet and spilled the rabbit from my lap. Pinky hopped down the aisle a few yards and a few women cried aloud. The Tibetan got to his feet and retrieved the rabbit, appologizing to the shocked women with a gentlemanly doffing of his hat. Once in his seat, he stuffed Pinky back in his cage and latched it securely. I was still upset.

"Calm yourself," he admonished me. "You should know that this was a past life experience. You were only temporarily allowed to 'visit' that existence in order to gain a lesson for your present growth. The man you were died more than two thousand years ago! You cannot help him now. Now sit down and behave rationally."

I crumpled into my seat and took some deep breaths, orienting myself again to the facts: I was in a mock-up of a train moving along the time track. I was no longer the man being pursued as I slept. I sighed deeply and looked at the Adept. "I'm O.K. now. But please, explain this to me."

Haurvata gazed out the window of the train and began. "In that lifetime you were a soldier. From a humble background, you worked your way to a captain's rank through courage, physical strength, and a talent for military strategy. You were quietly charismatic, and your men developed great loyalty to you. In service to your superiors, you waged a war on surrounding city-states which destroyed towns and killed many people, leaving the survivors to become slaves. You did not once consider the human consequences of your acts. You were not cruel, but you were morally naive. Your sole purpose was to blindly serve the cause of your leaders.

"One day, however, you chanced to overhear a conversation that changed your life. On your way to meet with one of your superiors, you heard two men talking in a courtyard. The coming war with a neighboring city-state was being discussed. Listening to them, it became clear to you that the politics among your own generals was not entirely straightforward. Instead of idealism, you found yourself face to face with a grim reality of power: scheming, double-dealing, and betrayal. It opened your eyes in a way you were not prepared for. As time went by, you pieced together much that was wrong with the way the war was being planned, due to the machinations of some generals for personal gain. In fact, you found that you and your own men were going to be sent into a battle that could not possibly be won.

"In the past, you had never questioned the necessity of dying for the sake of victory. Now the knowledge of what was behind this sacrifice embittered you. It made your usual isolation among men of better breeding more unbearable, and exacerbated your tendencies to brood. Eventually, you became involved with a plot to overthrow a faction of the generals most responsible for the problems you perceived. The plot failed, however, and your confederates were executed. You escaped, but before long they found you and, outnumbering you, killed you as well.

"One of that party of riders you detected in the cloud of dust just now was your lover. He had been forced to ride with the group and take part in the attack on you. The man charged at you with his sword, and you automatically swung with yours to defend yourself. At that moment, you knew he had acted only in order to die at your hands. As you stared at his blood-spurting body with shock and grief, another soldier slew you from behind. Many of your problems in subsequent incarnations stem from this lifetime. They form a pattern which tends to repeat itself due to the emotional charge the seed experience still holds for you. I want you to contemplate on this experience and learn what the pattern is. Then you must release it once and for all by blessing it and going on to more constructive things!"

Something inside me was shaken loose by my glimpse into this past life and all that I was being told. It rattled around in my consciousness like an object in an otherwise empty box, disturbing and agitating me. I allowed myself to sink down into these feelings, which came in waves, until I was weeping openly and uncontrollably. I opened my purse and found a dainty lace handkerchief which I promptly used up with one good honk of my nose.

"Here," said Haurvata, pressing a man's handkerchief into my hand. "This one is more practical."

I used it and still the tears kept coming. Waves upon waves of grief and anger, mixed with thoughts I could now name, broke upon me. Finally, I began, "It's so complex, Haurvata. I . . . it's hard to know where to start."

"Start anywhere, my dear," said the Adept gently.

"All right," I quavered, taking a deep breath. "I guess I felt like a pawn in that lifetime. People in authority used me to fulfill their personal agendas, against my own welfare and the welfare of other people, including my own men. But I was too naive and ignorant to see it. My egotism blinded me from looking too closely at what I was doing. I accepted the goals I was handed by my superiors because it was convenient for me. I liked being a soldier. No, maybe I wasn't cruel, but I was responsible for a lot of senseless butchery nevertheless. It made me really angry to realize what a fool I had been. Then, at the point of death, the horror of having killed my own lover and being slain from behind filled me with total rage. This was not how I wanted to die!

"My last thoughts were ones of bitterness and helplessness. In this lifetime, I've had to work to control my reaction to resist and criticize authority. My basic belief has been that people who give orders are generally serving themselves, not others. I hate bureaucracy, rules whose only purpose is to control others, and authoritarian people in general. Passive people who just do as they're told drive me wild, too. It's difficult for me to have compassion for those two types of people: the followers and the bullies. I guess it's because I haven't forgiven myself for having been both!"

I laughed, a little weakly.

"The irony is, after years of destroying other people's lives, I came to know how it felt to be hunted down like an animal . . . yes, it was divine retribution all right! But the strange thing is, for two thousand years I've carried this grudge!"

Haurvata nodded. "Your anger became an automatic and ingrained attitude, and therefore a stumbling block for Soul. You went so far with it that you became suspicious even of God! Frankly, my dear, this pattern made surrender to the Holy Spirit next to impossible for you, and day-to-day obedience difficult. Because of this handicap, you were forced to exert an enormous amount of will power to cooperate with the Higher Self, instead of following its guidance naturally. This in turn exhausted and depleted your spiritual vitality and stamina at those very moments when you needed it most. Now you must surrender your anger and mistrust to Spirit. You cannot go any higher on the spiritual path without shedding this archaic aberration.

"It goes without saying that you must exercise watchfulness with all authoritarian structures within the human domain. The government, the church—nothing human can be exempt from ignorance, vanity, greed, and lust for power. But the authority of the Holy Spirit is different. It serves the whole, including the individual Soul, and therefore when you serve it, you also serve the whole. The Holy Spirit will never ask you to do harm to others or yourself. Nor does it 'use' you in the sense that you object to. The relationship between the individual and this life force is a reciprocal one. It is more like two lovers who give pleasure to each other, than a hand that employs a tool! Do you see the difference?"

I was silent for a while, searching myself for the answer. After a long time, I answered. "Yes. I see the difference. I think I'm going to let go of this baggage right now. Do you have any advice?"

Haurvata shrugged. "What do you think you should do?"

"Well," I said, taking a deep breath, "what about going back to the man and communicating with him? I'll make him see his experience in light of the whole, and he will realize that he was not a victim. He has learned something and now has the experience to do better. Do you think it will work?"

"Yes," said Haurvata. "I think so. But remember, daughter, communicate all this on a current of love. The mind powers do not reach Soul. Then bless him and surrender him to God."

I closed my eyes and found myself in a silvery plain with the man, fresh from death and very angry. I approached him cautiously and did as I planned. Haurvata was right. The current of love that passed from me to him allowed the wisdom I now carried to penetrate his resistance and sink in. The man thought I was an angelic spirit or goddess. I didn't disabuse him of this idea, but merely smiled and pointed to the bright white path that beckoned him to his place in the heavenly worlds. He left me and walked swiftly out of sight.

Back in the train, I was quiet. Finally, I said to my teacher, "Haurvata, I really do think he absorbed what I communicated."

"Of course," smiled the Tibetan. "I had no doubt that he would."

"Then . . . that should change everything in my lives up until now. But how could that be?"

"The naturalistic events that occur in time and space are not susceptible to change," answered Haurvata. "They are fixed in place by their own self-limited laws. But the subjective side of life does not operate within time-space laws. It exists, instead, as an accumulation of impressions from experiences, rather than the experiences themselves. These impressions survive as images with varying degrees of spiritual energy, both positive and negative, attached to them. Images with strong energy tend to survive longer and cause you to repeat similar experiences in the world of time and space. Weaker images fade and eventually disappear altogether. The relative energy behind these images is the feeling component they contain.

"When you change your subjective viewpoint about a previous experience, you do not change the physical events that comprise the experience, but the kind of impressions you store in your inner bodies regarding it. As a result, the meaning of the experience and the effect it has upon you is altered. For example, a childhood disappointment may be borne with grief, but as years go by, the individual may realize that greater strength and understanding came as a result of this early setback.

"In your own childhood, you desired arts experiences and lessons but could not have them because your family was not cultured or rich. But later you saw that this limitation was Spirit's way of guiding you to take up writing, and to depend upon inner, rather than outer, teachers. By taking a higher viewpoint on this outward limitation, you did not actually modify the 'facts' of your case. But today you think about, feel, see, and express these same facts very differently than you did, say, ten years ago. Don't be surprised if your interpretation continues to alter with the passage of time and increased awareness. Therefore, in essence, your life has significantly changed. Your inner growth has 'rewritten' the past, in the spiritual sense, if not the physical.

"As inner growth takes place, the destructive images are dissolved, one by one, and replaced with ideals of love, surrender, and service. But, as we've shown you, this is a delicate process and must be done gradually and carefully so that the structure of the personality is kept intact. And so it has been with you. We have had to move slowly so as not to collide with your fixed ideas and throw you into inner rebellion against your own teachers! If we made a mistake and triggered one of your negative images, we could easily have caused you to dig in your heels or even backslide into guilt and hopelessness. So you see, my friend, being a spiritual teacher is not easy! The self-proclaimed gurus and preachers of your world have no idea how complex it is to assist anybody to make a single real inner change.

"To conclude, when you went 'back' to speak with yourself after the soldier's death, you did not change anything in time and space. But you did alter something far more important: your attachment to attitudes of anger and suspicion against authority, and self-hatred for the mistakes you made. No one can actually alter anything within you but yourself. The higher beings can assist by providing the proper tools and teaching you to use them, but only you can fix your own problems and take another step along the path to God. When you become one of us, you will understand more about this sacred relationship between the inner teacher and his or her student.

"By the way, you haven't mentioned anything about how you felt upon discovering that you had a male lover in that lifetime as a soldier. Did this surprise you?"

"It sure did!" I exclaimed. "Everything else was so overwhelming, I just forgot to say anything about it. The funny thing is, it didn't feel strange from 'his' point of view. In fact, I felt a really deep affection for my lover. It wasn't just lust."

"No," nodded Haurvata. "Many people seem to think that homosexuality is necessarily based upon lust, but that isn't so. There can be real love between any two people, and when this is true, sex can be a normal and balanced expression of that affection. It is sexual excess that is an aberration, not sexual preference. There is probably as much or more heterosexual lust as homosexual lust, but one is accepted while the other is not. This is a societal matter and not a spiritual one. As far as the Unmani Dhun are concerned, sex is only another area for lessons in love, awareness, and responsibility, not any more or less important than any other area of life.

"Most people have been homosexual in one lifetime or another. The irony is that they often return in subsequent lifetimes to persecute the very thing they enjoyed in former lifetimes. These persecutors have often been excessive in their own previous homosexual incarnations and have not yet cleared up the emotional charges and imbalances from those lifetimes. Other people who may not persecute homosexuals, but who are unsympathetic toward them, simply lack tolerance for differences due to a relative want of spiritual experience, or due to stereotyped ideas of what homosexuals are like.

"The man who attacked you on the lower astral was clearly one of the imbalanced type. You had this experience due to a small debt you carried yourself from a lack of compassion for homosexuals in this lifetime. The opening up of your own homosexual incarnations will soon balance this deficit in you. Such personal knowledge would not necessarily work the same way on others, however. It might further inflame, rather than pacify, them. Therefore, knowledge is always a carefully guarded commodity in the lower worlds. It is not because we of the inner community are stingy with our wisdom, but because so few of you can use it safely and constructively. Yet, when Soul is ready, nothing will prevent it from finding its golden opportunity for growth."

"Haurvata," I began, thinking aloud, "I'm wondering how Soul learns to gain understanding through male and female, heterosexual and homosexual, experiences. Based on what you said, we learn through impressions made on our inner bodies. Do these impressions survive as male and female images? Or are they more generic than that?"

"Images survive carrying whatever is subjectively signficant about them," answered the Tibetan. "Therefore, the crux of the matter is, you can identify with your sex or sexual preference and interpret all your experiences from that point of view. Or, you can identify with Soul and understand everything as steps to becoming a co-worker with God. We have put a great deal of attention on your understanding of masculine and feminine currents to help you to understand and balance these aspects within yourself. This has helped to neutralize your identification with both sexes and free you to take a higher point of view. The study of male and female is not an end in itself, but a means to discovering the imperishable part of you: that is, Soul.

"In the future, remember that men and women seek each other instinctively for a sense of wholeness and never find it. But they can also reach out to each other with love, and begin the inner healing that makes them each complete. Love between two people can be a granting of space, a giving of respect and dignity, and a helping hand on the path to self-mastery. It does not have to be the quicksand of attachment and emotions that the Shangra Raj would have it be. However, never stand in the way of anyone who chooses the negative side of love for himself out of a desire to rescue him from pain. Pain is often the only way for Spirit to carry a strong enough impression into the inner bodies to trigger understanding and growth. But this you should know from your own lives! Do not let your own wisdom make you foolish. Keep to your own path and your progress will be swift."

The Tibetan looked deeply into my eyes until I felt as if I were sinking down into the blue-green waters of the basin fed by the Sword of Light. For a few moments a slight buzzing filled my ears, as if a tiny bee had found its way inside the hive of my brain. Then the buzzing spread all over my body, becoming a subtle vibration from a current of spiritual energy surging through me. I instinctively closed my eyes, centering myself in the Soul awareness.

I was standing on the peak of a mountain of molten white light. Below me its slopes angled sharply and plunged far below. Streams of colored lights, mainly pinks, roses, and shades of blue and violet mixed in turbulent waves back and forth at the base of the mountain. Some of the colored streams reached upward and traveled a distance, until they finally became transformed into the white hot light that did not burn.

Suddenly I realized that I was not only upon the mountain, but I was the mountain itself! As I perceived this, my awareness grew to encompass my body—bright white light, with swirls of color reaching upward at the base. I felt many things very vaguely: emotions, thoughts, memories, desires. They seemed to come from far away, below me. As I moved my attention higher up the mountain of light, which was also myself, these voices grew quieter, then fell silent. Finally, I felt myself lifting above the pinnacle of this mountain like an eagle circling on wind currents. I felt only an inner peace and a tremendous love for life.

All too soon, I was back in the train, Haurvata's eyes still upon me. "What did you experience?" he asked me gently.

"It was a triangular-shaped mountain of light," I answered. "I was on the mountain of light . . . and I was the mountain!"

"Yes," repeated the Tibetan, with a change of verb tense, "you are the mountain. You saw yourself as the complete spiritual being you have become, my friend—the trinity of positive, negative, and neutral, or male, female, and Soul. You have become whole—a perfect one."

The Tibetan fell silent. I looked out of the window of the train as it rushed by a wilderness of plains and scrub brush. Then a sight caught at my throat: an Indian on horseback, far away on a low knoll. He held his lance proudly, watching our phantom train rumble past, alone with his thoughts. Did his warrior spirit reach out to mine? Or did mine reach out to his? I strained to hold a last glimpse of him before he disappeared from sight. His image rose in my heart and shone there as clearly as any star.

Suddenly, I no longer felt so insecure, so alone. Beyond time and space, something of me existed that could never be extinguished by death, no matter how brutal, or peaceful, or ignoble. It wasn't simply a matter of the survival of Soul. That I had already known and accepted long before. But now I realized that through all of the many ups and downs of lives, something precious had been growing. It was Soul's individuality. For me, this meant that I could stop measuring myself against some generic and illusory standard of spirituality. Instead, I could begin to discover and explore my own place in the universe. It meant that I could learn to be myself. I could become Real!

I told Haurvata of my perception. "I'll miss my little woodenhead," he laughed, patting my knee. "But I shall get used to it!"

The train came to a stop and we got off, leaving Pinky behind to arrive at his next lifetime. A little boy on board waved to us and Haurvata and I waved back. The train rumbled by, covering us with a fine layer of dirt. I shielded my eyes and sneezed once into my hands. When I looked up again, I was lying on my back in the grass above the thundering Pacific Ocean. Overhead, three seagulls screeched and hovered on the updrafts. The wind had picked up and the afternoon had turned decidedly chilly. I sat awhile longer, gazing out into the horizon that stretched out farther and farther until it blended into the universe. Soon the whales would come, breaching along the invisible road they followed to their breeding grounds in the hospitable waters of a far country.

The whales were the travelers of the open sea. I, too, was one of them, following the inner path wherever it led me, with the instinct of Soul.

About the Author

Ariel Tomioka (*pronounced Toe-mi-OH-ka*) was born in Honolulu, Hawaii. She is a published poet and for several years was a writer-in-residence at many California public schools. She now devotes herself full-time to writing, speaking, and presenting workshops on the subjects of male-female relationships, dreams, creativity, and the processes of individuation and self-mastery. Ms. Tomioka welcomes letters from readers who wish to share their insights and experiences. Please write to her in care of Helios House.

Index

THE WAY OF THE WRITER
by Ariel Tomioka

A Unique Study Course for Writers and Spiritual Students

A very special twelve lesson course focusing on the spiritual foundation for the art of writing. The course aims to develop a broad and unique perspective—that of the writer's life as a spiritual path, as well as an artistic endeavor. Lessons are sent at six week intervals; the course may be studied individually or in a group (a roster of other course participants is sent to each new participant).

The course covers development of the inner faculties as well as the physical senses in order to write with originality and creativity; the spiritual power of language; distilling and condensing language through poetic training; the elements of fiction; how spiritual literature has developed in modern times; and much more of interest to all writers and spiritual students. Each lesson includes an in-depth essay on the subject of the particular lesson, spiritual exercises specifically for the writer, writing assignments, questions for further study and discussion, and an annotated reading list of pertinent books for follow-up.

The cost of the full twelve lesson course is $120.00, which includes all postage and handling (outside the U.S., the cost is $130.00). The first two lessons may be purchased on a "trial basis" for $20.00 (outside the U.S, $22.00). The introductory lesson set includes the full course syllabus and a three-ring binder for the course materials. To order, complete the Helios House book order form in this book.

WRITING TOWARDS WISDOM:

THE WRITER AS SHAMAN

by Robert Burdette Sweet

Robert Burdette Sweet, author and a teacher of creative writing, explores the elements of fiction, not merely as techniques, but as tools for personal integration and worldly understanding. Using the metaphor of the writer as shaman—a guide to our inner worlds—Sweet offers insights to keep your writing fresh and dramatic from start to finish. Includes tips for story structure, tapping into archetypes, and using personal material as the stuff of writing. This book will intrigue those who write and read for pleasure as well as those who are planning to make a living at writing.

Writing Towards Wisdom
The Writer as Shaman
By Robert Burdette Sweet

"Some of the most brilliant observations yet written about the craft of fiction." John Clark Pratt, General Editor, Hamilton Press

"Rarely have I seen the intuitive process of writing articulated so well." Alan Soldofsky, San Jose Poetry Center

"The world would be a much better place if everyone read *Writing Towards Wisdom.*" William Packard, Editor, *New York Quarterly*

ISBN 0-923490-01-9   **U.S. $9.95**

HELIOS HOUSE ORDER FORM

PLEASE SEND THIS ORDER FORM TO HELIOS HOUSE OR USE IT TO PREPARE A CREDIT CARD ORDER. TO ORDER BY TELEPHONE, CALL 1-800-765-4354 FROM ANYWHERE IN THE U.S. (INCLUDING HAWAII) AND CANADA.

❏　Please send me _____ copies of *On the Breath of the Gods* by Ariel Tomioka @ U.S. $9.95 each.

❏　Please send me _____ copies of *Writing Towards Wisdom* by Robert Burdette Sweet @ U.S. $9.95 each.

❏　Please register me in the *The Way of the Writer* study course by Ariel Tomioka @ U.S. $120.00 ($130.00 outside U.S.), including all postage and handling.

❏　Please send me the Introductory Lesson Set (Lessons 1 & 2) of *The Way of the Writer* study course by Ariel Tomioka @ U.S. $20.00 ($22.00 outside U.S.), including postage and handling.

❏　Please send me _____ copies of *Integrating the Male-Female Energies for Self-Mastery* (audiotape) by Ariel Tomioka @ U.S. $9.95 each.

❏　Please send me _____ copies of *The Hero's Journey* (audiotape) by Ariel Tomioka @ U.S. $9.95 each.

❏　I do not wish to place an order at this time, but please place my name on the Helios House mailing list to receive your newsletter/catalog.

Name _____

Address _____

City _____ State _____ Zip _____

Country (if outside U.S.) _____

VISA/MC No. _____ Exp. Date _____

Total Due for Books/Tapes/Study Course _____

California Residents add 6.5% Sales Tax _____

Total Due for Shipping (see last page of book) _____

Total Amount Due (or to be Billed to Credit Card) _____

INTEGRATING THE MALE-FEMALE ENERGIES FOR SELF-MASTERY

Thought-provoking talk by Ariel Tomioka on giving and receiving profound interpersonal love. Ms. Tomioka explains the need to live with "creative discomfort" and shares how she came to realize this through her own life experiences. Ms. Tomioka discusses the obstacles to self-mastery, the conflict between the ideals of "balance" and "wholeness," reconciling the opposites and oppositions in our lives in order to transform our consciousness, setting authentic goals for ourselves, how to become "real," and more.

Recorded Live in Toronto, Canada
90 minutes $9.95   ISBN 0-923490-04-3

THE HERO'S JOURNEY

Each of us is the hero or heroine of our own story. Our day-to-day objective life and our subjective life—in dreams, conscious inner travel, or imaginative experiences—form equal parts of our story. On this tape, Ariel Tomioka advocates following one's own instincts for wholeness and freedom. When we do this, we live richly, love deeply, and create a world in our own image. The hero's journey is the pursuit of our authentic purpose, the transformation of our whole Being, and every one of us can step onto this "path."

Recorded Live   90 minutes $9.95   ISBN 0-923490-05-1

Helios House
Retail/Wholesale Ordering Information

On the Breath of the Gods and other books and tapes published by Helios House can be ordered directly from the publisher if not available from your local bookstore. Discounts are available to individuals, teachers, health professionals, and organizations as well as to bookstores for quantity orders. Call or write Helios House for complete information.

Helios House, P.O. Box 864, Carmichael, CA 95609
Toll-free Customer Service number: 1-800-765-4354

In Australia, *On the Breath of the Gods* may be ordered from Aquarian Book Distributors (02) 319-3555 Sydney

Postage and Handling — Direct Orders

Within the United States

Surface	$ 1.50 (each additional book/tape $ .75)
Airmail	$ 3.00 (each additional book/tape $ 1.50)

International

Surface	$ 3.00 (each additional book/tape $ 1.50)
Air Mail:	
Canada/Mexico	$ 4.00 (each additional book/tape $ 2.00)
Europe/So. America	$ 6.00 (each additional book/tape $ 5.00)
Asia/Africa/Australia	$ 8.00 (each additional book/tape $ 7.00)

HELIOS HOUSE

"Helios" refers to the Greek god who drove the sun across the heavens in his chariot. Our name and our logo thus summarize our goal as a publisher—to shed light on how each of us can live up to our full potential as a spiritual and human being.

Write or call our toll-free Customer Service number to receive our current newsletter/catalog describing books, tapes, workshops, and study courses being offered by or through Helios House.

Helios House does not release its mailing list to any organization or individual. Helios House and its publications are not endorsed, sponsored by, or in any way affiliated with any religious organization or teaching.